Forthcoming by Robert Rowe

THE RAZOR, *a novel about skiing, December 2019.*
THE DAY KAL AIKENS STREAKED DOWN MAIN STREET,
poems & lyrics, January 2019.

Also by Robert Rowe

THE ART OF PERSUASIVE WRITING, a textbook of
persuasive writing essay assignments for high school
students, 2016.
THE ART OF PERSUASIVE WRITING, VOLUME 2, a
textbook of persuasive writing essay assignments for
middle school students, 2017.

Garage Songs

a novel

by Robert Rowe

𝓑𝓟

Bellhorn Press

Wellesley, Massachusetts

2018

ISBN 978-1-949064-00-1
Library of Congress Control Number: TBA
Cover design by Jose Lucas, stargazingstudio.com
Cover photograph by Paul Specht
Author photograph by Holly Hinman
Editors: Michael Jones, Jean Teillon, and Joan Crothers

Bellhorn Press
New Voices in Fiction Series
P.O. Box 812142
Wellesley, Massachusetts 02482
Phone: 781-214-0425

Publisher: Michael Jones.
Contact: mjones@bellhornpress.com
To order copies, please email: info@bellhornpress.com
To order copies for libraries and schools, please contact:
libraries@bellhornpress.com
For author readings and appearances, please email:
media@bellhornpress.com
Visit bellhornpress.com for more information.

10 9 8 7 6 5 4 3 2 1
First Edition

****

.

For my brothers and sisters

Prelude

Two Violins Dueling in the Staves

A college dormitory in New Hampshire

EVEN THE SOUND OF A GUITAR CASE UNSNAPPING IS music, so I do it slowly. In my dorm basement, I lift my big brother's Telecaster from its velvet case and plug it into my amp. It's got that thin maple neck with dual Humbucks— which is why a ton of players choose Telecasters for rhythm. When I'm not playing Donk's guitar, I keep it hidden in my closet 'cause his buddy Crispin tried to swipe it after Donk's car wreck. I had to chase that long-haired troll six miles through Somerville, and I lost a patch of skin the size of Vermont on the tar—just to get my own brother's guitar back! But I go way into that stuff later. Right now, I'm tooling on the tunes in *Garage Songs*.

If you hear the way a conductor can, the notes rise off each page and hum inside your skull. Do you hear the two violins dueling in the staves while my guitar paints the soundscape leafy-greens and birch-bark whites? Did you catch the drummer carving time with his hi-hats, cymbals, snare, and toms? Do you feel the bass player's chestnut notes throbbing in your gut? If you can, then picture a trumpeter swan lifting off Newfound Lake as my sister's voice rises above the bass:

We donned our pirate suits
And crashed the house of love.
With pilgrim hats and discount maps
We searched for treasure in our chests.

As I strum and bend the steel strings, Raina mainlines blood into sleeping words. Electric waverings spiral through our dorm basement. We return to the intro. Again, the two violins wrestle. Maybe the notes form waves of bees that sting all over again. Maybe they form charms of hummingbirds that cover your skin with an emerald sweater. Or maybe the notes slip through a vent, sneak down a heating duct, and float off into the New Hampshire night.

Beautiful collectors with an eye for fine guitars, strum these silent strings pulling the world where it must go. Brilliant listeners with an ear for paper music, hear these ragged melodies and piece together your own songs. Luminous singers with lava oozing from your windpipes, open your glorious mouths. Let us burn in the fires of our own passing.

The Gordian Knot

ANY DECENT COMPOSER WILL TELL YOU THAT A HEAD scratcher is a Gordian knot of contradictions woven into one song that seems unsolvable, and therefore false, but in reality coheres and even has a melody of truth. Was it love or anger that drove my big brother Donk? Confidence or self-disgust? "Anyone can love a girl who's beautiful," Donk would say, "but can you love a screwed-up person?" Then he'd go and say, "Nothing motivates a human more than hate." A few hours later, Donk was hugging strangers at a Bim Skala Bim concert, letting drugged-out idiots pass his body above my head. The next ding-dong day Donk goes and clotheslines the captain of the Woburn football team. Then, Donk ran across the attic and stopped Raina from pulling the wings off a Luna-green moth. After that, he picked a fight with Morley, grabbed his hair and thumped his head against the tar. It's all one big monkey hump. Either way, by the time I could crawl, my big brother's being was fused to mine tighter than Bondo on a dented hood.

But this isn't about Donk. It's about *me*, Kuba, and my nineteen-year love affair with myself. But I could never figure out who I wanted to be, and Abe Lincoln's hat keeps falling off my head. Sometimes I don't love myself at all. In fact, I can often be seen punching myself in the head to amuse Donk's buddies, but Donk told me to "stop acting like a tool." Although Donk was a senior and I was a sophomore at Merriam Hill High, I had at least three inches on Donk. "You're getting up there, skinny boy," he'd say and punch my arm. "If you ever want to dance with the devil, come on over and take a few swings." Donk began weaving and bobbing, thinking he was Hagler; then he ducked and reached for my ankles. I shifted left. "Too slow," I said. "Oh please." Donk sniffed his fingers. "If this were *real*, I'd snap you in half." He was right. My big brother didn't give two tin tits about his body. Plus, he had more manic juice than a squirrel. Sometimes, when Donk was at his desk reading his humongous red dictionary, it looked like Donk might self-levitate. And if he thought someone was a snob? After a few Heff talls, Donk would bullrush the kid and smoosh his face into the grass. I admit, it wasn't very nice of my big brother, but you've got to admit, some dickheads deserve it.

But forget about Donk. I'm the kid who lost a sneaker running across the half-inch ice on Granny Pond. At Coos Canyon I climbed fifty feet up the tallest cliff and jumped in. But Donk shinnied up a pine tree another thirty feet, swayed back and forth, then arc'd into the river. Donk wasn't bad at ballet either, pavement ballet. Let's face it, those Ivy League suckbags on the Charles with their skinny canoes—they couldn't shadowbox their way out of a phone booth. But those Woburn football playing, dungaree wearing, anabolic injecting, bench pressing, bee-pollen popping punks—they're a bunch of loo-loos. More than once, my big brother came to breakfast with an eggplant glued to his eye. "Sometimes you bite the bear, sometimes the bear bites you," he'd say and drop his fork on the floor when Dad walked into the kitchen.

But screw him. I'm the one I want to talk about. Sure, Donk can play Alvin Lee's second solo in "I'd Love To Change The World" note-for-note and half-juiced too, but without my *Garage Songs* who would know? In one night, I ripped off more street signs—speed limits, stop signs, yields, Lee Ford, First Trust (where I had to hang and swing), IGA, Arcadia Auctions—than Donk ripped off in four years at Merriam Hill High. But when Chief Swan's cruiser pulled into our driveway and he bluffed saying he had witnesses, I sang like a rock dove. Donk didn't.

Moth rescues mixed with fist fights, balls big as grapefruits fused with self-disgust, sixty-second keg stands followed by all-night dictionary read-a-thons: why did Donk weave such a twisted Gordian knot?

Once after a Patriot's Day parade with maple leaves and oak leaves unfolding in their branches, I pushed through the screen door, walked into our den and asked Dad what he knew about Donk. Dad looked up from the Sports page. "Let's see, Donny hated eggs. He looked a little bit like Babe Ruth. Once he stayed in bed for four days when I cut down that sick elm in the backyard. That's all I know." Dad turned the page and studied the box scores. "Ooh, Clemens struck out twelve."

On Route 10 in Hanover, New Hampshire, I steer my Chevelle (the one with Bondo in all four quarter-panels) to Pushkoff's frat house. Inside Sigma Nu, Pushkoff twists open a cold soldier and drops a fistful of photos onto a glass table. I shuffle through the images like cards. In my coat I carry a wad of used envelopes. Sometimes I scribble on them.

The Smoking Pillow

(Four years earlier, Merriam Hill, Massachusetts)

"Bayonets! Hold the left flank! There's a bulge in the left flank," Donk hollered. "Send in Moran's unit!" Captain Moran's men rushed in from the rear to fortify the line. A boa of smoke slithered through the air.

"By Grant, we've got to turn them back," said Donk. A comrade slumped to the grass. A Confederate cannon flashed bits of color onto the dark troops.

"Charge, boys, charge!" their captain ordered. A wall of gray-clad soldiers surged up the hill. Donk raised his musket and fired. A lead ball whistled through the air.

"Galvin, did you hear that?"

"Hear what?"

"You gray scumbags!" my brother yelled. A Confederate soldier dashed up the embankment. Donk steadied his bayonet. Warm fluid filled his pants.

"One of the children." Mrs. Brice switched on the bedroom light. "I smell smoke."

"What kind of smoke?" Mr. Brice sat up.

A bayonet burned through Donk's bicep. "You want a row with me!" Donk heaved his gun butt into a bearded man's face.

"Donny?" Mom opened Donk's bedroom door. A wave of smoke spilled into the hallway. "Quickly, Galvin, call the fire department."

"Somebody get a stretcher," Donk called out. Gripping his neck, a Union sergeant squirmed in the grass. A flag jerked madly amid the fighting soldiers and horses.

Grabbing his pajamas, Mom dragged Donny out of his bedroom and into the hallway.

"What's going on?" said Donk, a rug burn forming on his back. She pressed her lips to Donk's. "Mom, what are you doing?"

Snapping the windowpanes with his ax, the fireman tossed a smoking pillow out our second-floor window onto the lawn.

Later that morning at Brice Used Cars, Galvin Brice circled a spoon in his mug. "His pillow fell on the heater and, I guess, he had just finished *The Red Badge of Courage* that night."

"The fireman couldn't just lift the windows up, huh," said Fallon, Galvin's top salesman. "One of them works in the hardware store, you know."

"What a life," said Galvin, resting his elbows on the roof of a Camaro parked in the showroom.

"Wait until one of them needs a second-hand sled," said Fallon.

"Are you kidding me." Galvin pointed to an elderly couple inspecting a Malibu on the front lot. "Go see what those customers want."

"Who, the Gillespies? They're *shoppers*. They've stroked every salesman from here to the North Pole."

"A real salesman knows how to turn shoppers into *buyers*," said Dad.

Fallon grabbed his NADA used car guide and walked out the door.

"Would you sign these, Galvin?" asked Connie, walking up to Dad with a pile of contracts.

"Sure thing, honey," said Dad, removing a pen from his tan sports coat.

Connie set the contracts on the roof of the Camaro. "I'm not your honey."

Dad signed each contract in four places.

"How's Donny doing?" asked Connie.

"Fine. They let him out of the hospital this morning."

"Where's he now—at home resting?"

"No, he went to the carnival with the Pushkoff boy." Dad signed the last contract and handed the pile to Connie. "Guess he wanted to ride the Ferris wheel."

Where Is The Ferris Wheel?

(Mount MacGregor)

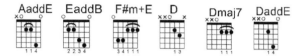

IN A GRASS PARKING LOT, DONK AND HIS BEST BUDDY Pushkoff sat on the hood of a Chevy Nova pounding soldiers. The windows were rolled down and the radio turned up. "Life in a Northern Town" by Dream Academy drifted through the night. Behind the boys on a practice football field, a Ferris wheel turned in the sky.

"Hey, girls?" called Pushkoff, taking a haul off his soldier in a way that best showcased his bicep.

"What?" Two women slowed in front of Donk's Nova.

"I'm over here."

The women looked at each other. "Well, you can just stay there," they laughed and merged into the crowd at the entrance gate.

"You've got the hot hand tonight," said Donk.

"Couldn't you tell by the tones in their voices? Those girls wanted a piece of *me*."

"Oh please." Donk twisted the cap off a fresh soldier.

"You're just jealous." Pushkoff punched Donk's arm.

"Those girls wanted to be as far away from you as possible."

"Shoosh, you're distracting the talent. Yoo-hoo, Miss?" A woman paused in front of Pushkoff. "Could you tell me where the Ferris wheel is?"

The woman motioned towards the carnival. "Look up in the sky."

"Could you walk me there? I have no sense of direction."

"I just went to the car to grab my purse. I came with my husband."

"I'm open-minded."

"Grow up." The woman hurried towards a fried dough booth.

"Pthhhhhfffff," Donk muffled a laugh.

"What?"

"I can't believe you."

"What? Tell me," Pushkoff asked.

"Where is the Ferris wheel? I don't know a guy on the planet who could get away with a crappy line like that."

Pushkoff killed his soldier and heaved the bottle into the darkness. "Listen, Donny boy, before I have to knock you out: if you're aiming to crush one out of the ballpark, you're gonna whiff a ton."

"Spare me."

"What?" Reaching into a cooler, Pushkoff pulled out a soldier and twisted off the cap.

"I don't think you could hit a single at this point in the game."

"Me?" said Pushkoff. "You're not even at the plate 'cause you don't have the seeds."

"And you do, failing on purpose like that?"

With the cap between his thumb and middle finger, Pushkoff snapped his fingers. The cap curved through the air above a row of cars. "Now you won't even talk with me straight."

"Hey, are you the guys who were bothering my wife?" A man in lawyer sandals walked towards the Nova. (Ivy League all the way.)

"We're just enjoying the sights," said Pushkoff, swigging his soldier.

"Well, if I ever catch either of you being disrespectful to my wife again, it'll be the last thing you do."

Pushkoff glanced at Donk. "Just walk away, pal."

"I will not. I'm a resident in this town."

"The carnival is here. It's almost midnight." Pushkoff set his green bottle on the hood. "Shouldn't you be enjoying yourself?"

"I would be if it weren't for jerks like you."

Pushkoff hopped off the roof. "Alright, if you're going to keep popping off like that-"

A surprise left caught Pushkoff's jaw. Springing off the hood, Donk knocked the man onto the ground. The two rolled around in the grass. Donk climbed on top.

"I pay taxes in this town. I pay taxes," yelled the man.

Grabbing hold of the man's hair, Donk thumped his head against the ground repeatedly.

"I'm a resident of Merriam Hill." The man flailed at Donk's back. "I will not be bullied in my own town."

Donk grunted and brought his fist down upon the man's cheek.

Pushkoff pulled Donk to his feet. "Donny, leave the guy alone. He's just protecting his wife."

"Let go of me." Donk shoved Pushkoff. "This guy's a self-entitled turd!"

The man rushed towards Donk. Hooking his arm under the man's crotch, Pushkoff lifted him up and carried him four cars away. A body thudded against the ground. "Take off now or I'll rip your head off and stuff it down your neck!"

The man walked towards the Ferris wheel trying to fix his ripped shirt. "I'll be back with the cops. I'm pressing charges."

Pushkoff wiggled his hands. "I'm shakin' like a leaf." He glanced at Donk and pretended to swat a bug off his neck. "God damn deer flies."

Donk clenched his jaw tight. Slowly the corners of his mouth turned upwards. "I shouldn't drink, should I? For some reason, a few beers and out comes the cape."

The Dollars Are Flying By

Donk says, "There are two kinds of work: one kind piles burgers on your plate, the other kind tries to unsnap the useless overcoats a person wears before they find their *inner-compass*."

For our burgers, Dad drives to Arcadia Auctions and bids on used cars. In the heat of bidding, the auctioneer tries to get dealers to bid a ton more than a sled's worth.

"Hibedy dibedy, hibedy dibedy, hibedy dibedy hibedy. Take a look at this one, fellas. It's a brass hat." The auctioneer whacks the podium with his jockey stick. "'83 Caprice Classic: air, cruise, power windows, locks, sunroof—all the toys. What's it worth, fellas? Do I hear twelve-grand?" Dad looks away. "Galvin, are you in the game?" the auctioneer hollers. Dad shakes his head and walks to the snack bar. "Sometimes the best deals are the sleds a person chooses not to buy," says Dad, making a hotdog disappear in two bites. When Dad wins, Donk and I drive the sleds back to Brice Used Cars where Fallon, the original shyster-meister, sells them. Once Fallon grossed two-Gs off his own aunt. "I figure each relative is worth at least a thousand bucks," says Fallon, his pockets stuffed with used car guides, his belly bigger than Babe Ruth's. Oh yeah, Fallon moonlights on a Brinks truck. A few years back, a guard tossed a 50-pound bag of nickels into his truck and it landed on Fallon's jewel box. Fallon couldn't work for three months. Dad was livid.

For their burgers the Pushkoffs bury people. They live across the street in a gray contemporary with a perfectly manicured lawn. I mean, their grass is thicker than the hair on David Lee Roth's chest.

Scott Pushkoff's a senior and plays running back for Merriam Hill High. He's convinced that every girl on the planet is in love with him. Before a raver, Pushkoff throws his T-shirt in a dryer on high heat so it shrinks and does a zillion curls. Then, at the raver, he stands in the doorway so partygoers have to swerve around him just to get inside. When a girl even remotely acknowledges his presence, Pushkoff looks over at Donk and flashes his twenty-tooth grin. "Oh please," says Donk. "Come on," Pushkoff protests. "That girl wants a piece of *me*."

His sister Noy is a sophomore and plays on the field hockey team. The coolest thing about Noy is she can have a conversation on just about any subject. One night Ferranti had a party and Noy stayed in the kitchen for an hour talking with Mr. Ferranti about Diane Arbus. On the babe-Richter scale, Noy's at least an 8.6 (but I'm nervous about dating a girl with bigger quads than mine).

Mrs. Pushkoff is always talking about tikkun olam: how people have a duty to heal the world. One time Donk was fighting Devlin behind the high school and Mrs. Pushkoff ran over and hugged Donk. Devlin walked away. "Why do people have a duty?" Raina once asked Mrs. Pushkoff at Thanksgiving dinner. "You have to find out the reasons why yourself," Mrs. Pushkoff replied.

Mr. Pushkoff slicks his silver hair back, so he looks like one of Whitey Bulger's hit men, but he only hits golf balls at Winchester Country Club. At Pushkoff Funeral Home the downstairs is lined with caskets. "This is the one John F. Kennedy was buried in," says Mr. Pushkoff, pointing to a mahogany casket. "Or if you prefer, your loved one could rest in a casket made of solid bronze with a hand-rubbed finish." Even though they're still in high school, Pushkoff and Noy have already arranged their own funerals. "I want to be buried with my cat and my casket must be lined with silk," says Noy. "I want a closed casket," says Pushkoff, "'cause if some guy's talking trash at my wake, I won't be there to body slam him."

Me, I want to be recycled. So when I croak, I want the Pushkoffs to torch my body, hike my ashes up Red Feather Ridge, and swoosh me around the summit. That's where I found my inner-compass on a hike with Raina. It took me nineteen years of guesswork to locate that damn compass and discover that the person I *am* is a ton cooler than the person I was trying to be.

If I mentioned my inner-compass to Dad, he'd probably pee his pants laughing and tell me, "I ought to be pushing sleds for him." Dad wants to be a bigwig *new car* dealer so he's going ball-deep in debt building a fancypants showroom so Chevrolet will give him a franchise and he can finally outsell the super-stuck up Skip Lee. Skip owns the Ford store just over the bridge in Arlington. In winter, he wears a full-length coat made of fox fur and sports a sick tan. At Acadia Auction when Skip wants a sled, he stands in front of the sled, legs spread like Clint Eastwood, and keeps nodding until the other bidders stop raising their cards. Years back, Dad tried to join the Rotary Club and Skip Lee blackballed him. That really fired Dad's fuse. "They're just a used car outfit," Skip told Mr. Pushkoff. "I'll show that prima donna and his Gucci watch," says Dad.

At Brice Used Cars a man in a hunter-green suit walked into Dad's office. "Galvin, old-buddy, how the heck are you?" Vince Irvine's hand sprung up.

"Let's see. Two-steps ahead of the IRS, one-step ahead of the wife, and just about even with the kids. Glad you came, Vince." Dad shook Mr. Irvine's hand.

"Tell me, how is Marna? You've got yourself quite a gal in her. She ever tell you I used to copy her answers during tests?"

"No, she didn't. Is that how you got into Dartmouth?"

"Probably, I didn't know what the heck I was doing." Mr. Irvine adjusted his glasses. "Marna had the best hook shot this side of Causeway Street. She once hit fifteen hook shots in a row against Woburn Catholic."

"Sounds like she was the one with holy connections that night. Have a seat." Dad motioned towards a chair.

"Swoosh! Nothing but net—fifteen times in a row."

"The bump-n-roll hook. Impossible to block," said Dad, leaning back in his chair. "My old man taught her that move."

"Is that right?"

"Sure is. About the time Jack Kennedy was picked off, we were playing two-on-two in my driveway when Marna sprang up for a jump shot and my buddy Noah slapped the ball into the bushes. So Pa comes out with a Globe tucked under his arm and shows her the bump-n-roll hook. You crouch down quickly so your fanny flies out and bumps your opponent out of your airspace. Then, you roll left or right, depending on your strong side, and lob a soft hook towards the basket. 'See if the fellas can block that,' said Pa—and we couldn't either."

"Well, I'll be damned." Unsnapping his briefcase, Mr. Irvine removed a bunch of papers and slid them towards

Dad. "Here you go. Twelve and a half percent, floating rate, tied to the prime, and spread out over fifteen years. I even typed it up myself. Give it a once-over."

Dad scanned the typed-in numbers. "How does Abigail like Dartmouth?"

"Very much so. Very much so. She rooms with a girl on the rowing team so they can drag each other out of bed for 5 a.m. practices. This Friday, Sally and I are driving up to Hanover for homecoming. Those numbers all right?"

"Getting closer, but I want to talk to you about the rate. Boston Northern is offering eleven and a half percent. Shave a half-point off that and it's a done deal. A few years down the road a half-point could make all the difference."

"Boston Northern. That's a naughty word where I come from. You don't want to bank with Boston Northern. They're fair-weather friends. One double-dip recession and they'll get all squirrel-eyed and start calling in their loans, or worse, they'll trim your air supply, and with no working capital, you'll shrivel on the vine. Seen it happen during the oil embargo. And once the dominoes start falling, you can kiss your assets goodbye. Boston Northern drove Luby Motors into Chapter 11. Don't you want to bank with your buddies over at First Trust, Galvin?"

"Can you at least match their rate? I don't mind you making a fair profit, but don't expect me to put Abby through Dartmouth," said Dad.

"I'll wiggle a few branches and see if any apples drop," said Mr. Irvine returning the papers to his briefcase. "Can we meet tomorrow, say two o'clock?"

Dad nodded.

"Good. We're bullish on you, Galvin. Will Marna be able to make it?"

"Why do we need her?" asked Dad.

"We always ask the spouse to sign a promissory note."

"I'll use the store for collateral. Besides, we have the house in Marna's name. You wouldn't take the shell off a turtle's back, Vince, would you?"

Outside, Donk guided his Nova into a *Customers Only* parking space.

"Galvin, it's me Vince. We sat next to each other in Mr. Brewer's history class. I wouldn't steer you wrong."

Dad studied Mr. Irvine's hands. "I don't know. Marna's had to put up with a lot of shenanigans over the years. I don't want to go dragging her into my chess match."

Donk hovered by Dad's office while I fished through Connie's desk for the keys to the soda machine.

"I know it's a lot to ask, but the higher-ups want the extra signature." Mr. Irvine leaned in towards Dad. "You are planning on paying us back, aren't you?"

"Course I am." Dad got up. "There's been a Brice pushing iron in Merriam Hill for twenty-eight years and, soon as this nitwit's old enough," Dad grabbed Donk and began scrubbing his scalp, "he'll be selling sleds too. Kid loves noogies, no fooling, asks for them all the time."

"Is that right, young man? Are you planning on going into the car business?" Mr. Irvine put his hand on Donk's shoulder.

Donk stiffened up.

"Donny, answer Mr. Irvine when he asks you a question."

Donk wiggled his fingers, but said nothing.

"Go ahead, introduce yourself to Mr. Irvine."

Donk stared at a photo of Dad standing in front of the showroom with the police chief.

"Kids these days—they don't have any etiquette." Dad steered Donk from his office. "Go grab your sister from voice lessons." Dad handed Donk a sawbuck. "Give this to Mrs. Jacobs."

"Hi Mr. Irvine," I said, stepping into Dad's office.

"That's my middle kid."

I pointed towards a loaded sedan parked out front. "Did you see what I picked up at the mill yesterday?"

"He didn't pick that up." Dad swiped at my arm. "I bought that at Arcadia last night."

Mr. Irvine turned around. "Which one?"

"Over there, Vince," I said. "The metallic-blue Park Ave. Get a load of this Christmas list: one-owner, 27K original miles, ice, cruise, new sneakers, delay wipers, the trinity of power: seats, windows, locks—all the toys—and the plushest velour seats you've ever laid your hands on. Go ahead, *touch* it."

Dad pushed me into the showroom. "Go clean the bathrooms, then help yourself to a soda."

I held up the soda machine keys. "You're going to lose a few handshakes to Boston Northern driving around in that relic of your youth." I pointed to Mr. Irvine's Fiat. "A man of your caliber ought to drive a Park Ave. You've got to give off an air of liquidity, Vince."

"Don't listen to him. He hallucinates." Dad laughed.

I held out a fin. "Go take Mr. Irvine down to the Red Onion for a root beer float and some fries. While you're gone: I'll phone Vince's insurance agent, switch over the plates, and get the Park Ave douched and inspected. When Mr. Irvine gets back, the Park Ave will be *ready for business* with a full tank of gas."

"Go play on the railroad tracks." Dad hucked his pen at me (the one he got for being 'salesman of the month' for nine straight years).

"Thanks." I caught the pen and slid it in my pocket.

"Oh ho." Mr. Irvine slapped my shoulder. "Die birne faut nicht weit vom stamm. You've got a stung bear here. Boy's going to be your retirement policy. Can promise you that, Galvin."

"First, I need to teach him a few things." Dad studied my face. "Hey give that back to me," he called as I walked out of his office.

Mr. Irvine rose to his feet. "I'll put in a call to our Cambridge office and get back to you. Stay away from Boston Northern. I could tell you a few stories about them that would freeze the blood of a walrus." Snapping his briefcase shut, Mr. Irvine strolled outside. Passing the Park Avenue, he came to a stop. Reaching inside, he ran his hand across the velour seats. Then he sat in the driver's seat and studied the instrument panel. A minute later, he climbed into his Fiat and accelerated down Mass Ave.

Out back in a wash bay, Fallon's son scrubbed the whitewalls on a Caprice Classic as the radio behind him played "World Leader Pretend" by R.E.M. In the showroom Fallon slid the cellophane off a cigar. "Think you're doing the right thing, Galvin? Remember what your old man used to say: 'Own your inventory outright and run a rat's nest into the ground.'"

"Dammit all, Fallon, we're gonna roll more tires than Skip Lee, and if that means putting all our burgers on the table, then that's what I'm going to do. I'm tired of chasing nickels while the dollars are flying by." Dad pointed to a man inspecting a Blazer by the flag pole. "Go see what that customer wants."

"He's a tire kicker," Fallon shot back. "He was here last week asking questions about a dozen different cars—wasting my time."

Dad motioned with his head. "Ask him what we could do to earn his business *today*."

Outside, Fallon popped the hood of the Blazer. The man studied the engine. "How much are you asking?"

"Go ahead, take it for a ride," replied Fallon, dropping keys into the customer's hand. "Then we'll talk price."

The Stars Formed Unknown Constellations

ALTHOUGH MY BIRTH CERTIFICATE SAYS KUBA, MOST people call me Spaz 'cause I'm a little bit tapped in the head. Doctor Van Dyne, humongous snob with his I'm-too-busy-to-breathe routine and tortoise-shell glasses, says I've got Meniere's—everything spins for no good reason: trail maps, goalposts, guitars, dictionaries, songbooks, Red Sox tickets. Once I stayed in bed for sixty days straight. That's when I learned to play Donk's Telecaster (the one Aunt Bee unloaded after Uncle Addy took off). So while Donk was at football practice with spit swinging from his mask, I was shoeless on his mattress with a stack of songbooks, a box of gingersnaps, and *his* Telecaster.

Now you might think I'm a mental case, but each chord has its own color: E-major is school bus yellow, D-flat a russet potato, and A-minor the clear ether from a Corvette's tailpipe. Donk almost choked on his popcorn when we were listening to Green Magnet School and I picked up his Telecaster and began playing the chords. I thought he was going to coldcock me on the spot, but Donk just wiggled his fingers, pulled out his cigarette maker, and licked a square of rolling paper. My big brother knew when words were no good.

"You think you're pretty pissa, don't you," said my sister Raina, lifting a wah wah peddle off Donk's dresser. No I don't. I'm no *snob*. In fact, I'll confess to a total douche bag: if identity is a warm sleeping bag you use when camping on Mount Washington, I'm always cold. If *rising* means walking into First Trust Savings and having Mr. Irvine squeeze your hand, I'd rather munch the bark off a birch. If cracking the cosmic code means finding a cosmic joke, then I'll crack that too. Donk knew exactly what he liked: reading every frickin' book about General Grant and the *Civil War*, being known at keg parties as a *sick unit*, decking kids on a football field, and afternoon-long jams with Crispin, Ferranti, and Janota, who play in the band Wet Towels on Wood.

Raina sings for Wet Towels on Wood. They're not known much outside Boston, but they're super stuck-up anyway. On stage Raina turns her back to the audience, so all they see is nutmeg hair reaching to her bum. Save me. You can bet a ton when most kids do things one way, Raina does them the other way. In the middle of winter, when most kids wear parkas, Raina walks to Strawberry Records in a Rory Gallagher T-shirt that Donk found in a convertible. Save me. Or during that key moment in "The Sound of Music" when they're hiding behind gravestones, Raina blurts out: "I hope they get caught—wa ha ha ha." Save me a gajillion times.

Donk says Raina knows how to "place a saddle on a person's back and ride them up the totem pole." I asked Donk what he meant. He said: "It's like the place in a forest that gets the most sunlight so pine trees grow the tallest." I didn't get that either. Besides, this story isn't about totem poles, how we buy and sell cars, Donk cracking the cosmic code, my sister's nutmeg hair, or all that Civil War stuff.

In our den Dad practiced his golf swing. I guess Dad had found some golf clubs in the trunk of a trade-in and had just played nine holes of golf with Mr. Pushkoff earlier that day.

"Shameless social climber," said Donk.

"Are you kidding me? I don't give a rusted nail what those Harvard barnies think. In fact, I bonked a ball off one of their carts today." Dad sipped his drink then pulled a putter from his golf bag.

"Then what's with the new showroom?" Donk sniffed.

"Go jump in a shark tank," said Dad, tapping a ball towards an imaginary hole.

Donk walked upstairs. In his room, he lifted up a window, crawled through the opening onto the roof. Then, he climbed up the slate shingles to the cupola. During the day, a patchwork of houses and lawns opened before our eyes. At night, streetlamps and stars formed unknown constellations.

"Hey Spaz?" called Donk.

"Yeah?"

"What are you doing up here?"

"Just checking out the sky."

Donk fished through his pockets. "What's that?" He pointed to a group of stars below the Northern Cross. "Poseidon's Mast?"

"No such thing," I said.

My brother took a glass vial from his pants and popped off the cap. "After nine o'clock the Russian bear comes out of his cave, huh?"

"He called me mental case, told me I was going to end up in jail."

"He shouldn't say that."

A satellite inched across the sky, too steady for a falling star.

"Donk, do you think I'm mental?" I asked.

My brother sniffed his fingers. "Remember that sandbar we used to drag our canoe onto and have a picnic—the one with the burnt sand? You filled a plastic bag with the stuff and kept it in your closet for years until Mom tossed it. Remember that?"

"Yeah."

"Well I think that's pretty cool."

"You do?"

"Yeah, I do. I even showed Pushkoff."

"That sand was a weird molasses color. I could never figure out how it got burned."

"Me neither. It looked like the middle of a Fig Newton or something. It all blows by me, Kuba, but you tuck everything away."

Below us a stream of headlights flowed through the maze of streets. "Look at all those streets and all those streetlights. There's some sort of mathematical grid laid over whole state."

"All those streets and all those *cars*." Donk slid the glass vial into his breast pocket. "Can you keep a secret, Kuba? You won't tell anyone, not even Raina?"

"You know I can."

Donk shifted on the wood slats. "The truth of it all is: I hate cars. Dad sells them and I hate them. I wish there weren't any cars. We could walk home from football practice, take the T to Fenway, even use our bikes to get groceries."

In Granny Pond a choir of carpenter and bullfrogs gave an improv concert for free: *Jug-o-rum, jug-o-rum, jug-o-rum. Pa-tunk pa-tunk. Jug-o-rum, jug-o-rum, jug-o-rum. Pa-tunk pa-tunk.*

"Why would I want to tell anyone?"

Next day, Raina surveyed the airways above our house from the cupola.

"You won't," said Donk.

"You don't have the sack," I said.

"Yes I do." Raina pulled a roll of duct tape from her coat and taped a tee between two slats. She set a golf ball on the tee. A golf club rose above her head. The golf ball skimmed down the roof and fell onto our lawn.

"Let me take a shot." Donk stepped in front of Raina.

"Stand back, doughboy." Raina elbowed Donk's gut. "It's my idea." She placed another ball on the tee. "It's all in the legs." She raised the club. The ball floated above the trees towards a house below.

"We shall never surrender!" I yelled.

"Shut your face."

We listened for an impact.

I reached for the club. "I've got the swing, smooth as butter."

"Strong as butter too." Raina dug her nails into my hand. Her body twisted in barber pole motion. A golf ball sliced wide-right towards the Pushkoff's house.

"Oh boy," said Raina, trying to steer the ball left with her body.

"You nitwit," said Donk as the ball struck the Pushkoff's house.

We slid down the roof, squeezed through Donk's window, almost fell down the stairs, and ran into the den. Donk clicked on the TV.

"Why are you three breathing so heavy?" asked Mom, standing in front of the TV, her hips blocking the blue rays. "Don't tell me." Mom hurried back into the kitchen.

Mrs. Pushkoff opened her sliding glass door and walked out to her yard. "What on earth?" By the doghouse she spotted what looked like a super-huge chunk of hail. Bending over to pick it up, an electric jolt raced through her spine. She fell onto the grass.

"Noy," Mrs. Pushkoff called. "Come over here and help me up. I threw-out my back."

How Much Will The Whole Menu Cost?

(Galena)

"This is going to be a palace, I tell you." Dad opened a canister of blueprints and spread them out on the hood of an Impala parked in the showroom. "We'll have enough space in our new showroom for six maybe seven sleds— glass all-the-way-around too. Our sleds will be visible from Mass Ave *and* Worthen Road. At night we'll shine lights on every car, so while we're sleeping, the sleds will sell themselves. How many sleds will you be able to roll then, Fallon?"

"My customers would buy their cars from me at the dump," said Fallon, puffing on his cigar.

"Oh, I forgot. God's gift to the motoring public over there." Dad traced the blue lines with his fingers. Outside, a backhoe dropped slabs of blacktop into a dump truck. "Take a look at the skylights—my own office too. I tell you, we're going to snake half of Skip Lee's customers. See how he likes it for a change. Him and his Gucci watch. Do you know what he said to my neighbor Noah Puskoff? 'You can't trust them; They're just a used car outfit.' Can you believe that bigmouth? Where does he get off questioning my scruples like that? I'm as honest as the next guy."

Fallon nodded.

"I'll show Mr. Skip Lee who the public decides to trust. We'll see who ends up in receivership. I just got off the phone with Jack Kelly at the regional office and he told me Chevy approved our application for a franchise. All I have to do is add five bays, finish the showroom, and we're golden." Waltzing to the coffee machine, Dad hummed a jingle: *See what's new today in a Chevrolet. See what's new today in a Chevrolet.* Tilting the pot, a stream of black liquid flowed into his mug.

"And how much do you think they'll charge us for that?" asked Fallon.

"That's turtle feed when you compare it to the cost of doing nothing." Dad scanned the lot. "Now do you think we'll stop those tightwads from driving into Boston to save fifty friggin' bucks? I can't stand those Ivy League liberal frauds. They stand up in our P.T.A. meetings and say: my son needs this. My daughter needs that. Me, me, me! That's why they're getting ahead, Fallon. They're leaving tread marks on our friggin' backs."

In the parking lot, the backhoe lifted buckets of cinnamon dirt into a dump truck.

"I'm going to gross fourteen-hun off every one of them," said Fallon.

"You should. In fact, go for eighteen. Trouble is, they're too smart for that." Dad set his mug on the blueprints. "In fact those Ivy Leaguers got us dancing like puppets." He moved in marionette motion. "Interest rates up. Interest rates down. Money supply tight. Money supply loose. But Fallon, I still want you to try. You just have to hone your bush league skills. That means: Don't ask customers how much they have to spend until you've got them hooked on a sled. That only frightens them and we *need* them."

"I never pre-qualify," said Fallon.

"Good. Make sure you wave me over so I can close every deal."

"What if we're two-Gs apart?"

"Blow the jokers out of here, but if there's a couple-hun on the table, I want to see the numbers before they drive across the bridge to Lee Ford." Dad scanned the lot.

Fallon removed a boiled potato from his coat. "I've been keeping them from buying out of town already."

"Oh yes, Mr. Wonderful over here. Well let me ask you this, Mr. Wonderful: Where did old man Tossy end up buying?"

Fallon bit into his potato. "I brought you in on that deal, but you couldn't close a zipper that day."

"That's because you didn't leave me enough room to maneuver. How come every time you bring me in on a deal you're only holding seven-hun? I couldn't close a deal for a snow cone with that amount of profit."

Fallon's face turned red. "I lowballed him so he'd come back."

"Lowball? How about highballing someone for a change. Remember, a good deal is a state of mind."

"Let me ask you this: Who's got twelve sleds out the door and the month isn't even half-over?"

A woman with rollers in her hair walked across the showroom. The two watched her until she turned right towards the Service Department.

"I know, I know, Fallon, you've got a little hitting streak going. Is this the month you finally break thirty units?"

"If we could get a real closer in here, maybe I could." Fallon thumbed through the prospect log.

~ 30 ~

Dad tightened his lips, but slowly the corners turned upwards. "You dirty Catholic. Let's pull out the old sales log when I worked the floor. We'll see who knows how to close a deal. One month after leaving Holy Cross I rolled twenty-eight sleds and interest rates were high enough to tickle a horse's nose." Outside, a Jeep drove into the lot and parked in front of a brown Z-28. A man in a dungaree jacket climbed out and walked towards the Z.

"Yeah, but you didn't have Skip Lee pushing sleds across the bridge," said Fallon.

"Are you kidding me? We had Luby Motors right in Cambridge and his sleds were flying off his lot at two-bucks over book. Try competing with that."

Fallon dialed a phone number and held the receiver to his ear. "I don't know, Galvin. If interest rates head north and people start holding onto their paychecks, we could be swimming in a sea of red ink."

Outside, the man in a dungaree jacket climbed into his Jeep and drove off.

"Damn, we missed him," said Dad, turning to Fallon. "I thought you were a lot-hawk?"

High up in our cupola Donk's shoelaces dangled above the slate shingles. In the sky the sinking sun glowed like a Corvette's brakelight. Moments later, the rows of houses were flooded by a river of night.

"Someday I'm going to cruise into the Red Onion and order the whole menu: Cajun steak, Jersey clams, eggplant parmesan, Mary's friends beans—everything." From his pants Donk pulled out a cigarette roller. "I'll clean out the entire desert rack: banana cream pie, coconut bars, raspberry cobbler, apple-rhubarb crisp."

With a rusted nail Raina scratched her name on a plank. "Jeez, Donk, that's really ambitious. Do you think you're up to it?"

Donk tightened his lips. "You just wait. Every pizza combo you can dream up: artichoke hearts, ham, peppers, pineapples, sausage. I'm going to point to their cooler and say: I'd like to buy every soldier marching in that fridge. Every Heff Tall, St. Pauli Girl, Heinie, PBR, mini-Mick, Old Swilwaukee—even Schlitz." Donk tapped a suede pouch. A trickle of shredded leaves fell into his roller.

"I'm in," I said, leaning against the chimney. "How much do you think the whole menu will cost?"

"Not enough." Placing a cigarette in his mouth, Donk removed a blue-tipped match from his pants and dragged it along his zipper. A flame erupted on the tip.

"How'd you do that?"

"Oh please." Below her name Raina scratched: *Wet Towels on Wood rules.*

Donk continued: "Eastern omelets, westerns, northerns, fiddleheads, Alaskan King Crab, fried flounder, and squid. Side orders galore: grits, sweet potato sticks, French fries and gravy, beer-batter onion rings—and give me some of that crabapple coleslaw. You can't miss a single item." An egret of smoke drifted into the night. "If the waitress forgets to bring an orange soda or one scoop of cottage cheese, the whole thing is a big donut hole." With his pointer-finger and thumb, Donk made a monocle and peered through it. "A giant nothing."

An evening breeze lifted wisps of water off Granny Pond and onto my cheek. "Do you really have the whiskers to do this?" I asked.

"Are the Kennedys gun shy?" Donk laughed, but it didn't sound like a laugh.

"You're twisted." Raina crawled down the roof and disappeared through a bedroom window.

"You feeling all right, Two-by-four?" I asked.

"She'll see. One small gesture could circle outwards and change everything."

You've Got To Own It

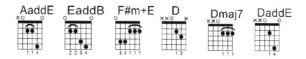

Me, Donk, and Raina lived on the top of Merriam Hill in a stucco house built during the Civil War. The thing needed a paint job bad. Worse, the roof was trashed. Every so often, a slate shingle would slide off the roof and explode in our driveway. But Dad stole it, offered half what the seller wanted. He was always doing stuff like that. "Let's see if there's a little wiggle room," he'd say and offer half. But houses were cheap then. Now all these Ivy League snobs are moving in 'cause the schools are good and jacking up the home prices. That means, the cool people—the ones who were here first—have to move out 'cause taxes are higher than Tiny Tim's voice.

One time we were buying shoes at DeSilva's for school and Dad started *negotiating* with the owner. Donk was so embarrassed he hid behind the sneaker rack. "We don't negotiate prices here," said Mr. DeSilva. "But you negotiated with me when you bought your van," Dad argued. "Okay, I'll give you ten percent off." Mr. DeSilva relented. "Twenty percent and you've got a deal," Dad fired back. "Everything's negotiable," said Dad as we walked to our car with shoe boxes swinging in plastic bags. "Never ever pay asking price."

My big brother was a wicked sick negotiator too, but the stuff Donk angled for were way different than the things Dad tried to get.

"You've got to own it," said Donk, guiding his Nova into a parking spot at Busa Liquors. "It's not the words you say that count, it's what's beneath the words. Now go out there and snag us a case of Heff talls."

I opened the car door and walked towards the entrance. A man wearing a baseball cap strolled past. "'Scuse me, sir, would you buy us a case?"

"Not tonight."

"Hello, miss?" I called to a lady. "Today's my birthday and my folks said I could have a party. Would you buy us a case?"

The lady shook her head.

A man in a dungaree jacket climbed from a Mustang.

"Hey, man," I said in my lowest voice, "be a guy and hook us up?"

He studied my face. "What if you boys got into a car wreck?"

Donk got out of the Nova. "Stand back and take notes. Yoo-hoo, miss?" Donk smiled and waved to a woman in a plaid skirt. "How are you. I left my wallet in my tool box at work and that Grinch behind the cash register wants me to drive eight miles back to the construction site to get it and my dad's surprise party starts in five minutes."

The woman studied my brother's face. "How old are you?"

"Twenty-one," said Donk.

"Is that the truth?"

"Yes it is."

"If you're lying and you get into an accident, I could go to prison."

"I'm not." Donk maintained eye contact.

"Well, okay." The woman walked towards the liquor store.

"Haffenreffer is my dad's favorite beer," called Donk.

Twelve minutes later, the door of the liquor store opened. The woman walked out pushing a shopping cart. Inside the cart was a case of Heff talls. Donk got out of the Nova, picked up the case, and sat back down in the driver's seat.

"Thanks again," he called, setting the case on my lap. He turned on the car and backed out of the parking space. "I could be dribbling nonsense—and I usually am—but if I use just the right tone, just the right pitch, then hidden messages are sent."

"But you had to string together a pack of lies to get what you wanted," I said as we drove down Mass Ave.

In front of Quimby's Supermarket a policeman sat in his cruiser and watched us pass.

"Don't look," said Donk, turning onto Merriam Street.

We drove up Merriam Hill and slowed to a stop in the Pushkoff's driveway. Donk pulled his keys from the ignition and grabbed the case off my lap.

"Hey, Two-by-four?" I asked. "Can I carry the case inside?"

Donk thought for a moment. "Okay." He handed me the case.

"Donny baby. Kuba with the soldiers," purred Pushkoff as we walked up the front steps.

"What's going on?" said Donk.

"Take a look at these bad boys." Pushkoff began flexing his tits, first the left one, then his right.

"You're whacked," said Donk.

Walking through the front door with a case of Heff talls on my shoulder, I felt like the big wahoo. I thought of Scott and Donk how we formed our own pack against the world. Our own private club. I imagined sixty pairs of eyes on me. A riff from Rory Gallagher's "Cradle Rock" leapt into my ears as I squeezed past the clusters of partygoers crammed into every space in Pushkoff's house.

"'Scuse me, buddy. 'Scuse me. Coming through. On your left," I called in my deepest voice. "On your right." I eased by two girls. "How are you ladies doing tonight?"

The two girls looked at each other.

"Hey, Spaz, throw me one of those," called DeSilva. I tossed him a soldier.

Raina reached over my shoulder and grabbed two bottles. "Thanks, Spaz."

"Oo, keep it working," I said.

"Pig."

In the den I sat on the case, half-listening to Noy and half-watching the party. Kids from the wrestling team gathered around Donk.

"You up for a swim later on?" asked Noy.

"Maybe after a few more of these," I said.

"Why are we sitting in the corner?" asked Noy.

"You're filling me full of shit," the captain of the wrestling team said, stomping his foot. "Tell me reality, not your personal fantasies."

"On every bible in this town, I swear," replied Donk. Gesturing with his hands, Donk continued his story. I couldn't catch the words.

"Naw haw haw haw." One of the wrestlers fell to the ground laughing.

"You can take that to the bank." Donk poked the captain in the chest.

"Want a soldier?" I asked Noy.

Noy leaned against me. "I'll try yours."

DeSilva pulled a CD from his coat and put it in the CD player.

Noy stood up. "Isn't this The Moxie Men?" Noy pulled me towards a bunch of kids dancing. "I love Slade Cleaves."

In the dark the dancers moved like a thirty-legged tarantula. Our bodies lunged for the notes pouring from the speakers. Amaranthine melodies woke dormant desires, filling our bodies, bending us, spinning us. Raina swigged her beer then spouted the cold liquid through the air. The amber bubbles floated with the notes. We moved through the icy spray, shifting and turning, our earthbound bodies endlessly shifting and turning. I placed my hands on Noy's waist. She moved closer. Her skin was damp. Her hair smelled sweet as fresh-cut grass.

"Everyone's pretty shitty, huh?" I said.

"They think they're so original." Noy rested her head on my shoulder. Blood rushed to my mid-section. That second Noy began to *really* exist. I nudged her ear. She looked up. I leaned forward and we kissed. Her warm and wet mouth surprised me.

Donk hurried to the keg, refilled his cup, then rejoined the wrestlers. "Wait until you hear this one. During summer vacations I used to crash at Pushkoff's house every night. We'd pitch a tent in his attic and sleep up there. So, one night I dreamed I was taking a whiz in the school bathroom."

"Hey, I dreamed that too," DeSilva said.

Donk nodded. "Next thing I know, the sleeping bag was soaked. So, quiet as hell, I snuck downstairs with my sleeping bag."

(Nine years earlier, 3:30 a.m.)

"What's that noise?" Mrs. Pushkoff sat up in bed. She checked the clock.

"What noise?"

"A high whining noise. Sounds like the vacuum cleaner."

Mr. Pushkoff pulled the blanket over his head. "At this hour? Certainly not our kids. They don't vacuum during the day."

Mrs. Pushkoff put on her bathrobe. "I'm going to find out what that noise is." She walked down the hallway.

"If it is the vacuum cleaner, Rachel, for God's sake, let them finish."

Mrs. Pushkoff paused in front of the bathroom door. "Noy is that you?" She knocked on the door. "Noy?"

Donk turned off the hairdryer. "It's me, Donny."

"What in Christ's name are you doing with the hairdryer at this hour?"

"Think I got swimmer's ear from being in the pool all day."

"Do you have an earache?"

"A little one, yeah."

"Open the door so I can take a look."

"No." Donk rushed to the door. "This happens every summer. Just a few minutes with the hairdryer and I'll be fine."

"All right, but wake me up if your earache persists."

Donk took a haul off his soldier. "I'm telling you, when I was done, Noy's sleeping bag smelled like Hitler's revenge. Next morning, I rolled up the sleeping bag and stuffed it in a toy box. When Pushkoff got up, I told him I had to mow the lawn and booked it home."

Outside, four lacrosse players climbed up the steps to the front door. Pushkoff lowered his arm. "Sorry, boys, house is packed." Behind the lacrosse players, two of Noy's friends gazed into their compacts. Pushkoff raised his arm. "Ladies, come on in." Pretty miffed, the lacrosse players stood on the lawn and talked with each other. Moments later, they charged into the house, knocking Pushkoff onto the carpet. Trying to avoid a hail of fists, Pushkoff thrust his head into the gut of a player and bear-hugged him. Chugging in from the den, Donk faked a haymaker, reached for a player's ankles, and tipped him onto the carpet. Grabbing the kid's hair, Donk swung his fist repeatedly.

"Get this guy off me!"

Pushkoff squeezed harder. A loud crack sounded.

Donk kept swinging.

Raina grabbed Donk's shirt and pulled him off the player. "Are you sick or what?"

"He deserves it." Donk spit at the player as DeSilva hauled him out the door.

Pushkoff tried to button his shirt, but the buttons were gone. Blood leaked from a gash above his eye. He flashed his twenty-tooth grin. "I love it. Just wait until we see those boys in school."

We unscrewed the screen door and hid the bent frame in the cellar.

At 12:40, a suburban rolled into the driveway.

Mrs. Pushkoff got out. "Who recommended that film anyway?"

"The Brewer's. Why?"

"It was a glorified soap opera."

"I don't know. I kind of liked the desert scene," replied Mr. Pushkoff. "Imagine dying of thirst like that."

"Your poor mother must have been a saint," said Mrs. Pushkoff, picking up a beer bottle off the lawn.

Mr. Pushkoff opened the door and switched on the front hall light. A trace of ammonia lingered. "There's something wrong here. It's too clean."

It Was The Maps. We Didn't Have a Damn One

(Fort Humboldt)

Raina dropped her backpack on the trail. "I quit. I can't feel my knees."

"But we're not even half-way," Donk protested.

"Go on without me," said Raina.

"Sheesh." Donk sat on a log and tightened his laces.

"What are you—a sissy?" I said, unscrewing the cap off my canteen and taking a haul.

Raina hawked a loogy. The loogy arc'd through the air and landed on my shirt.

"What the-" I grabbed Raina's ponytail and pulled her towards me. Using her ponytail as a rag, I wiped the loogy off my shirt. Raina reached down, grabbed my jewel box and squeezed. I fell to the trail in a fetal position.

"Who's a sissy now?"

"Screw you," I said, clutching my jewel box.

Raina raised a rock above her head.

Rushing towards her, Donk smacked the rock from Raina's hand. The rock thudded on the dirt. "Are you sick or what!"

Raina took off down the trail.

Donk pulled on his backpack and headed up the trail. "I can't take this. I'm going to the summit by myself."

"Wait for me." I hurried after Donk.

Back home Mom poured vinegar, poppy seeds, sugar, corn oil, and salt into a blender. "I don't understand it."

Dad tilted a brown bottle. "Just a splash here and there."

"What was your sister Beatrice like in high school?"

"Just enough to navigate between the ting and tang." A spoon clanked in Dad's glass.

"Bee never liked me." Mom pushed a button. The blender whined. "Who is this Crispin fellow anyway? Why haven't I seen the Pushkoff children lately? Are you listening to me?"

"Whoa, Bessy, nice and slow." Dad sat down at the kitchen table. "What was that, hon?"

"I found a prophylactic in her purse. Do you think she's having sex?"

"I hope not." Dad sipped his drink and looked up.

"I don't want her behaving like your sister. All that runnin' around."

"The thing about Bee is it's all about Bee, and if the sidewalks don't rise up to greet her feet, she's willing to toss the baby, the bath water, and the whole bucket out the window."

The summit of Red Feather Ridge is a sneaky mother because of all the gullies and crests before the real summit. Hikers are often tricked into thinking they've reached the summit when they've only peaked another crest. Adding to this prank are the disappearing trails. Since most hikers turn back after two or three crests, the higher up a hiker climbs, the more overgrown the trails are. It's not unusual for hikers to veer off a trail for half-a-mile and not even know it. If that wasn't enough, the size of White Mountain National Forest is a nightmare. It stretches umpteenth miles north towards Quebec. Last summer a few hikers disappeared for days until they stumbled onto a logging road near Copperville.

Donk dipped his canteen into a stream. "Damn hikers are always swiping signs for their bedrooms."

I inspected an arrow painted on a rock. "Which way does it point?"

"Can't tell," said Donk.

"How 'bout we use the right rule: when in doubt, turn right. That way we're assured of being right at least half the time."

"Where'd you get that from?" asked Donk.

"Mr. Brewer."

"Don't believe everything Mr. Brewer tells you. Remember, he's a football coach. To him, life's a humongous game of football."

"What's wrong with that? It works for him."

"I don't know." Donk felt inside his pocket and pulled out a glass vile. "I just don't want the tangled parts of my life defined by a quarterback sneak or an all-out blitz." Donk unscrewed the cap and gingerly poured a yellow pill into his hand. "All this team spirit dog-doo. If I'm feeling like a piece of human garbage, I want the freedom to slither on my back."

We climbed over a toppled birch. "Yeah, but how would you feel if I slugged you in the face?"

Donk popped the pill into his mouth then slid the vial back into his pocket. "If it's sincere, bring it on. I probably did something to deserve it. There's all this tip-toeing going on in our family. It sucks. We've been tip-toeing so long, I forgot what we were tip-toeing around."

"But Mom cries so easily and Dad goes ballistic."

"Look, if you don't feel it, don't say it. Period."

"Sounds like we need to alter our running game."

"Yuck, yuck, yuck," said Donk, bouncing a pine cone off my head.

"How about Fallon? He doesn't candy-coat anything. Remember the time he and Dad got into a shoving match on the 4th of July?"

"It's a start," said Donk. "Trouble is, Fallon hasn't felt an emotion in so long that his brain needs to send a telegram to his body just to make sure they're still attached."

Above us, a tiny stream flowed off a granite ledge. Wisps of spray stuck to my face. We continued up the trail.

(Three months earlier)

"Donny, Kuba, come here." Dad motioned us to the showroom window. *"Take a look at Fallon. He just sold a station wagon to that family. Do you know how I can tell? Look at the way he's swinging his belly and whistling—that's Fallon's victory walk. He's got what it takes to be an ace salesman: shark skin and the heart of a whore. Last month he grossed twelve-hun off his best friend."*

Fallon walked into the showroom, reached into his desk and pulled out a sold tag.

"Did you send that sled down the road, Fallon?" asked Dad.

"Just in time to reach my incentive and earn my monthly bonus."

"But this month is old news. How many sleds can you roll next month? Twenty-five?"

"Was Mayor Curley on the take?" Fallon licked his pinky and walked towards Dad. "Wet Willie?"

"Beast. You stay away from me." Dad hurried into his office.

Outside, Fallon slid a sold tag under the wiper blade of the wagon.

As we descended into a gully the hardwoods grew farther apart. Donk knelt down and searched amongst the fallen leaves for a trail. We turned right.

"What do you think of Noy?" I asked.

"She's mint, but don't forget, her dad's an undertaker. Surround the casket with flowers. Wear a black suit. Glue the lips shut for the wake. Make sure the flower car leads the hearse. To undertakers, it's not what you do that counts, it's how you look doing it."

"Reminds me of a lot of bands."

Donk cracked a smile. Ahead of us, a salamander scuttled under a leaf.

"She's been working hard, if you know what I mean," I said.

"That could be a padded bra. Girls do those sorts of things. You have to beware of falsies."

"How can you tell?"

"Simple, if there aren't any seam lines and they're too round—definitely falsies. Damn, I thought this was a day hike."

"Tell me the truth, Donk." Without stopping, I reached around and unzipped my backpack, then pulled out a can of soda. "Have you ever gone past first base?"

"What do you think?"

"I don't know." After taking a haul, I handed Donk my soda. "Well?"

"Well, what?" Donk demanded.

"What was it like?"

"Those things are hard to describe. My hands felt disconnected like they were someone else's hands."

"But what did the actual touch feel like?" I asked.

"Surprisingly warm like a ram's horn."

I had never felt a ram's horn. "What the heck does a ram's horn have to do with anything?"

"You ask too many questions. Go pester Raina."

"Why? What does she know?"

"Oh please," sneered Donk. "She says it makes you forget to think."

Balancing ourselves on a log, we walked over a brook. On the other side, triangles of sunlight covered the forest floor.

"What's so fun about that?"

A Dapper Honest Abe
(Ten years earlier)

Mom washed dishes as she balanced a phone between her chin and shoulder. "Yes. Okay. Uh-huh. Twenty-inch inseam. Twenty-four-inch waist. Okay."

Donk tapped Mom's shoulder.

"Just a minute." Mom cupped the receiver. "What is it, Donny?"

"Big black hat."

"Oh yes, we need a stovepipe hat. Head size?" Mom felt Donk's head. "I don't know, eighteen inches? Ten years old. Sounds about right. Do you have any cotton beards? Uh-huh. Good. Tomorrow after four. Uh-huh. Great, see you then." Mom hung up the phone. "All set, honey."

"Yeah." Donk circled around the kitchen.

"What do you mean you gave Raina the compass to hold?" said Donk.

"How did I know she was going to act like a psycho?"

"Let me see those." Donk grabbed my binoculars and climbed up a tall pine.

"See anything?"

Donk shook his head.

I checked my watch. "We should head down."

"I'm not going to blow a whole day hiking so you can be a wuss."

"But it could take another hour to reach the top."

Donk shinnied down the pine. "If we don't reach the summit, then what's the point?"

I started up the trail. "Okay, but we'll probably end up lost and they'll find our bodies up in Canada." Above our heads a red-bellied hawk floated in the sky. "I bet that red-bellied nutbag can see the entire forest."

(Ten years earlier, continued)

"They've banned funeral homes in Massachusetts from doing in-house cremations," said Mr. Pushkoff, wrapping a popcorn ball in wax paper. "And I just bought a retort. If the MFDA doesn't grandfather us in—we're out 30,000 clams."

The doorbell rang.

"I'll get the door." Carrying a tray of popcorn balls, Mrs. Pushkoff opened the front door.

"Trick or treat," said Donk.

"Well hello there, President Lincoln. I didn't know you lived in Merriam Hill."

"I live next door," said Donk, adjusting his cotton beard.

"And you know Marna Brice too? Hi Marna."

"Hi Rachel," said Mom.

Donk slid a popcorn ball off the tray and into his pillowcase.

"What a dapper Honest Abe," said Mrs. Pushkoff. "A carbon copy. Now Abe, what do you have to say for yourself?"

"We are engaged in a great Civil War, testing whether any nation so conceived can endure. The world will little note, nor long remember what we say here, but it can never forget what those men-" Donk's eyes began to well up. With his pillowcase, Donk wiped his face.

"Oh Marna, did I say something wrong?" Mrs. Pushkoff reappeared with a box of tissues.

"He says people can tell his beard is fake."

"Fake? Why that's a real beard, isn't it? Noah, go grab your razor; Donny needs a shave."

Mr. Pushkoff appeared with a can of shaving cream and a razor.

Donk hid behind Mom. "Do you really think so?"

"Honest to goodness," said Mrs. Pushkoff.

"God, the sun practically runs from the sky after 7:30," I said, squeezing through a thicket of spruce.

"What do you think, left or right?" asked Donk.

"Straight down. If we don't stumble onto a trail, we'll start yelling. If no one answers, we'll build a humungous fire. They'll definitely spot that." My shin thumped against a fallen tree. "Cruddy buckets of crap," I yelled as blood dripped down my shin.

"All this climbing and not one vertigo ledge, not one valley of spruce spread out before our eyes," said Donk.

"It was the trails. They just disappeared," I said, unscrewing my canteen and splashing water onto my shin.

"It was the crests. There were friggin' too many."

"It was the maps. We didn't have a damn one."

How Did The Horses Know?

CAN YOU LIFT A SONG OFF THE RADIO AFTER ONE LISten and go play it on your Fender? After a few Heff talls, would you bull rush a herd of Ivy League fencing snobs and try to rub their faces in the grass? How fast can you shadowbox? Could you trade guitar solos with Crispin till a fork twisted in your gut and lava oozed out? In the wee hours, would you pull up sixty-three street signs and dump them on your best buddy's lawn—just for the chance to be considered? Because in Merriam Hill certain titles needed to be given to you by your friends. Just calling yourself a *sick unit* wouldn't make it so. It's like being popular, if you have to say you are, buddy, you aren't.

So Donk and his buddies concocted a series of nutbag stunts in order to put themselves in the running to earn the prized title. Soon a point system sprung up. Now a kid needed to do more than just pull-off a sick stunt, the stunt needed to be performed with a fearless gusto that highlighted the pilgrim talent of the doer. For instance, backing up onto your buddy's lawn and heaving a pile of street signs would earn the doer twenty points, but standing the signs upright and planting them in fresh cement would earn a much higher score. Likewise, tackling a couple posers at a Tufts wine tasting party would earn just an average score, but bull rushing the entire Harvard men's rugby team in a Salem State t-shirt would land the doer a whole truckload of points. In time, the stunts became even nuttier and required outrageous sack. Streaking past the police station on a horse head broomstick while wearing a tricorn hat and reciting "The Midnight Ride Of Paul Revere" was one of many such stunts attempted during Donk's senior year at Merriam Hill High, a stunt that landed Pushkoff in jail and cost Mr. Pushkoff a pile in lawyer's fees, but the bar had been raised and a new goal emerged: not who was merely a sick unit, but who was, in fact, the sickest unit. A furious race had begun and the clock was ticking.

"You coming, Spaz?" called Donk from the driveway.

"DeSilvaaaa," I said, squeezing in the back seat of Pushkoff's Diplomat. "How's it going?"

"Little Brice." DeSilva punched my arm. "You going out with the big boys tonight?"

"Someone's got to teach you Girl Scouts how to swill a few soldiers," I said (never having swilled more than two soldiers at a party before).

"But we're not downing soldiers tonight," said DeSilva, arching his eyebrow like John Belushi. "We're drinking scorpion bowls at Peking Gardens in Woburn. Then we're going to see who can hoist the most bowls. We're building a collection for prom night."

"Let me grab my gym bag first," I said, hurrying into the house.

"Hurry up. We have to go," called Pushkoff.

"Okay, all set." I climbed into the car. Donk shut the door.

"They're going to check your bag," said DeSilva.

On Route 128, Pushkoff signaled right and veered to an outside lane. A Blazer swerved in front of us. In the breakdown lane Pushkoff buried the pedal. His Dodge chugged past the Blazer. Pushkoff made a Howdy-Doody face at the driver. "Use a blinker much?"

In the parking lot, streetlamps beamed cones of frozen light onto the cars. Pushkoff turned off the engine and coasted into a parking space. We walked towards a tall wooden door with carved elephants and brass knockers.

"I don't have an ID," I said.

Donk pawed through his wallet. Amidst guitar picks, Bim Skala Bim ticket stubs, Heff beer caps with their secret puzzles, and a squished condom, Donk fished out a license. "Try this."

"Where'd you get that?" I checked the birth date: 8/03/44. Then I recognized the photo. "Hey, this isn't going to work." I handed Dad's license back to Donk.

"Will too. The owner Heston Chu just bought a van off Dad and told him the waiters barely speak English. He picks them up every morning in Chinatown and drives them out."

"But the photo doesn't look like me."

"We'll give them all our IDs at once. Besides, they don't look at the picture, only the numbers."

"They're not going to turn away business," Pushkoff added.

Inside, the waiter set four menus on our table. "Would you like drinks?"

"Four scorpion bowls," said Pushkoff.

The waiter studied our faces. "Can I see IDs?" he asked.

Quickly, Donk handed the waiter our IDs.

The waiter set four ceramic bowls on our table. On each bowl, women in grass skirts danced in front of a Buddhist temple. Donk glanced at me.

"DeSilva, how'd you miss that tackle today?" asked Pushkoff. "See a ghost?"

"I think you need to stop sniffing hair gel. It's only six games into the season and Bart Graph already has a full boat to BC. Graph has more sick moves than the mayor of South Boston. How do you expect me to tackle a running back like that?" asked DeSilva.

"Fill him in," said Pushkoff.

"You don't follow the eyes, you chase the body. That's where the runner's really going," said Donk.

"It's true," said Pushkoff. "If my helmet points east, I'm probably heading west."

"I'm rolling up my pants the shit's so deep," said DeSilva. "If it were that easy, I'd be playing for the Patriots."

"I never commit to one direction until the runner commits," said Donk.

"But what if the runner pretends to commit?" I asked.

Pushkoff and Donk looked at each other. The buzz of human voices filled the restaurant.

"That's when you hit the film room to see which way the runner usually goes," said Pushkoff.

"Kid's got a point. We can study our nuts off, but in the end, we never really know which way the runner's going," said Donk.

The waiter set four more scorpion bowls onto our table. He reached for the empty ones.

"Still working on that." Donk held onto his bowl.

Pushkoff shook his head. "No way. Look at Fernandez. He leads the league in tackles every year. If you put in the work, you'll make the plays."

"Who's got time to think?" said Donk. "If a player hesitates, even for a split-second, it's a blown tackle. There's got to be a better way."

Pushkoff felt his biceps. "So tell us: what is it?"

"When I figure it out, I'll let you know."

"Aahhh."

"I knew it."

"He's tossing us like salad."

"I heard something once," I said, slipping an empty bowl into my gym bag.

Donk looked surprised. "What?"

"Meriwether Lewis wrote in his journals that when they reached the Waterton Mountain Range, the expedition turned south in search of a pass. A few days later, when they saw a low cloud-belt beside Mt. Stimpson, they began to climb. But Lewis observed that the horses kept tugging their reins south. Eventually, with a good bit of whipping, they forced the horses up the ridge. The decision to cross the Waterton Range at that point was a disaster. The south ridge of Mt. Stimpson rises almost 9000 feet through incredibly deep snow and treacherous ravines. The crossing took six days. Four men and eleven horses died from exposure. It wasn't until almost forty years later, when a second expedition arrived at the south ridge of Mt. Stimpson, that guides discovered Maria's Pass only two miles south of where Lewis & Clark had crossed. Maria's Pass rises 5,216 feet and could easily have been crossed in one afternoon if Lewis & Clark had only followed their horses." I sipped my scorpion bowl. "How did the horses know that Maria's Pass was there?"

In his jean jacket Donk buried a scorpion bowl. After glancing at the cashier, Pushkoff slipped a bowl under the table, then undid his pants. The waiter scribbled on our check and tore it from the pad.

"Everyone cough up eighteen bucks," said Donk.

A pyramid of crumpled bills formed on the table. Donk and Pushkoff got up and walked towards the exit. Stashing a second bowl in my bag, I followed, then veered off towards the bathrooms. Mr. Chen waved Donk and Pushkoff over. In his ski coat, with a bowl under his armpit, DeSilva walked past them and out the door. In the bathroom I removed the contents from my bag.

In the parking lot, Donk sat on the hood of his Nova. "What did you expect with an eight-inch bowl down your pants?"

"Me?" said Pushkoff. "What about that hump in your jacket? You looked like the python who swallowed a pig."

DeSilva cracked a Heff Tall in the back seat. "Next time, take notes from five-fingers DeSilva. Hey, where's little Brice?"

"Probably frisking him right now. Dumb gym bag."

The carved door opened and a garishly thin, tall woman walked out.

"That's the ugliest girl I've ever seen," said DeSilva.

"Yeah, but look at the talent," said Pushkoff, pointing to the woman's boobs.

The woman walked towards Donk and Pushkoff and put a cigarette between her lips. "Hey, boys?" she asked, adjusting her hemline. "Will you give a light to a lonely lady?"

Pushkoff and Donk rolled off the hood and fell onto the tar. Grabbing his crotch, DeSilva ran into the bushes.

From behind two double-D cups I removed a pair of scorpion bowls. "What's the record for swiping scorpion bowls anyway?" I asked.

"Where'd you find him, Donny?" said Pushkoff, resting his arm on my shoulder.

"You're dead, little Brice," called DeSilva from the bushes.

"You're one *sick unit*," said Donk, wiping his face.

At that moment, a bottle rocket blasted off from my feet, surged through my body, and soared across the sky towards the stars.

The Rosary Bead Crossover Step

(Quincy)

In the front lot at Brice Chevrolet a guy in a hardhat hooked a cable to a Chevrolet sign. A crane lifted the sign upwards. When the sign reached the top of a signpost, two guys guided the sign towards two metal clasps on the post. Meanwhile, on Mass Ave, a transport vehicle filled with new Chevrolets slowed to a stop. The driver got out, set traffic cones in the street, and pulled out two long steel ramps from the back of the transport. One-by-one, he drove each car down the steel ramps and onto the car lot. At the wash bay, he got out of the car and handed Raina and me the keys. After inspecting each car for damage and missing parts, we washed each car then drove it to the front row.

In the showroom, Dad excitedly spoke into the phone. "I want a hotdog machine, popcorn popper, and cotton candy spinner. Send me a couple boys too. Dad peered through the window at us. "Actually, I'm all set in that department." Dad listened. "We already explored that. I tried to get Jim Rice to come and sign balls, but his agent wants three-Gs. Cam Neely? How much does he want? Oo, kind of steep. How about twelve-hundred? Let me kick it around for a while. Sure thing. Call you this-after." Dad hung up the phone. He and Fallon walked outside to the car lot. "Raina, do you know how to make cotton candy?"

"Do you know how to pour a glass of milk?"

"Oo, my lungs are icing over." Dad inhaled in a hyper way. "Good, make sure you're ready to walk out the door at 6:59 a.m. this Saturday." Turning to me, Dad faked a punch.

As I tried to shift right, Dad stepped on my sneaker and slapped me across the face. "Think quick."

"Cheater," I said.

"Always watch the feet. Think you're ready to take your first up?"

Suddenly, I became aware of the smallest details: the green algae growing on the walls of the wash bay, the triangles of missed dirt on the car we had just washed, the eight magnetic license plates stuck to the safe in the showroom, and, for the first time, I noticed Dad's sport coat was made of cotton and not wool.

"Who me?" I tried to play it chill. "Definitely. I've already got my nickname: King Gross, 'cause I'm going to gross eighteen-hun off every Harvard barney that steps onto the lot."

"Keep it down. The walls have ears, ears have lips, and lips flap." Dad turned to Fallon. "He's not lacking in confidence, is he?"

Fallon clipped the tip off a cigar. "Cocky bean pole like his old man."

Dad watched the crew fasten the sign to the pole. "I'm mailing discount flyers to every used car owner in Middlesex County. We're busting out of the minors and heading for the big leagues. Hey Fallon, how many tires do you think you'll be able to roll now?"

"How many mistresses do the Kennedy's have?" said Fallon with a laugh the sound of a broken gear box.

Dad circled around the showroom with a pretend dance partner. "You just wait till Skip Lee gets a load of us. We'll show him. Just a used car store. We'll see who the public decides to trust. We'll see." Dad gathered up Raina. "Come on, honey, it's easy."

Natten går tunga fjätt, runt gård och stuva
Kring jord som soln förlätt, skuggorna ruva
Då i vårt mörka hus, stiger med tända ljus
Sankta Lucia, Sankta Lucia.

"This is a two-step: one two, one two, one two-. Think of a train pulling out of North Station. Hey, you've got pretty good rhythm. Your Mother's not so bad either." Dad lifted his knees higher. "This is great. Fallon, I want to personally speak with any customer who drives in here with a Ford. I'll lose money on a sled to steal a deal from Skip Lee." Dad and Raina danced around the showroom. "Ma played this song when I was a kid. Thought I forgot it, but now I remember it. Can you believe it? I can remember every single word."

That night in our backyard Donk ran through a tire grid wearing his cleats and padded pants. On the porch Dad thumbed through *The Boston Globe*.

"I'm spent," said Donk. "I'm going inside."

"Like fun. You don't get ahead watching TV. Another twenty," said Dad.

Donk walked towards our house. "But I've got homework."

"Tell me another one." Dad put down the paper. "Listen, the only way a kid learns the crossover step is to do it six hours a day for seven to eight years until the old patterns break and response becomes instant. Think of rosary beads. You don't think anything's happening, right? Then one day time turns into molasses. You don't have to think anymore, you just *do*."

"Sounds loony to me," said Donk. "Did you ever feel that?"

"No, but I was a hack. But Jerry Kramer of the Green Bay Packers, they should freeze his body and put it in an art museum. When Kramer dropped his shoulder and pushed off on the outside foot to fill a hole, his cleats were half an inch off the turf. Go look at the old films."

"Gee, I didn't think you respected anybody," said Donk.

"Quiet." Dad's belly wiggled. "That's because respect lasts about as long as a Styrofoam cooler. You better find a better motivation than that, son."

"Like what?" asked Donk, throwing a block at a pretend opponent.

"Like the mind clear as a windshield for one simple task. God, Kramer did it better than anyone who ever laced up a pair of cleats."

Dad picked up the sports page and began to read. "Tell me smarty pants, what technique do you favor for a downfield block: a roll block or a forearm shiver?"

"A roll block. That way, if you miss the defender, he still backs up enough to miss the tackle."

Behind the sports page, Dad made a face of approval. "Not bad."

Knees pumping like pistons, Donk ran through the holes in the tire grid.

The Haymaker

(Paducah)

At the gym Pushkoff lowered and raised a steel bar with 260-pounds of barbells attached while his buddy DeSilva stood over him and counted: "Three, four, five, six, seven, eight, nine, ten, eleven, twelve, thirteen, fourteen—one more, big guy."

Pushkoff tried to raise the bar.

"Come on, don't be a wuss."

Pushkoff's face shook fiercely.

"Fifteen," called DeSilva as the bar clinked.

After another set of bench presses, Pushkoff walked over to the mirror and began a rep of curls. By the bleachers a girl with nutmeg hair covered her face. Pushkoff set down his dumbbells and walked over to the girl. "Hey, what's going on?"

"Nothing, I'm having a crappy day," said Raina.

"I can see that. What's happened?"

"I don't want to talk about it."

"Come on, who am I going to tell?"

Raina pulled a tissue from her purse and wiped her face. "You swear?"

Pushkoff nodded.

"You know Tossy? Well he's been spreading rumors through the whole school."

"What's he saying?"

"Noy said he blabbed to the hockey team that I'm easy."

"Why, whud you two do?"

"We drank a few beers at Keenan's Park—we didn't go all the way or anything."

"Don't worry, no one'll believe that peckerhead. Besides, he won't be able to run his motor mouth if his jaw's wired shut."

"He's such a dick." Raina pulled a brush from her bag and began combing her hair. "I can't believe I let that maggot touch me."

"Let me finish my workout, then I'll go looking for him." Pushkoff walked towards the mirror and picked up a pair of forty-pound barbells. "DeSilva, do you know where Tossy lives?"

Across the street, Donk was sprawled on our couch, Donk read the Sports page. "What's the scoop?" he asked.

"Mrs. Hunger says I'm not working up to my potential so they booted me from orchestra till I pull up my grades."

"Whoop-dee-doo. Who wants to play worn out Broadway tunes anyway. Did you hear what Rice did last night?"

"What'd he do?"

"He checked his swing and snapped his bat in half," said Donk.

"I'd hate to get punched by him. Anyway, you know what Raina and Noy did Friday night?"

Donk scanned the Red Sox batting averages.

"Raina told Mom she was sleeping over Noy's and Noy told Mrs. Pushkoff she was sleeping over our house. Then they stayed out all night partying with the hockey team."

"Ask me if I care."

"Look, this is important. You know a kid named Tossy?"

Reaching under the couch, Donk pulled out a tray of éclairs. "Check out what I found in the fridge."

"Better not. Mom and Dad are having company."

"I'm powerless." Donk opened his mouth.

"Give me one of those."

Donk moaned. "Chocolate from the mountains of Switzerland. Bavarian cream from the milk maids of Germany." Donk fell off the couch and rolled around the rug. "Oh my god, I'm climaxing."

"I hope Mom and Dad have an all-star team of shrinks lined up for you."

The screen door opened. Mom walked into the house with grocery bags and fresh cut orchids. "What are you two doing?" She removed a vase from under the sink. "Where's your sister?"

Donk nudged the tray of éclairs under the couch.

"Raina's across the street with Mrs. Pushkoff. Guess she's pretty cut up," I said.

"What?" Mom set down the bags on the kitchen counter.

"Some guy on the hockey team's been bad mouthing her."

"You mean that greasebag Tossy?" said Donk.

"Stay away from the fridge. We're having the Irvines over for dinner. Vince Irvine is high up at First Trust and a good contact for your father." Mom walked to phone and dialed. "Hello, Rachel? Have you seen Raina?"

"What do you think I've been trying to tell you for the past century? Take the cotton out of your ears and stuff it in your mouth. Noy heard that Tossy's been blubbering to his hockey buddies that Raina's an easy lay."

"How does Noy know?"

"Noy's seeing Stan Bates. He's the goalie," I said.

Donk wiggled his fingers and felt inside his pocket. "Do you know anything about Tossy?"

"His Dad's a mechanic at Skip Lee's. I guess he's loo-loo on ice. Always getting kicked out of games. He even slugged a ref once."

"Did the ref go down? Hey we've got to figure out a way to get these éclairs back into the fridge before Mom notices we scoffed a few."

"Just give me a minute in the bathroom with a ketchup bottle." I hurried to the kitchen. "Mom, will you come in here for a sec?" I called from the bathroom.

"Just a minute, Rachel." Mom cupped the receiver with her hand. "What is it, honey?"

"I think I'm bleeding internally."

Mom leaned over the toilet and studied the rose-colored water with red clumps in the bowl. "We'll have to call Dr. Van Dyne." She fingered through the phonebook. "When did you first notice this?"

"Well, I'm off to practice," called Donk after closing the fridge door. "You're gone," he mouthed to me. Then he kneed the screen door open.

"Rachel, can I call you back?"

In his Nova, Donk pushed an Indigo Girls' CD into the player. The song "Closer To Fine" floated from the speakers. Down Merriam Hill my brother's car shifted and turned towards silence.

At the table I held my stomach.

"Hi, Marna Brice here. Can I have a word with Dr. Van Dyne? My sixteen-year-old is passing blood. Ah-huh. No, I think this is the first time. Should we bring him in?"

The screen door opened. Dad walked into the kitchen. "Donny passed me going at least thirty miles over the speed limit. I almost had to swerve into the woods to avoid him."

"Just a minute, hon. Uh-huh. Yes. Have you noticed any weight loss?"

I shook my head.

"Oh, for the love of Christ," said Dad, sliding his briefcase into the closet. He unscrewed the cap off a Seagram's bottle. "What the heck happened to you?"

That Friday, when the C-period bell rang at Merriam Hill High, Donk walked to the part of the quad where his buddies hung out between classes. "What are you sick puppies up to?" said Donk, dumping his books on the walkway.

"I had this dream last night," replied DeSilva. "Your girlfriend kept mailing me her bra with a bunch of love letters. So the Brice boys came over to my house wanting a piece of me. You sick puppies were in my driveway clanking empty beer bottles together and calling: 'DeSilva, come out to play-ay. DeSilvaaaaa, come out to play-ay.' So I came out in my slippers and knocked out all three of you with one punch. Then I woke up and thought: hey, this could be reality."

"Yah, yah, yah, very funny—you skinny twig." Head faking DeSilva, Donk wrapped his arms around DeSilva's thighs, picked him up, and walked around the quad. "I'm laughing so hard I could puke."

"Hey put me down, Brice," DeSilva called.

"How are you going knock out all three of us when you can't even take one of us?"

"Let go of me before I scratch you a new set of eyes."

"Hey Donny?" Pushkoff tapped Donk's shoulder. "There he is." Pushkoff pointed to a kid in a cracked leather jacket. "By the payphone. That's the guy who smeared Raina's name all over Merriam Hill."

"You mean the peckerhead with the shitkickers?" Donk set DeSilva back on his feet. "Let's take a walk over there and see what's going on." Donk walked towards the payphone followed by a stream of his buddies. "Hey pal, what's going on?"

Tossy looked up at Donk, but continued talking.

"Who are you talking to?"

"Hold on a sec." Tossy smiled at Donk, revealing a chipped tooth. "What do you want?"

"Are you the guy who's been talkin' smack about my sister?"

Tossy gripped the receiver tight. "Maybe, what's it to you?"

Donk balled his fists. "Well next time I hear your rubber lips flapping—"

"Your sister's a hosebag—what can I tell you."

"You piece of human garbage. My sis—"

Tossy swung the receiver. Donk threw a haymaker. The receiver struck Donk's cheek. Donk's fist caught Tossy just above his eye. Tossy slumped to the ground, the receiver dangling above his body.

"My sister deserves to be treated better than that," said Donk, walking back to the quad with a blue welt forming on his cheek.

Track 12

Touch a Dirty Dish

Dad carefully folded a piece of paper on his desk. "Hey, Fallon." A paper airplane floated towards the puffy-faced salesman. "I think it's the Irish Air Force."

Fallon drew back a rubber band. A paperclip ripped through the airplane's wing. "Eagle-Eye Moran strikes again."

"Tell me, Eagle-Eye, what deals are you working?"

"I'm trying to hawk the DeGeneres deal, but she's radioactive. No bank will touch her. She's got sixties and nineties coming out her ears."

"Call Joel DeSilva at the Credit Union. We practically gave him his last sled."

"Already tried, but he's only buying A and B paper. Guess a few big shots from the regional office paid him a visit." Fallon's belly jiggled. "They've got the highest repo rate in the state."

"What did Mayflower Savings say?"

"They want another grand down," said Fallon.

"Cheapskates." Dad scanned the lot. "Show them a phony-G down."

"Already am."

"What are you holding?" asked Dad.

"Eleven-hun."

"We can't afford to lose any deal." Dad chewed his pen. "Send the deal back to Mayflower showing another five-hun down. If they go for it, stroke a check to Ms. DeGeneres for fifteen-hun and have her sign a promissory note. If they still balk, send it back showing eighteen-hun down."

Fallon pulled out a fresh credit app from his top drawer.

Outside, a Corvette slowed to a stop. Dr. Van Dyne climbed out in his hospital scrubs and hurried over to a new Suburban. He hurried into the showroom. "Hi Galvin, I'm on call so I only have a minute, what's the best you can do for that Suburban?"

"Good to see you, Neil. Are you trading in the 'vette?"

"Don't know. Probably sell it outright, but give me a price both ways. My kid just got his license and I don't want him getting any ideas."

"Have a seat." Dad motioned towards a chair. He opened the inventory book and pulled out the Suburban's invoice. His fingers tapped a calculator. "You know, Neil, anytime you sell a vehicle privately you risk a lawsuit."

Dr. Van Dyne glanced at his wristwatch. "How so?"

"The Mass lemon law states that sellers have to stand by their vehicles for thirty days. That means, some joker could hotdog around Revere Beach in your car for twenty-nine days, then drop it off in your driveway—and you'd have to take it back."

"It says that?"

"Yup. What year is your 'vette?"

"82."

"How many miles she got?" asked Dad.

"Around fifty-thou."

"Let me get the exact number," said Dad, hurrying towards the door. "Could make a big difference."

* * *

At 6:05 p.m. behind the old train depot in Merriam Hill center, two girls smoked cigarettes.

"I'm going to wear black for a year," said Raina. "Nick Shabbot is a jerk for swallowing those pills. I could have helped him out."

"Yeah, what would you have done?" said Noy.

"We could have hung out and talked and I would've really listened—not just pretend to listen. That pisses me off. Most people pretend they care, when in reality, if A & B were legal, there'd be one non-stop brawl."

"If that's true, I'm glad they're pretending," said Noy.

"Trouble is, when enough people are doing it, you can't tell where the pretending ends and the real feelings begin."

"How do you know?" said Noy. "Name one person who's admitted this to you."

"Don't have to. Their faces give their guts away. Everyone's pretending they're not in pain."

On Mass Ave a Corvette signaled left and turned up Merriam Street. The girls dropped their cigarettes.

"Who's this snob?" said Raina, smoke flowing out her nostrils.

The Corvette slowed to a stop in front of the girls. The driver motioned to Raina. "Hop in." She climbed in. The driver turned to Noy. "Want a lift, Noy-toy?" Noy shook her head. The car sped up Merriam Hill.

"You embarrassed the heck out of me, Dad," said Raina.

"Who me? I had to sweet talk Dr. Van Dyne for forty minutes—just to get him to trade this popsicle. Showed him the auction slips. This sled's got 49,828 miles. After 50,000 miles, the trade-in value plummets faster than a Russian rocket. Listen to this." Dad down-shifted. The Corvette lunged forward.

"Hey, slow down, Evil Knievel, you almost smooshed that squirrel. Where are the seatbelts in this thing?"

Dad glanced over at his daughter. She wore a white tee-shirt on which she had handwritten the names of bands and albums all over it. He tried to read the words, but it all seemed gibberish. "What's the matter? Don't you trust my driving?"

"I don't trust anyone's driving."

"Good," said Dad as the Corvette careened into our driveway. "I'll remember that next time Crispin Degenerate hotrods over here to drive you to a keg party."

"It's *DeGeneres,* Dad. Get the name right." She shut the car door.

Dad studied Raina strutting up the walkway, flipping her hair back, a clump of bracelets jangling. What did all those bracelets mean? "How 'bout a little thanks for the lift?"

"No one touch a dirty dish," declared Mom after dinner, sliding a carrot cake out of the fridge. "Everyone on the porch. Kuba, grab the forks. Raina, grab dessert plates."

Donk began piling dirty plates on top of each other.

"Bup bup." Mom slapped his hand. "Leave them on the table."

On the porch Mom served slices of carrot cake, its cream cheese frosting thicker than cement.

"Mom?" asked Raina.

"What is it, honey?"

"When you were my age, did something ever happen to you that was so painful you never wanted to show your face in school again?"

"Let me think." Mom turned to Dad. "How do you like the frosting?"

"Tell me the truth," said Raina.

"Honey, do I ever not tell the truth?"

"I just mean, I don't want to hear a story about being a waitress and dropping a tray of dishes or something weak like that."

Mom closed her eyes. "Let me see."

(Christmas Eve, 22 years earlier)

"Okay Janet, Marna—you too, Neil." *Nunny's fingers moved across the piano keys.*

> *Une flambeau Jeanette Isabelle*
> *Une flambeau, courons au berceau.*
> *C'est Jésus, bonnes gens du hameau*
> *Le Christ est né, Marie appelle.*

"Alright, who's singing sharp?" asked Nunny. "Janet, you sing the bass cleft."

"Bass is too easy. Why can't I sing melody?" asked Janet.

"Not tonight, dear. Marna only knows how to sing melody. Be a sport. It's a gift to be able to sing the bass."

Janet made a face, then dropped her voice to low A.

> *Ah! Ah! Ah! Que la mère est belle*
> *Ah! Ah! Ah! Que l'enfant est beau.*
> *Qui vient là, frappant de la sorte?*
> *Wui vient là, frappant comme ça?*

Nunny turned to Neil Van Dyne. "I graduated with honors from the New England Conservatory."

Neil smiled and continued singing.

"When Rachmaninoff performed at the conservatory, I was hand-picked to play a duet with him. I was chosen out of eighty-two students by the man with octagon glasses."

"Oh Mother." Her eldest daughter's face flushed salmon. "Let Neil sing."

"I just thought Neil might like to know that he's not singing with any old Sunday school pianist." Nunny ended the verse with a fancy trill. "After our recital, when I had finished playing "The Polonaise," the man with octagon glasses walked over and tapped me on the shoulder. I quietly followed him onto the stage."

Neil leaned towards Nunny. "Rachmaninoff is my father's favorite composer."

Nunny looked down at the keys. "Your father has good taste. We played on the same stage." Nunny switched keys to F-minor. "I think it's time for 'Oh Come, Oh Come, Emanuel.'"

Neil checked his watch. "I'll have to get going after this."

Oh come, oh come Emanuel
And ransom captive Israel
That mourns in lonely exile here
Until the son of God appears.

"Oh dear, can't you stay a while longer," asked Nunny. "I'd feel better if you did."

"Thanks, Mrs. Clauson. I'd love to, but I promised my folks that I'd take them to Midnight Mass at St. Brigit's."

"Couldn't you tell your parents that it would mean the world to me if you stayed?"

"Mother," said Marna, "will you stop hounding Neil. His parents are expecting him. It's Christmas Eve."

Rejoice! Rejoice! Emanuel
Shall come to thee oh Israel.
To us the path of knowledge show
And cause us in her ways to grow.

~ 73 ~

Nunny stood up. *"I get nervous this late at night with just us girls here. Christmas is a dangerous time of year."* She placed her arm around Neil's. *"Why don't you stay with us. I just put fresh sheets on the bed in the guest room."*

"If your mom's really concerned, I'll call my parents. It's no problem. Father Feeney gives me the creeps anyway. He wears makeup."

"No, I won't have you held hostage. Now Mother, Neil's parents are waiting for him so they can go to Midnight Mass together. He can't just not show up."

Nunny chewed her lip. *"I don't know, dear. I'd feel better if Neil spent the night in the guest room. I just bought a half-gallon of eggnog."*

"Nonsense." Marna opened the door. *"You can leave, Neil."*

"Oh dear, I wish he wouldn't," said Nunny. *"Terrible things can happen on Christmas Eve."*

"We can take care of ourselves," said her eldest daughter as Neil crunched over the snow on their walkway. *"Neil, did I leave my gloves on your dashboard?"*

"I'll check."

Lifting a lit candle off a Yule log, Nunny rushed towards the Christmas tree. *"If he leaves, our tree could catch fire."*

Crackling needles popped in the pine branches.

"Mother, what on earth are you trying to do!" yelled Marna, grabbing the candle.

A wave of smoke rolled over the living room furniture.

"I don't know," said Nunny.

Dropping the gloves and running up the walk, Neil grabbed a shovel, propped open the front door, and rapidly pitched snow onto the flaming tree. A few moments later, he *dragged a smoldering tree out of the house and onto the front lawn.*

"I wish he wouldn't go," said Nunny on the couch, fidgeting with the steel strands of her Beethoven hair.

"I could have died," said Mom, finishing her carrot cake. "We had to take my mother to McLean's that night—on Christmas Eve."

"Did Neil still want to go out with you?" asked Raina.

Mom nodded. "It didn't bother Neil one bit, but I didn't know that at the time. I felt he had seen an unflattering side of me. So I avoided him at school and didn't take his calls at home. When your father asked me to the prom that spring, I said 'yes.'"

"So you might have married Dr. Van Dyne if it weren't for grandma's spells," said Raina.

"Oh I don't know, honey," said Mom.

We stared at Dad.

"What?"

"Dad's jealous."

"Don't make me laugh. Neil thinks the reason he's got a buck is because Jesus is rewarding him for his superior moral fiber."

"Well, maybe he is," said Mom.

We continued staring at Dad.

"Okay, so maybe I am a little. Neil's a decent guy too, always telling stories, but he's got to be the big cheese in every single one of 'em. He could be buying frozen peas at the supermarket when, suddenly, Neil's leading Pickett's Charge—right through the frozen foods."

A choir of musical honkings filled the sky. We looked up. Below the clouds, a v-fold of Canadian geese flew across floated through the sky. flapped their wings

~ 75 ~

"Why don't they crash into each other?" I asked.

"Because they're a lot farther apart than they seem," said Mom.

Dad stood up. "Well I'm goin' inside to catch the Sox game."

"Oh come on. Don't be a stick in the mud. Don't you remember any embarrassing moments?" asked Mom.

"Who me, I've got a million of 'em," said Dad.

"We're waiting."

Dad scanned the yard. His eyes fixed on the cars parked in the driveway. "Well this isn't really an embarrassing moment, but it's one I'm sure not proud of."

"You mean you never got caught," said Donk, snagging a moth from midair and sticking it in a spider's web.

The corners of Dad's mouth turned upwards. "You're right, smart-ass. You seem to know something about everything—why aren't you cutting hair or driving a taxi? Let me think." Dad looked down at the slats in the porch. "It happened my senior year. Each day at lunch, Stan Wardwell and I used to sit in his car puffing cigarettes. We were too cool to mix with the rest of the kids. So one time, I was about to snuff out my cigarette in the ashtray in the car door, only there wasn't an ashtray, just a hole where the ashtray had been. So instead of tossing the butt out the window, I casually dropped it into the hole. A few periods later, I was in chemistry class when I heard sirens. So I walked to the window. Outside, a fire truck was parked in front of Wardwell's car and a fireman was spraying water into the flaming console."

"What did you do?" I asked.

"Nothing. I walked back to my seat and sat down."

"You did?" asked Donk.

"Yeah, I didn't know if Wardwell had seen me drop the butt in his door or not. What would you have done?"

"If Wardwell was a good kid, I would have 'fessed up," said Donk.

"I'm not sure," I said.

"Did he have insurance?" asked Raina.

"Galvin!" Mom exclaimed.

A couple hours past midnight I poked my head into Donk's room.

"Donk?"

"I'm sleeping."

"Want to raid the fridge?"

"Leave me alone, Spaz. I just scoffed down a box of gingersnaps."

In the kitchen I put frozen waffles into the toaster, cut up a cantaloupe, and boiled a few eggs.

Donk thumped downstairs in a blanket. "I was half-awake anyway."

"Look." I showed Donk my hands. "They won't stop shaking."

"What's going on?"

"They were like this when I woke up."

"Here." Donk handed me a slice of cantaloupe. "Have some food."

The ceiling began spinning. In my head, waves rolled towards a distant shore. "It won't go away."

"What if we take a walk around Granny?"

"Don't think I can leave this chair."

"Waffles are ready." Donk opened the fridge and took out the syrup. The fridge light cast his shadow across the linoleum floor. "Eat until it goes away."

Next morning Raina refused to go to school. Dad was livid.

"What are you going to do, pump gas?" he asked, cutting into a block of cheddar.

"If I need to. What's wrong with that?"

"First of all, the fumes cause brain damage. Second, every wrench-turner in Merriam Hill will try to put the make on you. Third, what will you do for money? Start dealing hooch like Fallon's son and end up in the can? Should I keep going?"

Mom brought over the coffee pot.

Dad covered his mug.

"I'm not saying I have all the answers, but if I have to spend one more minute with those big-haired, designer-jeaned, two-faced, football callgirls and their sack of puss boyfriends, I'm going to jump off Concord Bridge with cinder blocks chained to my ankles." Raina's eyes darted from face to face.

"Father Feeney! Doesn't anyone like growing up anymore? This is supposed to be *your* time to fill your tank with stories: sneaking into movies, sleepin' on the beach, best friends. Someday you'll need to draw on those reserves."

"If you want to know the truth, it sucks," said Raina.

"Oh balls." Dad began pacing the way he did the day Key Bank cut his credit line.

"Honey, you don't want to be a high school dropout," said Mom, setting a bowl of sliced pineapples and bananas on the table.

"Think of whitewater rafting," said Donk, who had just come back from a rafting trip with the Pushkoffs. "If you hit a rock, keep moving 'cause there's another one flying up the river."

"I'm not going back."

"You will go to school—even if I have to place a saddle on your back and ride you there myself." Dad walked over to Raina. Now I've got to open the garage. Let's go."

"No way."

Grabbing Raina by her shoulders, Dad whisked her out the door. "If you're not going to school, then you're gonna work."

"Get your hands of me, you bully."

"Quiet." Dad looked at the neighbors' houses.

Raina tried to dig her heels in the walkway.

"Don't even try," said Dad, guiding Raina into the Corvette. The car disappeared down Merriam Street.

He Can Mix Things Together

(Fort Henry)

"Who was the first person killed in the Revolutionary War?" Mr. Brewer glared at the round heads of his students.

I raised my hand. "Crispus Attucks."

Mr. Brewer nodded. "Who cast the crucial vote in the Senate to acquit Andrew Johnson of his impeachment charges?"

I waved my arm. "Edmund G. Ross."

"Who discovered Natural Selection?"

"Lord Alfred Wallace," I said.

"Kill him," a classmate called out.

"String him up by his underwear."

"Quiet down, class." Mr. Brewer lifted a note card. "Who was western civilization's first monotheistic god?"

I looked around the classroom. No one raised a hand. "Akhnaton, God of the Sun," I said.

"Name the first medical team to perform open heart surgery?" Mr. Brewer scanned his student's faces. "DeSilva, do you want to make a guess?"

DeSilva shook his head.

"Okay Brice, who were they."

"Lillehei and Lewis."

Mr. Brewer shuffled his note cards. "Okay, someone else. Who was Anne Boleyn, and what was her nickname?"

"I know." Noy raised her hand. "She was Henry VIII's wife."

"Good," said Mr. Brewer. "Which one? And what did they call her?" The classroom was quiet. "Anyone know the answer?"

I wiggled a finger. "Anne Boleyn was Henry VIII's 2nd wife, otherwise known as 'Anne of a Thousand Days."

"He's making stuff up," a classmate said as the bell rang. (For unknown reasons school bells are usually in the key of G-major.)

"Pipe down, class. Now don't forget, oral reports begin Monday." Mr. Brewer tapped me on the shoulder.

"Yeah, Mr. B?" I said, strapping my textbooks together with an old belt.

"Will you stop by my office after lunch?"

"Sure. Do you want me to bring the stuff?"

"Yeah, I bet you will." Mr. Brewer whapped me with a text book. "Just bring those stilts you're walking on."

At Brice Chevrolet Dad pointed to a man with a cane, walking towards the service department.

"There's old twelve-bucker." Dad waved to a woman through the showroom window. "Oo, and there's nine-bucks and a hee-haw."

"What's he saying?" Raina asked Donk.

"Oh, Dad calls his customers, not by their names, but by the amount of profit he made off them." Donk slid a hanger into the mouth of a candy machine and tried to unhook a pack of Caramel Creams.

"What does a hee-haw stand for?" Raina asked.

"I think it means the customer bought an extended warranty."

Dad stepped outside to speak with the woman. "How have you been, Cindy?"

At Merriam Hill High I poked my head into Mr. B's office, catching a whiff of stale coffee, body odor, and wet tobacco. "You wanted to see me?"

"Come on in." Mr. Brewer brushed a stack of papers off a chair. "Have a seat. I wanted to talk to you about your plans after graduation."

"Okay." I sat down.

Mr. B peered over stacks of manila folders and graded essays on his desk. "Do you have any?"

"Not really."

"What are your interests?"

I scanned the books on Mr. Brewer's shelves. "I kind of like music."

"But you're not in school orchestra or jazz band," he said.

"I like a different kind of music. History's not bad either."

"History's a fine stepping stone for law school." Mr. Brewer fiddled with his beard. "Why don't you join the debating team?"

"Those brown-nosers, please."

"What's your game anyway?"

"What do you mean?"

"There's an open door here, Brice." Mr. Brewer's chair squeaked.

"I'm just repeating things I've read. For some reason I can remember facts. I can remember every Civil War battle in order and every lyric Joni Mitchell ever wrote, but I'm not like my brother. He can mix things together and come up with something new."

"Tell you right now, facts are the raw materials for ideas. If you fill your brain with facts, someday you'll start to see patterns. Do you think I'd still be coaching high school and teaching history to kids who think Lincoln's a kind of car if I could remember one-tenth of the facts I've ever learned?"

Avoiding Mr. Brewer's eyes, I slid a biography of General McClellan off his shelf and walked home.

At the dinner table, Aunt Bee scooped a boiled onion from a dish and set it on her plate. "The greatest thing about singing harmony is the freedom. You can sing the line any way you want and there are millions of variations."

I nodded.

"I add at least a dozen harmonies to every song. At the conservatory we'd stay up late into the night dreaming up harmonies."

"How many singers were in your a cappella group?" I asked.

"Are you going to let me have the floor or not?"

"Okay," I said, handing Aunt Bee a hunk of floor.

"Hey, put that back," said Dad.

I wedged the plank back.

"And make sure you stay away from thirds and fifths. Every singer and their Aunt Sally sings those."

As Aunt Bee blabbed, Chuggles leapt onto the table and began sniffing Donk's plate.

"Whack that cat off the table," said Dad.

"I don't mind. Her mouth's cleaner than most humans," said Donk.

"I'm sick of that cat always begging." Dad knocked Chuggles onto the floor.

"I wouldn't call it begging," said Donk, shoveling a boiled onion into his mouth. "Begging has a negative ring to it. When we see a person on the sidewalk begging, what do we do? We swerve around them and think they should be working."

"They should," said Dad.

"Well let me ask you this: Did Chuggles ask to be placed in her current situation? No, she didn't."

"I disagree with that," said Dad.

"We took Chuggles from her natural environment, paved over her forests, and kept her locked in a house till, what other alternative was there for Chuggles but to perform the role assigned to her by society. That's not begging at all; it's role playing."

"You think you're pretty sharp, don't you?" said Dad.

"It's not too hard around here," said Donk.

"Oh yeah, who was the 17th vice-president of the United States? Not quick enough for that one."

"What key was Beethoven's Fifth Symphony written in?" Donk shot back.

"C-minor?"

"Lucky guess." At the sink, Donk rinsed off his plate, then trudged upstairs to his bedroom.

"When the snow melts, we'll see where the signs lie," said Dad.

From the landing Donk called out: "Schuyler Colfax."

"He looked that up."

"How did you know what key the Fifth Symphony was written in?" asked Aunt Bee.

Dad smiled and pointed to his head. "It's all in here, Beezy. A bit jumbled up, but it's all here."

"Hey, Two-by-four?" I walked into Donk's bedroom. "I talked with Aunt Bee for two hours and couldn't squeeze in one word." Taking Donk's Telecaster out of its case, I played the song "What I am."

"Oh Auntie—she's a *floater*," said Donk, gingerly turning a page of his dictionary.

"What's a floater?" I asked.

Donk glared at me like Clark Kent trying to peer through a steel safe. "Floaters hover above their bodies the way astronauts float outside their ship. They're searching for a way back. Hey, who wrote that tune? The climb section ended on a leading tonality that set up the resolve in the chorus."

"Edie Brickel and New Bohemians," I said, sitting on Donk's bed. "They played The Middle East last night. Where were you?"

"Not at The Middle East."

"Why does Aunt Bee practically vomit words?"

Donk resumed his reading. "I guess for Bee silence stings, so she murders it."

"Oo, it's clammy in here." I grabbed a sweater from Donk's dresser. "What's so painful about silence?"

"Figure it out, Spaz."

So I tried to remember a time I had felt silence. One April vacation we were in New York City and Aunt Bee steered us into St. Patrick's Cathedral. We wandered up and down the aisles, past statues of sad men with their arms open, past stained glass windows glowing with ruby-reds and cobalt-blues, past bleachers of candles. We even paused to light a few, but the silence didn't hurt. "I can't."

Donk looked up from his dictionary. "Look, the way I see it, there are sixteen types of talkers, and eight are worse than sucking on an anthrax lollipop."

"You're making stuff up."

"Can it for a sec. The first type, as I mentioned, are *floaters*. Number two, beware of the *ketchup passers*. They're the type of talkers who, when you're having dinner with them and you share a huge secret—I mean a real blood raspberry—they stare at you wall-eyed and say: Hey man, pass me the ketchup, will you?" Number three are *information pumpers*. Information pumpers believe I have nothing better to do than be their live, in-person encyclopedia. Urrugh!" Donk's face scrunched up. "Number four makes me want to spew chunks: *sentence finishers*. They cut me off in the middle of my sentences and try to finish 'em so they can get back to what they really want to do, which is talk about themselves. The creed of sentence finishers is: I've only got a minute, so let's just talk about *me*. The fifth type, *bellhop whistlers*, lure you over and pile their luggage in your arms so high that you Peter Pan down a staircase. Then what do they do? Whistle for another bellhop. I call number six the *strategically aloof*, maybe the biggest scumbags of all. No matter how much go-go juice you give them in a conversation, they always give less—every friggin' time—to make you feel as if there's something you just don't get. Number seven, *contrarians*, are always dropping mustard gas into your air supply. It doesn't matter how good your songs are—they'll object— because in order for contrarians to feel up, you must feel down. Take my advice, Spaz, when you see a contrarian, reach for your weapons. Number eight are *black holes*. They can't generate their own light. All they can do is absorb other people's sunlight. Give black holes a wide berth." Donk got up and walked into the closet.

A few minutes later, I banged on the closet door. "What's going on in there?"

"Just a sec." Donk opened the closet door and walked to his desk. He unzipped his gym bag and pulled out two bible-sized books. "Look what I sort of borrowed from Coach Brewer: The OED Compact Edition; eighteen volumes in two." Donk took out a magnifying glass and began reading the A-section.

"What about the decent types of talkers?"

"What? Oh yeah. Run to the kitchen and grab me a jar of peanut butter first."

At the kitchen table, behind the Boston Globe, Dad dipped a cracker into a jar of peanut butter. "Hey Kuba, Fallon's bringing a customer up to see the 'vette. Will you give it a quick douche?"

"I guess."

Dad pulled a black box from his pocket and pressed the button. Outside, the garage door began to open. "These new things are great."

I backed the Corvette out of the garage and began scrubbing it with a soapy rag. The sun sank behind a clump of pines and I never got to ask Donk about the eight decent types of talkers.

Dance Until You See the Sun's Fingers

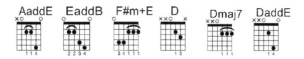

AaddE   EaddB   F#m+E   D   Dmaj7   DaddE

The fourth-period bell rang. Mr. Brewer closed the door.
"Okay, who's on for today?"
I raised my hand.
Mr. Brewer motioned for me to come up to the front of the class.
"Hi, the subject I wanted to learn more about was ghost dancing," I said, walking to the podium. "My research paper is titled:

The Promise of the Ghost Dance
by Kuba Brice

A ghost dance appeared in the Nevada desert in 1870 when a Northern Paiute man, Tävibo, prophesized that all Europeans would be swallowed by the earth, and the Plains Indians' ancestors would rise from the dead and once again roam the American West. Tävibo urged his followers to dance in circular movements, already a tradition in the Great Basin area, while singing ecstatic songs. Tävibo's movement spread to California and Oregon, but was short-lived.

However, in 1888, on the Walker River Reservation, a Paiute medicine man, Wovoka, revived the ghost dance.

Legend has it that Wovoka fell into a trance during a solar eclipse and the Great Spirit revealed a dance that could bring their dead brothers and sisters back to life and return the great bison herds.

"Do not tell lies," Wovoka told his congregation. "You must make a feast and dance for five days and four successive nights, and on the last night, dance until you see the sun's fingers. Then all must bathe in the Wassuk River and then disperse. When you reach home I shall give you good cloud and good paint, which will make you feel strong. But you must not fight anyone. When your friends die, do not cry. Jesus is now upon the earth. He appears in a cloud. What's more, the dead are still alive. When the time comes, there will be no sickness, and everyone will wear braids again. When the earth shakes, do not be afraid. It will not hurt."

Like other end-of-time visions, Wovoka's prophecies stressed the connection between worshipful behavior and imminent salvation. Salvation was not to be passively awaited, but welcomed by a routine of ritual dancing and upright moral conduct "for the ghost dance created energy that had the power to lift the dead," promised Wovoka.

Desperate for hope, native leaders sent envoys to Walker River to learn from Wovoka. The ghost dance spread quickly among western tribes who upon performing the ghost dance fell into trances, had visions, and gained the ability to self-levitate. Local bands adopted the core message to their own circumstances, composed their own songs, and danced their own dances. In 1889, some Lakota, Arapaho, and Cheyenne warriors returned from trance-induced spirit journeys with visions of 'ghost shirts,' which were deer skin garments painted with sacred turtles, eagles, and stars. In their visions, the ghost shirts made the dancers invisible to the bluecoats' bullets.

In December 1890, partly fueled by sensational newspaper accounts of the frontier, but more likely by a fear that the true measure of atrocities committed against Native Americans would come to light, the U.S. Government sent the Seventh Cavalry to the Badlands, the same cavalry which was routed at the Battle of Little Bighorn by Sioux Warriors led by Sitting Bull and Crazy Horse. The result was the Wounded Knee massacre, where over 200 Sioux women, children, and warriors were gunned down on a cold December night. As their corpses lay frozen in the snowy fields, it appeared that the ghost shirts worn by the natives were ineffective in warding off bullets. Wovoka quickly lost his congregation and lived on as Jack Wilson until sometime in 1932. The Ghost Dance is reportedly still being performed in some isolated regions.

"Now, I'm going to give you a demonstration." I nodded to Janota.

Janota began beating his congas: *Dim dim dun dim, dim dim dun dim, dun dun.*

In circular movements, I danced around the room, singing an Arapaho ghost song:

> *Ninaä´niahu´na, Ninaä´niahu´na,*
> *Bi´taa´wu hä´näi´säi,*
> *Bi´taa´wu hä´näi´säi.*
> *Hi´naä´thi nä´niwu´huna,*
> *Hi´naä´thi nä´niwu´huna.*

A few kids laughed. Mr. Brewer glanced at the clock. Leaping and spinning, I sang the song in English:

I circle around, I circle around,
The boundaries of the earth,
The boundaries of the earth.
Wearing the long wind feathers as I fly,
Wearing the long wind feathers as I fly.

Janota began mixing-in new rhythms. One reminded me of the flutter of a woodcock's wings. I sang a Cheyenne ghost song and tried to follow the invisible beats.

Ehä´n esho´ini, Ehä´n esho´ini´.
Hoiv´esho´ini´, Hoiv´esho´ini´.
I´yohä? Eye´e´ye´! I´yohä? Eye´e´ye´!
I´nisto´niwo´ni? Ahe´e´ye´!
I´nisto´niwo´ni? Ahe´e´ye´!

I sang the song in English:

Our father has come, Our father has come.
The earth has come, The earth has come.
Are we rising? Eye ye! Are we rising? Eye ye!
I am humming. Ahee ye! I am humming. Ahee ye!

Sweat flew from Janota's hands as I circled around the room. Noy flicked the lights on and off rapidly.

Mr. Brewer leaned towards Janota. "How long's this gonna last?"

"Don't know. Spaz told me to keep playing till something happened."

"Hey, Donk," called Raina, walking into Donk's room with a helium balloon. Chuggles followed. "Watch this." Raina let go of the string. The balloon hovered in the air.

Chuggles swiped at the string repeatedly. "There's just enough helium in the balloon to keep it from rising or falling."

Donk looked up from his desk.

In rapid motions, Chuggles batted at the string with her paw. The string swung back and forth. Again, she boxed with the string, but the string continued to float in the air. Chuggles stared at the string. A hand always held the string. How was the string suspending itself?

Donk turned away.

"What's the matter, Two-by-four?" asked Raina.

He didn't answer.

"Want me to take the balloon away?"

Donk nodded, wiping snot off his face with his sleeve. Raina carried the balloon into my room. Chuggles followed, hypnotized by the floating string.

The Greatest Invention of All-Time

(Fort Donelson)

IF A PERPETUAL MOTION MACHINE COULD EXIST, IT would mean a ton of stuff was working all at once to create an endless flow. Same thing's true with a mint song. Every section's sown so tight: intro, verse, climb, chorus, bridge, solo, and fade, that the song recreates the feeling of rising in your body—every time you play it.

The Elizabethans (sick units, all of them) practically burped mint songs. I want to hang out with the Elizabethans and their *deus ex machina*: the actors fly up, but the audience cannot see the straps. Forget about that self-aware stuff. Screw those posers. I mean, is it really going to help me figure out why the Red Sox are the biggest blowhards since Custer if I shine my flashlight above the field lights at Fenway? Am I any closer to knowing why Coach McNamara didn't yank Bill Buckner from game six of the '86 Series even though Buckner had slower foot speed than Captain Ahab? I-I-I d-d-don't think so.

Someday, I'm going to build my own perpetual motion machine. Then note by note, riff by riff, verse by verse, chorus by chorus, and song by song, I'll build an ageless car, and listeners who slide into my sick Chevelle and cruise these ink highways will come to know the feeling of rising, or let my tires burn down to their rims trying.

"What's going on?" said Donk, plugging his Telecaster into his Ampeg.

"Donny," said Crispin.

Crispin brushed past me on the cellar stairs I listened.

Crispin opened his guitar case. "Wait until you taste my new riff. It's sort of in Dorian mode. I swiped it from Al DiMeola."

"Nice." Donk switched on his amp. His fingers moved up the neck of his Telecaster. By the eighth fret the vacuum tubes in his amp warmed up, sending notes tumbling through the cellar air.

After a few practice scales, Crispin joined in. Their fingers climbed the neck from the first fret to the sixteenth, then back to the third fret, then way up to the eighteenth fret before racing back to the nut.

"You scumbag," said Donk, loosening his E-strings to D. Donk began playing a chord progression: Fm, D-flat, E-flat, B-flat, C^{7+13}, adding diminished-thirds, raised-fifths, and elevenths.

Crispin layered a solo over Donk's guitar.

After switching the chord progression to Am, F, D-flat, E, B, D^{9+11}, Donk began messing with the rhythm: splitting eighth notes into sixteenths, fusing quarter notes to form half-notes, and pausing in a pool of whole notes.

"Watch this." Crispin started playing lead in Dorian mode. Snakes the color of mouthwash slithered from his amp.

So Donk began throwing in off-beats at regular intervals. Then he played an F^{11sus}, then a D-flat$^{11+13sus}$. Did I hear an $E^{13+15sus}$? All this tonal mud. Then Donk went free-form nuts, breaking down patterns, strumming crazy flurries of thirty-second and sixty-fourth notes. Then surprisingly Donk stopped. A wave of silence rolled through the cellar.

Four or five seconds later, another chord progression: Am, F, C#m, Bm9, D, poured from Donk's amp.

This time Crispin hitched a ride on Donk's car, fingering variations of the chords, then arpeggios, then staccato, then staccato-arpeggios. Gradually, Crispin ventured from the chords into tiny riffs. The riffs grew longer. The tone fatter; then sweeter I don't know captured the taste infused with tennis ball yellows and bubbling boiling caramel poured onto snow. Then he broke free with a spontaneous melody. A swirling helix of honey bees flew from his amp and circled the basement.

Diving below the melody, Donk added dissonance when the melody got too cute and consonance when it got bogged down in muddy tones.

"What in John DeLorean's name is that awful noise?" said Dad in the driveway. In the kitchen a wave rippled in Chuggles' dish. "Marna, tell the boys to turn those monotonous guitars off before we have a couple cruisers out front."

"Did you say something?" asked Mom, holding the phone to her chest.

Opening the cellar door, Dad banged a broom handle against the stairs. "Donny, I've got a migraine you wouldn't believe."

The broom landed in front of Crispin's sneakers. A bloom of silence filled the cellar. Grabbing a towel from his guitar case, Crispin wiped his guitar neck. Behind the oil heater Donk pulled out a can of Johnson's Wax and popped off the lid.

"What've you got in there?" asked Crispin.

"Let me ask you this," I said, plunking down on Raina's bed. "Would you marry a guy who was a world-class biologist, had Morton Harket's cheekbones, and owned a beach house on Peak's Island, if he had one weird hobby?"

Raina looked up from her sheet music. "What's his hobby?"

"He likes to run over squirrels with his car."

"Gross. No way."

"How about this guy: he's a drummer in a big-name band, tells jokes like nobody does, and can bench press three-hundred pounds, but he has one minor drawback?"

Raina exhaled loudly. "What's his drawback?"

"His laugh. Every time he laughs, the whole room turns and stares. He sounds like a complete psycho."

"Hmmm." Raina picked turquoise nail polish off her toe nails. "Obnoxious laughs are hard to take. Still, if he wasn't *really* a psycho, I might go to a concert with him."

"Here's a great one-"

"Cut it with the dumb questions," said Raina. "I've got to learn this song."

"Just one more. He's a heart surgeon-"

"Spaz!" Raina growled.

"Kids," Mom called from the landing, "will you give me a hand with supper?"

In the kitchen I pulled a loaf of garlic bread from the oven. With a spatula, Raina slid squares of lasagna onto moon-shaped plates.

In the dining room we tore into the lasagna.

"Donk?"

"Yeah."

"What do you think is the greatest invention of all time?"

"Not sure those kinds of distinctions are worth making, Spaz," said Donk.

"Come on, don't be boring."

"Answer's easy." Raina cut in. "Gunpowder."

"Says who?" sneered Donk.

"Shut your face." A piece of garlic bread bounced off Donk's head. "Before gunpowder, if a country wanted to be the big wahoo, all it needed was a huge population, but after gunpowder, countries needed to make cannons, bombs, guns—all sorts of advanced stuff."

"Sounds like you've given this some thought," said Mom, placing a salad bowl on the table. "Galvin, we're waiting."

Donk plunged two wooden spoons into the salad bowl. "But Raina, didn't steel need to exist in order for gunpowder to be important?"

Raina made a face.

"What are you cookamungas talking about?" said Dad, walking into the dining room.

"Raina says the greatest invention of all time is gunpowder," I answered.

"What does Donny think?"

"He's too stuck-up to answer."

Dad picked up a square of lasagna, tilted his head backwards, and shoved it into his mouth. "I'd have to say the assembly line. Because of old man Ford, even poor schmucks like me could afford to buy a new sled."

"Ford didn't invent the assembly line," said Donk. "Singer did."

"Like fun. Pass the dressing, honey. Henry Ford used to say: 'You can have any color you want so long as it's black.'"

"Not bad," I said, placing my hand on Dad's shoulder. "What are you doing later on, handsome?"

Dad pushed my arm off his shoulder. "What's wrong with you?"

"All your telescopes are pointing to the wrong star." Mom sprinkled pepper on her lasagna. "Before the printing press, only monks and kings could afford to buy books. After the printing press, a whole universe opened up to millions of people and the return of democracy became a certainty. Do you really think weapons and cars were the key agents of change?"

"Yes," said Raina.

"I said assembly line, not cars," Dad protested.

Resting his chin on the table, Donk pushed the remaining bits of salad and lasagna off his plate and into his mouth.

"Sit up, Donny, this isn't a stable," said Mom.

"The greatest invention of all time is discontent," said Donk.

Raina laughed. "Are you a psycho or what?"

"How so?"

"I bet the motivation behind most bigwig inventions was a lingering sense of discontent and the belief that a better way had to exist," said Donk. "Plus, I'm not sure we should be focusing on one invention. Most huge leaps forward are, in reality, hundreds of small steps. I mean, without all those amateur naturalists before him, Darwin would never have discovered natural selection. But it's too confusing to remember all those amateurs, so we don't. Instead, we focus on one magic person who puts it all together 'cause we can't."

That evening we watched BC play Maryland in the den. On TV Len Bias dribbled a basketball around three defenders, pulled up, and launched the ball over a fourth defender. The ball arc'd through the air and swished through the net.

On the couch Dad sipped his highball. "Unbelievable. If Bias comes to Boston, we could win ten championships."

The Magic Oven

Donk's mattress-sized red dictionary says: "to *improvise* means to compose, utter, or perform a task on the spur of the moment without prior thought." The word comes from the French word emprouer, which means to turn a situation into profit. How can I call myself a musician? Every time I try to improvise, my fingers refuse to play what my body hears. When I try to sing, Mom shuts the windows. At a keg party, when a kid's poppin' off like a total douche bag, I turn into Mr. Freeze. Donk's totally different. In a tight spot, he can shuffle through his mind—every friggin' time—and pull out sick things to say. When he's playing his Telecaster and the climb starts heating up, threatening to outshine the chorus, Donk cools it off with a few muddy chords, say a 6th and an 11th chord.

One time, Aunt Bee was in my brother's room turning over piles of laundry, looking for a music book, when she opened the closet and found Donk—lips glued to a humungous water bong. Donk looked up like it was normal and said, "There's always hope with a bag of dope." Aunt Bee closed the door. She didn't even squeal on him.

Then on Christmas Eve, Mr. Pushkoff and Donk got into a verbal brawl. Before he was an undertaker, Mr. Pushkoff studied History at Beloit and, I admit, knew quite a bit. So Mr. Pushkoff was in our den saying Lee was a better general than Grant. (I admit, I kind of agreed.) But Donk wheeled around, mouth full of apricot torte, and said, "Are you talking about the general who ordered a frontal assault at Gettysburg on a heavily entrenched Union Army in broad daylight up a 48° hill?"

Mr. Pushkoff fired back. "No, I'm talking about the general who was so hungover on the morning of the battle of Shiloh that he was surprised by Confederate troops and almost lost his entire army."

"But then Grant counter-attacked and finished the day with a draw. Next day, Grant 'whipped' 'em pretty good." Donk wiped whipped cream off his face. "After that, Grant body-slammed Vicksburg."

Mr. Pushkoff volleyed. "With more than a two-to-one disadvantage in manpower, Lee racked up an unrivaled string of victories, including Fredericksburg where Lee divided his army twice and chased the Army of the Potomac off the battlefield. The bacon is sizzling."

Cornered, Donk opened a new line of attack. "Grant was not handed his rank. He earned every star through battlefield victories. If Lee had been born poor as Grant, we never would have heard of Lee."

"That's not true. Lee earned his rank in the Mexican-American War." Mr. Pushkoff steered the argument back to his original claim. "Most historians agree that Lee single handedly extended the Civil War two years with his generalship."

"And what else did Lee extend?" Donk veered again. "Just think if Lee had gotten his way. Any state with a beef, North or South, would have simply seceded and started their own country. The U.S. would have been carved into a dozen smaller countries like Europe. As a result, every generation there would have been a new war. Lee wasn't a great general; he was a criminal and should have been hanged."

"Lee fought for honor and to preserve a way of life."

"Yes he did. He fought to save *his* mansion, *his* slaves, and *his* money. What honor is there in that?"

I almost had to run to the john.

Mr. Pushkoff tugged on his moustache. "Must be lonely up there in your ivory tower. Down here we've got to fight and scheme for every buck."

"So why aren't you fighting now? Think how many schoolbooks that Volvo in your driveway could buy all those kids without shoes in Louisiana," Donk said.

Soda dribbled out my nostrils.

"Is that so?" Mr. Pushkoff walked to the cabinet and pulled out a bottle of gin. "How many measles vaccinations could one of your Brice vacations buy?"

Ouch. That one hurt.

"What about your new pool? I bet that body of water could pay for a dozen irrigation systems in Sudan," Donk replied.

"See that amplifier by the TV?" Mr. Pushkoff pointed to Donk's Ampeg. "I bet you could trade that amp for eight bushels of wheat."

I'm of two minds there.

"Touché," said Donk, clinking his soda against Mr. Pushkoff's glass.

So Donk suggested I try writing songs. I don't hate writing that much. After Uncle Addy booked it from Merriam Hill, Aunt Bee left a milk crate of journals in our garage. Most of the pages are blank, so I fill them in with music. If I'm on a hike and I see salamanders hiding in pine needles, I'll scratch the notes on a used envelope, then transfer them to my journal. When I'm hangin' out on

Pushkoff's couch and a melody floats through my mind, I'll run to the garage. Music comes from messed up places. Sometimes I'll be strumming my guitar in our driveway and I'll stop to watch a herd of ants marching towards a distant feast. Other times, I'll be raking our lawn and I'll freeze when I notice the bees are having sleepovers underneath the oak leaves. Raina swears I'm the Son of Sam 'cause I'll even hover near Fallon to catch a sing-songy phrase when he's got a couple seated at his desk and he's trying to close the sale. You probably think I'm Lizzie Borden's brother, but that's how I get my songs. I snatch them from the compost of my days. But that's Bush League stuff. Putting the pieces together right, that's the only ticket to the Major Leagues. Now if I could only learn to improvise.

The Magic Oven
(Eight years earlier)

In Mrs. Cook's class, the third graders gathered around Raina, who stood behind a small desk.

"First, you've got to choose the right apples: Cortland if you don't mind peeling off the skins, McCoun if you do." Raina removed six apples from her desk. "You cut them just so in pinkie-sized wedges. Next, you set the Magic Oven at 400°." Raina turned an invisible knob on her desk. "Any higher and the apples turn to mush. Any lower and the apples get that grainy taste."

"Now you need dough for a crust. In a bowl, measure 2½ cups of flour, 3/4 a cup of shortening, 3 tablespoons of orange juice, 1 teaspoon of vanilla, and a pinch of salt. With a fork, mash it up, then roll the dough into two balls: one smaller, and one bigger." She held up two dough balls. "Don't forget to rub flour on your rolling pin. Then squish the big ball round and flat till it's two inches larger than your pie tin." Lifting the rolled dough, Raina set it in the pie tin. "After that, trim your edges." My sister ran a knife around the edge of the tin.

"Next, pour the cut-up apples, 1 cup of granulated sugar, 1 cup of cranberries—which have been cooked the night before in 1/2 cup of sugar, 2 tablespoons of tapioca—it thickens everything, 1 teaspoon of cinnamon, and three pinches of nutmeg in a ceramic bowl." Raina removed a wooden spoon from the desk. "Mix everything up until the apples have brown specks on all sides." Raina tilted the bowl to show the class. "When you're satisfied, dump your pie-filling into the empty pie crust."

"Now flatten the small dough ball and place it on top of your filling. After that, flute the edges together, but make sure you press your fingers in opposite directions." Her fingers pinched their way around the tin. "Lastly, poke a fork though your pie six or seven times, unless you're making a mile-high pie." Raina stabbed the pie. "My Mom usually places a fruit pie in the oven for 42 minutes, but today I'll put it in The Magic Oven." Raina slid the uncooked pie into her desk. "Wait seven seconds aaaannnd—voila." My sister slid a baked pie from her desk and held it up for the class. "And that's how you bake a Brice Family cranberry-apple pie. Who would like a piece?"

A classmate raised his hand. "What if you baked the pie without apples?"

"What if you were born without a brain?" said Raina.

"Now that's enough kids. Good job, Raina." Mrs. Cook held her hands together. "Next up, we have Noy Pushkoff. What's your oral report on, Noy?"

"My report is titled: How To Conduct A Funeral."

In the garage I laid a door on two wooden horses. On my makeshift desk I stacked my journals and sheet music. I threw my picks and pens in a pickle jar. Between two gallons of paint I placed a row of books. In the row: *Keys to Arranging* by George Martin, *The Craft Of Lyric Writing*, guitar tabs for *Electric Ladyland*, *Principles Of Harmony*, a bio of Rogers and Hart, *Freeing The Human Voice*, a sound engineer's notes from Springsteen's "Jungleland" sessions, *Writing Music For Hit Songs*, and *Secrets To Counterpoint*. On Dad's workbench (which I never saw him use), I plugged in a hotplate and snagged a kettle from one of Aunt Bee's crates for a caffeine fix. For my water supply I pulled a garden hose through a broken window that Raina had hucked a rock through. At a yard sale I coughed up sixty-five bucks for an Alvarez six-string. (That was before I got Donk's Telecaster and his Ampeg too.) Eventually, Donk, me, and Raina squeezed enough dough from Mom and Aunt Bee for a condenser mic, eight-track, and PA. On weekends and after school, the three of us hung out in the garage.

"Ready? One, two, ready, go." I pressed record.
The lyric in hand, Raina sang into the mic.

> I'm high on this mountain
> Where I skied as a boy.
> My arms flapping like a falcon's,
> But I can't hear your eternal voice.
> Oh, sing your sweet voice in my ear
> 'Cause I'm afraid to hear.

"Wait a sec." I pressed stop. "If you dip low on the last note, you lose momentum going into the chorus and the chorus sinks like a lead balloon."

"I like the line sung low. It's a depressing lyric," replied Raina.

"The chorus should have a fifty-yard-dash feel. It's not a torch song," I shot back.

"Life isn't one big pep rally."

"It's not a giant funeral either. Music needs to-"

"This isn't music. This is mass market goop."

"You'll say anything to feel superior." I walked into the house and up to Donk's room. "Did you hear what that fleabag said?"

"What the hey?" Donk slid something under his bed. "Spaz, knock before you come in. What are you babbling about?"

I plopped on his bed and told him.

"So Raina doesn't think your song is real music. Let's visit our old friend Mr. Dictionary and see if Raina knows what she's talking about, or if she's just spewing smoke through her keyhole." Donk opened his red dictionary:

Music (myoo'zik), n. **1.** The art of combining sounds of varying pitch in time to express emotions and ideas in significant forms. **2.** An agreeable succession of tones occurring in a single line (melody) or an accordant combination of simultaneous tones (harmony) and their disbursement through time (rhythm). **3.** A composition to be sounded or sung by one or more voices, instruments, or both. **4.** The written score of a musical composition. **5.** Such scores collectively.
Music 2 (myoo'zik), n. **1.** Any sweet, memorable sounds; *The music of the waves.* **2.** Belonging to the Muses; any art over which the Muses preside over; especially lyric poetry set to music. **3.** The appreciation or responsiveness to musical sounds or harmonies; *Music was in her very soul.* **4.** *Zoology;* A more or less musical sound made by many of the lower animals; striudulation. **5.** In fox hunting the cry of the hounds. **6.** Face the music;

Informal; To meet, take, or accept the consequences of one's actions or mistakes. **7.** Magic music: a game in which each player is guided to finding a hidden article or doing a specific act by playing music louder and faster as the player approaches success, and slower and softer as he or she recedes. **8.** Music box: a gallery for musicians, as in a dancing hall. **9.** Music of the spheres, the harmony said to be produced by the accordant movements of the celestial spheres. **10.** *Informal;* Chin Music: in baseball when an opposing pitcher throws a pitch near or at a batter's head in an attempt to cause the batter to stand further away from the plate.
Musical, (myoo' zi kel), *adj.* **1.** Resembling Music. **2.** Having the qualities or powers of producing music. **3.** A melodious, harmonious person.
Musical 2, (myoo' zi kel), *n.* **1.** A drama, usually a comedy, in which both dialogue and lyric songs are performed.

"Let me take a look." Donk studied my sheet music. "Straight into the chorus, hey?"

"I wanted to give the listener a jolt," I said.

Donk made a pained expression. "Think about a movie that opens with the actor crying. You want to puke, right? 'Cause the director didn't show you how the actor got there—same thing with mint songs. I've heard bands get away with biffing the climb, but you didn't pull it off in this song."

"Why not?"

"For one thing the leap in pitch from the last note in the verse to the first note in the chorus is one heck of a Peter Pan. You've got to compose a musical bridge."

"The both of you can rotate," I said and walked back to the garage. But Donk had a point. Mint songs needed to recreate the Houdini routines, the many ways people hide from themselves, so listeners could relate. The process needed to be hidden too—'cause that's part of the routine.

Let listeners think it's just a dumb pop song till the notes sneak past their own private Maginot Lines, and they sing along and wonder: who made the maple leaves glow again?

It's Got Ice

Behind Brice Chevrolet by the dumpster, a man climbed down from his tow truck and inspected a Dodge. Fallon opened the showroom door and walked around the building towards the man.

"Ralston Tuttle, God's gift to the motoring public, what can I do you for?" said Fallon, removing a cigar cutter from his pocket.

"Easy, dry charge," said Ralston, reaching under the grill of an F-150 pickup and unlatching the hood. "Whud do ya got for wholesale this week?" he asked, pulling out the dipstick.

Fallon clipped the tip off his cigar. "That whore needs a gasket."

Ralston tasted the oil. "Needs more than that. Whud else ya got?"

"How about that Cutlass?" Fallon nodded towards a gray Cutlass as he slid a lighter from his pocket.

Ralston walked around the Cutlass. "Car's been whacked. There's spray paint in three wheel wells. Call the Governor."

"Why do you think I'm wholesaling it? I'll treat you right." Lighting his cigar, Fallon's cheeks puffed like a tuba player.

Ralston slid out from under the car. "No chance. Ever try to straighten a bent frame? You end up bending it the other way."

"How about this brass hat I bought at the mill?" Fallon pointed to a Park Ave. "Some bigwig in Detroit drove it. All highway miles. Clean title too, if you know what I mean."

"Got ice?"

"What do you think." A python of smoke uncoiled above Fallon's head.

"Not a recall is it?"

"So what if it is? Been fixed."

"Whud do ya need to get out of it?" Ralston removed a greasy NADA book from his shirt pocket.

"Forty-nine hundred."

Ralston stumbled back. "Easy, you'll short circuit my pacemaker."

"What do you mean? This whore will bring fifty-four-hun at the mill *all day long*."

"Only if you're standing there jacking up the prices."

"Oh come off it, I was thinking of putting this sled in my showroom."

"What if I take the Cutlass, the brass hat, and that Diplomat over there?" Ralston pointed to a Diplomat that looked like it'd been caught in a hail storm.

"I'm listening." The two men stepped behind the dumpster.

At the entrance to the dressing rooms at Marshalls, Raina held up a pile of belts, scarves, shirts, and jeans to the clerk. "Hi, I'd like to try these on."

"Sure," replied the clerk. "How many pieces?"

"Eleven."

The clerk handed Raina a red tag. In the dressing room, Raina did a half-turn in the mirror. She studied her legs, bum, and hips as she pulled a belt through the loops in her jeans.

"I'm all set," said Raina, handing the clerk a handful of clothes.

The clerk folded the clothes.

Out front, Raina opened the door and walked towards the parking lot.

"Pardon me, miss." A man approached Raina. "Would you come back inside?"

Raina clenched her fists. "You stay away from me."

"Don't make me call the police. Will you step back inside?"

"You keep your scumbag hands off me." Raina swung at the man.

The man raised a walkie-talkie to his mouth. "We've got a Code Six in Lot B."

"Mother of Mary, I can afford a pair of jeans," said Mom, pulling into Brice Chevrolet. Raina got out and walked inside.

In his office, Dad flipped through a stack of mail. "Let me ask you this: how many pairs of pants do you own?"

"Seven." Raina fiddled with an ashtray made from silver dollars on Dad's desk.

"How many days in a week are there?"

"Seven."

"Then what's the problem?"

"Dad, you're out of touch with reality."

"Of course I am. Nobody knows reality but Raina. And all at the tender age of sixteen too. You stay put." Dad hurried to the showroom. "Hello, can I help you?" Dad held out his hand. "I'm Galvin Brice."

"Hi, I'm Gary Zohn. This is my wife Sharon."

"Hi Gary. Hi Sharon."

"Our car was stolen last week at a Red Sox game. My brother-in-law bought a car from you folks, and he told me you treated him right."

"Who's your brother-in-law?"

"Bing DeRaps."

"Old Boom Boom DeRaps. I know Bing well. He's got a fist as big as a softball. How's his sports bar doing?"

Twenty minutes later, Dad walked back into his office. "I'm losing the famed Brice charm," said Dad, tossing his coat on the filing cabinet. "I couldn't give a sled to that couple. I'm telling you, the older I get, the more I'm convinced that price is irrelevant. People are looking for something else. A connection of some sort." Dad looked out the showroom window at the steady flow of cars driving down Mass Ave.

"Dad."

"What? Oh. Getting back to this morning's incident. When I was nine—the same year GM introduced the Corvette—I used to slide down every banister I could. My parents would say: 'Don't slide down that banister. You're going to split your head open.' I didn't listen. So one day I hopped on a banister at the town library, but I didn't notice a tiny nail was sticking up at the bottom. Sliding down I went—dumb as a stump. At the bottom, where the rail curves up, the nail ripped an eighteen inch gash in my pants. The next day I couldn't go to school. Do you know why?"

"The nail tore up your leg?"

"No."

"They were your favorite pants?"

"Don't be fresh." Dad lowered his voice. "I couldn't go to school the next day because they were the *only* pair I owned." Dad scanned the showroom. "If you want to steal, get a job on Wall Street. Until then, you're only stealing from yourself." Dad glanced down at his watch. "I've got an auction to go to."

Sitting on our front lawn, Donk hucked acorns across the street at the Pushkoff's mailbox. "See that's your first mistake right there," he told Raina as Noy braided her hair. "Teenage girls should not perform five-finger discounts at Marshalls. They're expecting it. A professional klepto goes to the hardware store. All those geezers with bifocals."

"What do you think: I want to wear a friggin' shovel to school?" said Raina.

"Is everything invisible to you?" said Donk.

"You don't have the seeds to lift anything," Raina replied.

"Are you screwin' with me?" said Donk.

"What about jail?" I asked.

Donk spit his wad of gum at me. "This is the key: what you steal must be totally useless and immediately given away." Donk wiggled his fingers. "Lawn fertilizer."

"You'll wet your pants." Raina stood up and walked to Donk's car. "Come on, let's go."

We climbed into Donk's Nova.

"Yeah, right." Donk started the engine. Soon the car was flying down the highway.

"Slow down." Raina yelled, snapping on her seatbelt. "I want to make it there alive."

Donk grinned as his Nova changed lanes and passed a white van.

"Knucklehead risks everything to save a few seconds," said Raina.

"You know the only thing worse than a backseat driver is?" Donk down-shifted and flew by a Vega. "One in the front seat. Take a powder."

Raina shuffled through Donk's CDs. "I'm not impressed. In fact, you bore me."

"Play the Titanics," I called from the backseat. Raina slid a CD into the player. The swirling opening riff from "Turn Around on a Dime" churned in my ears.

"Six-hundred and go." The auctioneer whacked the podium with his jockey stick. "Hibady dibady hibady dibady hibady dibady. Gimme six-hundred for an '81 Chevelle?"

A man with a Ford emblem on his coat raised a card.

"Six-hundred, seven-hundred, eight-hundred. Do I hear a thousand?"

A man in cowboy boots nodded.

The auctioneer's arm swung back and forth. "One-thousand, twelve-hundred, thirteen, fourteen. Hibady hibady dibady hibady dibady. Fifteen, and a half! Gimme sixteen boys! And a half, seventeen, and a half, eighteen! Roll this piece of steel outta here." The auctioneer pressed a button. The garage door began to lift. A lot boy hopped in the Chevelle and drove it outside. "And a half, nineteen, and a half. Two-grand? Do I hear two-grand?" The auctioneer pointed his long finger at Dad. "Galvin, are you in the game? Nineteen-seventy-five?"

Dad raised his card.

"Two-grand? Do I hear two-grand? Two-grand? This one's a keeper, fellas. Going once. Going twice. Sold to number fifty-four for nineteen-hundred and seventy-five?"

Dad walked to the podium and signed for the Chevelle.

"Son, what can I do for you?" asked a white-haired man at Scribner's Hardware.

Donk nervously picked his cuticles. "I'm in the middle of making a model tank and I ran out of glue."

"Follow me."

"That'll be a dollar eighty-eight." The white-haired man took two dollars from Donk. "And there's twelve cents for you. Have a good day, son."

"See you later."

"I knew it. Gutless wonder." Raina whispered to me out front.

"Do you have a bathroom I could use?" asked Donk.

The man closed the cash drawer. "All the way out back, you'll find a set of stairs. Go down the stairs. Bathroom's on your right."

Donk pulled the chain in the bathroom. Then he walked up the stairs. But instead of walking towards the front entrance, he turned right and walked though the "Employees Only" door. In the warehouse Donk slid open a wooden door and piled four bags of Quick Grow and two bags of clay pebbles onto the loading dock. Then he closed the door and hurried back to the front of the store.

"Thanks." Donk waved to the cashier.

In the car Raina poured a pixie stick into her mouth. "I figured as much."

"Listen, Mom wants us to grab a couple bottles of ginger ale." Donk pulled a few bucks from his wallet. "You two grab 'em. I'll wait here."

Stuffing the bills into my jeans, I noticed I had at least three inches on Donk.

Donk's Nova flew down Route 2A. Raina slid a CD into the player. Bim Skala Bim's "Wise Up" pulsated from the speakers.

"Damn these yield signs screw me up," said Donk, swerving into the breakdown lane to avoid a Volvo. The Volvo driver mouthed obscenities at us.

"Yeah, F-you too." I rolled down the window, undid my pants, and mooned the driver as Donk passed the Volvo in the breakdown lane.

"Are you telling him off or offering your services?" Raina laughed.

"What do you mean?"

A raccoon rambled across the street.

"Watch out," yelled Raina.

Donk cranked the wheel left.

"Whaaaaaa."

The raccoon scuttled underneath the car and continued into the woods. We looked at each other.

The auctioneer wiped his microphone with a hanky. "You won't want to miss this one, fellas." A Caprice Classic pulled in front of the podium. Dealers circled the car. "Fleet car, wire wheels, velour seats, sunroof. What do you wanna pay for it? How about three-grand? Hibady dibady hibady dibady dibady hibady."

Dad looked down at his feet.

"Do I hear twenty-five?"

Skip Lee held up two fingers.

"Two-thousand and go. Hibady dibady hibady dibady dibady. Twenty-two?"

Dad raised his card.

"Twenty-two."

Skip Lee held nodded.

In weathervane motion, the auctioneer swung his arm from bid to bid. "Twenty-four, twenty-six, twenty-eight, three-thousand, thirty-two, thirty-four, thirty-six. Thirty-eight?"

Dad wiggled his card.

"Four grand? Hibady dibady dibady hibady dibady hibady."

Skip nodded.

"Four grand, forty-two, forty-four. Forty-six?"

Skip shook his head.

"Come on, Skip. Look at that paint!"

With his hand Skip made a cutting motion.

"Forty-five, and a half, forty-six, and a half. Forty-seven?"

Dad walked to the food booth.

"Galvin?" the auctioneer called. "Game's not over. Forty-seven? Forty-seven? Come on, boys, it's got ice! It's got ice."

A bag of popcorn crinkled in Dad's hands. "Loony bidders. They're paying telephone numbers for those sleds."

"Did you hear a ping in the engine?" asked Donk, lifting his foot off the gas.

"No," I said.

Donk veered off the street into an empty parking lot of a seasonal farm stand. "I'm gonna check the oil." Under the hood, Donk slid out the dip stick. "Hey, Kuba, pop the trunk and grab me a quart of oil, will you?"

In the front seat, Raina pressed the forward button on the CD player. "This song needs a better singer."

"Raina?" I called from the rear of the car. "Come check out what this sick unit did."

"You paid for those," said Raina, peering at the bags of Quick Grow and clay pebbles in Donk's trunk.

"Go milk a bull. Now give me a hand." We stacked the bags on an empty produce table as a six o'clock sun painted a flaming crown across the horizon.

"When they spot those bags, I wonder what they'll think happened?" Raina mused.

"They won't notice," said Donk, pressing on the gas. The Nova fishtailed in the dirt before grabbing hold of the tar and accelerating down the street.

"When I get my license next year I'm going to pull off the heist of the century," I said from the back seat.

"Oh yeah, what will you take?" asked Donk as the needle climbed past seventy.

"I'm thinking." We passed an apple orchard. Washed in sunset, the branches drooped with glowing bulbs. "I think you should swipe something useful and keep it."

"Me too," added Raina. "I'm bored." I know what we can do. Let's sing one of Kuba's songs in three-part harmony. The one that has the 'merry wanderer' in it."

"I thought you needed a melody to sing harmony?" Donk smiled, or was it a wince? "Just kidding."

"My songs are like a virus. They invade your body and don't ever leave, but the results are pure interplanetary pleasure." I turned to Donk. "Do you like pleasure?"

"You're dreaming," said Donk.

"If you do, then I'm your go-to-guy." I covered Donk's eyes. The Nova swerved.

Donk batted my hands away. "Don't make me pull this car over."

"I'll sing melody. Kuba, you do call and response. Donk, you sing bass. Okay ready?"

"Huuumm." "Dooooooo." "Aahhhhhh."

Donk began: "Dum doo doo doo doo, dum doo doo doo doo, dum dee dee da da, dum dee dee da da, la la lee li lee, la la lee li lee, da da da da dee dee nee nee nu nu nu nu."
Raina sang the lyrics:

> *Who's that merry wanderer*
> *Laughing on a frozen pond?*
> *We're driving through this concrete desert*
> *Searching for the ice cream man.*

I tooled around with call and response:

> *Merry wanderer*
> *He's laughing, we're laughing*
> *Living in a desert*
> *He's in a white van*

Our voices joined in the climb:

> *But I'm not surprised*
> *I saw you dancing in your cage,*
> *Turning in the candle light*
> *Momentary statues in your wake.*

Donk wandered from the key. "Ma na ma naw mee, ha nah ma naw mee, ka cha, ka cha nee."
Raina frowned.
Donk returned to G minor. "Dum doo doo doo doo, dum doo doo doo doo, dum dee dee da da."
In the chorus Donk sang the fifth above, so I sang a third below.

> *Oh life, I don't know who you are*
> *I try to hold you in my mind.*

Like wine and sand with swerving cars,
You're gonna crash so take a scenic ride.

"Roll this go-cart outta here!" The auctioneer pressed a green button. A garage door began to lift. Autumn wind rushed under the door. A lotboy drove the Caprice outside. "Forty-seven, forty-eight, forty-nine. Five-grand?"

A woman with a plaid scarf tilted her card.

"And a half, fifty-one, and a half. Fifty-two?" A bidder followed the Caprice to the parking lot. "Come on, fellas, this one's a fleet car. Never been registered!"

Skip Lee nodded.

"And a half, fifty-three, and a half."

The women raised her card.

"Fifty-four? Fifty-four? Fifty-three and two-thirds?" The auctioneer rapped his jockey stick on the podium. "Fifty-three and two-thirds? Come on, this title's cleaner than a baby's bald head. Do I hear Fifty-three and two-thirds? Going once? Going twice?"

Who Wants To Wreck Their Knees?

"Hey, Two-by-four, wait for me," I called to Donk and booked it across the Merriam Hill High parking lot.

"What's going on?" Donk lifted his shoulder pads from the trunk of his Nova.

"Thought you were going to quit," I said as we walked towards Danforth Field.

"Want to, but Dad's paying me twenty bucks a game."

"Why?"

On the bench Donk laced up his cleats. "He's too cheap to pay for college so he's going to ride me like Rex Trailer till I get a scholarship."

"Where do you want to go to college?" I asked.

"AFC."

"What college is that?"

"Any friggin' college." Donk stretched his calves. "Well not any. Guess it matters some. Dad says linemen have a better shot at scholarships because—who wants to wreck their knees so some super stuck up quarterback can get their picture in The Globe?" On his back Donk raised his pelvis and did neck rolls.

"Yeah, but what about those three-hundred pound, corn-fed Nebraska boys?" I asked.

"Hard to tell."

A whistle colored the air a vivid orange.

"What key do you think that whistle's in?" I asked.

"Gotta go, Spaz." Donk hurried onto the practice field.

"Huddle up, guys." Coach Brewer dropped his cig in the crushed stones and stepped onto the practice field. "You puked your guts out against Concord. Pushkoff got 110 yards—just what we needed. Brice, you kept his lanes open. DeSilva surprised the heck out of me with five open-field tackles. Not half-bad. Now I could stand here and feed you the usual lip service: you guys are going to be Middlesex League champs, then you're going to waltz into Foxboro and win the Super Bowl. But you're not. Sure, you won big Friday, but you gave up eighteen points. You coughed up the football three times." Coach Brewer lifted his clipboard. "I counted nine blown tackles and damn near as many missed blocks. Those boys from Woburn are going to mount your heads above their fireplace. And talent has nothing to do with it. In fact, talent only gets in the way. How can you value something if it's dropped in your lap?"

Donk looked at Pushkoff and began to wiggle his ears.

"Everything sloshes together," said Coach Brewer. "Nothing stands out. So you coast."

Pushkoff looked away, but had to peek. Donk's ears and nostrils were flapping like moths.

"Till one Sunday, you're racing through The Globe and there on the Sports page is the kid who couldn't catch a pass in eighth grade. How did he become the go-to-guy at BC?"

Pushkoff looked down, but couldn't help it and looked. Now Donk's ears, nostrils, and his eyebrows fluttered in a concert of flesh.

"Boys, the question you have to ask yourselves is: what's invisible to you because it came too cheap?"

A muffled snort came from where Pushkoff stood.

Coach Brewer bent down and picked up a stone off the field. "I want to know what's so damn funny, Pushkoff?"

"Nothing, coach."

"Nothing is funny?" The stone arc'd over the empty bleachers. "Then let me give you something to laugh about. Okay, twenty laps around the practice field for everyone. Let's go. You can thank Pushkoff for all the fun, frickin' fun, fun, fun. The last player does an extra five laps compliments of me." Coach turned to his assistant. "Shaw, you take over. I have to go grab a few things in my car." Coach walked through the front gate towards the parking lot. On the other side of the fence, a man gazed through the iron bars. "Jesus Caity, if it isn't Galvin Brice." Coach Brewer held out a maroon pack of smokes.

"No thanks, trying to quit. Doctor's orders."

"What brings you out here? Checking up on Donny?"

"Any scouts sniffing around?" asked Dad.

"They usually show up later in the season."

"Think any colleges will throw a few dollars his way?"

"He's shorter than most offensive linemen, but I think the switch was a good move. He's got a quick outside-step."

"I want him to be realistic about the position he'll be playing after high school. If you're a running back and not from Florida or New York, no one's interested."

On the field, Donk and Pushkoff rounded the end zone.

"I wish I had known that," said Dad. "But I chose running back. I traded in my chance to play college ball for a few pom poms and a Thanksgiving Day hurrah."

"That's not true, Galvin. They would have found a spot for you. I had a tryout all lined up."

"Yeah where: left, right, or center bench?"

"Safety at Holy Cross. They're Division 1 too," said Coach Brewer.

Dad watched the practice.

Coach started towards his car. "I'll push him. Be right back, just getting the first aid kits—left them in my trunk. Don't go anywhere. I'll bring you on the field and tell Donny you're our new assistant. That ought to put the fear of Jesus in him." Coach returned with two oversized tackle boxes covered with Red Cross stickers. "Ready?"

"No, no, I don't want him to think that I've got nothing better to do than watch a high school football practice."

"Hey, Noah Pushkoff stops by every week."

"How's he going to get along in the world if I turn him into a mommy's boy?"

Coach Brewer held out his hand. "Alright, but you'll be here for Friday's game, won't you?"

Dad nodded. "What do you think our chances are?"

A Dumb Swede

"Left, left, crossover. Left, left, crossover," yelled Coach Brewer. A dozen boys side-stepped across the field. "Left, left, crossover. Left, left, crossover. Get those goddamn arms in the air, Brice!" Coach Brewer slapped a clipboard against his leg. "Okay, change directions. Right, right, crossover. Right, right, crossover."

Arms waist-high, Donk shuffled over the grass.

"No, no, no! Are you listening to me, Brice? Get over here." Coach Brewer grabbed Donk's facemask and pulled him through the drill. "You side-step twice, then cross with your outside leg. Like this." With a whistle in his mouth, Coach Brewer side-stepped across the field. "Now forty more times till you're practically floating over the grass. Right, right, crossover. Right, right, crossover..."

In the kitchen Mom grabbed a drink from Dad's hand. "I think you've had enough for one evening."

"That was only my second one," Dad protested. "And it's two-thirds water."

"And I'm the Queen of Sweden."

"Nice to meet you, Queen Brigitte."

"That's enough." Leaning over Dad's plate, Mom poured milk and a slice of butter into his baked potato and mashed the insides. "Have you heard from Fallon yet?"

"Bonny stopped by the showroom. They're keeping him overnight for observation."

"Is it serious?"

"You kidding me? Fallon's head is harder than a turtle shell." Dad shoved half the potato into his mouth. "Car's been totaled though. That's the third demo I've had to scratch off the books because of his boozing."

"You should let him go. He's more trouble than he's worth," said Mom.

"I would," said Raina.

"Quiet. Fallon taught me how to sell. Plus, Bonny would leave him. I'm sure she would."

"What if he plows into someone and they sue us?" said Mom. "They could take everything we own, our house too."

"As it is our premiums are higher than the Hancock tower," said Dad.

Chuggles hopped onto the table and began sniffing Raina's plate.

"Whack that cat off the table."

"It's okay." Raina put her plate on her lap.

"Must have done something awful in a past life." Dad lifted Chuggles off the table, walked to the side-door, and tossed her into the dark.

"What if you hurt her?" Raina ran to the side-door. "You know, Chuggles isn't a yo-yo."

"Don't you talk to your father that way."

"Then don't huck Chuggles 'cause you're mad at Fallon."

"Do you hear what's coming out of this Philadelphia Lawyer's mouth?" Dad asked.

"You shouldn't throw the kid's cat like that. She'll learn not to trust people," said Mom.

"Good. She shouldn't." Dad quickly cut his steak into pieces. "If I ever talked to my father that way, he would have ripped out my larynx and served it to me on a platter." Dad gripped his knife. "Those kids don't know what the real world is. They're in la-la land. Never had to skip lunch for three years straight just to outsell Fallon. You made it too easy for them, Marna, always rushing them down to Mass General with the smallest scrape, but they will find out what the real world is like, and when they do, it's not going to be peanut butter sandwiches with the crusts cut off." Dad shoveled the steak into his mouth. "Kuba? There's something terribly wrong with that boy. He's going to wind up in jail just like Fallon's kid. Donny? He's got a manic look in his eyes. Raina? I know her type. And that friggin' lush Fallon, he's going to single-handedly drive me into chapter eleven."

"Leave your foul mouth at the garage. Do you think Neil Van Dyne talks that way about his kids? I swear, when you're up, you'll lend a car to a total stranger—for a month!—then a switch goes off and you act as if your own family's plotting to cart you off to McLean's."

"I'd like to see a little more effort, Marna, a little more spit and shine. Rachael's kids make the Honor Roll every term. Skip Lee's kid's in medical school and his garage is cleaner than Fort Bragg. This house looks like a tornado rolled through it."

"You clean it then—and make dinner while you're at it." Mom got up and left the table. "Neil Van Dyne's a great cook. He makes dinner all the time, but you couldn't boil an egg."

"That's skirt work."

"I don't think I know what makes you tick."

"You don't want to either." Standing up, Dad tipped the table on its side. Forks, a gravy dish, potatoes, steak, green beans, my soda—everything—slid onto the floor. Dad charged out the door towards his car.

"Where do you think you're going?"

"Anywhere away from this rotten house." Dad's engine whined.

"Over my dead body." Mom ran outside and laid down in front of Dad's car. "You kids get back into the house."

"Marna get the hell off the tar!"

Raina booked it towards the car. "Don't be stupid, Mom."

"I swear if you don't get up off the driveway this instant, I'm going to run you over."

"You're a real class act, just like my aunt said, 'a real thoroughbred.' Go ahead, punch the gas. Go run to your pals down at the Elks."

"I'm going to count to ten and if you're still there, I'm backing up."

Raina grabbed Mom's ankle and pulled. Mom's shoe came off.

"You better not," I said.

"Don't just talk about it. Go ahead and do it, you gutless slug."

"I'm warning you." Dad revved the engine. "Ten, nine, eight, seven, six, five, four-"

"Thirty-three, sixty-eight, twenty-nine, sidewinder twelve." The quarterback placed his hands between the center's legs. "Ready, hike one, hike two, hut, hut, hut." Hurrying backwards, the quarterback shoved the ball into Pushkoff's gut. Pushkoff faked left, then ran straight ahead. Three yards in front of Pushkoff, Donk threw his shoulder into the belly of a linebacker. Pushkoff shifted right and ran towards the sidelines.

"Pushkoff, hit that goddamn hole!" Coach Brewer pointed towards the fallen linebacker.

By the sidelines, three redshirts climbed onto Pushkoff's back and rode him into the turf.

"Jesus-Catie, follow your block. On your feet, Pushkoff." Coach Brewer ran over and pressed his face against Pushkoff's facemask. "Do you think I spent the last eighteen years designing plays so you could make up your own play at the last second? Wait for your goddamn block."

Rejoining the huddle, Pushkoff muttered: "That hole appeared after I passed it."

"What was that, Pushkoff?"

"I thought we had the option to bounce to the outside?" Pushkoff gurgled through his mouthpiece.

"I'll tell when you have can improvise. Let's get the basic sweep down first." Coach Brewer put a whistle in his lips and blew. "Okay, boys, let's do that one over."

"Oh balls." Dad threw his keys on the dashboard and stormed into the house. The screen door slammed. In the kitchen he poured a drink the color of molasses. "She's lost it, just like her mother, a couple of wingnuts. What kind of people leave their Christmas trees up till June? In fact, they're all touched, the whole clan, always smiling like they've just rolled back an odometer. Come to think of it, I have never met a Swede who didn't have a long crack in their overhead cam. Something about living near the North Pole cooks their brains." Dad balanced his glass as he walked to the den. In the den he switched on the TV. At Fenway Park, 'Oil Can' Boyd leaned back and fired a fastball towards the batter.

I sat on the couch and didn't say a word. "She should be hauled away in a straightjacket." Dad turned around and screamed towards the driveway: "That's a hell of an example to set for the kids." Dad peaked over his rim at me. "The pace of the boss is the pace of the gang. You want to remember that. I think your Mother should see someone very expensive." "I'll take that." Mom grabbed Dad's drink. The drink spilled onto Dad's shirt. "Look at your handiwork—you've soaked the couch—and I left my Valium at the office. I'm going to bed." Dad stomped up the stairs. "How much do you charge to haunt a house!" he yelled over his shoulder.

"Everybody set?" The quarterback looked over the shadowy figures on the defensive line. "Fifty-eight, twenty-six, liberty twelve. Hike one, hike two, hut, hut, hut." Stepping backwards, the quarterback faked a pass, rolled right, and shovel-passed the ball to Pushkoff. In the open field a linebacker slipped and fell to the grass. Donk hurdled the linebacker and threw a roll block at the free safety. The free safety stepped back. As Pushkoff ran up the middle, the fallen linebacker reached out and tripped Pushkoff.

"Jesus-Catie, what kind of hole are you trying to open up, Brice, a mouse hole? Get over here." Coach Brewer ran up to Donk. "Do you think I want to spend my whole career coaching at this rinky-dink school? I'd rather stay home and collect food stamps. When the football leaves the center's hand, you take their middle linebacker out."

"My blocking assignment tripped so I went after the safety," Donk answered crisply.

"Is that right." Coach Brewer slapped his clipboard against his leg. "Is there anything dumber than a dumb Swede?"

"Yes there is, coach." Donk clicked on his chinstrap. "A smart Irishman."

"A regular Bob Hope." Coach Brewer tightened his lips, but slowly the corners moved upwards. "Get back into the huddle." Coach pushed Donk towards a circle of players that in the dusk resembled Stonehenge. "If we don't neutralize their linebackers, our halfback never reaches daylight."

Track 20
From Elm To Elm
(Donk's track)

I KNOW SPAZ TOLD YOU HE'S TAPPED IN THE HEAD. He flatters himself. Our family is more normal than he'd like to think. We go to Pastor MacDonald's church on Sundays. Our lawn is always trimmed. Dad wants to buy a summer home on Peaks Island. When I'm driving I always swerve around stupid cats and dumb squirrels.

Just last week, I was on my way to Crispin's to check out a few Rory Gallagher bootlegs when a gray squirrel, it couldn't have been more than a few weeks old, tried to leap across Merriam Street from one elm branch to another. What a nut. Obviously, it missed the branch and fell onto the street. The squirrel was lying motionless on the yellow line when a Volvo 780 turned the corner and drove straight towards it. I hate Volvos, especially those self-entitled Ivy Leaguers behind the wheels. They don't stop for squirrels 'cause they've got their chins jacked so high in the air they can't see them. So I scooted out in front of the Volvo and scooped up the squirrel. It's tiny legs didn't move, must have hit the tar pretty hard. A horn blared.

"Same to you, eagle nuts," I said, flipping my South Boston *hello*. The Volvo's brake lights lit up. I clenched the bottle of soda I was holding, even though I was really thirsty. He batted an eyelid, so I knew the squirrel was alive.

The Volvo waited like I was going to crap my pants and run home. They always do that *I'm about to hop out of this car* sort of thing, and if they do, guess who's the first one to call a lawyer? I didn't move. Plus, I was near DeSilva's house and I didn't want him to think I was a wuss. Otherwise, I admit, I might have booked it into the woods.

"Hey peckerhead," I called. "You got something to say?" I waved my soda and held the squirrel. Although most Volvo owners are math weenies, sometimes they're stock broker jocks, and when this guy got out, I admit, he could have played offensive line for Holy Cross. In these situations, I run a ton of scenarios through my mind. Did the Volvo guy know karate? If so, I'd probably want to take it to the ground and outwrestle him. Or was he the type to throw a lazy roundhouse? If so, I could step inside and land a few quick snaps to his face and hope a trickle of blood would be enough to send him back inside his finely engineered automobile. Or maybe—arrrgh! I wish I could vaporize my thoughts and just *do* 'cause time's a '65 Pontiac GTO with a 389 cubic inch V8 pumped with nitrous, blowing by you and no one (as of yet) has been able to find the brakes to slow the friggin' world down enough so I can string together a series of mint moves and build a pearl necklace of destiny.

Same thing with telling off snobs. You've got to fire back while their voices are still in the air or you're a 'poor sport.' Screw those posers. No snob is going to poke toothpicks in my airbag, then change the subject. Forget your mom's advice. Any time you see a snob, drop your soldier and reenact Pickett's charge.

But he might fake a haymaker and reach for my ankles. Then I'd have to knee him pretty hard in the face. Still, he might take the shot, knowing he'd have me pinned, then smoosh my head into the tar. Then I'd wake up a bunch of minutes later with dried blood and sand stuck in my hair. That's what my Uncle Addy used to do. The ankle grab was his signature move. I heard Babe Ruth would miss a high fastball on purpose so the pitcher would think he was hung over (and he usually was), but on the very next pitch, Ruth would ride a fastball over the right field fence. Is it true? My Uncle Addy, who's a diehard Red Sox rooter, says it is. But I don't believe him 'cause most people are liars (especially your relatives) and I'm not talking cheating on your taxes either. I mean the secrets you don't even tell yourself. We don't mean to. A creative omission here, a slightly polished fact there. No big whoop. But fifteen years later, we open our freezers and can't explain how the frozen body parts got there. This Ivy League pinhead in his Volvo with his 'trying hard not to look like he's trying hard' understated clothes—screw him. Screw his burgundy slacks and hunter-green polo shirt. I bet he went to Dartmouth, and if the bear bit him, he would lie his pecker off to his wife. That's a fact.

"What happened, honey?" his wife would say, pretending not to notice the stylized torn shirt and custom hairdo.

"Oh, I had to knock out this jerk from Merriam Hill," he'd reply, inspecting his biceps as he poured a potent drink.

The taller the glass, the larger the lie. That's why all Ivy Leaguers deserve two shiners apiece, so they'll stop acting so super-stuck up. On the other hand, I bet most wives know about their husband's G.I. Joe fantasies. The hilarious part is: the wives know, but they don't give a fouled spark plug about being tough. At least if they're like my Mom, who has the sickest straight-arm I've ever seen. I hear their secret laughs: 'Oh let them have their dungaree ant hills.'

But Mom didn't laugh when Dad faked a kick to my balls, then tomahawked me with his drink—glass, ice, and all. Then he kicked my balls. So while I was on the den floor clutching my jewel box, Mom rushed towards Dad, straight-armed him, and knocked him onto the couch. This was my plan: fake a left, then follow up with a soda bottle to the Volvo guy's head. That way, even if the peckerhead managed to block the bottle, his arm would definitely be out of commission. I set the squirrel on the sidewalk. If a bicyclist pedaled by, I'd tip him over. Bicycle riders always look for squirrels. The hose-head walked forwards. He wore a crew cut. Not a good sign. His fists were unclenched. An even worse sign (means he's probably done this before). Maybe he'll lower his hands like Hagler to draw me in. Then, after taking a few snaps to the face, he'll catch me with an uppercut. Then, with bees buzzing in my brain, he'll take careful aim and finish me off with a meat hook.

Pushkoff throws meat hooks too. When he's downed more than a rack, he serves up his 'rights only' special. If the chumps had any balance at all, they'd step inside and use Pushkoff's face for a speed bag. One night in Nantucket, Pushkoff and I were feeling pretty sloppy after trying to break the two-person case-drinking record. We nearly beat it too—nineteen beers—when Pushkoff yuked all over the kitchen so we were DQ'd. Pushkoff could barely walk when a guy in wire-rimmed glasses bumped into Noy and had the sack to tell her to "watch the hell where she was going." Since a sneeze could have blown the guy over, Pushkoff tipped him on his back, sat on his chest, and demanded he apologize.

The self-appointed pillar of Nantucket kept popping off, saying: "When I get up, I'm pressing charges. You're a bunch of goddamn tourists."

He was right. We are. But I'd like to ask him this: who isn't a tourist? I mean, if a gypsy moth rests on an oak tree for a week, the moth's lived there its whole life. Does that mean the moth owns the friggin' tree? So you tell me: who's got the Edsels parked in their driveways? But Spaz felt sorry for the guy, so he pulled Pushkoff off him.

"Maybe he donates money to save the whales or something," said Spaz.

"I doubt it," said Pushkoff, hocking a loogie at the guy as Spaz led him away.

But what if two quick jabs and a kick to the balls works better? Or maybe I should grab the Volvo guy's shirt with both hands, push him back, then quickly pull him forward off his feet? The old push-n-pull. These are the conversations I have with myself every tussle. I reel through the choices, but never swing because my mind blows. For every triple-hook combo my brain concocts, another section of my body is left exposed. I can't choose the best way to win. What if I grab his shirt with my left hand and pull him forward—straight into my fist? He won't expect that. Why should he? It works for Fallon. "Surprise," Fallon says, "is two-thirds of a good strategy." What Union Commander could have guessed that General Lee would divide his army three times at Chancellorsville? Or in the '65 AFC Championship, that Bart Starr would try a quarterback sneak and not even tell his running back? Chuck Mercein actually believed he had the ball. So did the Dallas defense. Same thing with sick songs. In Jimi Hendrix's version of "All Along The Watchtower," who expects the rippling curtain wah wah pedal right after the screaming dyads?

The Volvo guy stepped forward. Do you know what's screwy? Every time I'm in a tussle, I always choose the same damn routine: the dance and jab, while I look for an opening to grab the guy's legs. If I own a canoe, why do I use the bridge? Mom does it too. She'll say, "Brown sugar is healthier than white sugar." I'll say, "Brown sugar is only white sugar with molasses." She'll say, "Molasses is healthier than white sugar." I'll say, "Molasses is only burned sugar with sorghum." She'll say, "Sorghum sounds healthy." Or after hearing Aunt Bee sing *"Two for Tea"*, Mom will say, "Beatrice is a bitter drunk, immature too." I'll say, "Actually, Aunt Bee is quite perceptive and she has a surprising voice." Mom will say, "Bee's voice sounds like sandpaper on glass, and what does anybody know in the big scheme of things?" I'll say, "But we're not talking about the big scheme of things, we're talking about Aunt Bee." She'll say, "We're just tiny ants on a log," and walk away.

By then I'm ready to headbutt a bus. For once I'd like to think new thoughts and do them too. If the Volvo guy's not from Petronelli's Gym, the dance and jab is okay. Though once in Old Orchard Beach I spit on this off-duty rent-a-cop, who was rassling a bunch of girls. He looked like a steakhead who I could land straight rights at will, and I was too. But then the rent-a-cop grabbed my hair the way Algerian's do and gave me a headbutt. My shirt and shorts were soaked with blood. Pushkoff said he was about to toss a beer bottle at the guy's head when I switched to wrestling and had the guy pinned. With one eye swollen shut, I brought my fist down upon the guy's face so many times we had to hide in a boathouse for the rest of the day.

"You need some serious help," said Pushkoff. "I'm talking a whole army of shrinks."

"Easy for you to say," I replied. "Mr. 'our Scott's going to Dartmouth.' Mr. 'I date someone on the field hockey team.' Mr. 'I walk around with my boots untied.' Well I've got some news for you, Mr. Potato Head." I cracked open a Heff tall. "Someone needs to stand up to all the douchebags in this world."

"And this is how you're going to do it?" said Pushkoff in the dry heat of the boathouse. "Pick a fight with every muscle head you come across?"

"I don't give a brass bra what you think."

"Listen, Donny, to get by in this world, you've got to learn to eat a little crap."

Screw that and there's still more a-holes than toilet seats. I clenched my soda bottle.

"Hey man," the asshole Volvo guy said.

"Back off," I said.

"Hey man, I didn't hit that squirrel, did I?"

"Nah," I said. "That crazy bushy-tailed mouse tried to leap eleven yards from one elm branch to another. That isn't normal, is it?"

Shadowbox

(Donk's track)

Shadowbox, *v.* **1.** To dance around a practice ring and swing your arms though the air with an invisible opponent. **2.** To make the motions of defense and offense in anticipation of a fight or challenge. **3.** A conditioning procedure. **4.** Indecisive action.
Shadowbox, *n.* **1.** A rectangular wood frame fronted with a glass panel in which tintypes, heirlooms, dried flora, and other personal objects are arranged in an order that tells a story.

At The Middle East I handed the bouncer a fin and shoved my way towards the stage as a wall of sound pressed against my face and clothes. On stage, Ferranti's bass throbbed chestnut notes. Janota ticked off eighth notes on his snare and hi-hats, stressing every fourth beat: *Tuh tuh ti ti tuh Koosh, Tuh tuh ti ti tuh chuhsh. Tuh tuh ta tuh ta tuh Koosh, tuh tuh chuhsh chuhsh ti ti. Te te te te Te te te te.* Dyads and triads flew from Crispin's amplifier. A girl with nutmeg hair grabbed the microphone and began to sing:

> *Light bulbs hanging from my ears*
> *Baseballs turning into tears*
> *Caramel time measured on a drum*
> *Salmon skin parts the air and hums*

What was Raina doing there? She was acting like she belonged, in fact, deserved to front Wet Towels on Wood. She had laid her jazz vocals in the trash for some kind of lyrical personality chant which, I admit, had that Houdini magic.

A kid in a Bags t-shirt ran across the stage and dove into the crowd. Next thing I know, I was on stage running from a bouncer. The meathead grabbed my shirt. I swung my elbow and felt it hit bone. Leaping into the crowd, I landed on a cluster of hands like the feet of an upturned centipede. Guitar riffs pulsed through my skin as the crowd passed me above their heads. On stage, Janota churned out sixteenth notes, slowed to eighths, then sped up to thirty-seconds till half-notes hung like punted footballs. He stopped stressing every fourth beat. A seamless flow of beats formed a sonic escalator, waiting for a kid to climb.

I craned my neck towards the stage, and there Raina was, a crimson-capped chickadee in a bramble of drums and guitars. Her voice dropped to her belly, flowed upwards into her chest, climbed to her upper-palate, and echoed in the nasal passages in her skull. *All* her chambers were resonating at once. It was pretty sick.

Ragged shoes hiking hidden trails
Vanishing as night rolls up the hills.
Alone in a forest with the darkened pines
My inner-compass tells me where to climb.

She had built her own scab. My kid sister was shadowboxing with no help from me, battling the airy spirits in her own invented way. That's when I saw them: the milk glass cords flowing from her chest, reaching out to any kid who could grab them. It was then I knew: I was the fool. I thought a person learned to *shadowbox* by keeping their gloves down, so they could lure the shadows out and make peace with them. Now I'm convinced only monks hidden behind forty-foot walls can do that. No one ever truly feels safe. To shadowbox, you need to circle your opponents, tilt your head forward, bare your teeth, and be ready to jab the soulsuckers when they expose a sliver of their chins. Better to build an amazing scab, than be an ordinary wound. No, Raina wasn't singing Pinocchio's Cantos, and she wasn't half-bad either.

The crowd kept passing me around the room. Just for a sec I felt a weird lightness, but I remained glued to the centipede of hands. There had to be more. This 4/4 stuff wasn't going to do it. What sequence of stressed and unstressed beats could make a person rise? What kinds of interweaving melodies needed to be stitched together? I concentrated super-hard to catch every passing note and crack their walnut shells. Wet Towels on Wood had stretched the caramel moment further than any band I had ever heard, but there had to be more. Running out of hands, I dropped head-first onto the nightclub floor.

"Hey Fallon?" called Dad, flipping through a pile of buyer's orders at his desk. "Will you step into my office for a minute?"

"What is it, Galvin? I've got a customer out on a test drive."

"Look at these buyer's orders: thirty-two hun for a pickup with 55,000 miles, seven G's for a loaded Eldorado. Here's another one: a late-model Caprice for sixty-six hun. Why so cheap?"

"You know how it works," said Fallon. "We have to sell them a few diamonds on the skinny side so they'll take all the rats."

"I understand you knocking off a few bucks to grease the sale, but ten or twelve-hun? You're gonna to send me to the poor house with those kinds of deals."

"Just think it's good business to keep our inventory fresh," said Fallon, maintaining eye contact.

"That's fine. Just make sure you clear each deal with me first," said Dad, scanning the accounts receivables ledger. "Don't get too chummy with the wholesalers. Remember what my old man used to say-"

"Yeah, I know, I know," said Fallon, walking out of Dad's office, "sharks in tow trucks."

"They'll take the rats, Fallon. They always have."

The Shoestring Snapped

(Shiloh)

IT WAS THEIR YEAR. AFTER STEALING ONE FROM Wakefield when DeSilva picked off a pass and dipsy-doodled sixty-eight yards for the winning touchdown, Merriam Hill High went on an 11-0 run, which included the big whomp of last year's champ, Watertown. In that game, Pushkoff ticked off 248 yards behind Donk's sick blocking. After that, the Merriam Hill Red Raiders played out of their minds with wins: 23-zip against Stoneham, 42-37 over Burlington, 35-18 at Winchester, and 54-20 over Reading. It was Coach Brewer's first perfect season in twenty-four years. A huge reason was his multi-option offense. "You've got to prepare for multiple courses of action so the ball handler can choose the best path at that particular moment," said Coach Brewer in the *Merriam Hill Gazette*. "Every time the quarterback takes a snap he has three options: handoff to the running back (the preferred), roll left and run downfield, or pass to an open receiver." If Pushkoff got the handoff (and he usually did), he had three more options: lower his head and barrel up the middle, run behind Donk (a good bet), or bounce outside and race down the sidelines.

On December 3rd, Merriam Hill played Woburn for the Middlesex League crown. In the locker room, Coach Brewer surveyed his players' round heads. By the soda machine, Noy snapped pictures for the yearbook.

"Huddle up." Coach Brewer motioned to his team. The players formed a circle around the coach. "I don't have to tell you how much this game means to me. To be able to say that for one season: no one could touch us—that'd be great, but it won't help us win. In fact, that kind of thinking will only help us lose. What do you guys need to do to win today?" Coach slid a snuff tin from his coat and dipped his pinky into the tin.

A player raised his hand. "Think we can?"

"I know that's what some of the higher-ups want us to believe."

"Don't make mistakes," said Pushkoff.

"Everyone makes mistakes," Coach Brewer shot back.

"Play together as a team?" said DeSilva.

"Come on. It's all strategic alliances."

The players looked at each other.

"It's real simple. The team that makes the most plays today wins. Everything else is garbage. You've got to focus on the *play* in front of you, then the next one, then the next." Coach snorted a cinnamon mound off his pinky nail.

Players began jumping up and down.

"Hold on, there's more. Some of you will go on to play college ball, then Pushkoff will shuffle off to mortuary school. Brice will probably sell me my next car."

"No I won't," said Donk.

"Okay, so maybe not. The point is: the road we travel down was probably picked before we were born."

Donk looked over at me like he wanted to tell me something, then sniffed his fingers, and turned back to coach.

"But there's a way out. A play so jam-packed with grace that all bets are off. You wake up the next day and can't recognize the face staring back at you in the mirror. You look up and the sky's a different shade of blue. That's one of the best parts about this game, and one of the worst parts too. One *play* can change everything. Now I've asked Pastor MacDonald to come in here and say a few words, so listen up."

With a blue and gold Merriam Hill scarf around his neck, Pastor MacDonald stepped forward. The players bowed their heads. "What are you looking down for? He's not down there." Pastor MacDonald pointed to the ceiling. "Jesus is up there." The players looked up. "Dear Jesus, protect these boys from injury. Give them guidance to pursue your grace during this contest, and in all that they do. Lastly, we pray for the endurance to pursue this heavenly prize. Amen."

"Amen," the team replied.

Placing their hands on each other's shoulder pads, the players began jumping up and down. Strange gurgling sounds filled the locker room.

"Now go out there and bring home the gold ball. You won't get that many chances." As each player ran out of the locker room, Coach Brewer slapped his helmet.

On Danforth Field, Donk got into his three-prong stance. The Merriam Hill quarterback, Troy Foley, placed his hands between the center's legs. "Sixty-three, twenty-nine, twenty-eight bullet. Ready, hike one, hike two, hike three—hut hut hut." Hurrying backwards, Foley stuffed the football into Pushkoff's gut. Pushkoff faked right, then ran up the middle. Two yards ahead, Donk threw his shoulder into the belly of a linebacker. Pushkoff sidestepped the tangled players and rumbled twenty-eight yards downfield. Merriam Hill fans cheered. Three plays later, Foley took the snap and scrambled right. A Woburn player fought off the blocker and lunged towards him. Foley wobbled a pass towards the end zone. In the back of the end zone, DeSilva and the cornerback leaped up towards the ball. In the air, the cornerback's hands clutched the ball, but DeSilva snatched the ball out of his hands. Merriam Hill fans wildly cheered.

"Alright, DeSilva," I yelled from the stands.

But on the following possession, Woburn drove the ball seventy-three yards downfield to tie the score. The lead changed hands six times that day. I guess it was a question of who was going to have the ball last, and it looked like Merriam Hill would too.

In shotgun formation, the Merriam Hill quarterback stomped his foot on the grass as he counted: "Twenty-five, twenty-two, thirty-three liberty. Hike one, hike two—hut hut hut." The center snapped the ball. Catching the snap, Foley flung his arm back to pass. Pushkoff grabbed the ball from his hands and sprinted up the middle. Eight yards downfield, he double-faked a linebacker. The player didn't budge, so Pushkoff lowered his helmet and ran full-tilt towards him. The linebacker dove at Pushkoff's shins. The sound of shoulder pads striking shins could be heard in the stands. Pushkoff somersaulted through the air over a group of Woburn players. Landing on his feet, Pushkoff continued running downfield.

Above Danforth Field, the sky parted as an *air sculpture* in the shape of Pushkoff's sick move floated upwards and took its place among the unknown constellations.

Surprised as hell, Pushkoff blew past the secondary, side-stepped a diving cornerback, and scrambled into the end zone for the go-ahead score. Cheerleaders body surfed in the Merriam Hill stands. Dad got a nosebleed. I almost swallowed my scarf. With his body, Pushkoff had carved something that would always glow.

In the fourth quarter Merriam Hill led by six points. Coach Brewer huddled with his kickoff squad. "All we've gotta do is play the whole field, make one more tackle, and we're Middlesex League champs. Go get 'em."

The players jogged onto the field.

"Watch out for forward fumbles."

The Merriam Hill kicker raised his arm and booted the ball. The ball tumbled through the sky towards a Woburn receiver. Catching the ball, the receiver took off down the leftfield sidelines. DeSilva lowered his helmet and dove at the player. Just before contact, the player turned sideways and heaved the ball across the field into a pack of Woburn players. In the middle of the pack, a Woburn player caught the ball and began running down the right sidelines. Fans watched in horror as Merriam Hill defenders changed direction and sprinted towards the Woburn ballcarrier.

The announcer called the game: "Godomski to the fifty yard line, forty-five, forty, thirty-five, thirty, twenty-five."

It looked like the ballcarrier had a free ride into the end zone too, but Donk, his legs pumping like pistons, chased down the pack of Woburn players and heaved his body skywards. In the air, he set his hand on a Woburn player's helmet and vaulted over the wall of blockers. Landing on the ballcarrier, Donk hooked his arm around the guy's waist. The ballcarrier rumbled past the twenty yard line. Donk's arm slipped down to the guy's thigh. A Woburn blocker jumped on Donk, causing his arm to slip down to the ballcarrier's shin. Woburn players pushed the ballcarrier past the twelve-yard-line. Donk lost his hold, but managed to grab the ballcarrier's ankle. The runner slowed. Woburn players kicked Donk's arm. He felt the ankle slipping from his hand, but clamped onto the ballcarrier's cleat. The ballcarrier jerked to stop at the six yard line and tried to kick his leg free. Donk gripped the cleat with a wolverine's fury.

Above Danforth Field the sky began to part, making a space for a newly minted air sculpture.

The ballcarrier toppled towards the grass. The ground flew up. But his shoestring snapped and his foot popped from his cleat. Propped up by his teammates, the ballcarrier regained his balance and stumbled into the end zone. The referee raised both arms. Tiny cardinals flew from his whistle.

In the sky the newborn space closed.

Woburn fans rushed onto the field. Players in maroon shirts formed a human haystack. On the ground, Donk gripped the ballcarrier's cleat, now minus a foot.

Track 23
Why Do You Two Insist Upon Making Up Your Own Words?

The day before Christmas, Aunt Bee moved in. What can I tell you about Bee? The second Bee rolls out of bed, she thumps down the stairs to the kitchen and stirs up a pitcher of Bloody Marys.

"Oh, it's *awful*," says Bee, clanging a long steel spoon inside a glass pitcher. "It's just so *terrible*." Then she cracks up.

"What's so awful?" I asked Donk, shoveling cereal into his mouth as if Brezhnev was about to outlaw food.

"What have you been taking, stupid pills?"

That blows. If people don't think exactly the way Donk does, why are they the ones taking stupid pills? I mean, just 'cause Donk got six Fs on one report card and still scored 1580 on his SATs doesn't mean I'm dumb. Have you heard my latest lyric: "Giggle Like The Dali Llama?" I bet Cole Porter is doing backflips in his grave. But this track isn't about Donk, it's about Bee.

Mom wasn't thrilled about Bee moving in.

"She calls me Polyester Marna," Mom whispered in Swedish.

"Says who?" replied Dad, peering out the kitchen window at the ice on Granny Pond.

"Oh don't give me that. Bee's been jealous of me ever since I won the Miss Massachusetts pageant."

Dad walked over to the fridge. "Am I going to let my own sister freeze?"

Mom fiddled with the safety pin on her favorite dress. "No, but Bee chose her life. She told Fallon: 'Marna Brice doesn't know what it's like to not be able to afford toilet paper.' Well Bee could have had her toilet paper gold-plated if she had wanted to."

"I'm not so sure." Dad opened the fridge and looked over the contents. "You or I could easily have married a philandering nitwit like Addy. All those golf trips down to Pebble Beach and late-night sales meetings."

"And what about Bee's little Houdini routine? Explain those: the letters postmarked from Chicago, the hotel soaps from Rome."

"I'm thinking," said Dad, snapping a broccoli bloom off its stalk. "Where'd you hide the onion dip?"

"That's for tonight."

"Just a taste."

Mom exhaled loudly. "It's in the drawer. Bee acts like she's on contract at Capital Records, but what's she really? An airport lounge lizard."

"She opened for Anita O'Day once," said Dad, dipping the bloom into the onion dip.

Mom scrunched her nose. "Bee hallucinates. Anita O'Day joined her on stage for one song. Her name wasn't even on the marquee. How come everything that comes out a Brice's mouth has to be a sales pitch?"

"Because you've got to fake it till you make it. You know that."

Mom growled. Reaching under the sink, she pulled out a bag of potatoes. "Kuba, will you peel these for me?"

"Huh?" I asked before the question had sunk in. "Oh yeah." Standing by the sink, I attacked the potatoes with a peeler.

That night, the Pushkoffs and a few cousins came over for dinner.

"Let me tell you about men," said Aunt Bee, draining her glass. "They only express half their doubts. The more attached you are, the more their eyes wander."

"Where's Uncle Addy?" Raina asked. Donk kicked her boot.

"And fair-weather friends?" Aunt Bee rolled her eyes. "There when you don't need them, but when you're down, please, don't let the screen door slam."

"Who's going to sing the bass part when we go caroling?" Raina bit into a wreath-shaped cookie.

"Just a minute, honey." Aunt Bee hurried towards the kitchen.

In the dining room, Dad lowered a radish into a bowl of sour cream. "Truman should have let MacArthur march right across the Yalu."

Mr. Pushkoff fiddled with his sideburns. "I don't know, that would have been a blood bath."

"They sent a million men after our boys," Dad protested.

"What would you do if the Chinese massed nine brigades on the Texas border?"

"A couple of Doolittle-style raids on Beijing and Shanghai would have ended the war in a week," I said.

Mr. Pushkoff studied my face.

"He's got rocks in his head," said Dad, popping the radish into his mouth.

Back in the kitchen, Mom cranked a wooden spoon in a bowl. "These potatoes really soak up the milk."

"Should I run to our house and grab another quart?" Mrs. Pushkoff asked.

"That's alright; I'll just add a little water. Would you find out how many people are having wine."

"What goes on the asparagus, Mrs. Brice?" asked Noy as she poured a pot of boiling water into a colander in the sink.

"Aunt Brigitte's béarnaise sauce. It's on the stove."

"Can I help with anything?" Aunt Bee poked her head into the kitchen.

Mom sighed. "We're just about done. You could ask Galvin to carve the turkey."

"The greatest hitter, no question, was Ted Williams because he could hit for power and average," said Mr. Pushkoff.

Dad slid a knife across the turkey's back. "I think you need an education, Noah. Willie Mays hit 183 more home runs than Ted Williams and has a comparable lifetime batting average," said Dad.

"Williams batted .406 in 1941 and still managed to hit forty-two home runs. Top that."

Dad piled slices of turkey onto a porcelain platter. "As a pure athlete, Williams doesn't hold a candle to Mays. Did you see that catch?"

Donk walked up to the table and piled a dozen Swedish meatballs onto his plate. "The best measure of greatness is slugging percentage 'cause it tells you the batter's total contribution to an offense. You'll notice that Williams' slugging percentage was .634 while Mays' was only .597. Also, Williams had the highest on-base percentage ever— even higher than Babe Ruth's."

"I'd like to see those calculations," said Mr. Pushkoff.

"Kid's got a point." Dad pulled the drumsticks off the turkey and set them on the platter. "Now go tell your mother the turkey's carved."

Under the table I ran my hand across Chuggles' back. "What a bunch of posers."

Chuggles purred.

"What's the secret?" I asked, setting a meatball in front of Chuggles paws. "Speak to me, Chuggles. I know you can."

Chuggles sniffed the meatball.

"Just one word and we'll thrill the world."

After dinner, Mom clanked two wooden spoons together. "Everyone in the den." Mom lowered the needle on a library record, two years overdue. A Swedish carol flowed from the speakers:

Nu är det jul igen, och nu är det jul igen,
och julen vara skall till påska,
Så är det påsk igen, och så är det påsk igen,
och påsken vara skall till jula.

Mom twirled around the den with an imaginary partner.

Careful not to spill his drink, Dad sat down on the couch. "Sounds loony to me."

"I think it sounds manic," said Aunt Bee.

Raina and I danced a made up jig. "Hoodly boodly boodly, hoodly boodly boodly."

"Hey, those aren't the right words." Mom grabbed Dad's hand and pulled him off the couch.

"What the-," Dad protested as a tiny wave splashed over the rim of his highball. He handed his drink to Bee.

"Dance with me, you old coot." Mom guided Dad around the den.

Dad's face turned three shades of red. "She's cuckoo."

"Dancing with you is like dancing with a piece of wood. When I visited Sweden, all the men could dance. How did I ever fall for a man who can't dance and buys so many cars with bad transmissions?"

"Like fun. I can tell a bum transmission without sitting in the driver's seat."

"Then, apparently, you must like bad transmissions."

"Get out-"

Mr. and Mrs. Pushkoff two-stepped around the den.

Raina and I kicked our legs into the air like marionettes. "Hoodly boodly boodly, hoodly boodly boodly."

"I already told you, those aren't the words. Why do you two insist on making up your own words?"

Around 11:20, Aunt Bee went upstairs to bed. The rest of us sat around in the kitchen drinking eggnog. Donk shook the nutmeg like a tambourine.

"Donny, easy with the nutmeg," said Mom.

"So how many eggs are in this stuff anyway?" I asked.

"Yoo-hoo, Galvin, I've got a surprise for you," Aunt Bee called from the landing.

"What is it?"

"Woo hoo hooooooo. Woo hoo hooooooo." Aunt Bee thumped down the stairs in her nightgown. "Woo hoo hooooooo. Woo hoo hooooooo." She rushed towards Dad waving her underwear. "These haven't been washed for months." Dad looked up in terror. Bee chased Dad around the kitchen table.

"Marna, tell her to stop."

"I'm staying out of this," said Mom.

"Oh, it's awful. I can barely stand the smell myself. Woo hoo hooooo. Hula bula bula." Bee chased Dad into the den. "Woo hooooooo hoo. Woo hoo hoo. Ah-ha!"

"You keep your distance or I'll run upstairs and grab my jockeys from the hamper," said Dad, backing up against the couch.

"I've got you now." Aunt Bee shook her underwear.

"I'm warning you, Bee."

She lunged forward.

Dad leaped over the coffee table and ran into the kitchen. "Someone tell her to put those away."

Bee followed. "Woo hoo hoooo. You can't escape."

Holding his chest, Dad climbed the stairs. "You'll give me a heart attack."

"I think I see stains," said Bee, laughing in her cigarette voice and shaking her underwear. "Oh it's awful. Yoo-hoo, Raina? I've got a present for you." Bee ran towards Raina.

"Gross." Raina sprinted up the stairs.

"You two can hide in your bedrooms all you want." Bee called from the landing. "But sooner or later, you'll have to come down to eat, and when you do, old Beezy will be waiting."

"Cowa bunga!" Underwear in hand, Dad thumped down the stairs.

Bee screamed and ran into the kitchen.

Dad followed. "Yoo-hoo, Beezy? I've got a present for you." A tennis ball rolled across the floor. Bending down to pick it up, Dad spotted a slipper underneath the table. "Ah-ha." He lifted up the table cloth. "Gotcha."

Aunt Bee burst out from underneath the table, knocking over a chair. She ran into the den.

Dad followed. "Yee-ha. Yaw! Yaw!"

"Oh god, I see stains," cried Bee over her shoulder. "Those look like the real McCoy. I was only fooling around."

Dad's belly jiggled. "I warned you. I wasn't bluffing."

"Get those things away from me. I'll never kid around again, I promise."

Dad chased Bee around the coffee table.

"Oh, this is awful," said Bee, her nightgown fluttering.

"I bet these have never been washed." Dad cornered Bee by the TV.

"Okay, I've had enough. Game's over."

Dad stepped forward waving his underwear like a poppet. "That's not the way it works."

The Salmon Nautilus

(Vicksburg)

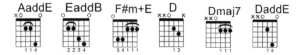

As I hurried down Merriam Hill toward the high school, a blue Dodge pulled next to me. A chorus of voices sang out:

"Get in."

"Want a ride, big boy?"

"Got any dough?"

"Hurry up."

I climbed in the backseat and sat on Raina's lap. "What are you psychos doing?"

"Get out of here." Raina pushed me off her lap.

"What does it look like?" said Crispin, sliding The Cult's "Nirvana" into the CD player. "We're biffing school and heading into Beantown to hang out at the aquarium."

"Have you seen the sea otters?" asked Donk.

"You mean the river otters?" I said.

Donk raised his fist. "How'd you like a charley horse?"

"What exit should I take?" called Pushkoff.

In the front seat Crispin unfolded a map. "That one." He pointed to a green exit sign.

Pushkoff cranked the wheel. A wave of coffee splashed over the edge of Raina's mug onto Donk's leg.

"Hey, watch it," said Donk. "Dang, look at what you did to my pants."

Pushkoff eyed Donk in the rearview mirror. "Better your pants than my seat." The car slowed to a stop at a tollbooth. Pushkoff handed the lady two quarters, then stepped on the gas. The needle climbed to fifty.

"Did you guys know that tollbooth operators have the highest suicide rate of any job?" I said.

Donk wiggled his ears.

"No, really, I read it in the Globe.

"It's because people are rude trolls," said Raina, "unless they're related."

"Come on. Then every waitress in the world would be offing themselves," replied Donk.

"He's got a point," said Crispin. "I think it's being stuck in a booth all day and watching people drive off to cool places. I'd rather scrub toilets with a toothbrush for a living."

Donk wiggled his ears and nostrils. "I bet working in a tollbooth is a transitional job," he said. "A job people take while trying to learn the skills needed to land a job they really want. And let me tell you, it's hard to learn new skills in a tollbooth, so after a few months—boom."

A few blocks from the aquarium, Pushkoff backed up into a parking spot. Donk lifted a parking ticket from another car and placed it on Pushkoff's windshield. "That's a decoy."

"Don't be a douche. They check those tickets," Raina said, pulling a tube of lipstick from her purse.

Inside the Aquarium, a footpath circled upwards around a huge Plexiglas tank shaped like a silo. We followed the path upwards.

"Hey Little Brice?" Crispin bonked me on the head. "I saw you at the Slag show. Why were you standing in the corner all by yourself?"

"Too many flying elbows."

"Whud you think of the show?"

"I kind of liked Moran's solo in "Needle Queen." He's got this breathing tidal-wave-of-fuzz going on that no one else is doing."

A chorus of voices hooted:

"Oh please."

"He's been sniffing glue."

"Yeah, right."

"Read another thousand books."

My face turned five shades of coral. "What do you turds know about a mint song anyway," I said, peering through the Plexiglas. On the tank's bottom, the bulbous eyes of cod poked through the muck and watched us.

"A mint song has lyrical sweeps in the melody," said Raina. "I prefer a range of at least two octaves."

Donk wiggled his eyebrows, but Raina had a point. A rollercoaster ride of notes puts a little helium in the blood. Pushkoff does it on the field when he shifts, fakes, spins, and sprints. Even my mom is intrigued—and she hates football. Why is Mom intrigued? Because a swerving Geiger counter finds more uranium.

"That's part of it," said Crispin. "A mint song also needs dissonant chords to provide contrast and give value to the harmonies."

Crispin was onto something. Most musicians write from one part of their body. You hear their songs and think: oh, those notes are coming from their ribcages or low in their guts. A mint song is different. The notes bubble up from places few composers go: the hollows in their hips, the capillaries in their hands, and the flaps of muscles that stretch across their chests. Those traffic-horn ninths, molasses sevenths, and pond-water elevenths give a song that full-bodied sound.

"You're pretty impressed with yourself, aren't you?" said Raina, kicking Crispin's sneaker.

"If that's your way of asking me for a date, I'm busy, but I might be able to pencil you in next month."

Raina chased Crispin up the footpath.

Pushkoff felt his biceps.

"Guards, guards, there's a crazy lady after me," cried Crispin as Raina punched his back.

In the tank, a shortfin mako swished its boomerang tail.

"Hey Pushkoff?" called Donk. "Give you a quarter if you hop in the tank and wrestle that shark."

"You first," said Pushkoff.

Donk pretended to dive through the Plexiglas.

At the top of the walkway, a guide stood in front of a shallow tank. The sign read: Northern Sea Stars and Spiny Sun Stars. We had about forty minutes to kill before the otters' feeding time, so we wandered over to the tank.

The guide walked towards us. "Starfish, also called sea stars, are not fish at all—they're echinoderms. Echinoderm means: spiny skin." She lifted a five-ray sea star from the pool. "Sea stars move by pumping water along their canals, then in and out their tube feet. Sea stars are carnivores; they eat mollusks and other echinoderms. When a sea star eats an oyster, it clamps its rays to each half of the oyster's shell and pulls. The oyster is able to keep its shell closed for long time, but eventually it tires out and the sea star is able to pry open the shell enough to insert its stomach and devour the soft meat inside." With her knife, the guide sliced a ray off and tossed the amputated sun star back into the tank.

Donk nudged my arm.

"One of the most remarkable abilities of a sea star is its talent for *regeneration*. A sea star that loses a ray can grow a new one given time."

"How many rays can a sea star lose without hurting its ability to grow whole again?" asked Donk.

"Most species can regenerate only if the central disk and one whole ray are intact, but a few species can grow whole bodies from a single ray. Those species, like *Linckia*, will regenerate several starfish from a single echinoderm. However, if the pieces are too small, they will not generate enough oxygen and the sea star will die." She handed me the cut ray.

I examined the ray. "What do you think, Two-by-four?"

Donk ran his finger over the ray. "A mint song makes your *salmon nautilus* hum," said Donk.

"Huh?"

"Shut up."

"Salmon what?"

"Salmon nautilus." Donk shot us a nasty glance. "It's the labyrinth of flesh and nerves winding through your body that receives and transmits the mojo juice that fuels the universe. Trouble is, most songs only resonate in your chest or in your gut, but mint songs make huge sections of your body *hum*."

We looked at each other.

"Give a listen to Rory Gallagher's "Walk On Hot Coals."" Donk closed his eyes. "The opening riff slips through my flesh like nickels dropped in a lake." Donk began dancing like captain weirdo. "The song builds and builds: intro, hook, solo, verse—by the time he hits the chorus, ginger ale's spilling from my ribs." My brother circulated around the walkway. "When he finishes the solo, my whole body's filled with the *feeling of rising*." Donk opened his eyes. "That's the whole point." My brother peered down at the mako shark circling in its tank, then back up at the sea stars. "Some day a musician's gonna write a song so filled with the feeling of rising that listeners are going to float away."

That klepto. *I'm* the kid who first used salmon to describe the body when Aunt Bee bought us a pack of airport salmon during one of her Houdini trips. The salmon glowed like lava. It's the tuh-tuh-truth. Plus, I'm the kid who got his salmon nautilus to hum on a hiking trip up Red Feather Ridge with the Pushkoffs, but Donk bootlegged it, gave it form, and placed it in a symphony of words. So who owns it? Now I have to come up with something new. Big brothers whack it.

"He's gone," said Pushkoff.

"Keep your acid trips to yourself," laughed Raina.

"How can a girl get her body to rise?" asked Noy.

Donk's face looked like a slot machine with its arm just pulled; you could see the reels spinning. "Remember the winter Spaz left his hockey stick in your mom's tulip bed?"

Noy nodded.

"In the spring the tulips rose up around the hockey stick till it was covered in a sea of green leaves. Remember that? Well, how did those tulips learn to rise?"

"Someone told them," said Pushkoff.

"Hardy har har—I aughta coldcock you," said Donk.

"You and whose army?"

"The tulips didn't need to learn," said Donk. "The know-how was already scribbled in their cells. It's in our cells too. Now if I could only figure out a way to get to that know-how."

I tossed the ray back into the pool. "Where do the tulips want to go?"

Donk picked at his knuckles. "The best I can figure is there's an Aloe vera river of pure awareness that floats through the universe and constantly wants to expand. During the Big Bang, the river poured from an unknown dimension and formed the universe. The river existed before the first Big Bang, it exists in Merriam Hill now, and will continue to exist after the universe collapses into it's original state." Donk studied our faces. "I'm serious, you peckerheads. When God particles began to acquire mass, they literally willed the universe into being. The same particles are inside Mrs. Pushkoff's tulips. They rise because the awareness inside of them wants to escape their bodies and merge back into the aloe vera river. The tulips want to go home."

Behind Donk a group of third graders walked towards the otter exhibit.

"Nice," said Pushkoff.

Raina leaned over. "I think I'm going to puke."

"What do you mean?" Donk asked.

"Phhff, pre-Big Bang consciousness—how the heck do you know?" asked Raina. "Did you ask the tulips? Do they talk to you?"

"You pretend everything means nothing, but you won't kill anybody to prove it."

"Only 'cause I'll end up in Walpole," said Raina.

"Shoot a whitetail deer. You won't end up in Walpole."

"Gross, no way."

Crispin flipped his dreadlocks from his eyes. "No, no. There's no hocus-pocus going on in the universe. It's a lot simpler than that. It's the same old conflict: our bodies grow old and die, but our minds want to live forever.

Luckily, our DNA keeps mutating. Naturally, with each new generation, humans acquire new talents, some very useful. Eventually, a whole new species of humans evolves."

"What are the talents?" asked Noy.

"A baby is born in Zhejiang with the ability to read minds. She can somehow perceive the synapses lighting up inside a person's brain like the veins on a leaf. Can you imagine the advantages? Naturally-"

"Naturally," Raina repeated.

Crispin did his best Blutarski face. "-her genes are passed on. A few centuries later, everyone on earth can read minds. Then, another baby is born. This time with an even wilder mutation: her thoughts can leap from her body and exist outside her body for a few seconds. As time passes, these clusters of consciousness are able to leap further and further outside of their bodies and exist for longer and longer periods of time as they learn to extract glucose from the sun. Then, one summer day in 32,000 A.D., a golden child permanently leaves her body and never needs to re-body again. This sets off a tidal wave of souls leaving their bodies, a reverse big-bang of the spirit as the human species evolves into conscious clusters."

"That's as good as anything else you can say."

"Stop chasing parked cars," said Raina.

Our laughter echoed down the corridor.

"I'm out of here," said Donk, walking towards the otter tank. We followed. By the otter tank a sign read: *Next Show at 11 a.m.*, so we stood in line.

"Kids, I overheard your conversations, and I have to say I disagree," said a guy with a Jesus beard and converse sneakers. (MIT all the way.) "Coding is rapidly overtaking the evolutionary process. While the mind could take a half-million years to evolve to the point of existing outside its body, engineers will pull it off in three centuries when programmers learn how to create personalized algorithms that can replicate a person's consciousness. People's minds will be preserved in algorithms. Then, the code will be downloaded to human droids. Presto, you've got immortality."

"How do we know this hasn't been done already and that's who we are, Mr. Stallman?" I said, reading the name on his badge.

"Hmm, you may have a point," Mr. Stallman said. "But I'm pretty sure if I cut into my skin I'd only find blood and guts."

The door opened to the otter show. We walked into the hall and sat down in the front row.

"Imagine living in a universe and not being able to figure out the reason why?" mused Noy.

Donk wiggled his fingers. "It's kinda cruel, if you really think about it."

In the rear of the otter exhibit, by the simulated riverbank, a door opened. A woman walked into the exhibit holding a bucket. She tossed hunks of fish into the water. The otters swam towards the fish. Setting the fish on their bellies, the otters began rolling like logs and taking bites each time they surfaced. Strange sounds filled the room.

"What's up with the spinning?" I asked Donk as the trainer placed the bucket on a high shelf and rushed across the hall into the polar bear exhibit. Ignoring my question, Donk climbed up onto the railing. Breathing in a weird way, Donk balanced himself atop the railing.

"You're gone."

"Nice."

"Hey, what are you doing?"

I reached for Donk's arm, but it was too late. Donk had splashed into the otter tank. The freaked out otters dove to the bottom. Donk grabbed a hunk of hake, set it on his belly, and began rolling like a Goodyear radial. The nutbag even ate a little. Friendly as hell, an otter swam up to Donk and began spinning alongside. Donk tossed a piece of his hake to the otter and let out a riff: "Dom keeherah, ayom keerah." Climbing over the railing, I leaped onto the riverbank, grabbed the bucket, and began tossing fish to the otters. Donk washed his pretend whiskers and cleaned his watertight fur. Soon six otters were rolling together. Donk dove to the bottom, and when he broke the surface, the strangest song sprang from his voice box: "Ree durreen, dom keeherah, ayom keerah, ree durreen." I heard a trace of Mike Scott's voice from the Waterboys' version of "Sweet Thing", just after the chorus when Scott freeforms, "Ah ee-ah oh ee-ah ah oh ah ee-ah sawheet thayang." The six otters joined in. The concert sounded like a musical translation of Kandinsky. If there was a pattern, I couldn't hear it. Still, it cohered—the sick units! A few minutes later, Donk's salmon skin began turning blue and his movements slowed. Oddly, his fingertips glowed a pale-orange color.

"What the hell do you think you're doing? Out of that tank—now!" The trainer pulled Donk from the water. "Otters die from human viruses all the time. You don't move." The trainer ran down the pathway. "I'm calling security."

"Grab him," I yelled. "You play dead," I told Donk. Carrying my brother's body, the five of us booked-it down the pathway.

"Out of our way."

We swerved around a stroller. "Someone call an ambulance!"

"Visitor fell into the pool."

"Anyone know CPR?"

"Stand back." Pushkoff forearmed a security guard.

"Call Mass General; we're on our way."

Running out the front entrance, we rounded the corner, reached the Dodge, and tossed Donk into the back seat. Our tailpipe spit out exhaust as we cruised up I-93.

"Did you see the expression on that security guard's face?" asked Raina.

"You owe me big-time," I said, tossing my coat on Donk as he shivered in the back seat.

Who's In Charge?

In the showroom, Dad rested his elbows on the roof of an Impala. He scanned the lot. The door opened. In walked Fallon with a railroad track of stitches across his forehead.

"Jesus Christ, you look like you lost an ice pick fight," said Dad.

Fallon set his briefcase on his desk. "Damn oak trees. They jump in front of you."

"How bad is it?"

"Totaled."

"Oh balls!"

"I'm gonna make this up to you, Galvin."

"That's what you said last time. Well, here we go again. We were just starting to get some meat on our bones too. How do you expect me to hawk a sled with a rebuilt title?"

Fallon looked down at his shoes.

Retrieving a cloth from the glove box of the Impala, Dad began wiping the dust off the hood. "I'm taking the deductible from your paycheck."

"That's fair."

"What did Dr. Van Dyne say?"

"Usual stuff: stay off my feet, plenty of ice and rest, call him if my dizzy spells persist."

Dad scanned the front row of new cars along Mass Ave. "Fallon, what I really want to know is: where are all the customers?"

"Give me a minute and I'll scare some up." From his briefcase, Fallon pulled out a copy of *The Merriam Hill Alarm*. "Let's see who's had a little fender-bender over the weekend." Fallon scanned the Police Log. "Here we go: Chet Holland of 31 York Street fell asleep while driving and his vehicle slammed into a stone wall." Fallon removed a phone book from his desk. "He was treated for light whiplash and released. Let's give Chet a call and see if he needs a new sled."

"Fallon."

"Yeah?"

"Hold off for a sec." Dad walked to the coffee machine. "Three sugars, right?"

Fallon set down the receiver. "Just two. I'm trying to drop a few tons."

Dad rolled his swivel chair across the showroom to Fallon's desk. "Did I ever tell you about the time my kid got booted from kindergarten? I know I've told everyone else."

"Heard something about it, yeah, but the details are fuzzy," said Fallon.

"A few years after Bobby Kennedy got picked off, I was at my desk with old man Rizzano closing a deal for a cube van when I get this call from the principal at Fisk Elementary. He tells me Kuba had a run-in with his teacher during story time and he can't reach Marna, so he wants to know if I can come pick him up. I guess, part-way through *Charlotte's Web*, Kuba gets up and walks over to the work bench and starts hammering and sawing as if nothing else mattered. So Miss Gage tells him to join the rest of the class, but Kuba keeps hammering and whacking away at the wood. So she hurries over, grabs his arm, and directs him back to the reading circle. But he refuses to sit down and demands to know: 'who's in charge?' So the teacher hauls Kuba down to the principle's office, his voice echoing down the hallway as she's dragging him: 'who's in charge around here anyway? I don't want to hear a story. I want to meet the person in charge.'"

The dark liquid jiggled in Fallon's mug.

"In the principal's office Miss Gage asks him: 'who do you think's in charge, Kuba?'"

"'He is,' my son says, pointing to the janitor. Remember Dick Foley?"

"Of course," said Fallon, reaching for his pen and circling Chet Holland's phone number. "He bought a Silverado off me two years ago."

"Well, he's the maintenance guy at Fisk. So the principle explains to my son that all adults hold some sort of authority, but in the classroom the teacher's in charge. But Kuba was convinced that behind the scenes Foley was running everything. Next day, same thing. He wouldn't take his place at the story circle. So, we had to pull him from kindergarten until the following year. Knew he was too young, but Marna wanted him to get a head start in the game of life."

"Why did Kuba think the janitor was in charge?"

"Don't know."

Fallon scanned the *Police Log*. "And I thought I had heard every Brice story there was. Look at this: Fran Valenti's Blazer was stolen sometime Friday night—right out of his driveway. Police found his Blazer in Woburn completely stripped. Let's give St. Francis a call."

"One more thing, Fallon."

"What?"

"I'm in charge. That means, when you're driving one of my sleds, lay off the sauce."

"I just spent the night at Mass General and I'm in no mood for one of your lectures. Remember, before I trained you to sell, you didn't know the difference between a slant-six and a straight-six," said Fallon.

"And now you're training me for the poorhouse."

"Poorhouse. You don't know what the poorhouse is. Back in South Cleveland, do you know what a six course meal was? Four potatoes, a glass of sour milk, and a punch in the face."

"I know, I know. My Dad built this rattrap and I was able to buy in at the ground floor. Never had a fired-up sales manager rubbing sticks together under my chair, but that doesn't mean I'm a nincompoop you can jerk around." Out front a woman inspected a Saab.

Fallon reached for his coat.

"You stay put," said Dad, grabbing a magnetic plate off the safe. "You'll probably scare her off with those stitches. Everyone already thinks salesmen are a bunch of lowlifes. I'll go see what she wants."

Raina poked her head into Donk's room. "Noy and I are going to the movies, want to come?"

"What's playing?"

"Bunch of stuff. We'll pick one when we get there."

Donk gingerly turned a page of his tombstone-sized dictionary. "Okay, call Dad and see if we can."

Raina stayed in the doorway.

"What?" demanded Donk.

"Only weirdoes read the dictionary for five hours."

"Eat a pillow. This is the greatest book ever written."

"Oh yeah, then why does this room smell like maple syrup?"

"Shut your face. Mom's in her bedroom."

"Maybe she should know."

"Come on, only scumbags fink on their brothers."

Raina fiddled with the guitar picks on Donk's dresser. "Don't worry, I won't tell."

"What did Dad say?" asked Donk, flipping another page.

"He said, 'go ask Mom.'"

"And?"

"We can go—whoo-hoo." Raina danced around the room. "When do you wanna leave?"

"We should head out early, so I can make a few pit stops."

Raina leaned over Donk's desk. "What new words did you learn today?"

"To be honest with you, I really didn't know any of them, so I'm focusing on words that begin with the letter C."

"I'm pretty good at vocab. Ask me the meaning of a word."

"Oh yeah, what does *car* mean?" asked Donk, dipping his hand into a tin of brownies.

"Are you for real? That's tit. A car is. . . give me a sec. A car is. . . hold on. A car is an automobile."

"Go on." Donk picked a crumb off his pants and put it in his mouth.

"A car is. . . a boxcar on a train?"

"Not exactly, but I'll give it to you. Keep going."

"I'm done. Give me another word."

"See. You barely know anything about a car. The idea of a car is a lot bigger than you think. Don't worry, I do it too."

"I'm not. You're a freak. Let me see that." Raina read the definition.

Car *(kar)*, n. **1.** An automobile. **2.** The part of an elevator that transports passengers up or down. **3.** *Poetic;* A chariot of triumph; a vehicle of splendor that travels through the sky. **4.** A perforated box floated in water for preserving live fish, lobsters, or clams. **5.** A vehicle moved on wheels and drawn by a person or horse; a wagon, coach, or shopping cart. **6.** The basket or cage suspended from a balloon that contains passengers. **7.** *Astronomy;* The seven stars also called The Great Bear, Big Dipper, or Charles's Wain. **8.** *Philosophy;* A collection of beliefs that guide a person.

Car 2 *(kar)*, n. **1.** A vehicle running on rails; a streetcar, omnibus, or farm cart. **2.** Railcars especially designed and furnished for the comfort of travelers; a palace car, sleeping car, drawing-room car, or parlor car. **3.** Dummy car: A railcar containing it's own steam power or locomotive. **4.** Funeral car: In a funeral the railcar, wagon, or automobile bearing the casket; a hearse. **5.** Car coupler: A shackle or other device used for connecting cars in a train.

Car 3 *(kar)*, adj. **1.** Unnatural. **2.** Disembodied. **3.** Left-handed. **4.** Sinister.

At the other end of the hallway, I walked into Mom's room. "Come here for a sec."

At her desk Mom paused from writing a check and looked up. "What is it?"

"Shhh, keep it down. I was in the basement playing floor hockey and I almost tripped over Mrs. Pushkoff."

"What's she doing down there?" Mom set her checkbook in the top drawer and closed the drawer.

"She's just sitting there."

"Rachael? Rachael?" Mom searched for the light switch in the furnace room.

"Hi Marna," said Mrs. Pushkoff.

"You okay?"

"Not really."

"What's wrong with your arm?"

"Can't move it."

"Let's get you upstairs." Mom placed her arm around Mrs. Pushkoff's waist and helped her up the stairs.

If Giant Sequoias Can Keep Rising, Why Can't We?

APRIL'S *BOSTON HERALDS* TURNED INTO MAY'S, AND May's turned into June's. June's were still folded in our driveway when Donk found himself on graduation day with no love letters from colleges or recruiters.

"I have a friend," said Aunt Bee, "who teaches music at Plymouth State. She's not half-bad. You can spend twenty years stumbling over the principles of composition, or you can go to college, study the great composers, and learn a heck-of-a-lot in four." Aunt Bee reached for the phone. "I'm going to give Lillian a call." She did. Donk enrolled as a special student for the fall semester.

In her office, Professor Ellis spoke with Donk. "If you can manage to get all Bs in the fall, we'll visit the dean in the spring."

Donk nodded. "What classes should I start out with?"

"Let's see." Professor Ellis studied Donk's transcripts. "Were you in the school orchestra?"

Donk shook his head.

"Jazz band?"

"Thought about it, but-," Donk's voice trailed off as he scanned the titles in the bookcases behind Professor Ellis.

That July Dad rented a beach house on Peaks Island in Maine, so we drove up I-95 to Portland and took the ferry across Casco Bay.

After the ferry reversed its engines and came to a stop, dockworkers secured the boat to the dock. We grabbed our suitcases and guitars and walked towards the shore.

"Look at all those lobster traps." Donk pointed to a stack of traps on a dock. "I wonder if they peg traps all winter?"

"Uhgh, that gives me the willies," said Raina. "What if their boat sank? You wouldn't last two minutes in that water."

"Actually, I heard drowning is the best way to go," said Donk. "First, your whole body goes numb. Then you sink. Then you fall asleep."

"How do you know? Did you ask someone who drowned?"

Donk picked up a clump of seaweed and hucked it at Raina.

"You missed." Raina ran down the dock. "You couldn't hit a cow."

"If you can't behave like civilized beings, I'll take you both home right now," called Mom.

"I'm not going anywhere," Donk stated.

"How about into the ocean, you sawed-off runt." Dad picked up Donk and carried him towards the water.

"Police! Police!" yelled Donk.

"Jesus, will you shut up." Dad set Donk on the dock. "You sure can dish it out, but you can't suck it up."

Donk began to sulk.

Mom grabbed my hand. "So, Spazzola, how do ya like Peaks Island?"

"How'd you know they call me Spaz?"

From her purse, Mom removed a pair of sunglasses and slid them on. "What do you think, I only exist when I'm talking to you?"

Dad placed his arm around Mom. "Boy, Marna, you're sassy on vacation."

"I used to think the world disappeared when I turned my back," said Raina.

"She still does," Donk said.

"But how do we know something exists when we're not there to see it?" I asked.

"Because when you're not seeing it, I am—nitwit," said Dad.

"But how accurate are our eyes?" I replied as a Painted Lady floated by. "I mean, how do we know I'm seeing the same colors on that butterfly as you are?"

Donk began wiggling his ears. "Actually, butterfly wings are made of structural pigments. They're colorless. The colors we see are only the different ways the sun bounces off their wings. Your salmon nautilus needs to second-guess your eyes," said Donk.

"He made that up," said Dad.

Raina circled around us. "Look, I'm a Monarch butterfly."

"I'm a Gypsy moth." Taking my guitar from its case, I followed Raina and began strumming "Orpheus With A Guitar."

Raina sang the first voice:

> The sky is smeared with ink and gin
> A barbed wire fence digs in my skin
> The sun blushed berries bump the ground
> A child's laugh will soon be gone.

"Hey, did you write that?" asked Mom.

I nodded.

"Three triple-rhymes in a row—pretty clever. What kind of butterfly are you, Donny?"

"A Black Swallowtail," said Donk, still sulking.

"Whose kids are you anyway?" mused Dad. "Honey, what time does the mailman deliver mail?"

Mom tilted her head back and got a face-full of sun. "I'm probably missing out on all the fun."

Dad snuck behind Donk and stuck his pinkie into Donk's ear. "Wet-Willie."

Donk chased Dad up the street towards the beach house. Guitar in hand, I followed.

"Don't forget your suitcases," Mom hollered. "Oh fudge. Give me a hand, Raina, will you?"

On the porch Dad turned off the grill and shuffled into the kitchen with a plate of burgers. "Supper's ready."

Mom dropped a handful of knives and forks on the table. "Where's your brother?"

"He's down at the dock. Wanted to see what the fishermen caught."

"Tell him supper's ready," said Dad. "But put on some fly dope or those black flies will lift you up and carry you away."

With my eyes closed, I walked down the street until my knee banged into a mailbox. At the local inn, I saw Donk peering over a fence at a lobster bake.

"Look." Donny pointed to a bunch of guys in aprons. "They're dropping lobsters into boiling water by dozen and people are lining up to eat them. Just think, those lobsters evolved over millions of years to survive in the freezing North Atlantic only to end up in boiling water."

"I read that lobsters don't have central nervous systems so they can't feel pain."

"I don't believe that for a second." Donk smooshed a black fly on his arm. "Look at their claws trying to pinch the cooks' arms."

"Probably an instinct."

"It's the desire to exist."

"Still, if they can't feel pain, how can they be suffering?" Donk clenched his jaw. "Can't you connect the dots?"

"Not in your head I can't." I crouched down on the ground. "Race me home?"

"What's that in the sky?" Donk pointed skywards.

I looked up.

Donk took off. "Made you look, dirty crook, stole your mother's pocketbook."

My sneakers flopped against the tar as I tried to catch Donk. Behind our backs, the sun's salmon legs ran off to California.

"What took you so long?" said Dad at the table. "I was just about to eat Donny's burger."

Mom studied Donk. "Why are you breathing so hard?"

Next day, Raina, Donk, and I laid our towels on the beach as a metronome of waves crashed against the shore. On the dunes, lyme grass, seawort, and darnel battled for space with milfoil, marsh rose, and foxtail. Further back, ring lichen dotted a cliff and milky lines of quartz ran through the granite, creating a stone map of unnamed places.

After kicking off his sneakers, Donk pulled a cassette player from his bag and pressed play. The opening chord progression from "Painted Yellow Lines" by Dispatch pulsed from the speakers.

Raina rubbed suntan lotion on her belly. "Here we are for a blink."

"A moth resting on a birch," said Donk.

"There's some kind of kooky symmetry," I said, taking off across the beach, filling my lungs with ocean air.

Donk checked the road. "No cars in sight. No human sounds to pollute our silence. This beach is ours!" He slid off his trunks. So did I.

"What the heck," said Raina, untying her bikini.

We fell into the wind, shifting and turning, notes spinning off our bodies. Then we raced across the beach, leaping into gusts of wind with outstretched arms. Moving in a circle, we kept time with our feet, shifting and turning, carving *air sculptures* with our bodies. They floated upwards and dissolved in the sky. Beside us, waves threw themselves onto the beach. Stepping into the center, our bodies intertwined: torsos twisting, skin touching, legs lifting; then our shadows flew up and spiraled towards the sun. In the bay, a ferry cruised back to Portland. A girl in a kayak paddled across the water. Floating seagulls rose and fell with the waves. Just as quickly, our feet touched down upon the sand. Still we wanted more. If giant sequoias could keep rising, why couldn't we?

"Car!" Donk screamed.

We dove into the ocean. Salty icicles pierced my skin.

"Water's friggin' cold."

Leaping from the water, we sprinted up the beach and searched for our bathing suits.

"Jesus, Joseph, and Mary—put your swimsuits on!" Mom yelled from the road.

I hid my privates behind a horseshoe crab. Raina held seaweed over her boobs. With a rock, Donk covered his jewel box. We search around the beach for our bathing suits, then put them on.

At the beach house, Dad looked up from the kitchen table. "So they were running on the beach naked. What do you think goes on in their loony heads? Maybe we let Beatrice stay above the garage too long."

"Beatrice? What about *you?*" Mom laughed. "What about your nude calisthenics every time Bee brought a new boyfriend to the house? No wonder she got stuck with that charlatan Addy."

"That's different."

"How?"

"It just is." Drink in hand, Dad walked out onto the porch. "God, I tortured my poor sister."

On the beach I collapsed on my towel. "Got to take a breather."

"You okay, Spaz-a-mataz?" asked Donk.

"Having a fast-spell. Think I'm gonna yuke."

"Want me to walk you back to the house?"

"Just let me lie down for a sec. I'll be alright," I said, closing my eyes. I woke up to the sounds of high-tide rolling in. Donk and Raina sat on the beach encircled by a wall of sand.

"Left wall crumbling," said Donk as a wave smacked their fort. Furiously, he kicked sand to the left wall.

"Reinforcements needed." Raina dropped pieces of driftwood in front of the wall.

"Flood diverted," said Donk as the retreating wave carried half the fort back into the sea. "Monster wave approaching," he hollered. "Increase wall thickness." He scooped up sand and packed it into the wall.

"Seaweed barrier in place," I said, dumping an armful of seaweed in front of the fort.

"Red alert! Red alert," said Raina as the wave rolled up the beach.

The wave poured over the wall and submerged their legs.

"Center wall washed out." I threw my body in front of the next wave.

It rolled over my body and engulfed the wall.

Raina hopped up. "Evacuate fort. Massive flooding." She ran up the beach and down the road towards the house.

"Destroy all evidence." I kicked over the breached walls.

Donk remained seated.

"You coming?"

"Going down with the fort," he said as seawater covered his legs. From the sky, hordes of ultraviolet piranhas flew down and gnawed on Donk's shoulders.

This is when I first felt it. The sand beneath me was moving. I was riding on the crest of an invisible wave. I jumped to a rear wave, but it merged with my wave and kept me hurtling towards the gray triangles of open ocean. I leaped to my left, but landed on an identical wave. That's when I realized, the waves were carrying *me* away. What good was a blink of awareness when everything we love gets carried out to sea? What good was music when every note was collapsing in its own placenta? I admit, beach houses and air sculptures, nutcase brothers and singing sisters added up to a ton, but the waves would whisk them away too.

The waves were up to Donk's chest, swallowing whole acres of beach. Foam eyebrows were everywhere.

"Come on, Two-by-four," I said, dragging Donk up the beach.

In the kitchen, Dad unscrewed the top off a saltshaker and placed a piece of napkin over the opening. With his finger, he pressed down into the napkin, forming a thimble-sized cup inside the shaker. He poured Cayenne pepper into the cup and screwed the cap back on. After picking away all traces of the napkin, he set the rigged shaker back on the dinner table.

"What do you think you're doing?" asked Mom as she diced onions and chives.

"Just wait until Donny goes nutso with the salt again. Not going to say a word." Dad danced over to the fridge. "Think I'll have one of those brewskis."

"Grab me the green bowl while you're in there."

Dad handed Mom the bowl then cracked open his soldier. A few minutes later, he cracked open another one. "If we sold our house, we'd probably have enough equity to buy a palace up here—cash on the barrel."

"I don't know. What if the economy continues to head south?" said Mom. "I read that fishermen up here are going broke left and right. They take and take and take from the sea and never give back. Of course George's Bank is going to get depleted."

"People need cars everywhere."

"Up here, I bet they wait until their cars die before buying a new one." Mom scooped mayonnaise into the bowl of potatoes, then added onions, peppers, and chives.

"You're probably right," said Dad, watching Mom's hands. How did they move so quickly? How did they get so wrinkled? He placed his hand on her waist and smelled her hair. "Thanks, Marna. Thanks for not taking off when sometimes I think you should." Dad turned away. "See, there it goes." He walked to the porch. "Can't say anything without turning into a damn mommy's boy."

Mom set the potato salad on the table. "Now why would I ever want to do a thing like that?"

During dinner, Donk reached for the saltshaker. His hand moved up and down like a piston.

"Well, honey, this is just about the best potato salad I've ever had," said Dad watching Donk scoff down his meal.

"Could use a little more mayonnaise," said Raina.

"Arrgh, great balls of fire!" Donk booked it to the sink and French kissed the faucet. "What did you put in that potato salad anyway?"

Dad laughed until his face looked like a scarlet ibis. "Little spicy for you?"

Later that night, Raina exhaled loudly on the couch. "Hurry up, it's just a board game."

Donk fiddled with his wooden squares. "Take a chill pill and observe greatness. I'm about to get the highest total in the history of Scrabble."

Raina crossed her arms and sat back. "I could get the record too if I took an hour."

"How so?" Donk laughed. "You don't know a single seven letter word."

"Handjob," said Raina.

"That's a lie."

"Don't worry, Donk," I said, "I know all about you and Pushkoff in the first grade."

Raina's eyes narrowed to slits. "You don't know squat."

Donk laid down seven letters horizontally on both sides of the word: THEN. "Meet the wordmeister." Donk got up and shadowboxed. "Jab, left-right, hook." His arms flailed. "I am the greatest of all-time, better than the champ Marvelous Marvin Hagler." Donk added up his score. "Three, eight, thirteen, nineteen, double-letter twenty-two, and two double-word scores equals seventy-nine, add fifty for using all my letters—that's 129 points! Top that." Donk took the last six letters from the pouch.

"That's not a word," said Raina. "I challenge."

"It is too a word: PANTOTHENIC. Go look it up."

Raina did. It was.

"Let me see that." I grabbed the dictionary from Raina, but instead of checking pantothenic, I casually flipped to the Z-section. "You don't say, but do you know what it means?" I asked, buying more time.

"Please! That's tit. Pantothenic acid is an oily, yellow acid found in plants and animal tissue."

I pretended to listen and searched for a word that would end the game and leave Donk stuck with six letters. I closed the dictionary. "He's legal and lucky."

"Come on, Spaz. You're as bad as he is. I'm getting a soda." Raina walked to the fridge.

Donk cleared his sinuses. "Grab me a can too, will ya?"

"Ciao oo, baby. The disco king is back." I thrust my hips back and forth like John Travolta (Donk hated Travolta) and laid all my squares on the board vertically beside the word: FAN. "ZYMURGY, that's ten times two for a double-letter score, twenty-four, thirty-one, thirty-five times two for a double-word score is seventy, add fifty for using all my letters, and nine points for the word FANG—that's 129 points. Take a back seat, sucker." I shadowboxed around the room.

"You cheated, peckerhead," growled Donk.

"Oh, do I see six squares in your holder, Donk?" I added up his letters. "That's sixteen more points, plus thirteen from Raina—158 points for the new wordmeister." I bowed to a pretend audience. "Thank you. Only cash, please. No checks. Crisp hundred-dollar bills."

"More like the sheister-meister." Donk grimaced. "There's nothing I can say. You abused me badly. You little." Donk got up and chased me around the den.

"The agony of defeat," I called as Donk grabbed my shirt and pulled me to the floor.

On the porch, two silhouettes leaned against the railing. In the tar-blue sky, brown bats swooped down onto mosquitoes. Past the sea grass and boulders that lined the road, waves unfolded up the beach, sending a salty mist floating through the air.

"Why are we slugging it out in Merriam Hill for?" asked Dad.

"I know it," said Mom. "But if we lived here year-round, the winters would spoil it."

"You know what they say up here." Dad mimicked a Down East accent, "If you can't take the wintahs, you don't deserve the summahs."

Mom made a face. "Wish it was that easy." She leaned against Dad. "Remember the first time we stayed up here in my uncle's cabin? We both had our shirts off when Ma pulled in the driveway."

"We should have known she'd come up early."

In the bathroom Donk removed a bottle of cough syrup from the cabinet and sprayed multiple blasts into his mouth.

"What's so fun about that?" I asked.

Raina rolled her eyes.

"Zing goes the strings of my heart," said Donk, spraying more blasts.

Next day on the beach Dad surveyed his receivers. "Ready? Hike one, hike two, hike three, hut hut."

Mom hiked the football. I sprinted down the beach. Donk chased after me. The football spiraled through the sky. I reached out. So did Donk.

"Dive," yelled Dad.

The ball spiraled past my hands and bounced across the beach.

In the huddle, Dad sketched a diagram in the sand. "Kuba, you line up behind me, take the handoff, and cover the ball with both your arms."

"Blitz," Donk whispered in the defensive huddle.

"Hike one, hike two, hike three, hut hut," Dad yelled.

Mom hiked the football and hurried towards the end zone. Raina chased her.

Donk and a kid we met on the beach counted: "One one-thousand, two one-thousand, three one-thousand." They charged us.

Dad caught the snap, turned, and shoved the ball in my gut. Arms raised, ready to block, Dad ran down the beach.

Donk faked inside, then ran outside around Dad.

I closed my arms around air. "What the heck?"

"Gotcha." Donk tagged me with both hands. "Where'd you put the ball?"

"Don't know," I said, scanning the beach for the football.

We looked down the beach, just in time to see Dad running into the end zone with a hump in his back—the shyster.

"Crazylegs Brice is back." Dad did an end zone polka. What kind of person does an end zone polka?

"Hey!" said Raina.

Donk exhaled loudly. "That's cheating."

"Where does it say in the rulebook you can't do that? Where?" Dad walked over to Mom and put his arm around her. "I'd like to read that chapter."

"Where'd you learn to pull a fast-one like that?" My body slammed into Dad's. I held on.

"That one? Let's see." Dad squinted as the sun bounced off the sand and stung our eyes. "Joe Bellino pulled the 'camel back' on me during a pickup game at Hanscom Air Base." Dad slapped the pigskin with his palm. "Go deep and fishhook right."

I sprinted down the beach. The football spiraled through the air. A gust of wind nudged the ball out over the ocean. I judged the ball's descent and dove over the waves. The ball spiraled downwards. In the air, I extended my arms. Just before hitting the water, the leather sphere landed on my fingers. I plunged beneath the water. Ice picks surged through my body. I emerged from the ocean holding the football and threw the ball back to Dad.

"They should put a photo of that catch in a museum." Dad's voice cut through the wind. "That catch is the tailfin on a '56 Chevrolet."

Fishtailing

In our backyard Dad clanged a wrench inside a grill.

"Hey Dad?" said Donk. "Pushkoff wants me to take him for a spin in the Corvette."

"You're dreaming."

"Why not? I won't let so much as a thumbprint get on it."

"I'm a thousand-percent sure of that 'cause you'll never drive it."

Donk walked towards his Nova. "Need anything at the supermarket? I'm picking up some hamburger rolls for Mom."

"All set. Damn, I can't seem to get this grill lit." Dad removed a piece of metal from the grill. "Hey, Donny, get back here. Swear on your mother's life that you won't take the Vette on the highway and I'll let you drive it to the supermarket."

Donk nodded. "I won't go near 128."

Dad tossed the keys to Donk.

"All right. I'll call Pushkoff."

"And no racing."

"Check out this." On Route 2, Donk swerved into the opposite lane and pulled alongside a fourteen-wheeler. Then he downshifted to fourth. The rear tires screeched as the Corvette leaped ahead of the truck.

"This bad boy gives your neck a snap." Pushkoff clicked on his seatbelt.

"Know what I'd really like to do?"

"I'm afraid to ask."

"Set cruise control to a buck-ten, fly through New York, Ohio, Colorado, all the way to San Diego, and not pass a single state trooper."

Pushkoff flashed his twenty-tooth grin. "With a trunk full of Heff talls."

"Then I'd check into the Hotel Del Coronado and spend a month swimming with the dolphins in the Gulf of California."

"I'd be at the mahogany bar downing soldiers and titillating the ladies with my universal talents."

Donk spit out a laugh.

"What?"

Donk stared at the yellow lines, blurring into one long stripe. "I love what speed does. It fuses things together. There's a straight-away coming after this bend, right?"

"Think so."

"How many cars ahead of us?"

"Six."

"Watch this. It's called a slingshot." Trailing a Camaro, Donk lifted his foot off the gas. The Corvette drifted back forty yards or so. Just before the bend, Donk punched the gas. The Corvette surged towards the Camaro. Coming out of the turn, Donk turned into the opposite lane and flew by a Camaro, Pinto, Le Baron, delivery truck, and two motorcycles.

"Did you see the expression on that lady's face?" Donk slapped the wheel.

"You are one twisted individual," said Pushkoff.

"I know. I can't help it."

Pushkoff rubbed his biceps. "Let's go back and get those rolls."

The Corvette passed an apple orchard that stretched alongside Route 2A for nearly a mile. "I wonder what this sled tops out at?" Donk buried the pedal. The odometer spun clockwise.

"Let's get those rolls. I'm starving," said Pushkoff. Ahead, Pushkoff pointed to a turn where the soft shoulder spilled onto the road. "You see that patch of sand?"

"Where?" asked Donk as the tires passed over the sand and the rear of the Vette began to fishtail. Pushkoff placed his hands on the dashboard.

Dad was setting apple sausages on the grill when Chief Swan's cruiser drove up with Donk and Pushkoff in the backseat. A door opened. Chief Swan stepped out.

Dad put the lid down on the grill. "Ernie, what the hell happened?"

"They were driving along Route 2A by the-"

"I want to hear it from the traitor's mouth."

Donk and Pushkoff climbed from the rear seat. "We were cruising out by Tate's Orchards and-

"How fast?" Dad glanced at Donk's chin.

"Around a buck."

Dad lunged forward. "Whoa, Galvin." Chief Swan stepped in front of Donk.

"Go on. What did you hit? I hope to hell you didn't hit another car."

Donk shook his head.

"So how'd you end up off the road?"

"When we hit a buck-ten, the Vette began to fishtail and the soft shoulder sucked us in. Then I over-corrected and we shot across the street."

"There were no skid marks so they must have been airborne by then," Chief Swan added.

"We hit a pair of boulders blocking the access road."

"They pushed a six-ton boulder back forty feet," Chief Swan added.

"Oh balls! Insurance company is going to love this. Didn't want to be a hard ass, so against my better judgment, I let my kid take the Vette for a spin and this is my reward. It's a miracle you didn't kill Scott."

Donk's eyes remained glued to his sneakers.

"He's right. Those boulders acted like shock absorbers. You two were very lucky. I've seen-"

"Then what would you have said to Mrs. Pushkoff?" Dad held up his arms. "Well gee-whittakers, Rachel, I wanted to be a big shot and race a Corvette. By the way, I killed your son."

Chief Swan put his hand on Donk's shoulder. "It's the kids who are always trying to get away with something, pull a rabbit from their hat when there isn't one, who end up needing the jaws of life to pry them from a wreck." Chuggles strolled up to Chief Swan and rubbed against his boots.

"What goes on in that useless head of yours?" asked Dad.

"I wanted to know if it was true. If Corvettes can go as fast as they say."

Chief Swan placed his citation book back into his belt. "There are appropriate places for that. You could join the racing club up at the old airport."

"Galvin, I want you to treat him like an adult," Mom called out.

"When he starts behaving like one." A drop of blood dripped from Dad's nose. "Jesus H. Christ. On my new shirt too. Honey, grab me a hanky—will you?"

Donk began hitting himself in the face.

"Whoa, son." Chief Swan grabbed Donk's wrists. "That's not going to undo what's been done."

"Thanks for driving him up here, Ernie," said Mom, handing Dad a hanky.

"We'll need to rent a backhoe to push those boulders back and a town sign was partially-"

"Send me the bill."

"Thanks. I'll hold off on writing this up so they won't pull his license. I'll let you and the mrs. decide the proper punishment, but I wouldn't-"

"He won't drive until he's got as many gray hairs as I do."

Chief Swan fiddled with the two-way on his belt. "Well, I better get going."

In his office, Dad opened an envelope with a car key and studied the monthly statement from GMAC. "These carrying costs are killing me. Hey Fallon, come over here. When are you going to start pushing the new sleds? I've got a lot full of Chevys waiting for a real salesman."

"Soon as Marna finds herself a real husband."

"You watch yourself, you dirty catholic," said Dad, opening another envelope. "I have a mind to tell Daphne about your little visitor."

"Keep your trap shut."

"Don't worry, Fallon," said Dad, pushing a pile of envelopes off his desk and into the trash. "I've got larger wars to wage."

"That's dirty pool. What about those high-mileage sleds you're shipping down to Houston that suddenly have 30,000 miles?"

Grabbing a lint-roller from his top drawer, Dad ran the roller across his suit. "Once they're out of my hands, I have no control over what over-zealous retailers do."

"That's not what Uncle Sam says."

"Keep quiet." Dad scanned the showroom. "They just closed down old man Libby for playing pinwheels with his odometers."

"Not sure I can. My conscience is killing me."

"Who you? Get the hell out of my office. And one more thing, put down the sports page and start reading the log book for a change before I'm standing in the unemployment line."

"Unemployment line? You don't know what it's like to not have a buck. Back in Cleveland when my sister was born three months early, Ma had to put her in the oven on low heat just to keep her from turning blue. You're riding on the gravy train, Galvin."

"I know, I know, Fallon. Now go roll a few sleds."

Fallon walked back to his desk. Mom pulled up in her station wagon. Donk hopped out and walked into Dad's office.

"What would you do if your son smashed up your prized car?" asked Dad. "Do you know what I pay for insurance premiums?"

Donk shook his head.

"Didn't think so. Tell me, Jackie Stewart, what's a just punishment?"

"I would-"

"Go on." Dad continued opening envelopes. "I want you to tell me what your errors in judgment were."

"Ground him for the whole summer."

"That's a start."

"And make him fix the Corvette?"

"You can't fix that car. I'm not sure an all-star body shop could. Try again."

"Put him to work and make him buy a new one?"

"That's right. It's time you take responsibility for your actions. Then maybe you'll proceed with more caution. Why can't we be born smart and progress towards youth and carelessness? Everything's backwards. Childhood should be the gold watch of retirement. What's the point of all this bumbling? I'd like to hear Pastor MacDonald answer that. Monday, you show up at 6:59 a.m. with a suit and tie on—ready to push some iron. When I was your age I was already outselling Fallon."

Fallon's ears pricked up. "When I was on vacation."

Dad poked his head out of the office. "When I want to hear from you, I'll rattle your cage."

"What about my scruples?" Donk asked.

"Can't believe you had the nerve to say that. Fallon, did you hear what just flew out of this Philadelphia lawyer's mouth?"

That Thursday, Dad and Donk slowed to a stop at the entrance of Acadia Auction. A guard inspected Dad's registration papers.

"All set." The guard waved them through.

After parking, Dad and Donk walked past six lines of used cars and trucks, each a half-mile long. With shoe polish, some sellers painted key selling points on the windshields: *Original miles! One owner! Leather seats!* or *All the toys!* Donk wiggled the hood ornament on a Cadillac.

Dad slapped Donk's hand. "Don't touch that. Some of those are glued on."

The six lines flowed into six open garage doors in a defunct manufacturing plant. All day, used iron rolled into the warehouse, past one of six auctioneers, and out the other side. As the sleds passed the auctioneers' podiums, scores of car dealers waved their numbers and bid on the sleds they wanted to buy.

Inside the plant, the auctioneers' voices boomed. "Hibady hibady dibady, hibady dibady—seventeen and a half?"

A woman nodded.

"Gimme eighteen?"

A guy with a beard waved his card.

"And a half! Nineteen? And a half! Two-grand?"

The woman shook her head.

"Do I hear two-grand?" The auctioneer whacked his jockey stick against the podium. "Hibady dibady, hibady dibady hibady."

Dad handed a fin to Donk. "Grab a hotdog and a soda. I'll come get you when there's a car to drive back to the dealership."

In the cafeteria, Donk set down a soda and beef stew on his table. Behind him, a guy in a Harley Davidson T-shirt and a retired couple argued about the Red Sox. Donk opened Dad's old briefcase, pulled out Grant's *Memoirs*, and began to read.

In August, Dad brought home a Virginia ham.

"Have you tried the ham?" he asked during dinner. "It's peanut-fed."

We passed around a tire-sized bowl of mashed potatoes.

"Noy, give the ham a taste."

"Dad, stop pushing your ham on everybody," said Raina.

"How do peanuts affect the taste?" I asked.

Donk shot me a glance.

"Makes the flesh very tender."

I tasted the ham. "Oh, I can't handle it." I fell off my chair and rolled around the floor. "So juicy."

"You think so?"

Raina stood up. "Let's split. Noy and I are going over Crispin's to watch *Rocky Horror Picture Show.*"

"Why don't you stay in tonight," asked Mom.

"Because I don't want to."

"You went out last night."

"So."

"Oh no you're not." Dad waved his fork.

"Why can't I?"

"Because life isn't one big smorgasbord for Raina—that's why. Why do you spend time with that degenerate anyway?"

"Dad, he's not a degenerate; he's a musician," said Raina.

"And I'm John DeLorean. Take a seat."

Raina walked towards the kitchen.

Dad stood up.

"Just going to the fridge to get something to drink."

Moments later, we heard a scream in the kitchen, then a thud. We booked it into the kitchen. On the floor beside a crimson knife, Raina was curled up like a squirrel. Mom's knees buckled, but Donk caught her and held her up.

Dad knelt down and felt Raina's neck. "That's not blood. That's ketchup."

Raina jumped to her feet. "I fooled you. Ha, ha. I had all of you fooled. Ha, ha, ha."

"You little guttersnipe." Dad's arm cast a shadow above Raina. Donk stepped in front of Raina. A knee flew into

Donk's jewel box. The two began pushing each other. Mom grabbed Donk's shirt and pulled him back.

"He was going to hit her. He would have hit her." Donk pointed to Dad.

Mom pushed Donk through the doorway. "Donny, you get back into the dining room."

"I'm not scared," said Donk.

"Yeah, big tough mommy's boy," said Dad, his hands balled into fists.

"Don't you have one ounce of gratitude in that thick skull of yours?" asked Mom. "Do you think he likes spending sixty hours each week trying to sell cars to people who think he's a checker-suited pickpocket? Do you think the caption in his high school yearbook read: 'I'm going to sell used cars?' Well I've got news for you, O lord of youth."

"Hey, we sell new cars too," said Dad.

"I'm not going to sit back and let him pop her, no matter how screwed up she is."

"Let me save you twenty years of traveling down the wrong road: you can't hate your way to self-respect," Mom yelled. "Millions have tried."

"Donk, want to walk around Granny Pond?" asked Raina.

"That's because most retreads hate the wrong things," called Donk, opening the screen door and walking down the driveway.

"That's the spirit," said Mom, wiping ketchup off the floor. "It's a wonder human beings reproduce as quickly as they do. Can't remember what I had in mind when I first got married and had kids, but it wasn't this."

In the den I sat down on the couch. "You okay?"

"Must have done something awful in a past life." Dad steadied his glass. "We had a good day at the office too. Wrote nine deals. It's beyond me. Maybe I'm being paid back for that whale oil scam." Dad clicked on the TV. "They've got this manic energy. Don't know where it comes from—probably from your mother. Her whole family is touched, bunch of actors and musicians."

"What about your elephant races with Aunt Bee?"

"Quiet." The ice in Dad's glass jiggled.

On the screen a fly ball bounced over Henderson's glove and rolled to the wall.

"Oh, for the love of Christ. Will you take a look at that. Why does McNamara let that mutt in the game?" Dad clicked off the TV. "When I was your age, things were different. When your grandfather said jump, you bet your mother's good name, I ran to the nearest cliff and jumped off. And let me tell you, he was a real piece of art. Do you know what that tightwad did?"

"What?"

"Well, in addition to cleaning the crapper and waxing cars at the garage, I bagged groceries and stocked shelves for three years at Quimby's IGA, saving up so I could buy my own sled. Had it all picked out too. A '56 winged-tip Buick. Those were the days when design meant something. You had Harley Earl at GM and George Walker at Ford. I had packed away almost two-grand when Old Kinderhook finds out. So you know what he does? He starts charging me rent. Eighteen bucks a week. You can guess who was able to buy a new sled that year—and did I ever get to take it out on Friday nights? Not on your life." A small crimson stream flowed from Dad's nose. "Oh balls. Get me a rag, will you?"

I returned with a napkin. "You alright?"

"I'm fine."

"Is it true that Pushkoff's Dad bought him a Camaro for getting in to Dartmouth?"

"Yeah." Dad folded the bloody napkin and stuffed it in his shirt pocket. "I never liked those Ivy League prima donnas. There's us, chained by the way we talk, and there's them, doing those little things we can never figure out. That's a fact." Dad waved a finger in my face. "They walk around their law offices and hospitals erect as champions. They watch us from their glass towers as interest collects. Meanwhile, we've got spit swinging from our masks. You don't want to forget that because they won't." Dad clicked the Red Sox game back on. "Oo, tie score."

The Clouds Rubbed Their Bellies On The Tips Of Elms

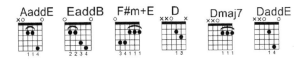

IN MID-NOVEMBER, DONK WALKED INTO PROFESSOR Ellis's classroom with his guitar case. In the middle of the room, two oak stools faced each other. Beside each stool was a music stand. Donk removed a classical guitar from its case and sat down on a stool. All scarves and flying hair, Professor Ellis breezed into the room, sat down on the other stool, and slid her guitar from its case. She placed her foot on a block of wood. On her guitar she played a passage from Chopin's "Prelude in D-minor." She looked up at Donk.

"Well?"

Donk began to play.

"Stop," Professor Ellis called after six notes. "Repeat that phrase, and place more emphasis on the *A-flat*.

Donk began again.

"Stop." She exhaled loudly. "Too much staccato. Also, pay attention to the D. You've got to anticipate the *A-flat*. Now try again.

Donk did.

Professor Ellis shook her head. "No, no, no. This isn't going to do. You're playing every note incorrectly."

Donk wiggled his fingers. "Are you sure?"

"Oh yes. You're fretting the correct notes, but as far as tone, volume, timing, and timbre, you've got wooden fingers. You're going to have to practice six hours a day, young man. I'm afraid you don't have the slightest idea how to listen."

"This went on for three months," Donk's voice traveled through the phone lines to Mom. "I didn't get to play more than eleven consecutive notes the whole semester."

On Fridays, Raina and I loaded our P.A., my acoustic, four mics, and two sleeping bags into my Chevelle. In a cooler we stuffed coldcuts, sodas, brownies Mom had baked for Donk, and a few apples. Then we drove up I-93 to Plymouth.

"Okay, play me one of the songs you've been blubbering about," said Donk in his dorm room.

"I wrote it for you, college boy. Ready, Raina?" I played the chord progression: A, E, F#m, D, DaddE.

Raina's voice floated through the room:

I know you're 'bout as open as a cellar door
Got your problems in a closet try to sell them as gold
If your friends don't mouth your hip views, you really take
offense / You think your Superman, you're really Clark Kent.

The room went dark. Raina's voice grew muffled. Donk removed his pillow from my face.

"Seventeen and he already knows everything about the friggin' universe," said Donk.

After three Heff talls, Donk's bookcase began to sway. Donk leafed through the sheet music to Elliot Carter's "String Quartet No. 1." Raina talked to Donk's roommate Barton.

"You keep your cruddy hands off her," I said, pointing to Barton.

"I'm not sure, but I think that's my decision—numb nuts!" Raina flipped her hair. "Donk, take him for a walk till he chills out."

The clouds rubbed their bellies on the tips of elms as Donk and I walked across the quad.

"You can tell me, straight-up, whud you think of my song?"

Donk tilted his head slightly. "I was kind of hoping you'd fiddle with the melody more, screw with the rhythm, make more patterns then swerve as far as you can, maybe even mess with freeform and flip-flop keys. Anything to create a little rising." The walkway forked. We veered left, away from the stadium, towards the auditorium.

"How about a little falling?" I said.

"Yeah, right. Hey, is Chuggles getting enough to eat?"

"Every morning, she claws my door till I feed her."

"Good." Donk removed a plastic container from his pocket and popped off the lid. "Don't let Chuggles play outside." From his other pocket, he pulled out a soldier. "She doesn't know about cars."

"What's going on, Two-by-four?" I asked.

"Kind of in a bind," he said as music flowed from open windows in the auditorium.

"You should go to the New England Conservatory with Crispin," I said.

"Don't you get it?" Donk wiggled his fingers, then made a fist.

I stepped back. A squirrel scurried across our path with an acorn stuffed in its mouth.

Next day by the mess hall exit, Raina and I beat a rhythm on our thighs. She sang melody. I sang a fifth below:

> *Feels so nice to be a god*
> *and know the thoughts in your head*
> *'cause everybody throws a curveball*
> *to keep the hounds off the scent.*
>
> *So you put your sneakers on*
> *and tried to win the marathon,*
> *but with every step you fake*
> *you're running further from the tape.*

Donk opened the exit door. "Okay, calmly walk to our table."

I leaned towards Donk and cupped his bum. "After lunch, you and I are going to go round and round and round."

"You're fried." Donk knocked my hand away. "Get your bony stilts inside."

We walked inside the mess hall. Barton waived to us from a table.

Donk pointed to the cafeteria line. "Pretend you're getting seconds and grab what you want."

Those Holy Loo-Loos

In our garage Raina sang into the mic:

My soul wants me to fly past these one-eyed pilgrims,
Past stained-glass motels to a ballroom in the sky.
You were the oil queen with Einstein's hair and Benzedrine,
And Santa's bag of secrets. I couldn't find the key.

She stepped back from the mic. "Bags don't open with keys. You can do better." Raina walked down the driveway and into the house.

"But ballrooms do," I called.

At my desk I tried to fix the line. "Knee, tree, breeze," I repeated a few times. *Tree* has potential. "And Santa's bag of secrets hanging from our tree," I sang. Gross. So I tried to rhyme with *sky*. "Why, fly, cry, eyes, collide." Maybe *eyes*? I sang the new line: "And Santa's bag of secrets flashing in your eyes." Cliché master. I opened Aunt Bee's rhyming dictionary. Maybe I could find a two-syllable word that rhymes with *key*? "Agree, chimney, debris, foresee, marquis." Got it. I walked into the house and handed Raina the revised lyric. "Does this please her royal highness?"

Raina scanned the page. "Hmm, this is much tighter—'cept for one thing: how do you expect me to sing 'stuffed in our chimney?'"

In the garage I filled the kettle with water, turned on the hotplate, and dropped a teabag into my mug. Each day, steam rose up and settled on my face as I composed new songs. Come winter break when Donk hears my latest stuff, he's gonna want to break both my hands.

* * * *

After final exams Donk rode a Greyhound bus home in February. That night for dessert Mom served Indian pudding that resembled the burnt sand in my closet.

"Hey, college boy?" I said, pushing my dessert bowl aside. "Raina says my new songs blow Townes Van Zandt's away."

"Yeah, right," said Donk, shoveling Indian pudding into his mouth.

After dinner, Raina and I cleared off the table.

"Crispin and Ferranti are coming over to jam, then we're going to The Middle East," said Donk, loading the dishwasher.

"You just got back," Mom protested.

In the den, Dad watched the evening news. Donk sat in the chair next to Dad, the chair adults sat in.

"Found out Fallon's taking C-notes from wholesalers. Your granddad hired him. What should we do?"

Donk focused on the TV. That was the deal: you never made too much eye-contact. "Remember what Grampy used to say, 'I'll pay you five-grand-a-month, plus-'"

"'-all the money you can steal,'" they said in unison.

Crispin's Toyota pulled into the driveway.

"Crispin's here." Donk stood up.

"Stay and chat," said Dad, turning to Donk. "Lot going on."

Donk turned to the front door. "Can't. Promised Crispin we'd hang out. Free tomorrow?" Donk turned to Dad, but Dad had already resumed watching the news.

In the garage I transferred notes onto a blank stave. Donk pulled up the garage door. In walked Crispin, Ferranti, and Donk with guitar cases and mic stands. Crispin and Ferranti walked back to their cars. A moment later, they wheeled in their amps.

Donk pulled his Telecaster from its case and fiddled with the tuning pegs. Then he plugged his patch cord into an amp and fooled around with the dials. "Spaz, do any of your new songs modulate to a closely related key? Otherwise-"

"I know, I know—listeners get bored after the second chorus."

"Let me see." Donk held out his hand.

I passed Donk the sheet music to "Winter Sand."

Donk played the opening melody, adding a fill at the turn-around. "Like this?"

I nodded.

He repeated the melody. "How 'bout going down to D instead of back to E?" Donk played the revised measure. "Sounds better, right?"

I nodded.

Donk played the climb, strumming the strings with his pinky while plucking the melody with his pointer, index, and middle fingers. "It wants to go to GsusaddC here."

I was ready to coldcock Donk.

Donk tilted his head. His mouth hung open. "I'd finish with a Bsus9, maybe a Bsus9+11." He played a version of Bsus9+11+13. "Hear the expectation for a resolve?"

"Maybe I don't want a resolve," I said as Janota walked in with his hi-hat and floor tom. After several trips to his station wagon, he set up his kit in the rear of the garage.

"Could be onto something," said Donk, pulling down the garage door. "You boys ready to practice or what?" Donk set my sheet music on a stand by the mics. "Let's give this song a ride." He turned to Ferranti and Crispin. "Intro's Em, Csus. Verse is A, B, BaddG, A, CsusaddF#. Chorus: C, Em, D, Am."

"Just play," said Ferranti.

"Okay, one two, one two, one two."

The tea in my mug shivered as guitar sounds and drums filled the garage. The band ran through the song twice. When they came back to the intro, Raina stepped up to the mic.

> My brother sits in the front seat
> Daring strangers to see
> Padlocked life in marble bones
> Roll our tires for hidden notes.

In the climb, Janota slowed things down with a stutter beat.

> On black ice highways our car swerves
> Into your separate universe.

I joined Raina in the chorus, singing fourths to her ninths, creating an unresolved-minor blend.

> Why aren't you at home in bed
> Midnight oil in your lamp?
> Don't you know the streets
> Are full of winter sand?

Janota played a drum roll, Crispin strummed six-string chords, and I hopped on keyboards.

Eight Heff Talls on the dashboard
Thirteen fingers on the wheel
Mustang swerving in the white lines
Light bulbs fading in your cells.

After the second chorus, Donk blew my skin off. He called it *trance*: a swishing series of chords on guitar that created hypnotic centers of energy. When it happened, Crispin was on lead, hogging all the air, when Donk's hand slid up the neck of his Fender, banked on a B-chord, then swished back and forth from Dsus4 to Emsus4, sending tiny tornados spinning down my ear canals. On musical skis, Donk swished up and down the neck, mixing chord progressions, creating a whole series of tasty repetitions. Then his hand slid further up the neck and further down till I was skiing on an icy ridge of sound. He even changed keys twice—the show-off. Having fully squeezed the juice from those moments, Donk snow-plowed to a stop with a C#sus11+13.

"Do that again," said Crispin.

Donk did, and on the fifth bank, half of me halted, while my other half kept skiing down a closed trail. I felt a rip. In my salmon nautilus, warm blood oozed onto frozen snow. By night's end, those holy loo-loos had concocted hypnotic swishings for every song, every section, every phrase, every *note*, competing in Darwinian fashion. Soon Janota was doing trance on drums, and Ferranti pulled-off trance on bass. It was all pretty sick. Now we had circles within circles, rhythms inside rhythms, and tiny-melodies woven into melodies.

"Okay, we've got to take off," Donk announced. Raina ran inside and grabbed her purse. Footsteps hurried down our walk, brake lights lit the side of our house, and an engine faded down the hill.

At The Middle East, the guitarist of the 360s played a nine-minute solo as Janota skanked his way through the mosh pit. By an exit sign, Crispin folded his arms into a pretzel shape and cycloned with a girl from Cambridge. Up front, Donk and Ferranti caught kids who ran across the stage and dove into the audience. One kid floated over the centipede of arms and dropped towards the concrete floor. Donk turned and dove. In the air he placed his hand under the kid's head. In the coal-colored sky above The Middle East, the stars began to shift. A space opened. The kid's head thumped against Donk's hand. Donk's knuckles filled with blood. The kid stood up and wobbled away. An air sculpture floated up into the sky and took its place amid the unknown constellations.

By the men's room, Raina hung out with the drummer from the Neighborhoods. When the 360s finished their set, Raina and the drummer, hand-in-hand, walked past the bouncers into the parking lot. She climbed onto the guy's motorcycle. The bike disappeared down Mass Ave.

Track 30
The Death Of The Death Of Love
(Cold Harbor)

DESTINY IS THE FORCE THAT DETERMINES THE COURSE of events. Pastor MacDonald says, a resistless force pre-planned by God. Dad says, by the address on your mailbox. Dr. Van Dyne thinks by the size of your noggin. To me, destiny is a '72 Chevelle with a 454 big block and chrome fuelies hauling down Merriam Hill at a buck-twenty, and even if you're a bench pressing, pill popping, human house, you yank the wheel hard and it only turns a quarter-inch. I admit, a quarter-inch blows. I mean, why can't hikers unroll their sleeping bags atop Red Feather Ridge for a few summers and learn to float with the sharp-shinned hawks? What control did Donk have when he drove his Nova down Mass Ave past Danforth Field, past Merriam Hill High, past Crispin in his house (no doubt, at this hour hunched over his Gibson), past Merriam Street where I'm up in the cupola with Noy playing my acoustic, past Dad's dealership (at 2:56 a.m., darker than a closed school), and straight through the last blink of a canary light burning to Pompeii red? When from the north, a Chevy Blazer, counting on a green flash, ignored the break and accelerated into a splash of headlights, chips of chrome, hunks of quarter-panel, and those awful perfect cubes of windshield spraying in all directions. Then a strange tinkling as torn parts, no longer a car, settled on the hoods of used sleds parked in the front row of Brice Chevrolet.

At 3:21 a.m. a cruiser stopped in front of our house. Raina woke to a tap on the door.

"Can I help you?" asked Raina in the doorway.

"Is your father home?" Chief Swan asked.

"He's asleep."

"Can I speak to him?"

"Just a sec." Raina climbed the stairs. She passed Donk's bedroom. His sheets were flat as home plate.

"Dad, Chief Swan's on our porch."

"What?" Dad sat up in bed. "What was that?"

"Chief Swan's on our porch," repeated Raina.

"Let him in." Dad lifted his pants off the door and thumped down the stairs. "Ernie, what is it?" asked Dad in the kitchen.

Chief Swan took off his gloves. "I just came from down-the-way and saw your boy's car all banged to hell."

"Is he alright?"

"He's unconscious. They've taken him to Mass General."

"Christ, what happened?"

"He was driving down Mass Ave, a bit too slow, and ran a red light. Other driver never saw him."

Dad studied Chief Swan's face. "Was he drinking?"

"They ran some blood tests. We'll know more when the report is filed. Bing Russell told me Donny was at the Red Onion early this morning with a group of teenagers, waving his arms, half-out-of-it, shouting something about wanting to order the whole menu. Bing asked them to leave. We're not sure where he ended up after that."

"How bad off is he? Should I phone Pastor MacDonald?"

Chief Swan nodded.

At the sink, Dad rinsed out a glass. He walked to the fridge and took out a pitcher of apple juice. Taped to the freezer door was a photo of the Holy Cross football team. Dad studied the photo. "Ernie, come over here. Can you pick out my face?"

Chief Swan walked to the fridge. He pointed to a player sitting on his helmet in the second row.

Dad shook his head and pointed to a player on his knees in the front row.

Dad filled his glass. "As a freshman, I started every game. Did you know that? Raina, go grab your mother."

"Is he going to be alright?" asked Raina.

"They called in Neil Van Dyne." Chief Swan explained that Dr. Van Dyne was one of Mass General's top neurosurgeons. "He'll do the best he can."

Dad snapped on his parka. "Stay with your mother. I'll catch a ride with Chief Swan. Will you drive me into Boston, Ernie?"

A subdural hematoma is a blood clot beneath the skull. Donk had one the size of a radish pressing against his brain. Dr. Van Dyne shaved Donk's head, chipped a hole in his skull, and drained the clot. But he didn't place Donk in a drug-induced coma. I would have injected 3000 c.c.s of Avakine into Donk's IV. I guess at the time, Donk's pulse had quickened and his pupils were a safe width. But on the second day the swelling spiked. A nurse lowered Donk's head into a tub of ice. Didn't help. The Blazer's impact produced alarming amounts of fluid. Donk's cerebrum was pinned against his skull, wiping out entire regions of gray matter.

Unable to send commands to his heart and lungs, the flow of oxygenated blood stopped. With no conductor, unoxygenated blood filled his lungs, his liver gummed up, and his kidneys clogged with piss. When Donk spit up a thimbleful of blood, his lips and fingers turned paler than the piano keys in A-minor. Dr. Van Dyne shined a penlight into Donk's eyes. If I could have aimed that penlight into Donk's chest, what would I have seen leaving? A swarm of screaming snow crickets? My brother's shimmering likeness? The hole inside a donut?

I'll never know what Donk felt when the space between his head and the door collapsed as the Blazer's bumper leaped forward five hundred times firmer than a human punch. And I wonder, was Donk's misfortune the steel orbit of our celestial cars careening down the blind highway of time? Or was his misfortune the residue of nineteen years of motion unguided by the reins of caution? Or was it something else? A sky full of pregnant mosquitoes waiting to give birth or a series of unplayed notes buried on the summit of a far-off monadnock that our steel-toe boots hiked over, swerved around, or in reality, never shared the same ridge?

I guess the green flowering tongues in Wilson's cornfields will continue their photo magic and the hooded warblers will still beat their wings south. But what if we could reach that summit? What if our atrium valves could pump nineteen times more blood into our brains? What notes would we find curled in those fossil beds waiting for a steel pick? What happens the moment a '68 Corvette L88 tops 160 mph and the protean gaps inside time vanish? Do the notes bloom into one hyper-sensating chord of eternity? Do they? I hate Donk. I mean, I want to hate Donk, but I can't. I need to ask him a few questions first: before the ambulance crew covered his face with a mask, before they wheeled him into a white van, before they sliced a hole in his windpipe and slid a plastic tube into his lungs, before the death of the death of love.

Next day, Aunt Bee began mixing Bloody Marys before breakfast. "Think of it this way." Bee stirred her drink with her pinky. "No matter how many toads you swallow in life, you will never be completely unhappy." Her belly wiggled. "Oh, it's awful. It's just so terrible."

"There must a reason why everything we love gets swallowed by the earth," I said.

"Everything we hate gets carried off too." Aunt Bee topped-off her Bloody Mary.

After Mr. Pushkoff lowered Donk into the ground and Pastor MacDonald sprinkled dirt onto his casket, everyone squeezed into our house in their Sunday clothes. Fallon rolled in a keg. On our table lay pinwheels of coldcuts, beehives of fruit, and more baked beans than a football team could kill. Me and Raina stacked pyramids of finger rolls. Mrs. Pushkoff brought a tray of kuchen cakes. Aunt Bee lifted the lid off a pot of Swedish meatballs. Resting on a crystal pie stand, mom's apricot torte (which Donk once ascribed to an out-of-body experience) waited. We didn't say a word, but piled our plates so high that our rolls tumbled onto the floor. We scoffed seriously. Ham in rolls, beans in rolls, Caesar salad in rolls, even plain rolls—it didn't matter. We dipped kuchen cakes in coffee, apricot torte in pale ale, coleslaw in milk—what's the diff? So long as there was *more*. On the porch, we began with Dunhill's and Carter's, then graduated to Gaulois, cloves, and hand-rolled Paddocks. After alternating between Jägermeister shots and milk shakes, we moved on to maple syrup root beer and Brixton port. Anything we could shove into our mouths was game. Still, we wanted more.

In the den, Aunt Bee walked to the piano, set down her mixer, and loosened up her fingers. I don't know why she didn't play much. I thought if you loved something, you did it every chance you got. I thought the louder someone sang, the more they loved music. I thought Donk was indestructible. He had taken so many body blows, crunched his neck on so many helmets, fallen face-first while crowd surfing at so many concerts.

Maybe I'm skewed, but love's in league with the Loch Ness monster. No one I know ever touched those cryptozoic scales. No one in Merriam Hill ever saw Sasquatch. Instead, some random camper in Hollis twists her ankle on a huge footprint curved as a question mark. Or in Fitzwilliam, a homeowner hears a high pitched growl and he wheels around—just in time—to see the back of a hairy cryptid running through the forest. Seekers crisscross America in their Winnebagos, film stuffed in their freezers. Somewhere there's a clan of bipedal hominids, an evolutionary sideshow, a missing link. They study the grainy photos. Is it a shaggy suit or not? Is it real? Until that day, I'll have to fuel my salmon nautilus with the shadow of a shadow of a shadow of a shadow. In the meantime, what the heck are we going to eat? When is the Fed going to lower the prime so Dad can make the interest payments on his loans? Or is love closer to an ivory-billed woodpecker— once here, now extinct—and all I can do is gaze at the stuffed specimens in glass cases at local museums. Once near Granny Pond, I spotted a woodpecker in a pine tree with a blazing tuft of red feathers on its head. "Over there," I whispered to Donk. "An ivory-bill." That was easy, I thought. Why were all the bigwigs wrong? But this bird had a black beak and didn't have the streams of ivory feathers on its wings—the ones that make it so damn beautiful.

Guess it was a cousin, the pileated woodpecker. Sure, there's hope. I heard a Cuban schoolteacher spotted one in the Sierra Maestras. If not, there's always cloning: removing the DNA from a stuffed specimen and injecting it into the egg of a cousin. But in the end it's a big whiff, a donut hole, a song of semibreves. The ivory-bill will never come back— not to this same place, not to this same time, not the perfectly messed up way my big brother was. Better chance that a tornado rolls through a junkyard and the flying parts form a 747 than of finding real love.

"Come on, Spaz, loosen up." Pushkoff punched my arm. "Grab another shooter."

I reached into the cooler and grabbed a cold soldier.

What kind of song can transform dime store vibrations, soup can rhythms, and a singer's tinsel puffs of breath into a celestial whirlwind that can lift listeners upwards with their shadows still clinging to their instruments and carry these pilgrims back to the Aloe Vera River of pure awareness where their massless particles can merge with the mind of God? What kind of song can do that?

What kind of post-Orphic song could kick-start my big brother's heart, force oxygen into his blue lungs, and allow his ghostly lips to talk? Are there a series of rhythms and melodies hidden in the strings of the universe that could do that?

I wandered into the den.

Rocking side to side, Bee began her song with a bass line two-octaves below the melody. In quick flourishes, she seeded the room with arpeggios: Amadd9, C#maddF, and Badd9, then dove into the melody. A helium wind passed through my body. Bee tossed in a wild F#6add13, which hung in the den. In the climb, she quickened her pace and swerved up a swan's neck. But in the chorus: G, Am, F,

Aadd9, she eased off the gas. A backdraft of quartals washed across my skin, and my salmon nautilus began to hum. A second chorus walked me up a mountainside, while the bass line led me through a cellar. The diverging harmonies tore off my skullcap and astral-projected me from my body. The awareness inside me floated upwards. I found myself looking down upon the round heads of our guests. Pastor Mac and Fallon stood next to the piano and talked. Rising higher, I looked down upon the red clay shingles on our roof and the clusters of lily pads on Granny Pond. Rising higher, I floated through a series of cloud banks till I reached the stratosphere. Below me, the cloud banks were schools of white whales swimming in the blue azure. Beside me, a nebula-shaped mass of light was rising towards the ionosphere. The strange light stung my eyes. I could not tell what it was. Far below me, I heard Bee playing the Overture from "No, No, Nanette."

On the piano bench, Bee lost the feeling of rising, lost the helium quality she had won when diverging harmonies are held in place by their opposites. I plunged back inside my body. It was February 1985 again. I was surrounded by relatives in their Sunday clothes. Some old guy was still president, and Donk had flown off into deep space. But on the piano, Bee had recreated one of the screwy head scratchers in life: I mean, if we're going to get knocked out, why does some puppet diddler let us climb into the ring in the first place?

I want to do what Bee did. I want to write a song that makes my salmon nautilus hum, a song when played just right causes the actual sensation of rising to pass through the listener's body. For eighty-four bars, Bee took the unwanted fabric of providence and pieced together a trampoline.

Slowly, the guests wandered to their cars and drove home. Still, we wanted more. So we climbed into Pushkoff's Dodge.

"What's more useless than lawn fertilizer?" I asked.

Raina made a dumb face.

"Wait a sec." I scooted into the garage. "Hey, Pushkoff, open your trunk." Pushkoff opened his glove box and pressed a button. The trunk flew up. I placed a shovel and an edger on top of his spare tire. "Here you go." I handed Raina a pair of gloves.

"What do I want these for?" she asked.

"Do you know that humongous colonial they just built on Saddle Club Road?"

Pushkoff nodded.

"That's a snob palace if I've ever seen one. Go there." I pointed down Grant Street. "Even Donk wouldn't have the seeds to do this."

"You mean Skip Lee's house?"

"Yeah."

Pushkoff turned left. "But what if they're home?"

"That's the point. They've got to be home. It's like picking a fight with a Quaker; if you win, you're still a wuss. Did you see the perfect lawn they unrolled a few days ago?"

"Yeah."

"I want their lawn. We're gonna hoist their perfect lawn. We're gonna roll it up and put it in your trunk."

"That's the stupidest thing I've ever heard," said Raina as Pushkoff turned right.

"Do I have to connect all the dots for you?" I said.

Raina frowned. "You try way too hard."

Pushkoff didn't say a word. Then his teeth flashed. "Nice."

"Pull over there," I said, pointing to a row of yew berry bushes on the edge of Skip's lawn. In grade school Donk and me used to pick the red arils to make blood pancakes. We'd smoosh them in a bowl and mix in dirt. We tried to sell them to our neighbors even though they're poisonous as hell, but they looked like they tasted good. Go figure. "Here's the deal," I said. "Raina cuts the sod, I roll it up, and Pushkoff lugs it to the car." We started by the sidewalk. Since the grass was just laid down it rolled up easy. Pushkoff lugged the rolls to the car.

"You are one twisted individual," he said. Judging from the tones in his voice, I think he really meant it. Twenty-odd minutes later, a third of the lawn was in Pushkoff's trunk. In fact, we couldn't shut the trunk. We went back and grabbed our tools. A shadow ran towards us.

"What the hell are you guys doing to my lawn?" Skip Lee yelled.

Dropping our tools, we sprinted towards the car. Pushkoff ran towards the house. Skip hurried after him.

"Hey, you—stop." He lunged for Pushkoff.

Pushkoff ran faster. "You missed."

Mr. Lee dove for Pushkoff's legs

Faking left, Pushkoff ran right.

Mr. Lee skidded across the dirt.

"Go—go!" Pushkoff booked-it to the car and dove through the open window into the front seat.

Raina juiced the gas. Our car took off down Saddle Club Road.

"That's what you get for having a perfect lawn, you stuck-up poser," I yelled.

Pushkoff righted himself in the seat. "I saved both your necks, and mine too."

Biffing a stop sign, Raina drove up Woodland Ave.

"Where we going to ditch this sod?" Raina asked.

"Haven't thought that far ahead," I answered.

"Think fast 'cause there's Chief Swan's cruiser," said Pushkoff.

Raina eased off the pedal.

"Don't slow down."

Raina sped up.

"Look straight ahead," said Pushkoff.

The police car continued down Woodland Ave.

"Got an idea. Drive up to our house," I said.

"Are you whacked? Cruiser's probably waiting out front," said Raina, turning onto Merriam Street.

"Go to the backyard."

She switched off the headlights and drove over our lawn into the backyard.

We dragged the picnic table and practice-tires to one side, then unrolled the sod over the hard dirt. My back killed, but when we finished the grass was greener than a golf course. Donk was dumb. How can you give something away if you don't own it first?

Standing in front of the closet mirror, Dad unbuttoned his shirt. He peered at the sudden portrait. "Come here, Marna." He hung his pants on the door. "Do I look different?"

Mom looked in the mirror. "I see what you mean."

"No really, my forehead looks massive. You could play nine holes of golf on this forehead."

Mom leaned forward. "My Aunty Olga used to say: 'a large forehead is a sign of character.'"

"That's a laugh." From his bureau, Dad pulled out a pair of peejays. He looked down at the floor for a long time. "Do you know what ambergris is?"

"A perfume?"

Dad nodded. "It's only the greatest lubricant known to mankind. Refuses to break down—even at temperatures that would melt a radiator. Comes from the intestines of a sperm whale." Dad began brushing his teeth. "That's why the sperm whale was nearly hunted to extinction. Used in all sorts of products: candles, perfume, clock lubricants, medicines. A few years back, we were able to buy 120 cases from a Japanese importer."

"Isn't that illegal?" Mom climbed into bed.

"It's a Federal offense." Dad rinsed out his mouth. "When a customer's car had a noisy lifter or rocker, instead of a costly valve job, we'd pour an eighth-pint of ambergris into the crankcase. Instantly, the engine was quiet as a distant plane. We'd charge customers a couple-hundred bucks. When they got their oil changed a few months later, the noise would return. That's when they knew they'd been rooked." Dad sat on the bed. "For some strange reason, ever since Donny's accident, all I can think about is ambergris. During Pastor Mac's eulogy, I thought how amazingly opaque and slightly ash-colored the stuff is. When we picked out a casket, I saw the sperm whale's block-shaped head. When we consulted Dr. Van Dyne, I heard the piston ring's quiet glide. When I picked up Donny's clothes from the hospital—I remembered the snake oil salesmen who claimed it was a cure-all. Signed the death certificate—ambergris. Got the tuition bill from Salem State—ambergris. I can't stop thinking about it." In the window the knotted limbs of an oak tree caged the sky. "Maybe I let a few things slide."

Mom placed her hands on Dad's shoulders.

"Why couldn't he be happy?"

"I don't know."

"Why couldn't he be happy the way we were?"

"One Christmas he took his toy truck—still in its box—set it in the fireplace and watched it burn. 'Why did you burn your toy truck?' I asked him. He said he wanted a race car."

Dad picked the dry skin off his elbows. "Things were going okay, weren't they?"

Mom nodded. "They were."

"We owned half our cars—free and clear."

"We did."

"Things were going okay and he made it go away."

Wheeling Through The Frozen Foods

At Brice Chevrolet Dad stood on the welcome mat and stomped snow off his boots.

"That speed demon Kevin almost ran me over with the plow truck. Is he into the nose candy again?"

Fallon looked up from his desk. "What was that?"

"Kevin. He looks whacked."

"Oh."

"What's gotten into you?"

"Nothing."

"Don't give me that." On his way to the coat rack, Dad stopped at the prospect log and read the entries. "So old man Douglass is interested in a van?"

Fallon picked at the cuticles on his fingers. "I'm tired of being a low-rent whore. For what? You don't learn anything. After a few years—you're on automatic pilot. There's zero upside. I've been cashing the same paycheck for twenty-two years. And those ungrateful, two-timing, double-dealing customers—they're 'bout as loyal as a jackrabbit. You know that, Galvin."

Outside, the snowplow scraped the frozen tar.

"I do."

"They'd buy from David Duke if he was cheaper.

"They would." Dad hung his parka on a hook.

"They'll drive across the bridge to save fifty bucks."

"They will."

"In fact, some customers buy out-of-town for plain spite." Fallon wiped coffee off his chin.

"They do." Dad kicked off his boots and stepped into his work shoes. "What brought this on?"

"Oh nothing."

"What do you mean *nothing*?"

"I'm just fed up."

"Fed up with what?"

"Bill Quimby has bought his sleds from me for fourteen years. When he forgot to change his timing belts and blew a rod—no problem—I let him use my demo for eight days. We buy all our groceries from his IGA even though it's a heck of a lot cheaper to drive fifteen minutes to DeMoula's. So last night after dinner, Daphne and I were out driving when we passed the Quimby's house, and do you know what we saw parked in his driveway?" Fallon's jowls shook. "A brand spankin' new Dodge Ticonderoga with temporary plates and Skip Lee's chrome insignia."

"That Benedict Arnold turncoat," said Dad. "They've been catering our Christmas parties since my old man ran the place. We played in the same backfield. I have to practically twist Marna's arm to shop at his IGA and he drives across the bridge to save fifty friggin' bucks." Dad reached for his parka.

"Where are you going?"

"Grocery shopping."

"Wait for me." Fallon grabbed his lighter off his desk.

"You watch the lot. And make sure Kevin doesn't plow into any customers."

"Galvin?" Fallon poked his head out the door.

"What?"

"You forgot your boots," said Fallon, handing Dad his boots.

"Oh yeah, thanks."

At Quimby's IGA Dad wheeled two shopping carts through the canned seafood section and slid ten rows of tuna fish, four rows of minced clams, and thirty-three cans of Atlantic salmon into his cart. In Aisle 9 he tipped a whole shelf of tomato paste and fifty-one cans of sliced mushrooms into his cart. By the cash registers in a bin marked 'Daily Special,' he quickly stacked forty-eight bottles of maraschino cherries in the children's seat. Wheeling through the frozen foods, he topped off a cart with eighteen Cornish hens, twenty-nine cans of frozen orange juice, and six stacks of TV dinners. He slid eight turkeys under the two carts. Rolling through Aisle 7, Dad stacked and packed sixty-six boxes of California raisins and forty-five bags of marshmallows before lifting a whole pyramid of Cortland apples from produce and dropping them into his cart. With two-dozen loaves of Wonder bread under both his arms, and six cans of lobster bisque stuffed into his pockets, Dad rolled both carts into the checkout lane.

At the cash register Mrs. Quimby's fingers fluttered with Olympic swiftness. Twenty minutes later, a long scroll of paper hung from the register. "That'll be $588.53 please," Mrs. Quimby said.

"I'll tell you what, I'll give you $480 even," said Dad.

Mrs. Quimby looked up. "Excuse me?"

"Okay, I'll give you $500, but not a nickel more."

"What do you mean?" Mrs. Quimby said, looking towards the Customer Service window.

"I bet DeMoula's would sell me these groceries for $500 dollars even." Dad pulled out five $100 bills and thrust them towards Mrs. Quimby. "Come on, I'll give you cash."

"We don't negotiate prices here," she said nervously.

At the Customer Service window Bill Quimby looked up.

"She's grinding me awfully hard, Bill." Dad waved the greenbacks towards the Customer Service window. "Last chance at 500 big boys."

Mr. Quimby shook his head.

"We can't," said Mrs. Quimby.

"Fine. I'll just have to buy out of town then—won't I." Dad stepped around the three carts of bagged groceries and hurried towards the exit. The electric door opened. He walked across the parking lot, climbed into his Suburban, and accelerated down Mass Ave.

In Heaven His Desk Is Next To Noah Webster's

Raina flipped through CDs at Strawberry Records. She read the list of songs, studied the artwork, wondered how they got signed. As the clerk rang up sales, she slid a Pixies CD into her coat, then an R.E.M., 360s, Swamp Oaf, Shawn Colvin, and Titanics. Strolling through the singles rack, she slipped Dinosaur Jr.'s "Water", Indigo Girl's "Kid Fears", The Bag's "Big Wig", Susan Vega's "Marlene on the Wall", and Tim Buckley's "Troubadour" into her purse. Then she walked to the cashier, paid for The Smiths "The Queen Is Dead", and strolled out the entrance. Reaching the sidewalk, she hurried to the T and caught a train home.

In her bedroom Raina folded a basket full of clothes.

"Your CD collection is out of control," said Noy.

"I borrowed those from Crispin," replied Raina, folding a ratty pair of jeans.

"I see." Noy studied the different titles. "And Crispin would buy an Indigo Girls CD?"

"Don't tell anyone, okay?"

"How many of these did you actually pay for?" Noy slid a Neighborhoods disc into the CD player. The opening guitar riff from "Dangerous" leapt from the speakers.

"I'm working on it," said Raina.

"Oh, I see, the 'have as many affairs as you can till you get it out of your system' approach to kleptomania." Noy began pulling socks from the basket and making a pile.

"Don't look at me that way."

"I'm not."

"Are too."

"Am not."

Raina walked to the dresser with a stack of folded jeans. "Okay, I admit it. I like the cheap thrill."

"Oh, that explains it. Phew, I'm glad everything's settled." Noy tried to match Raina's socks. "Why don't you just ask your dad for the money?"

"No way."

"Why not?"

"Don't want to."

Noy dropped the pile of unmatched socks into the basket and walked out of the room.

"Where are you going?" called Raina.

In Choates Dormitory, Pushkoff got my letter:

Dear Scott:

The world's suddenly new, but not what I expected. One million motes of dust rest on the frets of my big brother's Fender. All day, I play guitar and read books about the Civil War, waiting for the sun to run off to California, so I can sleep and wake up to yesterday. But the traffic's jammed on Mass Ave. Delivery trucks are double-parked, unloading their boxes as if none of this matters. Fallon rises to his burnt toast and grapefruit, and we're left with a few fireflies in a dark closet. Maybe if you're not too busy with football practice, we can hang out during spring break.

Your buddy,
Kuba

"Hell yeah," Pushkoff spoke into the receiver. "Wait until you get a look at me—I'm ripped."

At Woburn Cinemas a tunnel of light hovered above the shadows of moviegoers in their seats.

I pulled a St. Pauli from my sleeve. Reaching up my other sleeve, I slid out a Heff Tall. "Want a soldier?"

Noy took a green bottle. She held up a tub of popcorn. "Want some?"

I reached into the tub and pulled out a fistful of popcorn. On screen a Russian spy chased a British agent on skis. "Do you know the sun could have burned out months ago and we'd still be getting the rays? Then one day, we'd be lounging on the beach and an ice sheet a mile-thick would flatten us. Then, even Led Zeppelin's third album, side-B, would have been for nothing," I said as my hand dangled in the space between our seats.

"What about bonfires in Willard's Woods and falling asleep with the radio on and waking up to Bourgeois Tagg's "I Don't Mind"? Those moments are worth something, don't you think?"

"Momentary breaks from the universal blah. It's like Hagler's pounding the piss out of you—nonstop. Then, one day, he decides to take a breather. So you feel pretty good, right?—'cause next day you know he's going to start in with the left hooks. Is that all the rising there is?" On screen the arch villain laughed.

"Go in the lobby if you want to talk," a guy snarled.

"Don't make me come down there and teach you some manners," I popped off (hoping the guy was a wuss).

"What do you mean is that all? We don't have to pick apples for fifty cents a bushel all day. We don't have to run through the jungle with an M-16. We don't have to haul twenty-ton blocks of sandstone for some idiot pharaoh's tomb." Noy put her hand on my leg. "We've got it made."

I took a haul off my soldier. "What if we're lower on the evolutionary ladder than we think? What if a new species of super smart humans evolves? Then, everything I've tried so hard to do, all my garage songs, will just be baby steps."

"I don't think those cave paintings in France are baby steps at all," said Noy. We munched on popcorn and downed our soldiers.

"If I died tomorrow, the news anchors would put on their makeup and smile into the cameras as if I never mattered."

"They'd smile into the cameras no matter who died."

I reached my hand into the tub. It was empty. "When I touched his face it was cold and hard."

"Don't feel bad for Donk. No way. In fact, he's much happier than us. In heaven if you need a place to live, volunteers build you a house on a mountaintop. If you're bummed out," Noy snapped her fingers, "angels fill your 'frigerator with Ben & Jerry's. What was Donk's favorite car?"

"A Corvette, a '63 split-window coup."

"In heaven everyone drives a Corvette down a twenty-lane highway and the trunk has a built-in fridge with three pony kegs. At every rest stop there's a whiffle ball game with all your friends while The Beatles play a six-hour concert. You don't have to worry about Donk at all. He was into dictionaries, right?" Noy snapped her fingers. "In heaven, his desk is next to Noah Webster's. Every time Donk puts on a helmet, it's Thanksgiving morning and he makes the winning tackle. No, Kuba, he's much happier than before." On screen the Russian spy leaned forward and kissed the British agent.

"And I believe you too," I said, wiping my cheek.

"Shush," a lady said.

Noy leaned against me. "It's the truth, I promise." She kissed my cheek. I turned my head and kissed her lips. She kissed me back. Placing my hand on the curve of her waist, we began to make out. She pulled me closer. Her long hair splashed against my face, and although I've never tasted them before, her warm-wet mouth made me think of lilacs in fresh-pressed cider. I moved my hand higher. We continued to kissing as the villain fled in defeat. When Carly Simon sang the closing song, I reached up and was holding the most amazing scoops of warm vanilla ice cream the world has ever known.

A Good Deal Is A State Of Mind

"Who's winning?" I asked.

"Hold on." Dad leaned forward in his chair. On TV the Yankee's pitcher wound up and threw a curveball. The Red Sox hitter checked his swing. "It's that new guy Buckner. Good pickup. Could help us bust The Curse."

"I saw Fallon hanging signs up in the showroom."

"How'd they come out?"

"Kind of plain."

"We're not selling art here. Grab me a couple ice cubes." I returned with a tray. Dad pointed to his glass. "Are you going to push a little iron this weekend?"

"Was planning on it."

"Don't forget your suit and tie."

On TV the Yankee pitcher threw a fastball. Buckner swung. The ball floated over the outfielder's head and into the bullpen. Buckner jogged around the bases.

We hopped off the couch and began kicking our legs into the air. "Hunya hunya, hunya hunya."

"I tell you," said Dad, catching his breath. "This year I really think we're really gonna do it."

Sell (sel), v. 1. To persuade or induce someone to buy something. 2. To pitch to a person for a valuable consideration. 3. To transfer to another in return for something, especially money: *If thou wilt be perfect, go and sell what thou hast and give it to the poor.*

Matt.XIX 21. **4.** To trade: *The defenders at Fort Henry sold their lives.* **5.** *Slang;* to cheat, betray, or make a fool of. **6.** To be employed to persuade or cause others to buy, as a salesperson or clerk. **7.** To have a specific price: *Apples sell at one dollar a bushel.* **8.** To win acceptance or approval of one's ideas. **9.** To dispose of entirely, usually at reduced prices. **10.** To deal; to offer for sale. **11.** *Informal;* to turn traitor to one's country, cause, ideas, or friends. **12.** *British;* to Sell up: to sell off entirely: *She was forced to sell up her entire stock.* [OE *Sellan:* to give or deliver. Icel. *Selja:* to cause to take. Goth. *Salja: to offer a sacrifice.*]

Sell 2 *(sel), n.* **1.** *Scottish;* Self. **2.** A house or cell. **3.** A saddle for a horse: *He left his lofty steed with golden sell. Spenser.* **4.** A throne or lofty seat *[Obsolete].* **5.** An imposition, hoax, or fraud.

That Saturday morning, the sales force gathered in Dad's office.

"Here's the deal," said Dad. "Everyone with a pulse in Middlesex County has been mailed a check for five hundred dollars, but they can only cash the check if they buy a sled from us. So we bumped each vehicle five-hun. It says right on the check: 'This is a factory authorized sale. The dealership is unaware of this offer. Negotiate the best possible price, then present the salesperson this check.' That means, act surprised when customers whip out their checks. Read the words slowly as if for the first time. We won't know which customers have checks and which ones don't—so assume they all do. And beware of the stiffs who'll ask to see the five-buck sleds. If I'm busy, let Fallon work the deal."

"Remember, boys," said Fallon, stuffing a used car guide in his pocket, "don't reject any offer. Get it on paper with a deep, and I'll work the customer up from there." Fallon scanned the lot. "We'll trade for reindeer today."

Dad slid a pill bottle from his jacket. "Thirty-three deals and we've got a clean bill of health." He walked towards the bubbler. "Thirty-three deals and First Trust can take a leap off the Hancock tower." Water leapt from the bubbler as Dad leaned over and drank.

In the showroom I scanned the lot for customers.

"Got your sale shoes on?" asked Dad.

I showed Dad my freshly shined shoes.

"Are you prepared to sell a woodstove to a Texan?"

"With five cords of wood too."

"Don't forget, you've got to ask just the right questions and really *listen*. If I see a salesperson doing ninety percent of the talking, it's a sure sign he's botched the sale."

I tightened my tie. "Got it."

"Let customers define their needs, then pair them with the right sled. Meet the need, earn the sale. And make sure they test drive it."

"Okay." I buttoned my jacket.

"One more thing, if a guy's arms are crossed or a woman's nervously stroking her husband's leg, don't try to close the sale. Read the body language. Continue to dig for hidden objections."

"Continue to dig. Got it."

Dad studied my face. "Most customers lie. They won't tell you what their real objections are. Makes them feel vulnerable. So when you're working a deal: mirror the customers' body movements, speak the way they do. Charm the objections right from their guts. Then, overcome each objection one by one."

"Overcome them one by one."

Dad picked a piece of thread off my sleeve. "Your mind is irrelevant. It's the customer's mind that has to do the thinking."

"Let customers think. Ready," I repeated.

"You sure?" Dad pointed out the showroom window. "Customer at ten o'clock."

Later that morning a customer set his pen down on Fallon's desk. "Think I'd feel more comfortable if I waited till my settlement check comes in."

"Don't worry, we'll finance the down payment," said Dad, entering the conversation. "You won't have to make a payment for thirty days."

"But I don't want to pay interest."

"Won't have to. Just pay off the deep in thirty days."

"I'd rather just wait."

"Jerry, we held this car for two weeks. We had to turn other customers away. Meanwhile, the car is racking up interest."

"I'll come in as soon as my check arrives."

"What about Fallon? He's got a family to support." Dad sipped his Maalox.

"Sorry, I just want to make sure my finances are settled before-"

"Should have thought of that before you asked us to put a sold tag on the dashboard, before Bonnie typed up the paperwork, before we phoned your insurance company and had our prep guy douche and wax the sled."

"I want my deposit back right this minute!"

"We're holding onto your deposit. Come back as soon as your check arrives."

The customer stood up. "Don't make me report this to the Better Business Bureau."

"Says right here on the buyer's order: 'Deposits are non-refundable after seven days.'" Dad walked back to his office.

Fallon sat down. "This isn't an art museum where you can just stroll around and see the pretty paintings. We've got to roll tires to keep our store open. That means keeping your word."

The customer got up and walked towards the door. "I'm going straight to the Attorney General."

"Go ahead, you schmuck." Fallon leaned back in his chair.

"Fallon," called Dad. "That customer has lips and you can bet he'll flap them all the way to the State House."

"But he wasted three hours of my time."

"Only three hours? Consider yourself lucky. I've spent weeks on mind deals only to discover that the clown couldn't finance a toothpick. You've got to pre-qualify your customers, separate the buyers from the tire kickers. When a customer walks into the showroom I can tell in three seconds if he's a buyer or not."

Fallon clipped the tip off his cigar. "A regular Joe Girardi over here. How?"

"Your father was supposed to pay for your education, Fallon, not me."

"My father. Do you mean the guy who hurried out the door at 5 a.m. and stumbled home each night lit up like a Christmas tree? You've been eating sirloin so long, you can't tell the difference between a silver bracelet and a hand cuff."

"You seem to have an answer for everything. So answer me this, twinkle toes: why does Daphne come to our house with melon-sized bruises on her leg?"

Fallon glanced at me. "I could say something but I won't."

"Go ahead and say it." Dad wiped spit off his lip.

"One of these days I just might," said Fallon as he walked outside and puffed on his cigar.

Dad poured himself a cup of tar-colored coffee. "Wife's right. I don't know why I put up with him."

In the parking lot I shook hands with a bearded guy.

"Buzz you tomorrow," he called from his car as he turned onto Mass Ave.

"What happened?" asked Dad.

"Guy wants the night to think it over."

"Kuba, we needed that sale. Do you know how you can tell when customers are lying?"

"How?"

"Their lips are moving. He's probably down at Skip Lee's right now signing a contract. Give him the deal he wants."

"I did. I was only holding eight-hun."

"It's not the better deal he's looking for, it's the better salesman. An ace salesman creates the conditions in the customer's head that allows her to make the decision to buy. A good deal is a state of mind."

After lunch Dad flipped through the prospect log. "I thought traffic would be heavier."

"Maybe they've all gone to the mall," said Connie.

Fallon scanned the lot. "They'll show up."

"How many sleds we move so far?"

"Six."

At my desk Mrs. Snelling looked over the buyer's order. "I like this Dodge and I like you too, Mr. Brice. Now if you knock off another five hundred, I'll take it home today."

"I don't think we can go any lower and still make a profit. Let me ask the boss." I walked into Dad's office. "I'm only holding five-hun and she wants another five-hun off."

"Why did you go so low?" Dad's chair squeaked.

"You know, she's our neighbor."

"She doesn't care. She'd go to Lee Ford to save fifty bucks."

"Even showed her the blue book," I said.

"What did she say?"

"That our markup is probably fifty percent."

"Jesus, let me talk to her." Dad sprung up from his desk and walked to the front of the showroom. "Barbara, how can I earn your business?"

"Six thousand, Galvin, and we've got a deal."

"Just pulled the buyer's slip. We own that car for six-grand, plus a hundred for the sticker. Got my boy helping me out today and, in his innocence, he lowballed you. We need a little profit to pay our bills. Can we write this deal at sixty-five?"

Dad glanced at me. I kept my mouth shut.

Mrs. Snelling fiddled with her wedding ring. "I don't know."

"We've always given you a fair deal. And we're right down the street if your transmission goes again."

"See, Kuba, he always does this to me."

"Glad you're on board, Barbara." With both hands Dad shook Mrs. Snelling's hand. "Pardon me. What is it, Fallon?"

"Should I let this joker walk? I've been working the deal for weeks, including three test drives, and he's chiseling me for two-hundred bucks."

"Who is he?"

"Larry Tate. Works for the water department. Got a couple daughters. Says one of them knows Raina."

"What are you holding?"

"Nine-hun."

"Hi Larry, Galvin Brice." Dad squeezed the customer's hand hard. "Fallon tells me you're interested in that tan Blazer."

"If the price is right."

"Let me ask you this, Larry. How did you come up with the figure twelve-thousand? Are you using a blue book? Has a friend purchased a similar vehicle?" Dad shot a glance to Fallon.

"I got that figure from my bank. Plus, the driver's door has a ding."

"We certainly want your business, Larry." With a bemused expression, Dad tapped figures into Fallon's calculator. "I've been in this business twenty-two years and we've really priced that blazer to sell, but I'll work with you, Larry. What if I fix the door, could we write this up at twelve-two?"

The customer stood up. "Call me if you change your mind."

"Larry, how can I earn your business?" asked Dad.

"By playing ball."

"Larry, I'm pitching you a slow curve."

"Not slow enough."

Dad lowered his voice. "Larry, do you want me to hate you for two-hundred bucks?"

I detected a surprised expression on the customer's face. He walked to the cooler and drank two cups of water. Then he re-read the contract. Fallon strolled to the Blazer with a sold tag.

At my desk I leaned back in my chair and spoke into the phone. "Look, I'll be straight with you, we just want to unload these cars. I'll show you the actual auction slip and just charge you a two-percent handling fee to cover our expenses. That's what I told the customer."

"You're kidding," Raina's voice chimed through the phone. "Whud the customer do?"

"Promised he'd come back with his wife, but he never did. So I phoned him a few hours later and he'd already bought a sled at Lee Ford."

Raina made a gurgling sound. "They don't even trust the *truth*."

"I tell you, customers want the circus routine. They want the sword swallower and the lion tamer. They need the trick ponies and the high-wire act. Reality makes them vomit. I couldn't give these sleds away at cost, but Fallon, who'd sell his own mother an Edsel—they all ask for Fallon because he sings the songs they need to hear, the songs already half-formed in their minds. They send their relatives. Their friends too. They all trust his reassuring pat and vulnerable cough from all those awful cigars."

"So what are you going to tell them now?" Raina's voice echoed through the receiver.

At 5:40 p.m. Dad flipped through pages of the prospect log. "Where are all the customers?" he asked. "Can't understand it. We mailed out four-thousand invites, we're up to our necks in inventory, and we've only made—how many sales?"

"Eighteen," said Fallon.

"That just pays our expenses."

At 6:35 p.m. I held up Dad's jacket. "Let's go home, Dad."

"Fifteen more deals and we could have put a little meat on our bones, gone a month up on the mortgage, put some distance between the wolves and our air supply. But fate has it I sell just enough sleds to keep my doors open one more month. Those Ivy Leaguers must spring out of bed in the morning."

"I'll help you."

"For once, I'd like to tell them what I really think. I'd say: you're right, Mr. Customer, the resale value of this sled drops faster than a bride's skivvies just by driving it off the lot."

"I'll bid on every car at the auction and fill our lot. Then we'll roll some tires."

"I'd tell newlyweds: don't buy that car. It's a depreciating asset. Put your money in a CD that collects interest and you don't lift a finger. Buy a rat-trap for a eight-hun and drive it into the ground."

"We'll rent the circus and let customers who test drive a sled in for free," I said.

"I don't want you in this racket. We're lower on the totem pole than meter maids."

"We'll make extended warranties mandatory for all used cars to increase repeat business."

"To the rest of the world we're a bunch of cheese-mouthed whores," said Dad.

"We'll hire a finance guy and jack up the interest rates another two points."

"Not a bad idea."

"We'll play musical chairs with the customer. Bring in a third face for every deal."

"What about after you graduate? What about college?"

"I'll take night classes at Salem State."

"What about your guitar?"

"I'll practice after work."

Dad looked me in the eye. "You mean, you'll start this summer? You'll wear a coat and tie and show up at eight, not a minute later?"

I nodded.

"Will you follow up on every lead? If you get the flu, will you play hurt?"

I nodded.

"Will you haunt customers till they buy or die?"

All That Garden Stuff

In the den Dad slept in his armchair. At his feet, Donk's CDs, tapes, and records were spread out on the rug. There were six Bim Skala Bim CDs, three by The Bags, a bunch of Tom Waits, a couple Neighborhoods, five by Rory Gallagher, some R.E.M.s, a Susan Vega, Indigo Girls, Asthmatics, Slag, The Cult's "Love", and a boatload of Grateful Dead bootlegs. Behind Dad, three high school portraits rested on the piano.

Mom put her hand on dad's shoulder. "Calling planet earth. Yoo-hoo, anybody there? Hello, anyone home?"

"What the—who's there?" Dad swung his arm. "Stay away from me." He opened his eyes. "Oh, it's you."

Mom clicked off the TV. "You fell asleep with the TV on again."

Dad stared at the fading light on the TV screen. Mom sat on the couch and sipped her whiskey sour. A few minutes passed. She fingered the beads of water on her glass.

"I thought they'd be around longer," said Dad. "I thought that if I could just get them out of my hair for a few years, I'd run the shop, keep a close eye on Fallon, then we'd buy a house on Peaks Island."

"We spent a week on Peaks Island."

"A week's not going to do it. I'm talking years, maybe more. Then they can do whatever they want to me. First Trust can have the store. Wholesalers can grease Fallon all they want. Where's Kuba? I haven't seen Raina for months."

"He's up on the roof."

"Had it all picked out too. The one with the lawn the size of Danforth field. We'd grill steaks and zucchinis. I'd send the boys out on passing routes and we'd see who could make the most jaw-dropping catch. I'd buy a sailboat and we'd visit all those tiny islands in Casco Bay. Who knows what we'd find. I heard Chebeague has its own deer herd. At night, the boys could play their guitars while you and Raina-" Dad paused.

"We'd sing two-part harmony. Is that what you wanted to say?"

Dad reached down and grabbed a CD off the rug. "When I was driving home, I heard a Bim Skala Bim song on the radio, one the kids used to play. I never listened to the song before, but for some reason I did this time. You know, it wasn't half-bad."

Quiet filled the living room. In Granny Pond a bullfrog bellowed: *jug-o-rum, jug-o-rum, jug-o-rum.*

Mom took a sip from her drink. "One night, I climbed up to the cupola with Donny. Don't know how I made it up there, but I did. Donny told me how Kuba won the Boy Scouts' Father and Son Baking Contest in the 4th grade. He put chicken wire in the middle of the cake, then he baked it."

"So that's how he got that Statue of Liberty cake to stand."

"He said, 'Spaz doesn't know it, but he's the musician in the family, not me. You watch, someday he's going to come up with a song that never gets old—even after fifty plays. It'll always sound like it was just released."

"Donny said that?"

Mom nodded. "He also said that Fallon couldn't close a zipper, but you were the best closer in Massachusetts, even better than Skip Lee."

"No kidding?"

"So you must have done something right to have him look up to you like that."

"I had my chance. Remember the summer he grew all those tomatoes and cucumbers? Each evening when I pulled into the driveway, he was there pulling up weeds and pounding in stakes. He'd look up at me as I walked past. Behind him were rows of tomato and cucumber plants and a wheelbarrow full of tools. Do you know what I did, Marna? I walked right past him, went into the house, and turned on the news. Next day, he'd be out there digging and planting again, dropping seeds into holes, waiting for my car. I even snapped at him once: 'Why the hell did you dig up the lawn?' He just stared back at me, wanting something, but I couldn't figure out what that something was. All that digging and planting, making rows, and watering at night. All that garden stuff and I barely looked."

Track 35

Milky Cords Were Flowing
From Their Bodies

"We're gonna sound like hee-haws coming on after Pat Metheny," said Raina, carrying a milk crate of patch cords into the rear entrance of The Rat. "Who chose the order of appearance anyway?"

"I hate to clue you in, deary, but you should be thanking me for this exposure," said Crispin, lugging in a speaker cab. "Who shows up before the headline act anyway?"

During sound check Raina stepped back from the mic. "Enough covers. Let's run through one of the originals we practiced last week."

"Let's just get through this sound check. We can add songs to our set later," said Crispin as a bartender began pulling chairs off tables.

"We've been playing the same stale songs for months. Anyway, I brought copies for everyone." Raina passed out sheet music to Crispin, Janota, and Ferranti.

"These are your brother's songs." Crispin studied the scores.

"Yeah, so what. We haven't written anything."

Crispin hummed a chorus. "Looks like he hasn't either."

"You need to stop smoking dope. Did you hear the reverse climb? What do you think he's doing—putting ink on a cat's paws and letting it walk across a page?"

"God, am I allowed to have my own opinion?"

"An opinion implies that you have a brain that's not cooked."

Crispin taped the sheet music to his mic stand. "Can you sing this?"

"What do you think. Just play and I'll jump in."

That night, Janota's drumsticks blurred as he carved time on his hi-hats, snare, toms, and ride. All bracelets, scarves, and hair dyed with Kool-Aid, Raina swirled around the stage as a melody in E-minor poured from Crispin's guitar. Ferranti filled in the ground floor with chestnut notes. Raina grabbed the mic:

> *The porch lamp never lights our lawn*
> *The wind blows towels off our dock.*
> *Oh how the moon still glows*
> *Why are we two fools alone?*

In the post-chorus, the song shifted keys to G. Raina improv'd a melody. The melody floated over to Crispin. He added a phrase and batted it back to Raina. She *volleyed*. He stroked another phrase back. She caught it and lobbed a response over the net. The phrase penetrated Crispin's gut. A flock of notes flew from his guitar. Raina swallowed the notes and swirled around the stage. Crispin joined her with his guitar. That's when I saw them: milky cords were flowing from their bodies, connecting them, linking their chests, hips, and bellies. They were *cording*.

Raina's voice painted the room the color of loneliness:

Out here in the rings of Saturn
I mainline sugar in my veins.
I float among the crimson patterns
and flap my arms with Heron wings.

Crispin tried to volley, but somewhere in the song the cords vanished. Raina improv'd another riff, but the particles were gone. Crispin cued Janota. Wet Towels on Wood played the coda. A strummed chord faded into silence.

"Thanks for hanging around," said Crispin. "We're Wet Towels on Wood. Come see us at the Middle East on Tuesday nights." The lights came on. The audience buzzed for a few minutes. Gradually, kids broke free and walked towards the exit. On stage, Raina placed her mic in a padded case. She lowered the mic stand and coiled up the cord. Crispin wiped down his guitar neck. Janota unscrewed his cymbals, lifted them from their stands, and slid them into circular cloth bags.

"Give me a hand," Mom called from the 2nd floor window.

I climbed down our roof and grabbed mom's hand. Up on the cupola, we leaned against the chimney.

"I'm too old to shinny up here. You waiting for sun up?"

"Just listening to frogs."

"Might as well wait for sun up now." Mom pulled a white stick from behind her ear and placed it in her mouth. She slid a lighter from her pocket and lit the tip.

"When did you start?"

"Just now."

"Why?"

"Just making it up as I go along." Mom coughed.

"But you're our mast, our rudder too."

"Look at where it got us. And I knew so much a year ago. Guess you'll have to be our rudder from now on."

In Granny Pond, a chorus of frogs sang in the velvet night: "Jug-o-rum, jug-o-rum. Patunk, patunk. Jug-o-rum, jug-o-rum. Patunk."

"It wasn't your fault. We never listened to a single word you and Dad said. You were in the kitchen every morning before dawn. Dad's car pulled out of our driveway at 7:50 a.m. on the dot. You gave us a couple rules, and we followed every boneheaded whim we had. Me and Donk even had a contest once: who could break the most expensive thing."

"Who won?"

"Remember that ceramic owl you and Dad got for a wedding gift? The one Donk stuck in a tree to see if it would attract a real owl. Well, I pegged it with a BB gun." I put my arm around Mom. "It wasn't you; it was us."

"I wouldn't trade you three for anything. Not one of you. When you and Raina sang for Pastor Mac on Easter morning I was the proudest parent in the chapel. But I never told you. I wanted my children to have humility. I'd say, 'if there are six people in a room, then you should do one-sixth of the talking.' Or if one of you argued a point, I'd say, 'have courage and face your faults, dear.'"

"Yeah, but who wants to raise a little snot."

"I only saw what I wanted to see. I had this screwball notion that I was above all the hair pulling and shin kicking, or whatever you want to call what we have here. And if something didn't gel with my ideal—poof." Mom waved her arms like Houdini. "Into a black hole it went. Donny even told me, 'we should talk about things the way the

Pushkoffs do.' But I was defensive. 'You don't know the half of it,' I told him."

We heard a racket and looked up. A murder of crows chased an owl through the sky.

"I have these infinite loops in my mind: What if we had kept him at Tabor? Not been so quick to help him out of jams? Let him spend a few months in jail? Had your father take him to work more often?" Mom leaned her head on my shoulder. "I bought him all those Time-Life books on drugs and how harmful they were. He read every single one. Then he used the information to experiment and make his own concoctions."

"Maybe things would have turned out the same no matter what you and Dad did?" I said. "He always had that manic twinkle in his eyes—even as a little kid."

"Promise me one thing, Kuba?" Mom asked, staring into the darkness.

"Yeah, sure."

"Promise me you'll never have kids. Promise you'll never be a parent."

I nodded.

"If you do, you'll come face-to-face with your own helplessness. You'll begin as the parent and end up as the child. God, everything was such a struggle." On the horizon a bead of sunlight squeezed through the darkness. "All except one time. The time the Pushkoffs took him water skiing on Winnipesaukee. He had only water skied a dozen times, but he always had to out-do everyone. 'I'm going to try one ski,' he said. One ski. When Mr. Pushkoff pushed down on the throttle, he got up too. He was a quick study and darted back and forth across the wake. Water skiers like to do that for some reason."

"I tried it once," I said.

"So after a couple times he says: 'I'm going to try no skis. You know, like Wide World of Sports.' So we're going thirty and Donny keeps sticking up his thumb, signaling Mr. Pushkoff to go faster. Now we're cruising along close to forty. Donny skis outside the wake and sets one foot on the water. Spray flies up everywhere. We could just see his face. Then he kicks off his ski and starts gliding across the lake, his heels carving tiny troughs in the water. That's when I saw his expression shift, just for an instant, from anger and battling against life, to a sense of calm and even grace, as if at last, the thousand aspects of his being were flowing all at once in the same direction. He must have skied barefoot across the water for half-a-mile. Rachael and I were standing on our seats. Then his toe caught a wave— or was it the wake from another boat?—and Donny somersaulted across the water. He couldn't stop talking when we pulled him into the boat."

Learn Your Lingo

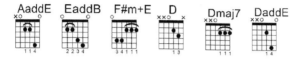

I'M NOT SCARED OF DONK. SURE, HE BUSTED TOSSY'S cheek—one punch—the telephone too. But what am I? A friggin' daisy stem? Would Donk streak through Merriam Hill during rush hour with a Halloween mask on? I don't think so. Sure he hucked a drink—glass and all—into a bouncer's face at the Paradise, then ditched three cops, but put a pile of blank sheet music on my desk and I'll knock Copeland's "Appalachian Spring" into next week—with a series of hooks and climbs. I'll body slam Elliot Carter's "Elegies" on the great green line that leads to Fenway Park. And Victor Young's "Street Of Dreams?" Phhff, I'll use his head for a speed bag. Forget about Donk. I'm the Brice who's going to lift your sleep. I'm a 454 four-barrel, huck-n-bucking, swinging-singing, Moxie-mainlining, nitrous Chevelle tearing up your highway with more sick moves on the treble clef than a jazzed squirrel. I admit, I was a tiny bit miffed when Donk invented trance and Raina figured out cording, but without my Garage Songs, who would know? Okay, sue me. Every time Pushkoff launches an air sculpture into the airways above Danforth Field, I start shadowboxing. But let me ask you this: what musician first slipped stop-time into a double chorus? What nutcase invented his own chords so he didn't sound like a Paul McCartney wannabe?

Who sprinkled freeform through a whole song? What I'm trying to say is: I don't have any buddies.

I want a ton of buddies. Who wants to walk into a keg party alone? Sometimes, I'll pretend I'm with the kids in front of me. I'll holler ahead: "Heeeeey, DeSilva, what's going on? Warrrrdwell, think you're ready to take on the big boy?" Must have been home with a thermometer jammed in my mouth the day Mrs. Gage taught our class the secret bosom-buddy Latin. Who needs buddies anyway. Not me! I'm a humming-strumming, moving-grooving musical ghost of Babe Ruth rising by the thrust of my own sneakers. I've got zillions of thimble-sized gasoline lamps spontaneously blazing in my body every goddamn, ding-dong day. Still, I feel as though I've been on vacation way up in Rangeley Maine, summer has ended, and all my buddies drove home, leaving me stuck in permanent winter up where the lumberjacks rumble.

If Donk were still here, he'd be my best buddy. You see, me and Donk were sliced from the same tread. "Hey Spazzola," he'd say, poking his head in my room, "want to see who can run across the half-inch ice on Granny Pond?" or "Let's borrow Aunt Bee's canoe and look for Blue Herons on the Concord River." Or at a raver, he'd punch my arm and say: "wanna try a keg stand?" Donk was the keg stand king. With Pushkoff holding his ankles, DeSilva pumping the tap like a psycho, and beer flying down his throat, Donk once sucked down brew for fifty-five seconds. He didn't even puke. Me, after twenty seconds, there's gonna be a pizza on the patio. So how do I find another buddy like Donk? Maybe I'll cruise up to Hanover and see if Pushkoff wants to be my buddy. "Get rid of those sugar-footed Dartmouth hoseheads," I'll tell him, then arc a beer bottle into a pep rally.

Does another buddy like Donk even exist? I mean, if I was teetering on the edge of a humongous cliff and a person might be able to save me, but it would mean he'd tumble over too, who would try to save me? I mean, if there weren't any witnesses, just me and him, who would try?

At Arcadia Auctions, Dad and I walked down a line of used sleds a quarter-mile long.

"Pop the hood," said Dad.

I pulled the hood-latch on a Chevy Caprice.

Dad leaned over the engine. "Come here. Listen to the pistons."

I walked over and leaned in.

"Hear that knocking? It's not a clicking sound—that's the belts. It's a knocking sound."

I leaned in closer. "Yeah," I lied.

"This whore needs a valve job. That's four-hundred bucks right there. We'd have to own this sled very right."

"Could it be a piston ring?" I asked.

Dad made a hotdog disappear in two bites. "Unscrew that oil cap."

I unscrewed the oil cap."

"Any white gunk under the cap?" he asked.

"A little."

"Let me see."

I held up the cap.

"Sled needs a new head gasket, maybe more. Let's move on." We continued walking down the line, stopping by a Chevy van. "What do you see, Kuba?"

"Looks okay to me." I called from underneath the van.

"Any oatmeal leaking from the crankcase? Oatmeal in the crankcase keeps a bum engine running for days."

"Can't see any," I called.

"Now go check the gearbox."

I wiggled on my back to the gearbox.

"Bolts been turned recently?" asked Dad. "Some sellers wrap the gears with pantyhose and you can't see that."

"Bolts look like they've been fiddled with," I said to be safe.

"Then crawl on out." We continued walking. Dad paused in front of a Chevy pickup. He studied a quarter-panel. "This isn't the original paint. Look at the overspray in the wheel-well. At the factory, wheel-wells are attached after the body's been painted." Dad took a magnet from his pocket and placed it against the quarter-panel. The magnet dropped to the tar. "See that? Magnets don't stick to Bondo. This truck's been whacked."

We walked past a dozen sleds.

"Check out this frame," called Dad, peering under a station wagon. "Frame looks like its been dropped off the Sears Tower. Once a frame's been bent, you can never get it straight. Let's move on."

"What other fast-ones do I need to be aware of before I can tell if a car is any good?" I asked.

"Wish it was that easy. We'd be loaded. But an engine could have a knock and, Christ knows, it could run like a scalded dog for years. You know that white gunk under the cap?"

"Yeah."

"Sometimes it's just condensation." Stopping by a Blazer, Dad opened the door and climbed inside. "You know, some dealers don't even look under the hood."

"They don't?"

Dad shook his head. "They buy their sleds based on a model's reputation or because it's what they've always bought and they've built up a customer base." Dad turned the key. The engine roared. He shifted the clutch to all five positions. We can't buy this dud." He turned the key and slid off the vinyl seat. "Clutch is ready to drop to the tar. Nothing fills the files faster at the Better Business Bureau than a bum clutch."

Inside the auction house the auctioneer covered her microphone with a hanky. "Alright, gentleman." She adjusted the volume. "We've got three miles of vehicles to unload by five o'clock."

"Auction's 'bout to start." Dad walked towards an open bay.

"So what cars we gonna bid on?"

"Most dealers keep the diamonds, you know that. We'll steer clear of the toilets and buy the sleds we can own right."

A lotboy drove a van in front of the podium.

"Hibady dibady hibady dibady hibady. Who'll give me three thousand?" The auctioneer hit the podium with a leather strap. "How 'bout a grand? Hibady dibady hibady dibady..."

"Here." Dad handed me a fin. "Go grab a hot chocolate. I won't be that long."

"What if I hold the card and you tell me when to bid?" I asked, but his tan coat had already merged into the herd of dealers.

In the cafeteria, I scoffed down two orders of fries. A few tables over, a dealer tossed last month's NADA price guide into a trashcan. When no one was looking, I reached into the can and grabbed the guide.

During lunch, Dad and I inspected a second line of used sleds.

"I'm ready to bid."

"It takes years to learn this racket," said Dad, inspecting a LeSabre with a missing hood ornament.

"Ask me the value of any sled. Go ahead, ask me."

"Okay, Mr. Wonderful." Dad removed a NADA book from his shirt pocket. "What's an '84 Impala with 70K worth?"

"Six-cylinder?"

"It only comes with a six."

"Does it have ice?" I asked.

"Yes."

"How are the skins?"

"Oh, for chrissakes, what are the skins?"

"The tires. Learn your lingo, big boy."

"Just call the car before I grow old."

"You're rushing the auction king." I added up the options. "Fifty-eight bucks?"

"Oo, we'll be bankrupt in three months."

"Just warming up. Give me another shot."

"Alright, an '84 Riviera—loaded—one owner and purrs just as smooth as a kitten," said Dad.

"Leather roof?"

"It's got all the toys. Everything but the kitchen sink."

"Any oatmeal in the crankcase?"

"Just call the car—you wingnut." We hurried towards an open garage door where an auction was about to start.

"Does it have a clean title—if you know what I mean?"

"Quiet. We don't joke about that."

"Why not?"

The auctioneer began gurgling. "Okay fellas, we've got an '85 Suburban. It's got leather."

"Because the state is cracking down on odometer magicians—big time."

"Fourteen grand and a queeeeee."

~ 258 ~

"You forgot to ask the mileage. By now First Trust has leans on our inventory, garage, and house too. They've also frozen our checking account. We're not playing horseshoes here."

"Well you've got the book in your hand," I said, pointing to Dad's NADA book.

"Who's going by the book? Look at Skip Lee." Dad pointed to a man in a coral suit coat who looked like he just returned from Florida, the same man who chased Pushkoff around his lawn. He waved to Dad. Dad smiled back. "I've been coming here for twenty years and—not once—have I seen a price guide in his hands. It's what John Q. Smith on Main Street is willing to pay that counts. The Riviera's got 57,000 miles on it."

"Ten-grand and six-hees?"

"I can live with that, but not a buck higher 'cause I'm seeing ads in the Globe for eleven-two, but you know that's without fenders." Dad leaned down and sniffed the Suburban's exhaust. "And you can bet the customer will chisel us down till we puke—the cheap pricks."

"Skip Lee's all show. I bet he sneaks into the crapper and checks his book."

"You may be right." Removing a magnet from his pocket, Dad stuck the magnet on the Suburban's door. The magnet dropped to the concrete floor. "Oo, this baby's had some work done to her."

A beam of light darted through the attic. "You up there, Chuggles?" I asked. "You sleeping?" A calico tail swung from the windowsill. "Why are you hanging out in this dusty place?" Chuggles looked at me, then resumed her bird watching. I lifted a box off one of Aunt Bee's chairs and sat down. "Think my songs are any good? If you heard one on the radio, would you buy the CD? Are you listening to me?" I smoothed Chuggles' fur. She began to purr. "If you are, say something. Say anything. I know you can." Outside, a robin swooped down onto a worm. Chuggles made a mewing sound. "Just one word and we'll thrill the world."

At Pushkoff's house I pulled open the screen door and walked into the den. "Is he back yet?"

On the couch Noy watched *As The World Turns* and scoffed down a bag of Fig Newtons. "Down the cellar. Got home last night."

As I walked down the stairs, I heard heavy breaths, then a clink.

"What's going on, Little Brice?" said Pushkoff on his back doing bench presses.

"Just got back from Arcadia Auctions."

"Buy anything?"

"Couple brass hats. Wanted to bid on a Z28, but my Dad wouldn't let me."

"Give me a spot me, will you?" Pushkoff lifted the bar off its mounts.

"Holy hell, how much are you benching?"

"Two-sixty." Pushkoff lowered the bar to his chest. "You think I'm a house now, wait until next year. I'll be running through those Ivy League ballet boys. No Harvard barney is going to solo tackle me." Pushkoff raised the bar. "Do you know DeSilva 's older sister?"

"Total babe."

"Guess who's taking her to the sorority ball?"

"Tossy?"

"Yeah, same to you. I am." Pushkoff lowered the bar. "She's always been in love with me."

"After all, she's only human," I said.

"That's right. Hey, that's a good one. I'll have to use it. There's only so much self-restraint a girl can have when I'm in the general vicinity. Sometimes, during games when I'm breaking a tackle, I get scared all the girls will start rushing the field and there'll be a babe stampede. I'll get trampled." Pushkoff raised the bar.

I tightened my lips, but couldn't hold a laugh.

"Don't worry, I'll deflect a few babes your way." Pushkoff strained to raise the bar.

"Come on, college boy, four more reps so you won't have to play left bench next year."

"Left bench? Coach Foley already told me: I'm the go-to-guy. You remember that, Little Brice, Scott Pushkoff is the go-to-guy."

"Yeah, you *go* to the dictionary and under the word 'narcissist' is your photo."

"But my photo is also under the word: *house*. Tell you right now, Brice: if you don't learn to charge your own batteries, when the elbows start flying you're going down."

"But who'll want to come within ten miles of you?"

After lowering the bar, Pushkoff tried to raise it. "Tell that to Tossy's sister."

I spotted him. "Come on, you wussy—one more."

Pushkoff 's face shook violently. Slowly, the bar rose, then it clinked. He stood up. "Do I look ripped or what?" Adding his own words to the "Theme From The Lone Ranger", Pushkoff sang and flex-danced around the cellar.

I'm a house, I'm a house, I'm a house, I'm a house.
I'm a house, I'm a house, I'm a house, I'm a house.
I'm a house, I'm a house, I'm a house, I'm a house.
I'm a hou hou hou hou house.

"More like a trailer," I said.

"Yeah, right." Pushkoff did sit-ups. "What are you doing for college?"

"Haven't thought about it."

"What do you mean you 'haven't thought about it?' You sit around all day playing your guitar and writing songs, and you tell me you haven't thought about it?"

"I haven't."

"Well get some chin whiskers and go to school for music."

"I don't know, maybe."

"...forty-eight, forty-nine, fifty." Pushkoff stood up, lifted up his t-shirt, and flexed his abs. "Got any laundry? I'll scrub it on my washboard."

"You're cracked."

Pushkoff walked back to the bench press. "Give me a spot, will you?" Team photos of the Celtics, Bruins, Red Sox, and Patriots covered the wall.

"What?"

"Stop spacing out and spot me. I'm going to bench two-seventy."

I stood behind the bench while Pushkoff slid a five-pound plate onto each side of the bar. "Donk wanted us to ride our bikes through Yellowstone and see a herd of bison. Did you know that forty million bison once lived in North America?"

"Oh yeah?"

I nodded. "Huge herds, some 200 miles long, roamed from Alaska all the way down to Mexico."

Pushkoff slid on the collars. "That far up?"

"Yup. Then the U.S. decided to wipe out the Plains Indians, so they went after their food supply. Riflemen spread out across the Plains and committed the largest animal genocide in history. The stench of rotting bison flesh could be smelled all the way to Philadelphia."

"No way?"

I nodded. "Donk used to say, 'Buffalo Bill's not a rodeo hero, he's a thug.' Now everything's one giant donut hole. All I can do is react. I have zero control."

"Yeah you do," said Pushkoff, tightening the collars.

"I do?"

"Donk loved to play guitar, right?"

"Every day."

"Then you've got to play every note he did and all the notes he would have played too," said Pushkoff, laying down on the bench.

"What was his favorite brew?"

"Heffenreffer."

"Then you've got to pound Heff Talls."

"Let's see, who really pissed him off?"

"Snobs."

Pushkoff wrapped his hands around the bar and lifted. "Then bullrush all snobs. Hmm, your brother owned twelve dictionaries—the nut. Well, you've got to read all his dictionaries. What about the way he wiggled his fingers? What was up with that? Do it anyway." Pushkoff lowered the bar to his chest. "Do all the things Donny did that made him who he was. If you want to stop a person from taking off, you've got to become that person." Pushkoff began raising the bar. His face turned purple and shook violently. Midway up, the bar stopped rising.

I slipped two fingers under the bar and helped Pushkoff lift it. "Come on, buddy, you can do it."

Slowly, the bar began to rise.

Track 37
Ghost Options

On Danforth Field, players in padded pants sprinted from end zone to end zone during spring tryouts. In the parking lot I opened my trunk, took out Donk's shoulder pads and helmet, and walked to the practice field.

"What brings you out here, Brice?" asked Coach Brewer.

"I was hoping to try out for the team."

Coach Brewer thumbed through the pages on his clipboard. "Most kids have been playing football since junior high. What position were you thinking about?"

"Who's playing my brother's old position?"

"Donny was an offensive tackle, but they usually run over two-hundred pounds. What sports have you played before?"

"Played little league baseball, hockey on Granny Pond, and summer soccer. I want to be an offensive tackle like Donk. Been practicing my crossover step six-hours-a-day."

Mr. Brewer fiddled with his moustache. "Alright, we'll give you a try, but don't look down when you're hit. Necks get broken that way."

The quarterback leaned over the center. "Ready, thirty-six, twenty-eight, forty-one, sweep, hike one, hike two, hut, hut, hut." The quarterback stepped backwards, faked a pass, then shoveled the ball to Bart Graph. Arms raised, I shuffled right, then ran forwards. Graph followed. A defender drove his helmet into my chest.

"You all right, Brice?" Mr. Brewer asked standing over me.

"Can't breathe."

"Don't try to breath. Keep your mouth open."

A kid named Tim Wardwell helped me off the field.

Coach Brewer waved his arm. "Okay, DeRaps, back onto the field." A kid the shape of a fire hydrant ran onto the field. All sweat and tobacco, Coach Brewer walked over to the bench where I sat. "That was our second-string linebacker and we're a small team compared to Woburn. You're just too lanky to play tackle."

"What if I start hitting the weights?" I asked.

"Most of these kids have been lifting weights and going to football camp for years. Even if you've got talent, it still takes ten years to master anything. Why don't you try soccer? I could walk you over to Coach Russian right now. What do you say?"

"Soccer's not going to do it. I really think I'm supposed to play football."

Coach Brewer scanned the field. "Now come on, don't do that. Some of these kids would pay big bucks to be able to crack a history book once and be able to remember who did what to whom."

"It doesn't help."

"Maybe not now, but someday all the glass beads will break and you'll string the pearls together. That's the way it works. Got to trust me on that point. Stick to what you're naturally good at." Coach Brewer gazed at the goalposts. "Hey, Wardwell?" Brewer motioned to his quarterback. "Go hold a few footballs for Brice Junior. See if he can paste one through the uprights."

With a fishnet of footballs, Wardwell and I walked to the thirty-yard line. Wardwell balanced the ball on the grass with his finger. "The key to kicking field goals is repetition. You repeat the exact series of movements every kick," said Wardwell as I kicked an imaginary ball. "Watch your foot actually strike the ball. Don't look up or you'll shank it."

Carefully, I took three measured steps backward and one sideways like I had seen on TV. My arms swung gently back and forth.

"Okay, this isn't the Super Bowl. Just kick the ball."

Taking two steps forward and swinging my leg forward on the third step, my foot struck the ball. The ball tumbled over the turf.

"Follow through with your kick. Really swing your leg."

Again, I took three measured steps backwards, and one sidestep. I took three steps forward. My cleat dug into the turf.

"Took your eye off the ball," Wardwell said. "Once your body's in motion, the world should vanish except for the ball. Watch your cleat actually strike the leather dimples."

I lined up, took three steps, and watched my cleat strike the ball. The ball hooked left.

"Your shoulders weren't squared with the posts. Straighten out your leg motion. Direct the ball with your whole body."

Lining up, I took three steps forward and swung my leg. The ball tumbled through the air towards the goalposts, landing under the crossbar.

"See, you learned something already. Now really swing your leg forward like a golf club. You get foot speed with a long rotation." Wardwell propped-up another ball. "Pretend you're kicking two footballs: one on the ground, and one in the air by your waist. Really give the ball a hateful kick."

With my eyes glued on the fat part of the ball, I took three steps forward and wildly propelled my foot forwards. While conducting wind sprints, Coach Brewer turned and watched. The football floated through the uprights eight feet above the crossbar and landed in the grandstands.

"That's it," Wardwell hollered. "You really cocked that sucker. Now repeat that exact motion."

I did. The ball floated through the uprights twelve feet above the crossbar.

"Too much height. Plant the tip of your cleat two inches ahead of the ball."

I planted my cleat just ahead of Wardwell's hand and followed with a long pendulous kick. My stomach, chest, thigh, and calf muscles tightened. The ball flew from my foot—straight through the twin posts.

"Now you're getting a sense of the rhythm needed for field goals." He handed me a plastic holder. "Fire a few dozen balls through the uprights and see if you can transform a rhythm into a routine."

Thirty footballs flew through the April air searching for the goalpost's middle.

"How'd he do?" Coach asked.

"Not bad for a newbie. Think he's worth a second practice." Wardwell punched my arm.

"Alright, Brice. Take a few balls home with you and we'll see how you do tomorrow with a couple defensive backs rushing at you." Coach blew his whistle. "There's concentration and there's game-concentration. I know kickers who can chip the ball through the uprights thirty times in a row during practice—from forty yards out too. But put the added pressure of a game on their backs, and I wouldn't bet my shorts on them." Coach Brewer slapped the clipboard against his waist. "Okay, all cornerbacks over to the practice field."

Dad opened the showroom door. "Vince, what can I do for you?"

"Can we speak for a moment in your office?" asked Mr. Irvine.

"Sure." Dad walked into his office. "Have a seat." Dad motioned to a vinyl chair, then sat in his own chair. "What's up?"

Mr. Irvine unsnapped his briefcase. "I've been reading through last month's list of repossessed vehicles and found some disturbing tendencies. Seven of them are from this shop. That's okay. It's only slightly higher than average. The problem is: we've discovered that these cars have far less equipment than stated on their loan applications." Mr. Irvine shuffled through his papers. "Here, take a look. The application states that the Chevrolet in question has a sunroof, intermittent wipers, and cruise control, but when our team repossessed the car for non-payment, we found out it just wasn't so."

"Maybe the owner removed those options?" said Dad.

"How can you remove a sunroof?"

"I tell you, Vince, I've seen it done."

Mr. Irvine looked flustered. "Here's another one." Mr. Irvine handed Dad a piece of paper. "An '85 Park Avenue. The application says it's got air conditioning—and thank God it does—but then someone from this garage penciled-in that the car has power locks and windows. It doesn't. Alloy wheels. No again. Here's another: leather seats. Double no. Galvin, we loaned $12,500 against this car because Brice Chevrolet said it had those options. Now

~ 268 ~

we're $2,200 upside-down. That car won't bring $9,300 at Arcadia. Dealers have an obligation to be accurate with their descriptions."

"We are to the inch with the odometer readings."

"And we appreciate that. That's the one item that's included in the contractual agreement between dealers and our auto finance unit. We've never had this problem to such a large extent. Our legal department is writing a new contract as we speak. Who filled in those loan applications?"

"We all do. Let me see." Dad studied the sheets of paper. "Hey, Fallon? Take a look at these loan apps. Who checked off the option lists?"

By the coffee machine, Fallon poured coffee into a Styrofoam cup, then shook in creamer. Stirring the tan liquid with his pinky, he strolled over to Dad's office. "I sold those sleds, just like every other piece of iron around here," said Fallon, stopping in the doorway.

"Oh, I forgot, God's gift to the motoring public over there. See what I have to put up with all day, Vince? Well it looks like you were a little over-zealous getting your sleds hawked."

Mr. Irvine held up a manila folder. "Mr. Moran, these vehicles are not equipped with the options you said they were equipped with."

"Oh those," said Fallon, scanning the showroom for ups. "In car sales, you have to sell customers on, not only the options a car has, but also the options a car hasn't got. If not, how will customers know which options are invisible?"

Mr. Irvine shifted in his seat. "I don't follow."

Fallon took a haul off his coffee. "Salesmen need to add *ghost options* or customers will buy over at Lee Ford."

"I still don't follow."

"FMC will finance a corpse, but you guys—after I've puked out my guts closing a sale—you guys won't finance average-retail. Poof, there goes my gross."

Mr. Irvine's face turned brick-red. "That's outright lying and thieving, Mr. Moran."

"But if the options are part of a car the customer wants, then it's not lying at all, it's supplying the conditions needed for *the sale*."

"That's alcohol logic, Mr. Moran. The point is: those options are not on the cars."

Fallon shook his head. "No, I don't think you understand. We're not selling cemetery plots. We're selling custom rides from point A to point Z. The sleds my customers decide to buy could set the course of their entire lives. But you guys needs to do your part and open up your vault so dealers can finance a profit. That's critical for our low-end customers who don't have a down-payment."

"What goes on in that head of yours? Do you know this practice of adding ghost options could ruin our business relationship, not to mention your line of credit?"

"I hope not, because in order to convince my customers a sled is any good, I must first convince myself. After thirty-some-odd years in the car business, the one truth I've learned is customers do not want the cars they can afford. They want sunroofs, cruise control, leather seats, alloy wheels, AC. Every customer wants them, so in a sense those options are already on the cars. Vince, I'm not trying to tell you how finance works, finance tells me. I'm just a player in the game."

"It's a crooked game at that." Mr. Irvine snapped his briefcase shut and stood up. "Galvin, talk some sense into that salesman of yours. We've got to make a buck too."

"I understand your having to clamp down on this practice of adding ghost options, or you'd have hundreds of base model sleds stuck in your hand at thousands over book, but I have to stand by my salesman because I firmly believe that he firmly believes that those vehicles have all the options he said they have."

"Oh Christ, you too." Mr. Irvine stormed out of Dad's office. "I want this practice of adding ghost options to stop."

"Fallon," said Dad, wiping his eye, "you heard the man."

At 3:18 a.m. Mom sprung up in bed. "Galvin, did you hear that?"

"What the-" Dad swiped at the air. "Hear what?"

"The noise on the lawn."

"Probably a couple squirrels mating. Go back to sleep."

"Can't."

"Want one of my sleeping pills?"

"No, I don't want a sleeping pill. There it is again. Sounds like a person's getting kicked in the gut." Mom slid out of bed and walked to the window.

"If they're out this late, they deserve it," said Dad.

In the backyard I set a football in a holder, took three steps backwards and one sideways. "Two seconds left. Merriam Hill down by two. Field goal would win it. Fifty-eight yards. Little Brice jogs onto the field. Check out at those quads, folks. Looks like he's been lifting. Here comes the snap. Kinda high. Brice lowers his head." I took three steps forwards and swung my leg. The ball tumbled into the night towards a tennis net (I swiped it from some snob's tennis court) strung between two trees. "Oo, Brice really got a hold of that one." The ball flew into the net. I pumped my fists. "It's good. Merriam Hill takes states." I

~ 271 ~

danced around the yard. "Were you nervous, Little Brice? Well, Howard, I've been kicking the ball well all week, so I knew if I could make solid contact and get full leg rotation, I'd have a chance to punch it through the-"

"What on earth are you doing up at this hour?" asked Mom, standing on the lawn, tightening the sash to her bathrobe. "Your father and I are trying to sleep." Her eyes scanned the plush green lawn. Something looked different.

"Just trying to get in a few extra kicks. I'll keep it down."

"Where'd this grass come from?"

I looked up at Mom and tried to think up a whopper.

"Don't tell me." She walked back into the house.

After gathering the footballs, I placed one in the holder, took three steps backwards, one sideways, and stared at the ball. I took three steps forward and swung my leg. The ball tumbled into the dark.

Track 38
Eraserback

In our kitchen the phone rang. (The ring's pitch was E_2. I guess, the phone company figures people might ignore a lower pitch.)

Mom picked up the receiver and placed it under her chin. "Hello?" she asked as she lifted plates from the dishwasher and stacked them in our cabinet.

"It's me," replied Dad. "I'm staring at the inventory; it looks like someone emptied their ashtray on the front row. Will you send the kids down?"

"I'll drop them off on my way to IGA."

"Oo, grab me some animal crackers."

In front of Brice Chevrolet Dad handed me a bucket. "Here's the soap and sponges. I'll go turn on the hose."

A few minutes later Raina aimed the hose at a car. Water ricocheted off the car and soaked my shirt.

"Hey watch it," I yelled.

"What's the matter—afraid of a little water?"

I plopped a soapy sponge on the hood and began washing the car. "Someone should invent a soap that washes and waxes at the same time."

Noy sprayed whitewall cleaner on the tires. "Better yet, how about a paint that repels dirt?"

"I've got an awesome invention," said Raina, rinsing off the hood. "Remember when we drove up to Maine to take

Donk and Pushkoff to football camp and no hotel would give us a room 'cause we brought Kayla? Well, since most families have dogs, I bet we'd make millions if we opened the Dog-A-Long Motel chain."

"Wow, you really went all out on that one," said Noy, making eye contact with me.

"I suppose you douche nozzles got a better one." Raina pointed her hose at me.

I booked-it beyond the water's arc. "You missed."

"I've got one," said Noy, scrubbing the whitewalls with a wire brush. "My invention's for teachers. You know how kids pass notes and throw airplanes when a teacher turns around to erase the chalkboard? Well, I'm going to invent a shirt with felt on the back, so during a lecture all the teacher has to do to erase the board is lean backwards and-" Noy wiggled her back, "presto, the board's wiped clean. I'll call it Eraserback."

My ribs began to hurt.

"Erasing the whole board when you're not even lookin' at it. That would be something," Raina sighed.

"Mine's a ton better," I said, dipping my sponge into the bucket. "Have you ever noticed how long it takes to rub on suntan lotion at the beach? Sometimes five, six minutes. Then, when you go swimming, it all washes off. People blow hours smearing on suntan lotion. That's why I'm going to build the world's first Suntan Lotion Shower Booth. Now, at the beach, all you'll have to do is drop four quarters in a slot, stand under the shower head, and you'll get sprayed with suntan lotion. I'll be loaded."

"You should have that patented," said Raina.

"You think?"

"No. Have you been snorting ants?"

I whipped my sponge at Raina. It pegged her in the face.

"You jerk, you got soap in my eyes."

In front of the showroom, Dad opened the door and motioned Pastor MacDonald inside. "Have a seat in my office, Gordon. I'll take a peek at your trade and run some numbers." Dad hurried towards us. "Clean up your language. This isn't a bowling alley."

"Kuba got soap in my eye."

Dad grabbed my arm. "Mental midget—use some judgment for once in your life." Dad turned to Raina. "Let me see." Holding the hose, he flicked water into Raina's eyes. "Better?" Raina nodded. Dad hurried towards Pastor Mac's van.

Later that day, I was sudsing up a Malibu when Raina snuck up behind me and poured soda in my hair and down my shirt. Then she poured coffee grounds at me. "Gotcha. We're even."

"Okay, you got me," I said, pulling off my Rory Gallagher t-shirt. I could feel the syrupy coffee grounds sticking to my scalp. "Hey, where's Donk's Telecaster? I haven't seen it for months."

"Crispin's got it."

"Crispin DeGeneres has Donk's Telecaster? Who gave you the right to lend it to that maggot?"

"I did. Besides, you barely play it." Raina aimed the hose at the sudsy car.

"How do you know? If you didn't need to eat, you'd never come home."

"Maybe he'd want Crispin to use it."

I clenched my fists.

"What's the matter, Kuba?" asked Noy.

"I just want Donk's guitar back, that's all."

"Well, I'm not asking for it back," said Raina.

A wave of rage washed over my body. "You tell that troll Crispin if it isn't on my bed by Friday, I'm driving my Chevelle through his living room."

"You tell him," said Raina as clear water washed across the car. "What makes you think you had this special thing with Donk anyway?"

"I know this doesn't mean anything to you, but he was our brother."

At Quimby's IGA Mom turned down Aisle 9 in search of condensed milk. Long florescent tubes poured light onto the shelves of food. She wheeled past bags of flour, boxes of brown sugar, vanilla extract, and baking soda before stopping in front of condensed milk. She scanned the cans. How many ounces did she need? What brand? Carnation was eighteen cents less, but only twelve ounces. That was eight cents an ounce. How much was Borden's? Which had a better date? Acid rose up from her stomach and burned her throat. Where could she sit without drawing attention to herself? She dropped a can of condensed milk into her cart and wheeled to the salt. The Shurfine brand cost seventy-five cents. Morton's, eighty-nine cents. Was there any difference? Did it matter what brand sat on their shelves at home? Why was that girl holding an umbrella? And what did salt have to do with girls in the rain? She remembered the same girl from her aunt's pantry. The aunt who made apricot tortes. Mom dropped the Morton's salt into her cart. A woman wheeled past with a toddler. Why bother when everything was being erased? Mom pushed her cart down the aisle. She picked up a bag of brown sugar and studied the ingredients. Brown sugar really was white sugar mixed with molasses. When people needed brown sugar, why didn't they just mix in molasses themselves? Maybe McIntosh, Macoun, and Gravenstein were all good for baking pies? Maybe their lawn was big enough to grow tomatoes, cucumbers, peppers, and squash? Who knew? She wheeled her cart to the dairy section and scanned the rows of cottage cheese. She hated cottage cheese. It was never on sale. The lids always broke, and the dates were never on the bottom. How then could she tell which ones were spoiled? How would she know? Except to *buy* and to taste. Mom took a thingy of cottage cheese off the shelf and searched for the date. Where the hell was the date? Everything was being erased and she was choosing cottage cheese. Her arm made a looping motion. The cottage cheese flew over aisles 10, 9, 8, even 7, and exploded against a glass door in the frozen foods aisle. Quickly, Mom pushed her cart out of the dairy section. A manager hurried past. She grabbed a box of animal crackers and pretended to read the ingredients.

Dad set his price guide in the top drawer and sat in his chair. "Sorry I kept you waiting, Gordon. My youngest boy squirted soap in his sister's eye. I don't know what goes on in that head of his." Dad handed Pastor MacDonald an appraisal slip. "You've really taken good care of that van. I'll go full trade on it."

Pastor MacDonald studied the appraisal slip. "Have him drop off the new van at Grace Chapel and I'll have a chat with him."

Later that afternoon Dad talked with a sales rep from The Globe. The rep pulled a folder of spec ads from her briefcase and laid them out on Dad's desk. Leaning over his desk, Dad evaluated the ads.

Connie poked her head into Dad's office. "Will you come to my office when you're finished?"

"What is it, honey?" asked Dad, sitting on the corner of her desk.

Connie closed the door and opened two ledgers. "I'm not your honey. I want to go over receivables so I can close out the month. Last few months have really drained our cash."

"Tell me about it. I had hoped by this time we'd own our inventory free and clear."

"We're floor-planning our entire inventory," said Connie.

Dad picked up a photo of Connie's two sons. "I know it. Interest rates are chasing customers off the lot."

"We don't have enough cash-on-hand to meet payroll."

"What do you suggest?" asked Dad.

"You know I can't suggest anything." Connie left a pencil on a green page in a ledger then walked towards a filing cabinet with a stack of deals.

"Okay, okay." Dad sat down on Connie's chair. With the pencil, he erased numbers and scribbled in new ones. "In like a tortoise, out like a hare. How long will this float our payroll?"

"Few weeks."

"Hopefully, we'll catch a little fire and sell our way out of this cesspool of red ink."

"Always have," said Connie.

"Now all we need is for Voelker to drop the prime to give our customers some fresh legs." Dad scanned the lot. "Connie?"

After filing the deals, Connie studied the new figures. "Yes?"

"What if First Trust starts sniffing around our books? They'll find out we've got a yo-yo balance sheet."

"Want me to keep the titles in my trunk?"

"Thanks. That'll give us a few hours. Has anyone figured out how to make duplicate titles yet?"

"Watch yourself. They put people in pinstripes for that."

"Just wondering out loud."

"What about the dates?" Connie walked back to the filing cabinet.

"Oh yeah." Dad erased the dates and penciled in new ones.

* * * *

That Sunday in Grace Chapel the churchgoers gathered in front of the stage as the piano player from Vertical Church sent arpeggios spiraling through the parish. Meredith Andrews stepped to the mic and began to sing the verse from "Come Holy Spirit." Churchgoers' arms swayed back and forth like quaking aspens in an April wind. After the last chorus, people ambled back to their seats and sat down. Pastor Mac walked up to the lectern and studied the round heads of his churchgoers. "My father liked to take our family on long Sunday drives. In our Oldsmobile Cutlass, we'd wind our way from Waltham down into Newton and into Chestnut Hill. When we drove past the elegant brick mansions and curved driveways in Chestnut Hill, my grandmother would lean towards me and say, 'They're not happy.' As a kid I'd picture dour-faced families sitting around mahogany tables, talking about golf, and passing around the Grey Poupon.

'Why aren't rich folks happy?' I'd ask my grandmother.

She'd look at me the way a jeweler studies a diamond and say, 'On the road to heaven there's a traffic jam of

Cadillacs and Mercedes, but to get to heaven you've gotta walk.'

I wasn't sure what she meant. That night Grandma read from her bible: 'In Luke 18:18 a ruler asked Jesus, 'Good Master, what shall I do to inherit eternal life?' Jesus replied, 'Thou knowest the commandments: Do not kill. Do not steal. Do not bear false witness. Honor thy father and thy mother. Do not commit adultery. Also, love thy enemy as thou loves thyself.' The ruler said, 'All these I have kept from my youth up.' Then Jesus said, 'Yet thou lackest one thing: sell all that thou hast and distribute it unto the poor, and thou shall have all the treasures in heaven. Come follow me.' The ruler was very sorrowful for he was very rich. When Jesus saw this he turned to the crowd and said, 'How rare it is for those who have riches to enter into the kingdom of God. For it is easier for a camel to pass through a needle's eye than for a rich man to enter into the kingdom of God.' Those in the crowd who heard Jesus asked, 'Who then can be saved?'

At seven, I was terrified. Our family went to Lakeview Church. We believed in Jesus, but we had not given all our things to the poor. In fact, we had only given the things we didn't want to a church tag sale. At Christmas time, my father pledged a fair amount to Sims Hospital, but he always had enough to buy me the G.I. Joe I wanted.

'Did Jesus only want the rich to give their possessions away?' I asked my grandmother.

She nodded.

'But why only the rich?' I asked.

'Because they're the ones with extra things to give,' she answered.

But we owned extra things too, I thought. What did Jesus mean when he said, 'Sell all that thou hast and

~ 280 ~

distribute it unto the poor?' Could we keep our Buick? Surely, Jesus would want Dad to be able to make his sales calls to support our family. Did Jesus approve of a Buick more than a Mercedes? What did Jesus think about cruise control or air conditioning 'cause, come August, it gets awfully hot in Waltham.

'You'll need AC for the fires of hell,' I dreamed Jesus replied one night.

What size house did Jesus prefer we live in? How about the Florida vacation our family took each winter? What did Jesus think about those?

Now my Grandma believed that fancy-pants cars and white-pillared mansions were roadblocks to our happiness. I guess I did too. When a Mercedes parked in front of Lakeview Church she'd whisper, 'Every time someone buys a Mercedes, blood is drained from Jesus' heart.' When we drove past Brae Burn Country Club, she'd point to the golf course and say, 'Lucifer is putting on those greens.'

In all honesty, I must ask myself: Did my grandma and I believe that rich folks weren't happy because we were jealous? 'Cause I don't know what I'm gonna do if I wake up one morning and find out that they are happy. On top of their seven-figure bank accounts, on top of their Roger Moore looks, that would be too much to take."

Bellies wiggled in the congregation.

"Oh, it's awful," Aunt Bee whispered in my ear. "If your grandfather had just stayed in Sweden, none of this would have happened."

Pastor Mac stiffened his back and peered into the congregation. Vince Irvine and his wife looked up from the front row. "So how can a person pass through the needle's eye? Perhaps the answer lies wrapped in Jesus' parable: 'It is easier for a camel to pass through a needle's eye than for a rich man to enter into the kingdom of God.' In Jesus' time, many cities had erected walls to protect themselves from invading armies and bands of thieves. These walled-in cities had small tear-drop entrances in the shape of a needle, so if an army showed up, only one soldier could pass through the opening at a time, and citizens would easily be able to overwhelm each soldier and defend their city. As you can imagine, travelers on camels couldn't fit through these needles. A traveler would have to dismount, walk through the entrance, and figure out a way to squeeze or push his camel through the entrance. Of course, the head and the long neck could fit through, but then the hump would get stuck. However, there was one way a camel could squeeze through the needle's eye: if it lowered its head, knelt down, and walked through the entrance on its knees."

Pastor Mac closed the folder containing his sermon and went into free-form. "Still, it's hard to have humility with life knocking on our doors. Every family has its myths, its set of exaggerations that paint a grander portrait in order to shield themselves from the cold realities of living. On one hand, these myths are fur coats that keep us warm. On the other hand, they're mirrors in a funhouse that distort our ability to truly see. So either you're confident or full of illusions, but you can't be both."

"It's just so terrible," Aunt Bee laughed.

"I sometimes wonder," Pastor Mac went on, "what would happen to a family if their myths were exploded, their fur coats were unceremoniously ripped off, and they were forced to look at themselves with clear unadorned eyes?"

A Stolen Fender

"Hi Mrs. DeGeneres," I called into the receiver. "Is Crispin there?"

"He might be in his room. I'll go check."

"Yeah?" asked Crispin.

"Hey, this is Kuba. I wanted to play Donk's Telecaster and Raina told me she lent it to you. Can I come over and pick it up?"

"It's kind of not here," said Crispin.

"Where is it?"

"I left it at our practice space in Somerville. My axe blew a pickup so I ordered a new one from Daddy's."

I took a deep breath. "Well I want it back, so take a trip to Somerville."

"Don't hassle me. You'll get it back as soon as my Les Paul is fixed."

"How long is that going to take?"

"Guy said it'd be a couple weeks. Anyway your sister said it was alright. Listen, I've got to meet Ferranti in Porter Square."

"You make sure a couple weeks doesn't turn into a couple months," I called into the receiver but only heard a dial tone.

That night, while cruising down Mass Ave, my buddy Wardwell pointed to a red Audi with a loose muffler. "There's Crispin's car."

My Chevelle U-turned and tailed the Audi through Arlington and into Cambridge. In Porter Square, the Audi pulled into a Quick Mart. In the passenger seat, Raina fiddled with the tape deck. Crispin got out.

I hopped out. "Hey, peckerhead, where's my guitar? You know, I don't like having to hunt you down just to get my own brother's guitar back."

Crispin walked towards the Quick Mart. "Calm down, will you. You'll get it." Inside, he handed the cashier a fin. He emerged with two sodas and clove cigarettes.

"I don't think you get it, you over-nurtured, self-centered, sack of puss. I'm not going anywhere until I get that Telecaster." I spit at Crispin's sneakers.

"Get out of my face, you stooge." Crispin shoved me, hopped in his Audi, and accelerated down Mass Ave.

My car left a patch of rubber the size of Texas on the tar. We tailed the Audi through Somerville. The Audi boffed a red light. We did too. The Audi cruised through Arlington. We followed. The Audi sped up. We sped up too. In Merriam Hill the Audi got caught behind a truck at a red light. I jammed my car into park and hopped out. Crispin got out too.

"Liver lips," I yelled.

"Rotate on this." Crispin held up his middle finger.

That pissed me off, so I kicked in the Audi's taillights.

"Hey!" Crispin hucked his soda at me.

I ducked. The bottle flew over my head and exploded on the tar. I brought my fist down on his rear window. Crispin bullrushed me. His sneaker flew into my gut. I caught his leg. He fell backwards. I jumped on him. Our bodies rolled around the street. Shards of glass sliced into my skin. Horns began blowing. Climbing on top of me, he jacked me in the head. Reaching up, I grabbed his dreadlocks and pulled. Crispin tipped forwards. I got up. We circled each other, fists raised.

"You're the biggest scumbag ever," I said.

"Why do you want his axe? You can't even play."

"Stuck up jerk." I threw a punch. Grabbing my arm, Crispin dug his nails into my skin. Water trickled down my face. I didn't give a crap. "Do you think you're so hot because your mom told you so, or did you learn to swim with barbells strapped to your ankles?" I yelled.

"You're cracked."

Aiming for his head, I threw a haymaker, missed and spun around.

Crispin grabbed me from behind. "Full-Nelson. Give up?"

"Screw you." Crouching down quickly, my bum flew out and bumped Crispin backwards. Rolling right, I threw a hook. Crispin fell sideways onto the tar. Knees on his chest, I grabbed his Adam's apple and squeezed. "I ought to fix it so you'll never sing again." Someone grabbed my shirt and pulled me to my feet.

"Get your paws off him," said Raina. "Crispin's not even the fighting type—he's a musician."

"He's a dirty fighter," I said, feeling the scratches on my arm. Jogging to the rear of Crispin's car, I kicked his brake lights, pulled the keys from his ignition and chucked them across Mass Ave.

"Are you sick or what?" said Raina. "You think the whole world cares if you act tough. Well, I hate to clue you, skinny boy, but no one gives a crap about a Merriam Hill punk. Do you get what I'm trying to say?"

I spit crimson saliva at Raina's feet. "Get away from me you Benedict Arnold piece of trash. What the hell do you do that's so hot anyway? You and your Jim Morrison strut. You and your Marlboro girl music. All for you. You. You. You. The amazing thing is: you live off your vanity. It actually gets you somewhere—'cause you convinced that if your clique thinks something's true—it really is. That's pretty sad."

A cruiser pulled up. Chief Swan climbed out and directed the traffic around our cars.

"Yeah and what do you do that's so great?" yelled Raina as blue lights flashed against her face.

"I don't murder my parent's sleep for a keg party. I don't ditch my own brother at the Middle East for a drummer I met five seconds ago. Yeah, I know all about that. Then Donk drove home alone. Why did you do that? How many people have to suffer so you can have a good time?"

"Donk left me stranded in Dorchester once at 2 a.m.."

"What happened here?" asked Chief Swan.

The divots in my arm killed. The divots in my arm killed. "You just don't get it, do you? Somewhere in your mind's inner-workings, amid the pools of self-deception, there's a process missing."

"That fellow vandalized my car," said Crispin.

"He tried to clock me with a soda bottle." I pointed to the glass shards.

"Did you throw that bottle?" asked Chief Swan.

"Well yes, but only after he kicked in my taillights." Crispin pointed to his Audi.

"What's your name, son?"

"Crispin DeGeneres, sir."

"What does your life have that mine doesn't?" Raina whispered furiously. In puppet motion, she raised and lowered her arms. "Kuba's so nice. Kuba's so down-to-earth. Because you're too much of a wuss to tell people what you really think. Stop sniffing daisies and see the world in all its glory: a giant poker-faced, chess match to pass on your genes and everyone loses. Only the nitwits think they've won. A beach house in Kennebunk—I am so impressed. A Dana Hall sticker on your Volvo—excuse me while I puke."

"If you really believe that, I feel sorry for you." A gas station attendant walked towards us and held out Crispin his keys. "But I know you don't—'cause you're shinnying up the glass totem pole just as fast as everyone else. You say nothing matters, but you won't streak through the center of Merriam Hill to prove it. You're a sham."

The skin around Raina's eyes tightened. "You think you know everything. Go spend your life watching reruns of "The Brady Bunch"—see if I care." She wiped her face. "You don't know squat."

That blows. Just when I'm about to tuck someone neatly into a category she goes and cries on me. That ruins the category and makes me feel like a big donut hole.

"Both of you." Chief Swan pointed his finger at us. "Get those cars off the street—now!" We pulled our cars into the breakdown lane. "You look hurt young man. Did she do that to you?" I shook my head.

"I'm pressing charges," said Crispin.

"That poser stole my brother's Fender. It's in his bedroom. I can prove that."

"If you two don't keep your mouths shut, you'll both be spending the night with me." Chief Swan pulled out his report pad. He turned to Wardwell. "Now what happened?"

"They're both lying, officer," said Raina. "They're embarrassed to tell the truth 'cause they're weaklings. We were followed out of Quick Mart by some guys on the Tufts football team. They made a crack about my jacket so I flipped them off. When the light turned red, they hopped out of their car and jumped us. We did the best we could, but there were six of them."

"Well why didn't you say so earlier. Did you get a license plate?"

"I think so, yeah." Raina looked at me. "129496B Illinois. It may have been 129496D. I'm not sure."

Chief Swan scribbled the plate numbers on his pad. "What type of car was it? How 'bout the color?"

"A black Dodge," I said.

"What direction did they go?" asked Chief Swan.

Crispin pointed east. "Down Mass Ave towards Medford." "Do I need to call an ambulance?"

"I'm all right," I said, hiding my arm.

"So am I," said Crispin, flipping dreadlocks from his eyes.

Chief Swan pointed to the Audi. "I want those brake lights fixed immediately—the windshield too. If you don't and I see you on the road, I'm gonna ticket you."

"I will, officer," said Crispin.

In Chief Swan's cruiser a woman's voice blared over the two-way. "We've got a report of a lost child in Willard's Woods..."

"I've got to take this call." Chief Swan walked to his cruiser and sat in the driver's seat. He spoke into the two-way, then leaned out the window. "And clean up that glass," he called as his cruiser accelerated down Mass Ave.

We looked at each other. Sitting in the Audi, Raina adjusted the rearview mirror, then fixed her mascara.

Crispin inspected his taillights while Wardwell and I kicked the glass cubes and plastic shards into a drain.

* * * *

A few days later I steered a new Chevy van into the parking lot at Grace Chapel. Pastor Mac stood by the entrance.

"Hi, Pastor Mac," I said.

Pastor MacDonald motioned for me to come into his office.

I sat down. "Van's been registered and has a full tank of gas. Here are the keys." I set the keys on Pastor Mac's desk. Then I opened Dad's briefcase and pulled out a clump of papers. "Here's the paperwork."

Pastor Mac studied me for a moment. "What's this I hear about you and Crispin DeGeneres fighting in the middle of the Mass Ave?"

I looked down at my combat boots.

"Smashed his window too. That's no way to behave."

"I know. My Dad's going to kill me, but I'll make it up to him. I'll be fine."

Pastor MacDonald began whistling a tune Aunt Bee used to sing. "And was your brother doing fine?"

"No, but I'm different. I'm not somebody's problem. I'm not a charity case people have to worry about. I'm not..."

Pastor Mac began shaking his head. "You've got to give them to him."

"To who—Donk?"

"You've got to give them to *Him*."

"Give what?"

"All those suitcases you're carrying. He can take them right from your hand, but you've got to ask him."

"I can carry them myself."

"Nobody can carry his suitcases all by himself. But if you ask Jesus, he can carry all the suitcases this world can pile on." Pastor Mac stood up. "See, light as a pillow. Go ahead, you try."

I stayed in my seat.

"Oh, I'll help you." Pastor Mac walked over and pulled me to my feet.

I lowered my head.

"Why are you looking down? Jesus is up there." Pastor MacDonald pointed towards the sky. "Oh, come on, don't be shy. Ask him."

On the walls, portraits of past clergy stared at me. "Dear Jesus."

Pastor Mac continued: "We ask for your guidance."

"I need some help."

"Because we cannot truly know your will."

"'Cause I can't make it."

"Truth is a blade of grass hidden in an endless field."

I had to think about it. "The world is big and I'm small," I finally said, noticing Pastor MacDonald had perfect hands for the piano.

"That's good. Now ask him."

"I feel stupid."

"Next to him we are. Go ahead."

"Hey, Jesus, if you were driving down the highway and saw me hitchhiking, but your friends didn't like me, would you give me a lift?"

The pastor nodded. "Don't stop. Ask him to take your suitcases."

I only managed to spit out the word 'suitcases.'

"Feel your body rising?" Pastor MacDonald squeezed my shoulders. "Young man, you're tighter than clam, but once you let him in, you'll never feel alone again. I don't— and nobody waits for me. That's the truth. Separated fourteen years and my only kid passed on." Pastor Mac studied my face. "But I have Jesus and he knows how to listen." A fist punched my arm. "Think you're tough enough to lace up the gloves with me?"

I tightened my lips, but the corners moved upwards. "I couldn't hit a minister."

"You don't have to worry 'cause you wouldn't get a shot in."

"Oh, please, I'm faster than Hagler."

A straight right nicked my ear. "Not quick enough for that one."

I held up both fists. "The trouble is, Pastor Mac, I can't decide if I should throw a quick jab or a right hook."

The room filled with laughter. "You sure are a con artist, but don't try to con *him*. If you want to roll with Jesus, you've got to move in just the right way. You've got to take a fierce moral inventory. You've got to come clean to him."

"Tell me, Pastor Mac, why is Jesus at the beach soaking up the rays with a couple cold soldiers while the world's policing itself down here—what's up with that?"

"We need the surprise uppercuts of fate because suffering knocks us off our high horses and brings us back to Jesus."

A likely story. I decided to stop with the wussy punches. "Why doesn't he just tell us? Why does everything have to be a mystery?"

"If there wasn't a mystery, there wouldn't be a purpose."

"Can't he give us a few clues?" I asked.

"Maybe he has, but you weren't listening."

"What does Jesus want from us anyway?"

"Jesus' secret wish is to create a being that can become aware of him."

I chewed my nails. "The gospels were written way after Jesus died. How do we know if Jesus is who they say he is?"

"We don't."

"Then why are you telling me this?" I reached for Dad's briefcase.

"Because in the stadium of shadows, I choose the shadow cast by the fastest runner."

Track 39.

I'm A Bidder

"I suppose you know who has to pay for that car?" said Dad, sitting at his desk. "I do. No way around it. Why'd you have to damage his property? I hate to put notions in your head, but next time wrestle him to the ground. That method's a lot less expensive. We count on local families for repeat business. A Brice destroying someone's car." Dad shook his head. "Doesn't look good."

"Look at what that dirtbag did." I showed Dad the divots in my arm.

"You were lucky. For every hundred stiffs and loud-mouthed jerks, there's always one ex-Marine with nothing to lose. Fallon found out the hard way. He was half-in-the-bag at Doc Grants one time when he mouthed off to a Navy SEAL. In the parking lot the sailor busted Fallon's cheek bone with a kick and proceeded to beat him into a pulp. 'Don't kill me,' Fallon pleaded with the guy. 'I have a wife and kids.'"

"How many Navy SEALs are there?"

"Doesn't matter. All it takes is one. Forget about those whisky-weekend, nutbag gutter-punchers. They're not tough. Real toughness is a lot different than you think. In fact, I've never met a tough person in my life. Have you?" The phone rang. "Brice Chevrolet, can I help you? Just a minute." Dad pressed the intercom button. "Hey Fallon,

~ 294 ~

Dottie's on line one." Dad put the handset back on the ringer. "Crispin was one of Donny's friends. Why'd you pick a fight with him?"

"That maggot stole Donk's guitar, and until I get it back, he's gonna have to carry around a suitcase of weapons."

"Do you mean this beat up thing?" Dad slid open his closet. Inside, Donk's Telecaster leaned against an old metal safe.

"How'd you get it?"

"Crispin dropped it off this morning."

I picked up Donk's Telecaster and checked the neck for cracks.

"Now don't you think you owe someone an apology?" asked Dad.

With natural harmonics, I began tuning Donk's Telecaster.

Dad studied my face. "Do you remember the time you borrowed the Pushkoff's tent and left it on the porch all winter? In the spring it got so moldy I thought it was a leopard's skin."

Pulling a pick from my wallet, I strummed a new chord progression I'd been messing with.

"Georgia DeGeneres has been a loyal customer for years. I suppose you know what this means?"

"Yeah, Saturday morning at eight with a coat and tie." My fingers moved up the neck.

"No, Wednesday morning at seven and don't be a minute late. We're going to Arcadia Auctions." Dad stood up and walked into the showroom.

I put down Donk's guitar and followed Dad. "We are? Awesome." I took out an old NADA price guide from my back pocket. "I've been studying the mileage tables. I can help you bid on sleds."

Dad inspected the prospect log. "It takes years to learn the wholesale racket."

Buy (bī), *v.* **1.** To acquire something by paying an accepted price. **2.** To negotiate a purchase. **3.** To obtain by giving any kind of recompense: *to buy favor with flattery.* **4.** To procure as a result of something done, literally or figuratively; to get at the cost: **a.** *To buy victory with blood.* **b.** *Buy the truth and sell it not. Prov. Xxiii.23.* **5.** To hire the services of: *The Red Sox bought a new first baseman.* **6. a.** To accept or believe an idea or point of view. **b.** To be deceived by an idea or point of view: *He bought the story, hook, line, and sinker.* **7.** *Theology;* To redeem or ransom a person's soul. **8.** *Cards;* To draw or be dealt a card. **9.** To acquire through devious means: *The governor bought the election.* **10.** *Slang;* Buy it: To get killed: *He bought it at Cold Harbor.* **11.** *Slang;* Buy off: To get rid of a claim by a payment; to influence to compliance or cause to yield through a bribe or consideration. **12.** Buy out: To secure all of a partner's shares or interest in a business. **13.** Buy in: **a.** To acquire shares of stock in a business or membership to an organization by paying a sum of money. **b.** To buy back one's own possessions at auction. **14.** *British slang;* Buy up: to purchase as much as one can. **15.** Buy on credit: to purchase on a promise or contract to make payment at a future date. [*OE Buggen, biggen. Goth. Bugjan. AS. Bycgan.*]
Buy 2 (bī), *n.* **1.** *U.S. informal;* a sensible purchase, a bargain; *That guitar was a real buy.* **2.** Anything bought.

That Wednesday Dad walked downstairs to the kitchen for breakfast.

"Where's Kuba?"

Mom poured Dad a cup of coffee. "Rushed out the door a half-hour ago. Didn't even finish his cereal."

"That Philadelphia lawyer." Dad reached into the closet and grabbed his coat.

"What about your coffee?"

Mug in hand, Dad hurried down the walk.

Dad's car pulled in front of the showroom. He waved me over. "Thought you stiffed me. Hop in."

"How many sleds we going to buy?" I asked as Dad's car pulled onto Mass Ave.

"We'll see. If the sleds are bringing telephone numbers, I won't buy any."

"I'm bidding on a sled," I said.

"You better not."

"I'm going to stand in front of the auctioneer and nod. 'Five-thousand?' Yup. 'Fifty-two?' Yup. 'Fifty-four?' Yup. 'Fifty-six?' Yup. Yup. Yup. Yup. I'm going to nod until the other dealers stop bidding and go home. Then they'll know who the big wahoo is."

Dad's belly jiggled. "I'm warning you."

At Arcadia, the auctioneer, Jeb Cardelli, covered his microphone with a hanky. "You won't want to miss this one, fellas," said Jeb as a lobster-red Camaro slowed to a stop in front of the podium. "One-owner, rally wheels, bucket seats, sun-roof." He lowered his voice. "It's got everything but a satellite dish." A cluster of buyers inspected the Camaro.

Sliding into the driver's seat, I shifted the clutch and revved the engine. "Transmission's tight. No music in the engine. I'm going as high as fifty-eight hun. This whore will fly off our lot."

Dad checked his price guide. "Soft like your mother. You don't buy hotrods this late in the year. They'll collect snow for three months while First Trust collects interest. You've got to follow the seasons."

"But if we wait until June, we'll pay an extra-G at the mill," I said.

"Okay, fellas, where do you wanna start? Hibady dibady, dibady hibady, hibady dibady. Give me four grand. Do I hear thirty-five?"

Stepping in front of the Camaro, legs spread like he was riding a horse, Skip Lee raised three fingers.

"Three grand and go. Thirty-two? Hibady dibady, hibady dibady dibady."

A dealer raised her card.

"Thirty-two. Thirty-four?"

Skip nodded.

Whirling in weathervane motion, the auctioneer's arm swung from bid to bid: "Thirty-six, thirty-eight, four grand, forty-two, forty-four. Forty-six?"

Skip nodded.

"Forty-eight?"

A man wearing sunglasses held up his card.

"Hibady dibady, dibady hibady, hibady dibady. Five grand, fifty-two, fifty-four, fifty-six. Fifty-eight?"

Skip shook his head.

"Come on, Skip, it's got a sunroof."

With his hand, Skip made a cutting motion.

"Fifty-seven. Fifty-eight?" The auctioneer looked at me. I raised my hand.

"No, no." Dad whacked my arm. "He's with me."

"Galvin!" called the auctioneer. "Are you gonna let the horses out of the barn? Fifty-eight?"

Dad shook his head, then pulled me aside: "I thought I told you I was going to do the bidding?"

"But I listened to the engine."

"You've got to work your way up. I started cleaning the crapper in sixth grade. In junior high I reconned beat-up trades. By the time I got to high school, I was doing oil changes and selling on weekends. I didn't get to bid on sleds till the day after my old man's wake."

"I'm not waiting a hundred years." I raised my hand.

"Put that hand down." Dad whacked my stomach. I grabbed my gut.

"Get this piece of iron out of here." The auctioneer pressed the garage door opener. "Hibady dibady, dibady hibady, dibady hibady."

"It takes years to figure out the auctioneer's tricks. Where are you going? Hey, Kuba, get back here." Dad followed me. Skip Lee looked over. Dad grabbed my arm. "Face me when I'm talking to you."

"Gordo, are you in the game?" The auctioneer pointed his bony finger.

The man wearing sunglasses shook his head.

"Fifty-seven going once?"

"If you can't behave, I'm going to have to ask you to sit in the cafeteria with the other drivers," said Dad.

"Going twice?"

"No," I said, yanking my arm free. "I'm not driving any more sleds back to your dealership. Do you hear me?"

Dad's eyes widened.

"I am not a lot boy. I'm a bidder."

The auctioneer slapped the podium with his jockey stick. "Sold to Lee Ford for fifty-seven hundred."

Skip Lee strolled to the podium and signed the transfer of ownership papers.

The Crossbar Chimed

After getting blown out by Brockton and barely escaping Bedford with a come-from-behind 15-14 win, Merriam Hill High surprised the heck out of everyone by going on a 10-0 tear. In a sick 44-20 win over Concord, Wardwell threw three touchdowns with a sprained wrist. During the streak I kicked nine field goals in thirteen tries, but blew a ton of point-after attempts. So in practice Coach Brewer fired up his chainsaw each time I lined up to kick. "If you can't control your mind, you can't control your body," he'd yell, revving up his chainsaw. At first I muffed every kick, but I quickly learned to retreat deep inside my body to a place no one else could go. That did the trick 'cause I bagged my next twelve kicks.

One team stood between us and the Middlesex League crown: Woburn, unbeaten, untied, and a bunch of whackos. We heard their linebacker Fernandez could bench a Volkswagen. Their receiver Dale "the giggler" Strout was a piece of art. Each time he caught a pass, Strout took off down the sidelines laughing-his-butt-off till he was tackled.

On game day the wind blew dead oak leaves across Danforth Field. Merriam Hill fans in blue and gold hats and scarves packed the stands. Across the field Woburn fans wore red and black.

The game was a bath of blood and dirt. The lead changed hands six times. With 1:38 left, Merriam Hill held on to a four-point lead.

The Woburn quarterback placed his hands between the center's legs. "Sixty-three, mailbox, twenty-nine, see-saw. Ready? Hike one, hike two, hike three—hut, hut, hut." The center snapped the football. Strout took off down the sidelines. Hurrying backwards, the quarterback faked a handoff, and fired a pass downfield. Strout and DeSilva leaped for the ball. In the air the ball bounced off DeSilva's helmet. Strout snatched it. Giggling all the way, he ran into the end zone.

The sound of a crashing surf erupted in the Woburn stands. But the Woburn kicker missed the point-after. The scoreboard flashed: Merriam Hill 19, Woburn 21.

On the next kickoff Tossy hauled in the punt, faked left, then took off right. A would-be tackler flew past Tossy. Behind two blockers, Tossy huck-n-bucked down the sidelines: "Tossy at the eighteen, twenty, twenty-five, thirty, thirty-five, forty," the announcer yelled. A Merriam Hill player roll blocked a defender. Tossy streaked past the defender. "Fifty, forty-five, forty..." Merriam Hill fans rose to their feet. But three Woburn players climbed on Tossy's back and rode him into the turf at the thirty-six.

On the sidelines the offense huddled around Coach Brewer. "Just what we needed." Coach Brewer slapped Tossy's butt and glanced down at his clipboard. "Okay, sidewinder twelve, tarantula, and flea twenty-three. You could run them in your sleep. Now it's time to execute." The players held hands and collapsed towards the middle. "We've got a little-under-a-minute left, so every hundredth-of-a-second counts. Now go out there and take the Middlesex League crown."

"I yoha-eye ye. I nisto niwo ni. Ahe e ye," I yelled as our offense ran onto the field. Coach Brewer pulled Wardwell aside and went over last-second adjustments.

"Thirty-three, sixty-eight, twenty-nine, sidewinder twelve." Wardwell placed his hands between the center's legs. "Ready, hike one, hike two—hut, hut, hut." Hurrying backwards, Wardwell shoved the ball into Tossy's gut. Tossy ran behind a blocker. The blocker slipped. Tossy lowered his helmet and tried to bullrush a defender. The defender dropped Tossy at the thirty-eight.

Merriam Hill players hurried to the line of scrimmage. Wardwell leaned over the offensive line and studied the defense. "Twenty-six, sixty-three, tarantula." He rocked forwards and back. "Hike one, hike two—hut, hut, hut." Taking two steps back, Wardwell pump-faked, then took off downfield. Just before being hit, Wardwell shovel-passed the ball to Tossy. Tossy caught the pass, tripled-faked, then sprinted down the sidelines. A defender wrapped his arms around Tossy 's legs, bringing him down at the twenty-nine. Tossy stayed on the ground holding his right knee. The ref called a timeout.

Our offense trotted onto the field with twelve seconds left. "Thirty-eight, sixty-eight, twenty-nine, flea twenty-three." Wardwell crouched down. "Ready, hike one, hike two, hut, hut, hut." Hurrying backwards, Wardwell scanned the field. A Merriam Hill receiver streaked towards the end zone. The football spiraled through the air. The receiver leaped to make the catch. Fernandez lowered his shoulder. The receiver somersaulted through the air. The ball skidded across the grass. Merriam Hill fans stayed in their seats. Woburn fans jumped up and cheered.

Coach Brewer studied his clipboard. Three seconds remained on the clock. He looked up at the goalposts. The flags on top of each post fluttered. "Get out there Tossy and run a slant sixty-eight."

As Tossy walked onto the field his knee buckled. Wardwell steadied him.

"Get back here. One damn title isn't worth you never walking again." Coach Brewer looked over at the practice net as I booted a ball into the net. "Okay Brice—get out there and punch one home."

I trotted onto the field. A man in a Chevy jacket and a chestnut-haired girl watched from the sidelines.

Woburn fans chanted, "Miss, miss, miss, miss, miss, miss, miss..."

On my knees I flattened grass and smoothed dirt where the ball was going to be set, but secretly I was praying my pants off. "Dear whoever's-out-there, sorry I'm a faithless nutcase, but right now I could use some help 'cause I'm having trouble trying to rise by the lift of my own sneakers."

"Don't listen to them," said Wardwell. "Watch your foot actually kick the ball—and follow through. A stiff wind's blowing left to right so I'd aim for the left post. But if the wind slows when you're kickin', you might want to aim closer to the middle. Ready, Brice?" Wardwell got down on one knee.

I nodded, placed my foot behind the ball, took three steps back, then one sideways.

"Ready, hike one, hike two, hike three," Wardwell yelled.

The center snapped the ball. As I stepped towards the ball, the canals in my ears closed. Noises from the fans and players softened to a swishing sound. Woburn players rushed me as if under water. I noticed hundreds of tiny dimples on the football. Wardwell caught the ball and set it at a one o'clock slant. I planted my left foot beside the ball and swung my right leg forwards. My cleat struck the ball. My calves, quads, and abdomen fired in unison. The ball flew off into the air. In the stands people stood on their seats. The ball tumbled through the gray sky, hooking away from the left post. I leaned right trying to will the ball back. A gust of wind whistled through my mask and straightened out the ball's path. The ball tumbled towards the left post. Silence wove through the crowd like a scarf. The flags fluttered faster, but it was too late. The ball would hit the post and Merriam Hill would lose to Woburn for the third straight year. It would definitely hit. In the parking lot a horn beeped. At least it was *near* a field goal. At least there had been a chance, an illusion of winning. The ball flew at the post. Maybe if I lied to myself and acted like we won, it would lighten the darkness to come? But it never worked. I can't control my own mind. On the field, the dead leaves lifted into tiny twisters. Helmut in trunk, I would drive home. Mom would say it didn't matter. But it did. I had the chance not to suck, but instead knit the same old knot of *almost*. I leaned further right, bumping into my teammate. Wardwell was a total douche. He told me to aim left. No, I was the total douche. I listened. A chime sounded as the ball banged the inside of the left post. It was *me*. Always underselling myself. Never winning 'cause it was safer to float and lose than take off my life vest and swim. I knew the wind wouldn't push a football four feet—so why did I listen? But the ball didn't bounce straight out. Not even close. It bounced sixty degrees to the right and fell towards the crossbar. I leaned forward. In the stands Pushkoff stood on his seat. Coach Brewer squeezed his clip board. Why hadn't I practiced more? Rummaged through libraries for impossible-to-find books from forgotten placekickers offering cryptic techniques? A gust of wind whipped across

Danforth Field and pushed against my back as the ball hit the top of the crossbar and bounced through the uprights for the winning score.

Merriam Hill fans flooded onto the field. Wardwell grabbed my waist and lifted me up. A wave of Merriam Hill players knocked us over and piled on top of us. I couldn't breath. When I got up, the sky, the school, the stands, our uniforms were a new color. Even the grass seemed alive.

Walking off the field, I searched for a Chevy jacket. Someone called my name. I turned around. It was Noy with her mom's perfume on. Her boobs pushed against my body. Her hair splashed against my face as I kissed her boiling watery warm-wet mouth. We walked off the field hand-in-hand. In my chest a tiny salmon chamber hummed for the first time.

"You really showed them today, Brice," said Coach Brewer, carrying his first aid box. "But what will you use for an excuse now?"

The Yo-Yo Balance Sheet

After showering in the locker room, I walked to my car. In the parking lot I dropped my gear into the trunk. A Mustang slowed to a stop. Wardwell leaned out the window. "We're having a little get-together tonight at Tossy's, you coming?"

At Tossy's house the Neighborhoods played "Out Of Your Reach" in the basement. I was in the kitchen trading tongues with Noy when partygoers began counting: "five, six, seven, eight, nine, ten, eleven..."

In the den two kids held DeSilva by the ankles above a keg. DeSilva gripped the keg with both hands. Wardwell held the nozzle in DeSilva's mouth. "Fifteen, sixteen, seventeen, eighteen, nineteen, twenty..." Tossy pumped the tap like a psycho. Beer dribbled out the corners of DeSilva's mouth.

"He's gonna lose it," a kid shouted.

DeSilva's face grew pale. "Twenty-four, twenty-five, twenty-six, twenty-seven, twenty-eight..." He was trying to beat Donk's record. The counting grew louder: "Thirty-two, thirty-three, thirty-four, thirty-five..." The whole party jammed into the den. "Thirty-eight, thirty-nine, forty, forty-one, forty-two, forty-three...," kids counted in unison. "Fifty-one, fifty-two, fifty-" Beer exploded from DeSilva's mouth and out his nostrils. Wardwell pulled the nozzle from his mouth. The two kids released his ankles.

~ 306 ~

DeSilva stood up and pumped his fists. "I'm the new keg stand king." He high-fived partygoers.

Just then my ears started to ring. The couch, chairs, rug, keg—every dumb physical thing—was floating in a sea of space.

DeSilva booked-it to the porch. A stream of gold liquid flowed from his mouth. Tossy followed with a wastebasket. The party erupted with cheers.

"Disqualified." "Lightweight." "Donk's record still stands."

What? They were saying *his* name. Donk was growing bigger, pinning me to the mat without lifting a finger. I walked out to the porch. "You alright, DeSilva?"

On his knees DeSilva leaned over the wastebasket. "Yeah, I'm okay. Almost had your brother beat, but I tried to pad the record by a few seconds and lost it."

There *he* was again. Donk pulled the eject lever way too soon, but still secured the win. What about me? Nine hours ago I launched an air sculpture into the sky and still I'm on stuck on Tossy's porch waiting to exist.

"Hey buddy, did I say something wrong?"

I shook my head.

DeSilva stood up and wiped his hands on his pants. "Ease up. Tonight's our night. We're Middlesex League champs."

I looked away.

"I bet your brother's record will outlast Pushkoff's rushing record."

"Do you know how you can tell if an engine block's cracked?"

"No."

"You look under the oil cap for white gunk. When you're buying a used sled, do you know how to factor in depreciation?"

DeSilva shook his head.

"You subtract three-hun for every 5,000 miles. I'm still in high school and I'm already bidding on sleds at Arcadia Auction."

"That's pretty cool," said DeSilva.

"I know all about the auctioneer's tricks. Auctioneers try to get dealers to compete with each other, so they'll bid a ton more than a sled's worth. So I set a ceiling for each sled *before the first* bid." Outside, two girls walked up the driveway towards the party.

"Is that right," said DeSilva, checking out the talent.

I nodded and killed my soldier. "I can tally up all the options without cracking a price guide: eight-hun for an automatic, buck-and-a-half for a roof rack, four-hun for a sunroof, buck-and-a-hee for cruise, two Ben Franklins for a CD player. But still I ask them, and they refuse."

"Who?" asked DeSilva. "Hey Spaz, let's go back inside and kill the keg—you and me."

"I'd never lowball customers just to get the sale. I'd sell myself. I wouldn't waste my time sending out fake checks. I'd rent the circus and hold the sale of the century. I'd tell them, 'set up the bigtop, fellas, right in the parking lot.' All those elephants standing on their hind legs and trapeze artists. We'd roll sixty sleds in one day. But still I ask them, and they refuse."

"Hey, there's your sister. Hey Raina?" DeSilva waved Raina over. "Make sure he gets home alright." DeSilva merged back into the party.

My sister opened the screen door. "What are you doing out here, Spaz?"

"You've heard "Soul Rocket," haven't you?"

Raina nodded.

"Who wrote it?"

"You did."

"That's right. I wrote it, not Donk. It's the first rock song in the whole friggin' state to use freeform in every section without trashing the melody. What about the chorus in "Wake Up You're The One"—it's a triple-chorus."

"I didn't notice."

"They didn't either. I'm going to walk up to them and make them say it. I'm going to walk right up to them and make them admit that I'm as good as Donk."

Raina put her hand on my shoulder. "I think you are."

"If they won't say it, I'm going to sit there and play my songs till they tell me why."

"Until *who* tells you why?"

"I'll play all week till the fret board's painted with my blood until they tell me why."

"Why what?" asked Raina.

"Why didn't they love me the way they loved Donk?"

"Come on, Spaz, people are looking." Raina poured part of her soldier into my empty cup. "Here, take a sip. It's just that when you're the first born a special bond forms. It's like the first kiss that somehow sneaks through all your barricades and touches something deep in your gut."

"But I can tally up all the options?"

* * * *

At Brice Chevrolet a Honda Accord pulled into a *Customers Only* parking space. A woman in a gray suit got out.

"What's she doing here?" Dad hurried into Connie's office. "She's supposed to be here on Friday." Dad slid

~ 309 ~

open a drawer, took out a stack of deals, and shoved them in his briefcase. "Give me that." Dad pointed to the accounts receivable ledger. He snapped his briefcase shut. "Tell her I've gone to lunch." Quickly, Dad walked through the Service Department. A bay door opened. Dad drove off in the parts truck.

At home Dad set his briefcase on the kitchen counter.

"What are you doing home at this hour?" asked Mom, gripping a potato peeler. "You look awful."

Dad opened his briefcase and removed three pill bottles. "The yo-yo balance sheet—that's what it's called and I'm screwed."

"The yo-yo what?"

Dad tipped a pill bottle. A yellow pill dropped into his palm.
"When a customer buys a sled with cash or check, by law we're supposed to pay off the floorplanned amount next business day. But sometimes we don't have enough cash-on-hand to make payroll, so we get a little free mileage off the customer's dough by depositing the check into our account. A week or so later, we pay off the floorplanned amount with the help of another customer's check."

Mom nervously peeled a potato. "Why have you been doing that?"

"'Cause customers have been rarer than dodo birds. Our cash-on-hand is nil. We're floorplanning our entire inventory. Someone ought to whack that bloodsucker Volker." Dad popped the pill into his mouth and swallowed. "So First Trust notices that our customers are registering their sleds a week before we're paying them off so I've got a bean counter camped out in my office right now."

Mom stopped peeling. "What are you going to do?"

"Don't know." Dad pulled the stack of deals from his briefcase. "Can't re-date months of paperwork in a forty-five minutes."

At Merriam Hill High I knocked on Coach Brewer's door. "Hey, Coach, you wanted to see me?"

"Oh yeah." Coach rummaged through his filing cabinet. "I want you to fill these out." He handed me a clump of college applications. "If you don't want to, then to hell with you 'cause there's plenty who would. Take your SATs yet?"

I shook my head.

"Well you better. There's one in Cambridge next week. Here." He handed me an SAT form. "I want this postmarked today. And don't go out partying the night before."

I shuffled through the application forms: Plymouth State, Berkley School of Music, Franklin Pierce, Salem State, UNH, Holy Cross, and Dartmouth. "Why do you want me to fill out this one?" I held up the Dartmouth application. "I have a better chance of winning Ted Kennedy's Senate seat than getting into that snobatorium."

"How do you know? Have you ever set foot on the campus?"

"No, but Donk told me some stuff. I can't stand the way those Ivy Leaguers smile all the time—like they're the only ones who know how to be happy. Besides, they chew at football."

"Just fill out the application. You can't kick a field goal if you're not on a team, and the you can't play on a team unless you're attending a college."

"Do they even give scholarships?"

"Don't you worry about that. If you get in, I'll squeeze your pop."

~ 311 ~

"But he's tap city."
Coach Brewer exhaled loudly.

In the garage I filled out the applications. For my essay I wrote about the time I got booted from kindergarten.

Who's In Charge
by Kuba Brice

"Who's in charge here anyway?" I asked my kindergarten teacher after she insisted I join the rest of the class for a reading of Charlotte's Web. Imagine a two-foot high, quarrelsome runt demanding that his kindergarten teacher justify her authority. At five, I was obsessed with finding out the reasons behind adult authority and their irritating rules. If a rule didn't make sense to me—*poof*—the rule vanished from my mind. During a lesson, if I wanted to go home and watch reruns of The Brady Bunch, I simply got up and walked home. If I got bored during story time, I simply strolled to the workbench, grabbed a few pieces of wood, and began hammering and sawing.

"Who do you think's in charge?" principal Como would ask me.

"He is," I said, pointing to the janitor.

The janitor had a mesmerizing array of tools: screwdrivers, tape measurers, all kinds of magic potions, power saws, and a hip existential attitude. He was the natural commander. On his belt, his key chain had hundreds of gleaming keys. No doubt, he could open any door he wanted. During recess, I'd watch him wielding a trowel, filling cracks in the brick school. I only dreamed of so much power. My teachers didn't agree, so I most of kindergarten in Como's office. Who does this joker Como think he is anyway? And who gave him the seeds to nail my power chair to the floor? In late-April I was in the principal's office, staring out the window, when I spotted the janitor high up in an elm tree, sawing off a dead branch.

"He's great. He's great," I shouted, bolting from the principal's office and running down the corridor with the principal hot on my heels.

"Get back here," demanded the principal.

"He's great," I yelled, turning a corner and sprinting towards the metal door.

Unable to stop, I slammed into the metal door, the door flew open, and I ran towards the elm tree so I could see a man floating in the sky.

Needless to say, I was expelled two days later.

These days, I'm obsessed with finding out the reasons behind...

* * * *

At the dealership Mom's wagon stopped in front of the showroom. Dad opened the door and walked to Mom's car. Mom lowered the window. "Any news?"

"She's still in there with Connie." Dad rested his arms on the door. "They've never taken this long."

"How long did the last audit take?"

"Can't remember."

"What if she checks the dates on your deposit slips?"

"They'll reel in my credit line faster than Perlman stiffs Revlon. I'll have to file for Chapter 11." Dad scanned the lot for customers. "We've got to kick start sales. I'm not talking cough drops here. We need major surgery."

Track 43
The Phantom Customers

Around 4 a.m. I kicked off my blankets and walked downstairs.

In the kitchen Dad pounded a calculator and scribbled figures into a ledger. "What are you doing up?"

"Got another fast spell." I opened the fridge. "Closing out the month?"

"Trying. We pulled in 177Gs, but laid out over 200. Those fair-weather friends at First Trust cut our credit line in half. How are we going to sell our way out of this mess with half the cars?"

"What about trimming a few expenses?" I took out a gallon of milk and set it on the table.

Dad studied account payables. "Already down to the bone."

"Maybe you-know-who should go?"

"Fallon would run ten blocks for a crooked nickel rather than walk across the street for an honest dime, but he doesn't cost us much. If he doesn't sell, he doesn't get paid."

I grabbed a cereal box from the cabinet. "He's still on straight commission?"

"How else is he going to have the incentive to sell?"

"Thought he'd be on salary by now."

"You'll see what it's like when you run the shop. Just hope we can hang on till this recession quits. People are starting to use the D-word."

I poured cereal and milk into a bowl.

"Coach Brewer stopped in the other day. Did you know he's a Freemason?"

"Yeah, saw him marching in the Patriots' Day parade," I said, shoveling cereal into my mouth.

"Well every year they hire a circus from Quebec to raise money for the Children's Hospital. It's only 6Gs, plus half the gate. Maybe we should try that circus idea of yours before our new credit line goes into effect?"

"Think so?"

"You're the one who thought it up. Do you?"

"Definitely. All those lions on stools and strong men lifting barbells—we'd make a ton. Customers want to be entertained. They want the high wire act and dancing bears. The everyday stuff blows."

"Then it's a done deal." Dad rapidly tapped the calculator keys. "Stop in at the end of the week and we'll go over the details. We need a huge infusion of cash to keep our garage from going bye-bye."

I put my bowl and spoon in the dishwasher and walked back to my room. Climbing the stairs, my legs felt like I could outrun Ben Johnson.

* * * *

At Brice Chevrolet Fallon poked his head into Dad's office. "Hey, Galvin, this lady wants to see you."

Dad peered through the tinted window in his office. "Tell her I've just started a sales meeting."

Fallon walked outside to Mrs. Pushkoff's Volvo. The Volvo disappeared down Mass Ave.

"What did she want?" I asked.

"Oh nothing—car problems." Dad held up a poster. "Here's the deal. You kids are going to hang up these posters in every supermarket and drycleaners from here to Newburyport. We're going after the mothers. The posters say, 'Each customer who test-drives a vehicle will get two free tickets to the circus—the tightrope walkers, trapeze artists, sword swallowers, lion tamers—the whole shaboom."

"What about their kids?" I asked.

Dad shot me a glance. "Customers who buy a sled will get free tickets for the whole family. Vince Irvine will be here from First Trust ready to approve deals on the spot. I want every customer to drive away on temporary plates or in an ambulance."

"What if they need time to think about it?" I asked.

"Steamroll the *stallers* into buying. This isn't an art museum. Customers don't pay us to gawk at the pretty pictures. If they're only here for the circus, take their name and number, then move on to the real buyers. The second a customer walks into my showroom, I can tell if she's a buyer or not."

"So what you're saying is you're a cherry picker," said Fallon.

"Go climb a skyscraper. I've matched wits with every tire kicker in Middlesex County," said Dad.

"Is that how you outsold Fallon—by taking all the pork chops?" I asked.

Dad's face turned red. "You better watch your step."

"Or was it because your name's on the sign? Buyers always think they're getting a better deal from the owner. You won't have that advantage with me." I flashed my twenty-tooth grin.

Fallon unwrapped his cigar. "I've been telling him that for years. He's an order taker."

"Arrogant punk. You think you can outsell me?" asked Dad.

"Maybe."

"All right. Go ahead and try. On the day of the sale, I'll take one prospect, you take the next. We'll see who ends up with the most checks on the board. Whoever sells the fewest has to lick the dust off the winner's shoes."

"How about this: if I win, I can bid on all the cars at the auction."

Dad thought about it. "Okay, but god help us if you win."

"I'll be the closer," said Fallon.

"We'll close our own deals. I need you on the floor." Dad gave me a noogy. "This nitwit thinks he can outsell me."

"But the boy couldn't close a zipper," Fallon whinnied.

"What I'd really like to learn how to do is to close your mouth," I croaked.

"How are you going to do that?" asked Fallon. "Hire John Hannah?"

"Stuff a boiled potato in it and a few kickbacks from wholesalers, if you know what I mean."

"You dirty son-of-a-" Fallon gave me the once-over. "Hey, Galvin, buy this kid a new pair of shoes. He can't sell in those scraggily lookin' things."

Dad studied my shoes.

I turned to Fallon. "Remember, this garage is bigger than one person. From now on, we'll work the wholesalers together. And when we pull out of this slump, you're on salary, plus commission." I put my pinkie in my mouth, then waved it at Fallon. "Wet Willie?"

Fallon didn't know what to say. He stepped back. "You Brices are all the same—bunch of loony Swedes." He walked over to the coffee machine. "Hey, Junior, how many sugars?"

"No sugar."

"Creamer?"

I shook my head. "Just black."

That night Raina walked into our den. "Mom, do you know where Spaz is?"

Mom sat at her piano with a stack of songs Donk had written in high school. "Try his bedroom."

"Spaz?" Raina knocked on my door. "Have you seen my mic? I'm supposed to lay down a few tracks tonight at Fort Apache and I want to use my own mic." She grabbed the knob. It didn't turn, so she knocked again. "Spaz, open up." Raina waited for a reply, but none came. She walked to the hall closet and grabbed a hanger. Poking the tip of the hanger into the doorknob's hole, she opened the door. On her brother's desk a lamp beamed a cone of light onto an open dictionary. Wind passed through a curtain. She heard a voice, so she climbed out the window. On the cupola someone was having a conversation.

"I told Dad I was gonna outsell him at the circus sale. How am I going to do that?" In Granny Pond a bullfrog replied: *Jug-o-rum, jug-o-rum. Jug-o-rum, jug-o-rum.* "I need to invent a sales technique that charms customers into buying after only one test drive. If I lose, Dad won't let me bid on cars till the next ice age."

Quietly, Raina crawled up to the cupola. Her sneaker loosened a tile. The tile slid off the roof and exploded on the walkway.

My heart jumped in my chest. "Who's there?" I turned around and saw Raina holding the railing. "Jesus, don't sneak up on me like that. I almost fell off the roof."

Raina ducked under the railing. "Who were you talking to?"

"No one."

"Liar."

"Shhh, I'm busy."

"Don't shush me. Tell me who."

I picked up my guitar and began strumming chords to a song I was tinkering with.

Raina frowned. "You were talking to Donk—weren't you?"

"No I wasn't."

"Were too."

"Was not."

"I get it. You don't have the seeds to talk to a real person so you conjure up a ghost 'cause ghosts always listen and can't give you any crap. How lame is that."

Frigginay. My sister was onto something. Phantoms respond just the way you want them to. Real people never do. I strummed a potential chorus to my half-finished song: G, D, DaddG, C, CaddB, C, CaddF#, CaddG, Em, CaddB, D. "Yowza, that's it!"

"What?"

"That's how I'm going to outsell Dad: phantom customers."

"You're cracked."

"Am not."

"Are too."

But I didn't care if was cracked. I strummed my new chorus. A rollercoaster car of neon light swooped down from my head and lit up my chest. This chorus had potential.

* * * *

At Brice Chevrolet, circus workers drilled holes into the tar and inserted tree-sized steel poles. A three-story tent rose up in the parking lot. From a pickup bed, guys tossed bales of hay into the tent. Behind the tent, elephants, lions, zebras, horses, a two-headed goat, and other animals waited in their cages to be fed. Carpenters in rock concert T-shirts assembled wooden booths. Generators hummed as booth attendants plugged in popcorn poppers, snow cone machines, pretzel cookers, caramel mixers, hotdog steamers, and other machines. Inside the tent, green-haired teenagers, tattooed men, and nose-ring-wearing women erected bleachers. Above the bleachers, steel cables crisscrossed the length of the tent. Trapeze swings hung above a safety net. In dressing room trailers, half-naked performers slipped on leopard-skin loincloths, jodhpurs, penguin suits, platinum-blond wigs, sequined skirts, lipsticks glossier than a Corvette's paint job, emerald-green eye shadows, lash thickeners, and rouges worn by girls who hung out in the smoking section of Merriam Hill High. Families formed a line at the entrance that wrapped around the tent. Parked cars on both sides of Mass Ave stretched further than an owl can see, but were they *buyers*? The ringmaster walked through a flap in the tent and began speaking into a megaphone. "Come see the circus. Come see the trapeze artists. Come on in and see." Families began to walk inside the tent.

In the showroom, Dad handed stacks of tickets to Fallon, Raina, and me. "We need to roll at least forty sleds to make payroll and pay down our debt." Dad pointed to a newly installed bell. "See that brass bell over there. When you're finished closing a deal, ring the bell and announce the sale. Then everyone stand up and clap."

"That's corny," said Raina.

"We're not selling tombstones here. Sell the sizzle. Plus, it sends the message: if customers diddle around, the car they want could be gone."

Later that morning a man in a baseball cap walked towards me. "Young man, are you a salesman?"

"Sure am. How can I help you?" I held out my hand. "Name's Kuba Brice."

"Hi." He shook my hand. "Tom Kenny. How much you askin' for that blue van?"

"$8495. Let me grab the keys." In the showroom I unhooked the keys and grabbed a license plate. Outside I began to work the customer. "This van has a 454-four barrel that cranks out 310 net horsepower. You could take a sledge hammer to that engine and it wouldn't quit on you." I noticed Tom's cap had a Little League name on it. "The van also has twelve seatbelts. How many people will you be transporting?"

"I'll be using the van to drive kids to games."

I pointed to the rear seat. "That extra seat costs $800 dollars when you buy it from the factory, but in a used van— it's free."

In his sports jacket, Pushkoff walked over to me. "Hey, pal, what's the price on that van?"

"$8495," I said.

"Not a bad price. Can I take it for a spin?" asked Pushkoff.

"Have a seat in the showroom. I'll call you over soon as this gentleman returns." I concentrated on my customer. "Would you like to take it for a test drive?"

The customer studied the van, then Pushkoff. "Alright."

I handed Tom the keys. "While you're driving, pay attention to the McPherson strut suspension system. It's rated for a ¾-ton pickup and rides smoother than a lovesick cow."

Tom climbed into the front seat. "I certainly don't want the kids bouncing all over the place."

I stuck the license plate on the bumper, then ran around to the passenger side and got in. Tom stepped on the gas. The van turned right onto Mass Ave. When we returned, Pushkoff was waiting. He took the keys straight from Tom's hand, hopped in the driver's seat, and started the engine.

"Would you like to come inside and discuss purchasing the van? I asked.

Tom watched the van disappear down Mass Ave. "Sure."

As we sat down at my desk, I heard clanging. I turned around and saw Dad ringing the bell.

"I'd like to announce that Jewel and Arthur Wardwell are the proud owners of a brand new '87 Caprice wagon." Dad began to clap. We joined in—the showroom shark!

"Are you trading anything in?" I asked, leaning forward in my chair to avoid looking too comfortable.

"No. My other van crapped-the-bed," said Tom.

We haggled back and forth over price. Before I could close the sale, Tom stood up.

"What can I do to earn your business today, Tom?" I asked, keeping eye contact.

"Let me sleep on it and I'll call you Monday."

"With the circus sale going on, this van's going to fly off the lot. Secondhand vans with a third seat are rarer than thirty-pound lobsters."

In walked Pushkoff holding the van keys. "If that van isn't sold, I'll buy it."

Inside the tent a whip unfurled above the elephant trainer's head. An elephant begrudgingly climbed onto its stool.

I clanged the brass bell. "I'd like to announce that Tom Kenny is the proud owner of a gorgeous Chevy Van." Everyone clapped.

Frigginay. It worked. Phantom customers turned *stallers* and *shoppers* into buyers. People needed to see the warm blood pumping and the game unfolding before their very eyes. Even *tire kickers* could be strong-armed into buying because they sensed deep in their bones that something was going to be taken away and never given back. I admit, there are zillions of cars, but no dealer had the exact sleds Brice Chevrolet did. Mrs. Tossy, Mr. Kenny, the Wardwells, Quimbys, and Kings—they all had reasons to buy *today*. And buy they did. I was going to win.

But then I heard Dad working a husband and wife. "I don't know if we can." Dad coughed nervously. "I'll go pull the invoice and see how close we are to cost." Dad reappeared with a folder. "But I'd like to earn your business." He rapidly tapped a calculator. "I've got First Trust on my doorstep demanding payment for a dozen titles."

That's when I saw the eddies swirling across Dad's face. He was letting the couple beat him up for a lower price, lower than a fair profit would allow. Across his forehead he emoted the brushwork of bankruptcy, the eye flutter of recession, the hunched posture of a small business vanishing. Dad was *telecasting*. The price began to rise. The wife stopped nervously petting her husband's leg. Dad kept his arms low to protect his ribs. "This Federal deficit is sending interest rates to the moon and tripling our carrying costs." The price rose further. The husband walked outside and inspected the car again. The wife exhaled. The husband walked in. Dad got up and clanged the bell.

Inside the tent an acrobat somersaulted through the air. A man on the trapeze reached out and caught her.

On the front lot a guy in a leather vest checked out a Camaro. Before he could climb back in his truck, I flagged him down. We shook hands.

"Is this the color you want?" I asked.

He nodded. "Wife likes red."

"How about mileage? This bad boy's got 47K."

"A bit high," the guy said, "but if they were highway miles."

"Like the T-top?"

"Yeah, definitely."

After asking a few more questions, I shut up and let the guy talk. Then we went on a test drive. When we returned, I had him park the Camaro in front of the showroom. Then I asked the guy inside. We walked to my desk.

Through the showroom window, while my customer watched, Pushkoff scrutinized every inch of the Camaro. He popped the hood, tasted the motor oil, revved the 3.6 liter engine, even took off the sunroof panels.

"You have first dibs," I told the guy.

"Tell you what." The guy pulled out his checkbook. "Throw a CD player in and it's a done deal."

The bell rang in G-major.

"How should I handle this do-nothing?" Fallon asked Dad. "I've been trying to sell Molly Alsup a car for three months. Finally, we've got a used car she likes and can afford and now she thinks I'm trying to send my kids to Boston College on her back."

Dad dusted dandruff off his shoulder. "You take it away from them. Drive the sled she wants behind the garage and drive back out in a real rat. After she pukes her guts out, she'll appreciate what she had enough to unlock her purse."

Fallon strolled back to his desk, grabbed the keys, and drove the car Molly was grinding him over behind the garage. Then he drove a lime-colored Yugo with a pretzel bumper and 134,000 miles in front of the showroom and parked it. "We could definitely get this Yugo in your price range," he told Molly.

A few minutes later, Fallon walked to the bell and clanged it with his knuckle. Raina, Dad, and I stood up and cheered as if Churchill had just delivered his "We shall fight in the hills" speech.

"A good salesperson lets customers make their own comparisons," said Dad between claps.

A hush swept through the tent as a woman in a sequined dress rode a bicycle thirty feet in the air across a steel cable.

At 4:51 p.m. the sales board read: thirteen checks for Dad, thirteen for me, eleven for Fallon, and seven for Raina. I needed one more.

Outside, a man with sideburns emerged from the tent and headed towards the new trucks. At the same time a beat-up Chevette slowed to a stop by the new cars. A woman, maybe a girl, got out. She opened the hatchback and took out a stroller. From the backseat, she retrieved a baby and snapped him into the stroller. The baby wore a white hat with a crescent visor. Dad hurried out the showroom door. So did I. Dad veered towards the man, so I veered towards the woman. "Hi, I'm Kuba Brice." I held out my hand to the girl.

She wheeled the stroller past my hand down the row of cars.

"Hi, I'm Ellen." She pointed to her child. "This is Donny. We need a new car. I'm tired of borrowing jumper cables from my neighbor." She stopped in front of a station wagon.

"This is a Cavalier RS." I tapped the passenger's door. "Each door is reinforced with steel. Very safe for kids."

She inspected the door.

"What type of transmission do you want?"

"I hate having to constantly shift gears."

"Need air conditioning?"

"No." She studied her baby. "I mean, yes."

"What's your favorite color?"

"I was thinking blue, maybe green."

I scanned the lot. In the corner was a teal-green wagon. After directing the customer to the wagon, I hurried inside and grabbed the keys and a plate. We strolled around the car. I slid my hand across the hood. "Car's got chip-resistant paint. Keeps it looking new. Go ahead, touch it."

Ellen slid her finger across the hood.

I knelt down and set my hand on a tire. "All-season steel-belted radials. They really hug the road. Great for winter driving." I pointed inside the wheelwell. "Rear antilock brakes too. When you jam on the brakes, your car won't skid off the road." I stood up and opened the driver's door. "Cloth seats with lumbar support. Great for the back. Go ahead, sit down."

Ellen sat down.

Pushkoff drove up in his car and lowered the window. "Excuse me, is that the only teal-green Cavalier you've got?"

I nodded.

"Still available?"

"I'm showing it now."

"Sold out everywhere. Call me if it doesn't sell." Pushkoff handed me one of his Dad's business cards.

"Sure." After a test drive, I led Ellen to my desk and brought her a coffee. I pointed to her baby. "Would he like some water?"

Ellen shook her head.

"What price range are you shooting for?"

"My grandma told me not to tell you."

Her grandmother's paying for the car, I thought. "Your grandmother sounds really nice."

Ellen looked at me funny. "She is. We live together. What would my monthly payments be?"

"Depends on how much you're putting down."

Ellen looked away. In his stroller Donny held a stuffed animal tightly.

"Most people come up with tax, title, and doc," I said.

"Let's try that."

My fingers tapped the calculator. "With tax, title, and doc for a down, you're looking at $332.55 per month for four years."

"Can't afford that. I was hoping to be closer to $250. My take-home pay is $255 a week." Ellen blushed. "I wasn't supposed to tell you that either."

"$250 is kind of low for a new car, but I'll see what I can do." My fingers tapped the calculator. "If I drop your interest rate to 8.9% and spread the loan out over five years your payments would be $267.19."

Ellen looked over the figures. "Can I call my grandma?"

"Of course." I slid my phone over to Ellen.

When I returned from the bathroom, she was waiting.

"Guess I can live with that." Ellen combed her baby's hair with her fingers. "Won't be a CNA forever. I'm going to nursing school. Anyway, you seem honest. My grandmother told me to bring home the paperwork and she'll cosign."

That was it? She wasn't going to ask me to knock off six-hundred bucks? I could easily do that. What about the interest rate? I could go as low as 6.9%. A clanging sound filled my ears. I turned around and saw Dad ringing the cowbell.

"Everyone take a moment to congratulate Alex Fisher who's the proud owner of a brand new Chevrolet truck." Dad put his arm around the customer.

"Good decision." I took a buyer's order from the desk and began filling it in. "When will you finish nursing school?"

"In three years, hopefully. With this little guy, I can barely handle two classes a semester."

"Oh." I lifted my pen from the buyer's order. What if Ellen never became a nurse? How would she make payments? I glanced over at the sales board. But if I didn't sell her a sled, some snake at Lee Ford would. "How much deposit would you like to leave?"

"Can I write you a check for $100?"

"We usually like 3%. Can you leave $400?"

Ellen looked away. "I don't get paid till next Friday."

At the sales board Dad added a fourteenth check by his name.

"$100 is fine." I took Ellen's check. As I finished filling out the buyer's order, I felt Donny staring at me. "He's a cute kid," I said, patting him on the head. He began to cry.

Ellen slid a pacifier into his mouth. "There you go. He's not used to being around so many men."

Inside the tent a lion tamer walked towards a lion sitting on a red platform. The lion opened its mouth. The tamer lowered his head into the lion's mouth. Gasps sounded in the audience.

"Buy a rat and drive it into the ground," I said.

"What?"

"A new vehicle loses 25% of its value—just by driving it off the lot. Buy a beater and drive it till the engine seizes."

"I'm sick of driving beaters."

"Join AAA. Do you want to cough up $267 every month for five years? After four years your car will be worth a few hundred bucks, but you'll still owe five-grand."

Ellen's eyes narrowed. "What kind of salesman are you anyway."

"Can't change your mind. Banks don't let people return cars."

"I don't know what trick you're trying to pull, but I want you to stop."

"I drive a beat-up Chevelle." I pointed to my car, parked beside the dumpster. "I have zero payments. I love it."

"How quaint."

"Take a few days to think it over. I can get another teal-green wagon in ten minutes."

"I don't have to take this." Ellen grabbed her check off my desk and began wheeling the stroller towards the door. She turned around. "I'm never coming back."

"Sorry you feel that way," I said, dropping the buyer's order into the trash.

Dad walked over. "What happened?"

"Oh nothing, just some cheapskate trying to chisel me down below cost."

"Why didn't you bring me in on the deal?" asked Fallon.

"I was about to. Then, she flipped out."

Fallon studied my face. "Next time, send me a signal. Your father used to drop his pen on the floor."

Outside, circus workers unhitched steel cables. The tent collapsed. A flatbed drove up. The workers pulled the poles from the tar and stacked them on the flatbed. They folded up the tent and loaded it on top of the poles. Then, the workers strapped the tent to the bed. A black cloud spewed out the exhaust pipe as the flatbed accelerated down Mass Ave.

After the last customer left the showroom, Fallon locked the door.

I looked up at the sales board, then back at Dad. "You beat me fair and square. Guess I'll never get to bid on cars."

Dad studied the sales log. "Any ding-a-ling can bid on cars, but not too many people can sell." He glanced over at Pushkoff, then back at me. "Maybe we should hire him too," Dad said, shaking his head. "We just might be able to ride out this recession after all."

Track 44

The Ball Skipped Past Buckner's Glove[1]

(The Wilderness)

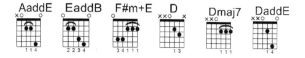

But on Monday morning Vince Irvine walked into our showroom with a couple lawyers and a court probate. "Sorry, Galvin, but you owe First Trust $266,310 which was given to you in good faith by customers to payoff all existing liens, including our floor plan. You failed to do so. Now we've got irate customers threatening lawsuits because they can't register their new vehicles until those liens are paid off. I'm authorized by the state of Massachusetts to collect this debt immediately or First Trust has the legal right to claim ownership of Brice Chevrolet at noon today and seek payment through the auction of your assets." Mr. Irvine handed Dad the court order.

Our circus sale had netted $71,940 so Dad frantically spun his Rolodex in search of untapped lines of credit, but as Mr. Irvine had guessed, the amount of unpaid liens was far larger than $266,310 and all of Dad's credit lines had been exhausted. So at 12:01 p.m. Dad handed over the keys to his dealership, the company checks, and all his credit cards to the court probate, making First Trust the new owner of Brice Chevrolet.

While Dad cleaned out his desk, Aunt Bee walked into the back office.

"May I help you?" asked Connie.

"Yes, I left some personal papers in one of the filing cabinets. I'll just be a minute."

"Legally, I'm not allowed to let you touch any files." Connie stood up. "I'll look for you."

"Oh, nonsense." Bee rushed past Connie towards a filing cabinet and slid open the top drawer. She removed a document from her blouse and held it up to Connie. "See. It's my birth certificate."

"Well, I'll be damned. Never saw that before." Connie went back to her typewriter.

"My father kept a personal file. I'll just be a minute." Bee opened a file and flipped through the documents. "Just want to make sure we don't leave any keepsakes behind." She removed three life insurance policies and slipped them into her purse. "Bye, Connie." Bee walked into the showroom. Stopping in front of a framed photograph of Dad with Tony Conigliaro, Bee unhooked the frame from the wall, carried it out to her car, and drove off.

Two weeks later, Aunt Bee walked into the showroom at Lee Ford. "Hello Skip, I'd like to see your new salesman."

"Let me page him." Mr. Lee picked up the phone. "Brice to the showroom. Brice to the showroom."

Dad walked into the showroom. "Who is it?"

Mr. Lee pointed to Aunt Bee.

"Hi Beezy. What brings you here?"

"I was doing a few errands, so I figured I'd stop in and see if you wanted to grab a cup of coffee?"

"Sure, why not." Dad held open the door for Aunt Bee.

"Galvin, don't you have a delivery at one?" asked Skip Lee.

"No, at three. Customer wanted to pick up her plates at the registry first," said Dad.

"Make sure you're back by two so you have time to prep the car."

"Why? Where's the washboy?"

"He's out today, so we have to prep our own cars."

"You mean, I have to prep the car. Alright, I'll be back by two." Dad and Bee walked towards Bellino's Donuts.

Skip opened the door. "And don't be late. Car needs to be gassed up."

Inside Bellino's, Dad and Bee sat down at a table next to a glass case of donuts.

"Did you ever think it'd come down to this, Beezy," mused Dad, "pushing iron for that jackhole?"

"I know it," said Bee, pouring a swirl of milk into her tea. "Little Mussolini ruling over his kingdom of cars."

"I tell you," said Dad, making his donut disappear in two bites. "It's not a silent hand watching over the economy. It's a silent fist."

At home Dad sat in his armchair with a glass of rust-colored booze, watching the pre-game show to game six of the World Series. "Raina, your mother's not feeling well. Go down to the supermarket and grab a few groceries. Here's the list. Oh, and take these."

Raina looked down at the red, green, and orange food stamps in Dad's hand. "No way, I'm not going anywhere with those things."

"Why not? You should be proud that your government takes care of its citizens like this." Dad thrust the stamps at Raina.

"Get those things away from me. You couldn't pay me a million bucks to use those things in public. You don't have the seeds to use them yourself."

"Like hell I don't, watch me." Dad pretended to get up.

"I'm watching," said Raina.

"Oh for chrissakes." Dad walked to the closet and grabbed his coat. "I'll show you. I don't give a wooden nickel what anyone thinks of me, not at this point, not one red cent."

"Oh yeah, then go ask Mrs. Pushkoff to come with you."

"That's dirty pool." Dad slammed the door. "Ungrateful wretch. My father would have paddled her behind and she would've deserved every whack."

"I'll go with you," I said, sliding into the passenger's seat.

At the Arlington IGA Dad wheeled a cart down Aisle 5. He studied the coffee and tossed a maroon-colored can into his cart. He pushed the cart to the meat cooler. He checked the percentage of ground fat in packages of hamburger. "Jesus H. Christ, $3.29-a-pound for 90% lean hamburger." He tossed a package of 80% lean hamburger into his cart. In Aisle 8 I grabbed a gallon of milk, orange juice, and cheese. In Aisle 1 Dad grabbed grapes and tomatoes. After locating potato chips and ginger snaps, we waited near the registers until a lane cleared. Quickly, he wheeled his shopping cart into the checkout lane and began unloading. The cashier rang up the items.

"Excuse me," said Dad. "The sign says .89 cents a pound for grapes, but you punched in $1.29."

"That sale ended yesterday," the cashier barked. Her fingers fluttered over the keys. "That'll be $32.40."

From his coat pocket Dad removed a stack of food stamps. He handed the cashier a $5, $10, and $20 coupon.

"These stamps have been removed from their booklets," said the cashier.

"I took them out because I thought it would be faster," said Dad.

"We're not allowed to take stamps that have been removed from their booklets," she said loudly. "Let me call the manager."

The intercom roared: "Manager to register four. Manager to register four."

Dad glanced behind him. Three customers were waiting. The cashier was holding up the food stamps so everyone could see.

The manager walked over. "What can I do for you?"

"His FDA coupons aren't in their booklets." The cashier handed the food stamps to the manager.

The manager inspected the stamps. "We're not supposed to accept stamps that have been taken from their booklets. We're supposed to remove them."

Now, five customers were behind us. Suddenly, I felt cool air against my face.

"Just take the friggin' things." Dad tossed the entire stack of stamps onto the cashier's lap. With one arm, he swept the unbagged groceries into his cart and hurried through the self-opening door.

"Don't be rude," called the manager.

"I have a job!" shouted Dad.

In the parking lot, we tossed our groceries into the backseat and drove off towards Merriam Hill. Four miles later on Mass Ave, we passed Brice Chevrolet and I saw the most surprising sight: *all the cars were gone, even the white* lines had been painted over. The lot was a black empty surface.

At home Dad opened the car door and hurried down the walk. "You grab the groceries," he called over his shoulder. With my arms full of food, I jogged to the front door. Raina watched from the second floor window. In the den, Dad sat down and clicked on the TV. Game Six of the World Series flashed across the screen. After tossing the perishables into the fridge, I ran into the den and sat on the couch. We watched the game. In the top of the tenth, Marty Barrett singled to center field, Boggs rounded third to score, and the Red Sox took a two run lead. We held our breaths. Could the Red Sox bust the curse and win, not just the tail and claws, but the whole damn lobster?

"You'll find a better job," I finally said. "Plus, you won't have to work weekends."

Dad sipped his drink. "Been in the car business my whole life. Don't know how to do anything else."

"How about another job in sales?"

"No one likes car salesmen. We're lower on the totem pole than funeral directors," said Dad as the Red Sox pitcher threw a slider to Gary Carter. Carter lined a single into left field. "You know, all my life I told myself it didn't matter if you had a buck or not. If you did, you bought a mansion in Merriam Hill. If you didn't, you bought a ranch in Woburn. If you did, you drove a Cadillac. If you didn't, you drove a Chevy. But tonight, standing in line with the cashier waving those stamps around, I felt it all right. I was a ghost living in someone else's dream." Dad glanced over at me. "I once saw a woman using those stamps at Stop-n-Shop. I remember being surprised 'cause she didn't seem to care what other shoppers thought." Dad looked down at his shoes, badly in need of a shine. "Now, I know how she felt.

She didn't care 'cause she had already crossed herself off in her *own* mind. That's the tragedy of it. You're erasing yourself in your own mind and you don't even know it. Do you know what the worst part is, Kuba?"

"What?"

"The worst part is, I didn't have the slightest idea what it meant to not have a buck, but I *thought* that I did." On TV Coach Morgan waved to the bullpen. Bob Stanley jogged from the bullpen to the mound. "So I never noticed those METCO kids riding the bus at five in the morning to Merriam Hill 'cause their schools didn't have books. Never thought about Fallon working key-to-key six, seven days a week, or that his kids might need him around a little bit more so his oldest son wouldn't end up in the can, which is where he ended up. "

"He did?"

Dad nodded as shadows and light from the TV shimmered on his face. "Only when I could see an emotion in myself, could I see it in others. I tell you, it's not just the generals and dictators whose heads balloon with power. It's the local hotshots who run their own real estate firms and the planning boards who rewrite codes to benefit their friends." On TV, Stanley threw a wild pitch. The catcher tore off his mask and chased after the ball. "Even the tiniest smidge of power can get to a fella's head." Dad sipped his drink. "Yup, that's the way it works down here. I remember marching through the gym at my high school graduation, tassel swinging, world glowing with promise. Two years later—whoo-hoo!—I was selling eight, nine sleds a week, pocketing four, five-hun a day. Then my old man gave me a piece of the action. *Look at all these jobs we create,* I thought. *Why don't those people want to work? Why doesn't government just get the hell out!* I said, not realizing that the magic hand of chance was really steering everything. I think about all the candidates I once supported, all the newspapers I once read, all the self-*congratulatory* slogans I once believed, and I tell you, I'm ashamed. Do you know what the real tragedy is, Kuba?"

"What?"

"The real tragedy is, the ones who have their hands on the steering wheel really think they're driving, so they never truly see who they're passing or what they're running over, so the spin cycle keeps on spinning."

On TV the announcer called the game: "Stanley winds up. Here comes the pitch. Wilson swings. It's a little roller up along first. Behind the bag. Buckner scoops it up—no, it gets past Buckner! Here comes Knight, and the Mets win it! The ball skipped past Buckner's glove and into left field. The New York Mets have magically risen from the dead to defeat the Boston Red Sox and force a seventh game. One strike from defeat, the New York Mets rally and score three runs in the bottom of the 10th to win game six. Bill Buckner misplayed a slow grounder and it rolled right under his legs."

"Jesus H. Christ!" Dad stood up. "If this isn't the crown jewel of a lifetime of screwups, I don't know what is. They stink. Marna?" Dad called to the kitchen. "Did you see what those mutts did? One strike away from winning the World Series and Buckner lets the ball roll under his legs. Every year these sorts of things happen, every damn year." Dad looked back at me. "We can't win."

"Calm down, honey," Mom called.

A commentator joined in: "With his bad Achilles' heal, I don't think Buckner should have even been on the field. The ghosts of Red Sox past are sure rattling their chains tonight."

"This is the last time I get my hopes up watching those choke artists. I refuse to watch." Dad turned his head towards the kitchen.

"McNamara is going to have some explaining to do," the commentator said.

"Oh, for the love of Jack Kennedy, why? Why do the Red Sox continually let me down?" Dad let out a moan that could have wilted a cactus. "Marna, I'm feeling out of breath." He tried to sip his drink. The glass fell onto the carpet.

"What is it?" Mom ran into the den.

"Can't breathe."

"Did you swallow something?"

"My jaw feels like someone jammed fifty needles through the joints."

"I'm calling Neil Van Dyne. Lie on your back. Here, let me loosen your collar." Mom picked up the phone and dialed. She listened for a sec then hung up. "I'm calling an ambulance."

The announcer's voice echoed through the den: "It was a soft grounder. I think Wilson just managed to get the end of his bat on the ball and slap it, but it was enough to befuddle Buckner and force a seventh game. Let's go to the Red Sox clubhouse."

"Hi Bob," said a commentator in the locker room. "A moment ago Bruce Hurst was standing here waiting to be named World Series MVP, but after the ball rolled between Buckner's legs, he quickly loaded up his gym bag and left for the airport. Stadium workers are now removing the Champaign that would've been uncorked had the Red Sox won tonight's game. It would have been their first World Series celebration since 1918—the year Paul Frazee shipped Babe Ruth to the Yankees and launched the greatest dynasty in sports history. Some of Boston's fans think the Red Sox were cursed when Ruth supposedly uttered the words: 'This town will never win a World Series again.' Certainly the curse of Babe Ruth is alive and well at Shea Stadium tonight."

Rapid knocks sounded on our door. Mom opened the door.

"Where is he?" a medic asked.

"In the den."

Two medics wheeled a stretcher into the den and lifted Dad off the floor. "Where is the pain, sir?" Unable to speak, Dad pointed to his chest.

"Get an oxygen bag in here. It looks like a cardiac event of unknown magnitude. Can you wiggle your toes, sir?"

Dad's big toe moved.

"How does your jaw feel?" the medic asked as another medic stuck an IV needle into Dad's arm.

Dad made a thumbs-down signal.

As the stretcher rolled down our walkway, the medic placed an oxygen mask over Dad's face. In the driveway, the medics lifted the stretcher into the ambulance. The driver flipped on the red light and the ambulance disappeared down Merriam Street.

In front of the movie theater, Raina and Noy watched the ambulance pass.

"Wonder who's in there?" mused Raina.

Two days later Dad sat up in his hospital bed and clicked on the TV. "What do you think of your old man having a duffer?"

"With all the hotdogs you eat, it's a miracle you haven't had one already," I said.

"I know it." Dad fiddled with the controls of his hospital bed. "Where's your sister?"

"She's at Fort Apache with Crispin working on a CD."

"I want you to watch after her."

"Dad, she doesn't even like me."

"But you'll watch over her, won't you?"

I nodded.

Dr. Van Dyne walked in and read Dad's chart. "Hi Galvin, you ready for tomorrow?"

Dad studied the doctor's face.

"Don't worry. We perform dozens of bypass procedures every day." Dr. Van Dyne attached the clip board to Dad's bed and walked out.

Dad muted the TV. "Remember the time Fallon sold two new sleds to the grocery clerk at IGA?"

"No."

"GM was running a special: *Buy a new car or truck and get $500 cash for your Christmas shopping.* Some customers bought sleds just to get the money to buy presents. After the kid bought a Z28, Ed Berman called me from Century 21 and said: 'I can't believe you sold that kid a new car. He just bought a house from us. It'll get foreclosed. How could you, Galvin?' But we just laughed at Ed and told him: 'Don't look now, Ed, but the kid just bought a truck and he's driving it home as we speak.' Three months later, both vehicles were repossessed. I guess, in the heat of making a buck, a few things got bent till we couldn't figure out what the original shapes were." Dad began to cough.

"Should I call a nurse?" I stood up.

Dad shook his head. "Before I forget. Bee was able to palm the life insurance policies I took out after your brother's car wreck. If something happens to me, make sure the insurance company doesn't screw your mother out of the proceeds."

"Dad, they do these bypasses all the time."

"That's what they always say."

"But we're gonna buy a beach house on Peak's Island. Noy and Pushkoff are gonna stay over. We're gonna play two-hand touch on the beach—the way we did with Donk."

"You do those things." Dad looked out the window. "Did you know I can name every vice-president in order? Go ahead, ask me."

"I believe you."

"Then ask."

"Okay, who was the 16th vice-president?"

"That's easy, Buchanan. Give me a harder one."

"Okay, name all the vice-presidents under both Roosevelts."

"You shyster, I always have a hard time with FDR's."

I noticed a grayish color to Dad's skin. "I'll give you a hint."

"No hints." Dad pointed to his head. "It's all in here. Just have to find it. Charles Fairbanks was Teddy Roosevelt's VP. Did you know they named Fairbanks, Alaska after him?"

"No I didn't."

"Let's see. Henry Wallace and Harry Truman were FDR's 2nd and 3rd vice-presidents." Dad closed his eyes. "A face is starting to come to me. He was a dour looking man. Came from Texas. Speaker of the House—got it: John "Cactus Jack" Garner. I should have been a lawyer. You know, history's a great background for law—and politics too."

"It is?"

"You bet, all those case histories they make you memorize. Had a line on a great internship too, but never applied."

"Why not?"

"Don't know. Guess you kids came along."

The Fishhook
(21 years earlier)

With a square hat on his head, Dad walked between the rows of seated parents in his high school gym. Grandma stood up. A camera flashed.

At home a banner hung from the bedroom window: *Congratulations Galvin!* In the backyard, Grandpa spread marmalade onto chicken legs and set them on the grill.

"Well, you big blockhead, you finally made it out of high school. Got yourself into Holy Cross. Bet you think you're big shot now that you're a college boy," said Grandpa.

"That's a laugh," said Dad.

"College has a way of changing you."

"Won't change me."

"What do you want to go to Holy Cross for when you could be earning good money working for me?"

Dad nervously kicked the grass with his sneakers.

"I'll give you a car too."

"I don't know. I'm not good at being pushy."

"Good salesman aren't." Grandpa flipped the chicken over. "I get it, you're too good for the car business."

"Didn't say that."

"I don't blame you, bunch of Philadelphia lawyers." Grandpa placed the lid on the grill and began weaving and bobbing. "Think you're tough enough to take the old man yet?"

Dad looked down at his feet. "Have another drink, Pa."

"Think you're a big college boy—don't you?" Grandpa punched Dad's shoulder. "Not so old that I can't whip you."

"Come on, Pa. I don't want to have to call an ambulance."

"Who you, Ichabod Crane's skinny brother?" Grandpa grabbed Dad by the waist and lifted. The two fell to the grass and rolled across the lawn. "Got you now," said Grandpa on top.

"Excuse me, I think I feel a fly trying to land." Dad straight-armed Grandpa. Grandpa tumbled over. Dad climbed on top. "Give up?"

"Will you two get up," said Grandma. "You look like a couple of slugs mating."

Grandpa tossed a clump of grass into Dad's face.

Dad closed his eyes. "I know all your tricks. Give up?"

"Not until the Red Sox win the World Series." Pretending to go for Dad's shirt, Grandpa reached for Dad's face and jammed his finger into Dad's mouth.

"Uurgh—you cheater!" Dad released Grandpa's shirt.

Grandpa yanked Dad's cheek. "What's the matter, don't you like the fishhook?"

"Cheater!" Dad protested.

"Remember, always keep your mouth shut." Grandpa got up off the grass and led Dad around the lawn. "Hey Beatrice, look at the tuna I caught."

"That's dirty pool," said Aunt Bee.

"No it isn't. It's being resourceful."

"Pipe down. I'm trying to catch the game," hollered Fallon.

On the radio Johnny Most's sandpaper voice called the game: "Five seconds left. Celtics up by one. Seventy-Sixers with a chance to win it. Greer putting the ball in play. K.C. Jones presses. Greer makes the inbound pass—Havlicek stole the ball! Havlicek stole the ball! Sam Jones takes it down the court. It's all over. It's all over. Havlicek has just stolen the ball. Celtics win it 110 to 109. Johnny Havlicek is being mobbed by fans. Bill Russell wants to grab Havlicek. He squeezes him. The Celtics have won the Eastern Finals. It's a bee hive at the Garden, folks. From out of nowhere, John Havlicek jumped in front of a defender and waltzed off with the ball, handing the Boston Celtics the Eastern Conference Championship."

"Whooo hooo."

"Hunya hunya, minkya minkya." Fallon did a jig. "Hunya hunya, minkya minkya. I tell you, that Havlicek's something else."

Releasing the fish hook, Grandpa joined in: "Hunya hunya, minkya inkya. Hunya hunya, minkya inkya."

So did Dad: "Oogady boogady, oogady boogady, oogady boogady boo!"

"That Havlicek could lift a yamaka off a rabbi's head. So are you going to push iron for me this summer?" Grandpa asked Dad.

"I'm not working for a cheater." Dad held a soda bottle against his cheek. "Commission or salary?"

"Commission, what else?"

"I don't know. I'm thinking of doing an internship at Ashworth & Conroy. A few guys on the team already have jobs."

"I know more people in law school than in high school. What do you want to represent rapists and murderers for when you could be earning good money right off the bat?

Look, I'll walk you through your first deals. You'll be an order taker. Besides, being on commission gives you the incentive to sell. Depending on the hours you put in, you can earn as much money as you want..."

Next day, the surgeon tried to fix Dad's heart, but during the procedure he accidentally nicked one of Dad's arteries. The blue pajama gang tried to slow the flow of blood with clamps, but they couldn't. So they stuffed in gauze. No go. They tried stitches. No luck. So after 39 years on earth, 266 months in sales, 14,516 breakfasts, 7,396 contracts, 943 auctions, 7 homes, 59 suits, 3 kids, 4 pets, and 1 wife, Dad waived the remainder of his lease and his heart stopped beating.

After the funeral, Mom invited everyone over to our house. Aunt Bee mixed the tallest pitcher of Bloody Marys in history. Mrs. Pushkoff brought over so much lasagna, scalloped potatoes, and tossed salad, I swear, she must have cleaned out Quimby's IGA.

A few hours passed. I was sitting at the piano, messing with a few chords, when I heard Aunt Bee calling me from the top of the stairs: "Yoo hoo, Kuba?"

"I'm in the den."

"Now that you're the patriarch of the family, I have a special initiation for you."

"What is it?"

"You'll see. Woo hoo hoooooo." Bee thumped downstairs, waving her hip-huggers. "Woo hoo hooooooo," she cried, running towards me

I sprung to my feet, faked right, then ran left into the kitchen.

Bee chased me through the kitchen. "Woo hoo hooooo. Woo hoo hooooooo. Hula bula bula. How do you like being the only male now?"

"Keep those things away from me," I said, bumping into Fallon. A bourbon wave splashed onto Fallon's arm.

"What the-" said Fallon.

"Oh, it's awful. These haven't been washed since August," said Bee, shaking her undies, her eyes tearing up.

"You keep your distance or I'll-"

"You'll what?" said Bee.

"I'll get Raina's dirty undies—and they've been around, I tell you," I said, running towards the bathroom.

"Jerk, I heard that," yelled Raina.

"Is it true?" Aunt Bee whinnied.

"Don't listen to him. He makes stuff up."

Locking myself in the bathroom, I dug through the hamper till I found a pair of undies. Then I dipped the undies into Chuggle's dish and smeared cat food on the crotch part. I charged Bee, waving the dirty undies. "Cowaaa bungaaaaaa!"

Bee caught sight of the brown gobs. "Gross." She booked-it into the dining room. "I was only pretending," said Bee panting. "But Kuba went and got the real thing."

"It's *real* alright."

Bee ran into the kitchen. "Oh, it's awful. It's just so terrible. Okay, okay, I've had enough."

I pointed to Bee's underwear. "Hey, Fallon, these skivvies have been to Rome."

Fallon looked over at Bee.

"Says who?" Aunt Bee asked with an O-gaped mouth.

I chased Bee into the den. "Says the mailman."

"They've also been to Les Deux Pieds en Le Quartier Latin on stage with Anita O'Day," Bee replied.

Mom, seated on the couch with Pastor Mac, looked up. "Not now, Beatrice."

Bee ran behind Raina. "Keep him away from me. He's got the real McCoy."

"You both need major help," said Raina.

I stepped forward, waving the dirty undies.

Aunt Bee raised her hands in the air. "Okay, I give up. You're worse than your father."

"It's gonna cost you," I said, taking another step towards Aunt Bee.

"How much?"

"Your condenser mic."

"The one from the forties? That'll be the day." Bee warily eyed the brown lumps. "Oh, the smell is awful."

"Your choice," I said, holding the underwear in front of Aunt Bee's face.

"Okay, okay—it's yours."

In the bathroom, I tossed the undies back into the hamper, then I strolled to the liquor cabinet. "Oo, I'm parched," I said, removing a lowball glass from the cabinet and lifting a V.O. bottle. *Bub bub bup bup bup.* I dropped two ice cubes into the glass. With two fingers, I tapped in the water. "Just a little ting for the tang."

---

1. Donk had scribbled in the word *effolia* into his humongous red dictionary right after the word: *effing.* He only gave it one definition, so I figured I'd add a couple more, but when I flipped through Coach B's OED I couldn't find the word. Figures. So that night I swigged a Heff Tall and made up a few more meanings.
Effolia *(ĕ-fōl-ĕ-uh), n.* **1.** A form of unknowing, often accidental but sometimes cultivated. **2.** The inability to perceive the hardships of others, often due to a lack of first hand observation, but not exclusively. **3.** The degree of shared intuition among musicians. *During the second set, our band slipped into effolia. Jerry Garcia 1980.* **4.** In music, a section in a composition in which the melody breaks down into dissonance, then returns to harmony.

Track 45
Everything You Own Can Be Repossessed In A New York Minute

"Got this yesterday from the insurance company." Mom held up a check. "Funny, there isn't anything I want to buy." Mom nervously fingered her wedding band. "Kuba, come over here."

Setting my acoustic guitar on the couch, I walked over to Mom.

"You to take this." Mom handed me the check. "Go up to Peaks Island and put a down payment on a beach house. Your father would have wanted that."

Next day, Aunt Bee and I drove north on I-95 towards Peaks Island. I turned on the radio just in time to catch the slow echo of Al Connelly's guitar in "Looking at a Picture" by Glass Tiger. At Exit 7 we turned onto 295. In Portland we boarded the local ferry and rode across Casco Bay to Peaks Island. On the ride over, waves crashed against the bow, spraying salt water on my face. Reaching the island, dockworkers connected the ferry to the dock. We walked up the hill to a realtor's office. Inside, a woman sat behind a desk reading a newspaper.

"We're here to buy a beach house," I said.

The agent didn't look up. "Aren't any houses for sale at the moment. Last house came on the market five months ago." She looked up. "But there are a number of condos still available in our Pine Acres development." The   agent drove us down a freshly paved road.   In a field purple loosestrife and devil's paintbrush danced in a strong wind. At the Pine Acres construction site, we got out and walked around the property. Stopping by the ocean, we watched a bulldozer level a bluff and push the soil into a pond. Further back, a skidder fed pine trees into a giant chipper. We walked toward a cleared section of earth. A man with a roll of orange tape drew the outline of one of the buildings in the dirt.

"This is the our most ambitious project yet." The agent unrolled blueprints. "It isn't everyday that a parcel of land this size comes on the market. An elderly woman passed away and willed the land to the catholic church. They turned around and sold it to a local builder who's bringing much needed development to the island. There'll be thirty-six units in all. Each unit will have it's own view of the bay, two bedrooms, an upstairs bath, and a full-size kitchen." The agent pointed to some blue squares on the map. "Here are the units still available."

I fingered the insurance check in my pocket. "How big are the lawns?"

The agent looked at the blueprints. "About 130 square feet."

"Is that big enough for a touch football game?"

"Well, you'll probably have to get permission from the condo association for that, but there's plenty of room on the beach for all sorts of games. If you think you might be interested, I would think hard about leaving a deposit today. These units are really moving quickly..."

"Let's go," I whispered to Bee.

On the ferry ride back to the mainland, I threw a cracker towards a great blue heron. Before it reached the heron, a seagull swooped down and snatched it from mid-air.

When we pulled into our driveway, Noy Mom, Raina, and Mrs. Pushkoff were standing in front of the garage.

"What's going on?" I asked.

Mom pointed to the place where the garage door met the ground. Pinned beneath the garage door was a lifeless calico cat.

"He must have tried to squeeze under the door just as it was closing," said Mom.

I pulled Chuggles out from under the garage door.

"Dumb cat. Don't you know the door would hurt you if you didn't make it? Now you'll never speak." I turned to Bee. "He was going to speak."

"What?"

"We were going to thrill the world."

"Put him in the cellar," said Mom. "I'll call the vet and see what we should do."

"First, I want to give clean him up a bit." I carried Chuggles into the kitchen and put him in the sink. Turning on the water, I spread shampoo all over his fur, then rinsed. Chuggles stayed cold. So I put more shampoo on his fur and washed him again. This time I rinsed with hot water, but Chuggles still stayed cold. I washed him again and scrubbed harder. Chuggles' body got stiffer. I kept washing till the shampoo was gone.

"Okay, that's enough," said Aunt Bee, handing me a towel.

I rubbed Chuggles' fur.

"Just think of it this way," said Bee. "Maybe a short life is a good thing. Maybe after a certain number of years, cats grow tired of living and they prefer to move on."

After drying Chuggles, I placed him in a garbage bag and carried him down the stairs to the cellar.

"I want to bury Chuggles next to Donk," I told Bee.

"I don't think cemeteries allow that," said Bee.

That night I snuck into Westview Cemetery with a shovel and dug a hole next to Donk. I laid Chuggles in the hole, filled it with dirt, and covered the dirt with hunks of grass. On Donk's headstone I scratched Chuggles' name with a nail. That night I knew truly and surely that I was alone in a universe expanding 46.2 miles per second. But the weird thing is, I didn't feel weak or bummed out, I felt kind of free. I was still *here* and there was a ton less to lose. That meant, far fewer reasons to be afraid. All my choices had dwindled down to one. When alone in the loser's circle, the only place left to go is inside.

But the whittling away wasn't finished. A week later a *notice of default and sale* was hand delivered to us. First Trust had foreclosed on our house. But Mr. Irvine was dad's friend. They had gone to Merriam Hill High together. I decided to head over to First Trust to see if I could change their mind.

At First Trust, Mr. Irvine's phone beeped. "What is it, Shelia?"

"There's a young man here to see you. He won't give me his name," said the secretary.

"What does he want?"

"He wants to discuss his parent's mortgage."

Mr. Irvine peeked through the blinds. "Okay, send him in."

I walked into his office. Mr. Irvine sat behind a walnut desk. His face was brick-red. Behind him, a large picture window gave a great view of Merriam Hill Center. Cars zipped by on Mass Ave. An Afghan rug stretched across the floor depicting strange animals with long torsos. On the wall hung a framed diploma: *Per auctoritatem ab actoribus est Dartmouth College. Pateat universis...*

Mr. Irvine stood up. "What can I do for you?" He leaned over his desk and held out his hand.

"Thanks for seeing me, Mr. Irvine," I said, shaking his hand.

"Have a seat." He motioned to a chair.

I sat down and rested my hands on my knees. "Hi." I heard the soft bustle of people depositing and withdrawing money in the other room. "Mr. Irvine-" I looked down at the Afghan rug, then up at his sunburned face. "I need you to take my mom's co-signature off my dad's loan."

"I'm not empowered to do that. A contract can't be altered without the expressed written consent of all parties affected by the change."

"I'll get the signatures," I said.

"How?"

Shyster. I tried a different tactic. "Look, the value of Brice Chevrolet will cover the loan."

Mr. Irvine shook his head. "There are lawyers fees involved and administrative costs. Besides, I can't undo a legal document. It's out of my hands."

"How convenient. My Dad banked with you because he thought you'd stand by him if the economy tanked. You practically grew up together. Doesn't that mean anything to you?"

"Friends are friends, but business is business."

"You mean, friends are friends until there's money involved. That's pretty sad."

Mr. Irvine rearranged the items on his desk. He slid a stein engraved with the letter "D" over to a baseball signed by Bucky Dent. "Look, there's an inherent risk when you borrow money. Half of all new businesses fail."

"Brice Chevrolet didn't have to fail."

"Mr. Brice, anyone with eyes could see that the market was overbuilt and a long corrective recession was imminent, that corporations—up to their eyeballs in junk bond debt—wouldn't be able to service their payments, bond prices would sink faster than Atlantis, and the real estate bubble would burst. Then investors, stuck with millions of square feet of unleased office space, would start fleeing like Union soldiers at Bull Run. Obviously, we have to call in our loans before other creditors gobble up their assets. Any business that misses a single payment is immediately foreclosed. It's either us or them. Our jobs or theirs. What would you do?"

I clenched my fists.

"On top of that, we've got this S & L fiasco. Speculators with a schoolboy's experience and milk-money down borrowed billions of greenbacks with help from Tammany Hall lenders—and guess who got stuck holding the tab? Uncle Sam. So what's Uncle Sam doing? They're auctioning off their foreclosed properties at pennies on the dollar. They're flooding the market further and property values are falling off the face of the earth. They're cranking up a pink slip tornado that going to swallow the middle class. Now even small businesses can't make their payments because customers can't afford to buy shoelaces."

I spoke with my teeth clenched: "You knew this could happen and still you asked my Mom to cosign."

From his desk Mr. Irvine took out a cloth and began shining his shoes. "Most borrowers refuse, but your father didn't."

"You threw my Dad a spitball to protect your pink bum and your fat Christmas bonus. We could have owned that house free and clear."

"No one owns anything," Mr. Irvine said.

"What?" I stood up.

"No one owns anything. If you were in this business, you'd see that. Everything you own can be repossessed in a New York minute. We don't even need a reason, just a good Harvard lawyer. Everyday, I hear customers say, 'Five more payments and she's all mine.' When does that happen? When the car is so beat up it's ready for the scrap heap. Or in the case of a house, the borrower is so beat up that their next purchase is a cemetery plot. All anyone ever owns is a drawer full of hand-me-down dreams. Sure, customers can increase their equity. Periodically, they can refurbish their investments. But miss one payment, let your insurance lapse once, create an environmental mess, forget to pay your taxes, or get sued? You'll wake up and find a lien on your house and your car's been repossessed—right from your driveway. That's when people find out who really owns what. It's the most pervasive myth since flat earth." Mr. Irving glanced at his calendar. "Listen, I have an appointment."

"I'm not leaving until you admit that First Trust loves money more than Jesus," I said.

An expression of surprise washed over Mr. Irvine's face. "Excuse me?"

"That's right, I see you in the pews on Sundays listening to Pastor Mac's sermons, but that doesn't change how you act when you put on a tie. I want you to stop pretending you're a friend to these people and start showing them who you really are—an Ivy League shark."

"Just leave."

I reached for Mr. Irvine's shirt. He stepped back. I grabbed the baseball off his desk and wound up.

"No!" Mr. Irvine recoiled.

I turned to his window and threw the ball as hard as I could. The ball smashed through the glass, flew through the air, and bounced across the street, striking a passing car. The car's brake lights lit up. A man in blue jeans got out and nervously looked around.

A month later, bidders lined up at the registration table in our driveway. In front of our garage, the auctioneer rapped the podium with his gavel. "Today we have a five bedroom, two-bath, stucco house with a full-size basement on the *top* of Merriam Hill." The auctioneer held up a certificate. "This dwelling passes full inspection according to Massachusetts housing codes 264 through 289. Inspection includes: sewage pipes, frame, roof, and oil furnace. Appliances include: gas stove, washer and dryer, microwave, dish washer, and a new refrigerator. Deed holder is First Trust Banking Corp. All bids are final. $20,000 bond needed before auction begins. Only bonded bidders can buy. Winning bidder's deposit is non-refundable. The remaining balance is due in five business days." The auctioneer waited for a family to complete a last-minute registration. "Where will we start the bidding at? Hibady dibady hibady dibady hibady." The gavel struck the podium. "Hibady dibady dibady dibady. Let's start at $20,000. Do I hear $20,000?"

In the bedroom, Raina and Mom packed clothes, shoes, books, and keepsakes into boxes.

Raina looked out the window. "What's he doing?"

In the backyard I danced in a circle and sang an Arapaho ghost song:

I circle around, I circle around
The boundaries of the earth,
The boundaries of the earth,
Wearing long wind feathers as I fly,
Wearing long wind feathers as I fly.

The auctioneer scanned the bidders. "How about $10,000?"

A man in golf pants raised his card.

"Hibady dibady hibady dibady hibady. $20,000?"

A woman with a child nodded.

"$30,000? Hibady dibady dibady dibady."

A card wiggled.

"Do I hear $40,000?"

The woman nodded.

The auctioneer's arm swung from bid to bid. "$50,000, $60,000, $70,000, $80,000, $90,000?" The auctioneer's gavel struck the podium.

The man in golf pants looked down.

"Come on, folks, this is a once-in-a-lifetime opportunity. Have you seen the view from the cupola?"

Running and leaping through the air, I sang a Cheyenne ghost song:

Ehä ´n esho´ini, Ehä ´n esho´ini ´.
Hoiv ´esho´ini ´, Hoiv ´esho´ini ´.
I ´yohä? Eye ´e ´ye´! I ´yohä? Eye ´e ´ye´!
I ´hihäsini ´ehi ´nit, I ´hihäsini ´ehi ´nit.

Skip Lee nodded.

"$90,000. Finally, a wise man. Hibady hibady dibady hibady dibady dibady—$100,000? Do I hear $100,000?" The auctioneer scanned the crowd. "Going once at $90,000. Going-"

Mr. Pushkoff raised his card.

"$100,000! Do I hear $110,000?"

Skip Lee nodded.

"$110,000. Hibady dibady dibady hibady dibady hibady. $120,000?"

Mr. Pushkoff held up his card.

"$130,000 to the gentleman in front. $140,000?"

Skip Lee nodded.

"$150,000. Do I hear $160,000?"

Mr. Pushkoff turned away.

Standing behind the podium, Mr. Irvine removed the deed from his briefcase.

"$160,000?" The auctioneer pointed his long finger at Mr. Pushkoff.

"Honey!" Mrs. Pushkoff elbowed her husband.

"It's only assessed at "$144,000. That's all the bank will give us."

"$150,000 going once, going twice," said the auctioneer.

In the backyard I sang the song in English:

> Our father has come, Our father has come.
> The earth has come, The earth has come.
> We are rising—eye ye! We are rising—eye ye!
> I am beginning to turn into a bird,
> I am beginning to turn into a bird.

Mrs. Pushkoff snatched the card from her husband's hand and waved it.

"$155,000. Do I hear $160,000?"

Without looking at the Pushkoffs, Skip nodded.

The auctioneer's arm swung from bidder to bidder. "$160,000, $165,000, $170,000, $175,000, $180,000,

$185,000, $190,000, $195,000, $200,000? Are we going to pass $200,000?"

Skip nodded.

"$200,000, $205,000?"

Mrs. Pushkoff lowered her card, then raised it."

"$205,000, $210,000?"

Skip frowned.

The auctioneer pointed his bony finger at Mr. Lee. "Skip to my Lou, my darlin', look at that red tile roof. They're getting harder to find."

With his hand, Skip made a cutting motion.

"$207,500, $210,000?"

Mrs. Pushkoff dropped her arm.

"$210,000? It's got a cupola. Probably can see all the way to Red Feather Ridge. $210,000 going once. $210,000 going twice."

Mrs. Pushkoff covered her face.

"Sold to bidder number six for $207,500." The auctioneer slammed his gavel on the podium.

Checkbook in hand, Skip Lee walked over to the registration table. Mr. Irvine laid paper work on the table for Skip to sign.

After the auction, still wearing my ghost vest, I walked past Raina's bedroom and heard sawing. "What going on?" I asked, walking into Raina's room.

Raina put down the saw and removed a piece of sheet rock from the wall. She dropped what looked like a perch into the hole and re-fit the sheet rock. "What does it look like I'm doing?" she replied, taping the sheetrock in place, her dolls staring up at us from a cardboard box.

"I don't get it?"

"Remember all those fish we caught in Granny Pond that we stashed in the freezer?" Raina cut a square of wallpaper and spread Elmer's Glue on the back. "Well, I'm sticking them in the walls."

I smiled. "The new owners will never be able to figure out where the smell's coming from."

"Correct, Watson. Now get out of here—and don't fink on me either."

"You're one twisted individual."

"They just can't take our house and expect nothing to happen." Raina placed the wallpaper over the sheetrock and rubbed the wallpaper till the hole become invisible.

"Skip Lee's a douche bag."

"Greedy ambulance chaser—that's what he is." Raina cut into another part of the wall. After removing the piece of sheet rock, she dropped a perch into the hole.

On a positive note, Mom was able to buy a three-bedroom in Arlington with the insurance dough. Raina and I got our own rooms, but Raina never slept there. In fact, we didn't see her for four months. Then in April I was walking past Strawberry Records and I saw a poster of Seedtime—right in the front window! I couldn't believe it. Seedtime had put out a CD on Cherry Hill Records and there was Raina on the cover acting like she belonged.

On the college front: Holy Cross said *no*; No go at Berkley School of Music; Franklin Pierce said *yes*; I got waitlisted at UNH; Plymouth State said *yes*; and Dartmouth—big surprise—said *no*. Worse, I didn't get a single love letter from a program to play football—not even a tryout. So, I decided to biff college and chase the ghost called music. Why not? I had written nearly thirty songs. That summer I practiced my songs and wrote a few new ones. When I got bored, I put on my hiking boots and cruised up Route 2 to Red Feather Ridge.

They Still Worship The Snow Statues Melting In Their Minds

Alongside Route 2 a girl was walking. Her thumb wasn't raised. The way her hips were moving made me think she had no place to go, rather it was the going itself. I kept my foot on the gas. But there was something familiar about her: the way her arms swung from four to eight o'clock, her heel-to-toe bounce, her nutmeg hair. I lifted my foot off the gas, steered my car into the breakdown, and came to a stop. Not wanting to frighten her, I stayed in my seat and watched her pass in the mirror. She looked up. I opened the passenger door.

"What the heck are you doing on 93 at seven in the morning?" I asked.

Raina got in and shut the door. I couldn't tell if she was trashed or not, but knew enough to keep my mouth shut. I stepped on the gas and followed the painted yellow lines stretching further than we could see. Above our heads, the sky was a sapphire sea. A half-hour passed.

"It was all supposed to be so easy," said Raina. "We were good. We practiced too. Then, Cherry Hill Records signed us. When our CD dropped, I thought it was a done deal. Look at Bim Skala Bim—we're as good as them."

Raina turned to me. "In fact, our songs blow their songs away, don't you think?"

"Bim Skala Bim is pretty tight, but I know what you mean. Your vocals have more surprises." A guardrail hovered above the tar, legless and free.

"That's what I say. Dan Vitale couldn't sing his way through a fire drill, but who gets picked up by Electra and who gets dropped by Cherry Hill after only one album? So we only sold two-thousand CDs. How much money did those tightwads spend on promotion? Wow, a few fanzines and a keg of Sam Adams at our CD-release party at some rinky-dink night club. All our friends showed up. We could have done that."

"Tons of bands get dropped," I said, turning off the interstate. "The Neighborhoods got dropped three times. Every major label passed on The Pixies and they're as good as any band out there. You guys'll get re-signed. Just keep cranking out new stuff—songs that make your salmon nautilus hum. That way, if you never sell another CD, at least you'll have the music."

Raina rolled down the window. A stream of nutmeg hair flowed from the side of the car. "But I want people to like us. Little did I know, hundreds of bands get signed every single sucky day. They lay down their best tracks and nothing happens—even if their songs solve the riddle of time travel. And what if a band does generate a buzz? All because some greasy-haired DJ in Worcester played their CD or a sound engineer salvaged one of their riffs from a mountain of demos. The point is, huge forces are at work and all our musical efforts amounted to zilch. When no one gave a hoot about our songs, my illusions melted and the shadows behind those illusions began their full-court press. Why did I want to be a bigwig singer anyway? Because a long lobster claw of sadness seeks us out, Kuba. So I laced up my sneakers and took off, only to discover that the faster I ran, the further I got from the finish line, and the whole race was just another false start."

We stopped at a gas station, filled up, then continued down a two-lane road.

"Crispin doesn't see it that way. He thinks we got dropped because my voice is too thin. Can you believe it? He does his bull moose howls and my voice isn't big enough."

I rested my arm on the seat behind Raina.

She leaned against me. "They kicked me out. They ganged up on me and kicked me out."

We passed a sign: Red Feather Ridge State Park.

"Now they call themselves Burn The Candle. I think that's a crappy name, don't you?"

"I've heard better," I said, turning down a dirt road.

"I thought I was irreplaceable, that's a laugh. Everyone's replaceable, even Neil Young."

"Forget about those working-class posers. You know Crispin's Dad's a lawyer, don't you?"

"He is?"

"Went to Cornell too."

"Why do people pretend to be poor?"

"Maybe because that's the way they feel. I say, if your parents are loaded, go with that."

"Really?"

"Hell yeah, and if you're voice isn't multi-layered and bruised, tool around with trance, try a triple-chorus, throw freeform into the mix, experiment with stoptime—anything to juice the song."

"You think?"

"I do. Forget about approval from strangers. What do strangers know anyway? Aunt Bee's got it right. Once Crispin saw Rory Gallagher at The Middle East having a few soldiers, so he pulls out his Les Paul and asks Rory to show him the lead to "Walk On Hot Coals" and Gallagher—the sick unit—did. As you can guess, three kids walked in and screamed: 'Oh my God, there's Rory Gallagher!' Five stools down, Bee looked up from her scotch and soda and croaked, 'Who cares.' Gallagher almost dropped Crispin's Les Paul on the bar floor he was laughing so much."

"Bee's lying. She does care what strangers think."

"But she tries not to. That at least gives her a chance. I mean, just 'cause a girl eats sunflower seeds every morning doesn't mean she's gonna wake up and feel the sun."

At the trailhead I searched the trunk of my car. "Here, put these on." I handed Donk's sneakers and shorts to Raina. In my backpack I stuffed a compass, trail map, water purifier, fly dope, windproof and waterproof matches, a bag of gorp, and a few oranges. Then, I put on a coal miner's hat with a light on top.

"Put that away. You look like a freak," said Raina, changing into Donk's clothes.

"I know I look like a freak, but we might need this." I shut the trunk.

"Why?" asked Raina as we walked towards the trail.

"Last time Donk and I hiked this trail, it got dark and we never made it to the summit. This time, unless Sasquatch tears my legs off, we're going to the summit."

Raina surveyed the ridge. "It looks tit."

"Yeah, right. Mallory's last words," I said as we disappeared into the woods.

A monadnock is a huge erosion-resistant dome of granite with sandstone and schist mixed in. In Abinaki, monadnock means 'mountain that stands alone.' In Mohawk, monadnock means 'rises up' which is what Red Feather Ridge does. It juts up 5,366 feet into the New Hampshire sky. The trails begin in a forest of maple, beech, and white ash. As hikers climb, the lower elevation trees give way to yellow birch and pines. Further up, the birches turn into red spruce. Gradually, the spruce shrink until the hiker is walking on pure granite.

Thousands of years of leaves and ferns opening in May then dying in November, have covered the ridge with a clove-colored loam. Only in the alpine zone (above 4,200 feet), where winds can exceed 160 m.p.h., can hikers see the granite surface. The granite contains all kinds of stuff. You can easily spot fool's gold and mica, but Donk put a piece of granite under a microscope and discovered hairstreaks of copper, specks of tourmaline, and pinpricks of garnet.

Above the treeline the granite is marked with map lichen, ring lichen, pixie cups, and reindeer moss, which give the alpine zone a lunar feel. When the weather is dry, the lichen provides a scratchy surface for your sneakers to grip. But when the lichen is wet, the surface becomes smooshy and slick. You'd think the monadnock was greased with green bananas. The smallest slip can send a hiker tumbling towards the cliffs that surround the summit. This explains the commemorative plaque on the fire tower that has the names of fourteen hikers who fell to their deaths.

As we hiked up the trail a kingbird sang in a pine: *Kit kit kit teery. Kit kit teery.*

"Why do you think birds sing anyway?" asked Raina.

"Probably trying to lure a mate," I replied. "But I'd like to think they sing because a feeling of rising is passing through their body."

"Where'd you come from. I think they sing because they're afraid," said Raina, stepping over a root.

Up ahead the trail forked. A lone arrow pointed at both trails.

"See what I mean. This place is loaded with disinformation. Grab the map in my backpack, will you?"

"Here we are," said Raina, putting her finger on the map. "Trail on the left looks shorter."

But the terrain is steeper, I noted as we swerved left. "So where are you living now?"

"Not living anywhere."

"What do you mean you're not living anywhere?"

"I'm couch surfing."

"Where?"

"At whoever's house I happen to be hanging out at when I want to crash."

"Why don't you stay at Mom's?"

"I like it this way. I like not having anything someone can take away or steal."

Beside the trail, tiny British soldiers were marching in the moss. I didn't say a word and kept on hiking.

"Do you know what I miss most?" asked Raina.

I shook my head.

"The smell of just-washed sheets, being able to store my stuff in the attic, the news guy's voice when Dad watched TV. I even miss that stupid red dictionary. God, I used to hate that book. Before this Donk thing went down, I was a little twit from Merriam Hill. What did I have the right to sing about?"

"Everyone should sing."

Raina smiled. "No they shouldn't."

Sing (si), *n* & *v*. **1.** To utter sweet sounds as birds do. **2.** To articulate musical inflections with your voice, especially words set to music. **3.** Pleasant humming, buzzing, or whistling sounds (a kettle, the wind). **4.** To be affected with a ringing sound in the ears. **5.** *Slang*; To turn informer, to confess. **6.** *Archaic*; To convince through singing; *Singing home the bride.* Longfellow. **7.** To portray, expose, or celebrate. **8.** To usher in or out with singing (a new year, leader, or style). **9.** To bring about a desired state through singing (sing a child to sleep). **10.** To cry out or complain; *They should sing if they were that bent.* Chaucer. **11.** *Sing up*; To sing more loudly. **12.** *Sing-along*; A gathering of singers.

I scaled a huge boulder, then turned and held out my hand.

"I can do it myself." Raina scaled the boulder then dusted off her shorts.

We continued up the trail. Yellow birches were suddenly everywhere.

"I didn't realize things weren't going to stay the same," said Raina.

Hesitating a bit, I put my hand on her shoulder. "You did the best you could."

Raina pushed my hand away. "Screw you, Spaz. I didn't do the best I could, so don't tell me I did. I had a first-class case of me-itis. In my world, I was the only star in the sky. Do you know what the craziest part is? I spent all my time circling my own nest and still I felt neglected. I'm the one who deserved to have that Blazer hop a red light."

"That's the way it works down here, people get the opposite of what they want."

"You know what an even scarier thought is? What if 'COZ had put our songs in heavy rotation? What if our CD had flown off the shelves? What would have happened then?" Raina raised her arms. "Seedtime owns the air waves, proof that my illusions are real. What a sad thought, that my childhood fantasies might have lived on for decades. Luckily, my screw-ups were so massive that every inch of my custom steel suit was blown off and I was left naked beneath a gray cloud of arrows. From now on, I'm not taking advice from anyone who hasn't had at least three nervous breakdowns."

"Try not to beat yourself up too much."

"Why?" Raina asked. "Like I have a choice."

"'Cause the real snobs are the ones who hate themselves. They hate themselves because they still worship the snow statues melting in their minds. I mean, they still believe. That's why it still hurts."

We climbed over a fallen birch and continued up the trail.

Caramel Time

(Appomattox)

"See anything?" asked Raina.

"Yeah, a whole mountainside of spruce," I called from the crown of a pine.

"Any arrows or scuffed up rocks?"

I lowered my binoculars. "All the rocks look scuffed up. Grab the map in my backpack."

Raina unfolded the map. "It says we're on Upper Gray Ghost. When was this thing printed anyway?"

I shinnied down the trunk and studied the map. "This map blows. We don't know where we are."

"I agree." Raina released the map. A gust of wind carried the map over a cliff.

"Hey, I was only kidding." I reached for the map, but it was too late. The map floated high above the valley. "What are we gonna use now?"

"Don't worry, I'm a regular St. Bernard." Raina swerved around a boulder and continued up the ridge.

"Hey, wait for me," I called, slipping on my backpack and hurrying up the trail.

After hiking up a crest and down into a gully we came to the base of a forty-foot cliff.

"This way." Raina began climbing up the cliff.

Instead of going Raina's way, I hiked along the base of the cliff for a while. I was about to turn back too, when I spotted a tiny stream flowing between two granite formations.

Near the top of the cliff, Raina ran out of crevices. "Spaz, get the heck over here," she yelled. "I'm stuck."

I squeezed between the two granite formations. There I found a crevice the stream had carved in the granite. I climbed up the crevice. Reaching the top of the cliff, I ran over to Raina and looked down upon her head.

"Why'd you try that way?" I asked.

"Just give me a hand, you nitwit."

I got on my belly and reached down the cliff. Our fingers were a foot apart. Trying to reach further, I lost my balance and fell forwards. My hand grabbed a root and stopped my fall. I got back on my feet.

"You're no help," said Raina.

"Take a Valium, I'll figure something out." I scanned the area for branches, but this high up, the spruce were shrubs. So I took a windbreaker from my backpack, tied one sleeve to my ankle, then tied the other to a root. Slowly, I lowered myself down the cliff face-first. Still, our fingers were an inch apart. "Jump," I said. "Jump and I'll grab your hand."

"Screw you." Raina lowered her foot and searched for a crevice.

"Come on, I'll catch you."

"I'm stuck."

"No you're not." I stretched further. A tearing sound came from my windbreaker. I pulled back a little.

Raina gripped the outcrop. "My legs are cramping."

"Hurry up, jump," I yelled.

She studied my outstretched hand.

"Just trust me."

Raina glanced at the rocks below. "Damn you," she called and jumped.

We're Just Tiny Ants
(six years earlier)

"Hey, Mom," called Raina, dropping her book bag in the hall closet. "Listen to me. I'm the best singer in the girls chorus." Raina began to sing:

> I dance in a circle where the flames leap up high
> I dance in the fire and I dance through the night.
> When the blaze burns my skin I care nothing for the pain
> In the spring I am Lord of the Dance again.

"Don't get too carried away, dear," said Mom, sliding a tray of haddock rolled in breadcrumbs into the oven. "In the grand scheme of things, we're just tiny ants marching towards a crust of bread."

"But we're not living in the grand scheme of things. We're living in Merriam Hill and I'm the best singer in the Diamond Junior High Girls Chorus. Mrs. Pushkoff even said so." Raina spun around the kitchen and sang the chorus:

> Dance, dance, wherever you may be
> I am the Lord of the dance said he.
> I live in you, you live in me
> I lead you all in the dance said he.

"Modesty is an endearing trait in a young person."

Raina looked up at Mom. "But I've been practicing my scales for four years?"

"We're just tiny ants, dear," said Mom, pouring croutons into a bowl of romaine lettuce.

I grabbed Raina's wrist and pulled her up.

"That was close," said Raina, inspecting a scrape on her knee. "Didn't think you'd catch me."

We continued hiking up the monadnock. My heart beat faster with each step. My mind felt clearer. In the silence I discovered a choral of birds singing, endless gusts of wind, and the scuffing of our own sneakers. The syrupy smell of spruce drifted through the air with the scent of decomposing leaves and whiffs of sub-baked granite. Below us, the valley opened up like a giant blue bowl.

"Take a look," said Raina.

I studied my sister's face. What before seemed defiant, now looked like fear, which no doubt was fronting for some other emotion.

"No, you loony tune, up there." Raina pointed up the mountain.

In the distance, hikers were walking along the granite ridgeline towards the summit Donk and I had tried to reach years earlier. We picked up our pace. As we hiked through the krummholz the spruce got shorter and shorter. Then they were gone. Now, we were hiking on pure granite. We passed a group of hikers resting on a boulder. I wasn't tired one bit. In fact, my muscles felt juiced and my body felt light as a helium pillow. Reaching the shoulder, we hiked along the ridgeline into a stiff wind. A half-mile or so in front of us stood the summit. We quickened our pace. Warm ginger ale filled my chest I was so excited. A lookout tower stood on the highest point. We walked faster, passing a dozen or so hikers. When we reached the summit an unfamiliar energy flowed though my salmon nautilus. My body felt like I could almost fly, so I began running and leaping off small outcrops of granite. In the air the wind cradled my body. I began carving air sculptures with my arms and legs.

"He's not my brother," said Raina.

With an eight or nine-step start, I ran and leapt off the largest outcrop. In the air I stretched my arms and legs the furthest they could go. I looked up and the sky collapsed into blue trapezoids; cascades of lemon triangles tumbled from the sun; emerald spears pointed everywhere; and the granite mountain turned into a sea of gray rectangles. Minutes unraveled into long strings of milliseconds stretching like caramel into the horizon. From the bellies of milliseconds, rivulets of piko-seconds poured out, forming momentary flowers of time, their ghostly shapes blooming then dissolving in flashes of another bloom. Seconds became caverns to crawl around in and stuff your pockets with strings of time. Lichen squished beneath my sneakers as I landed. Still there had to be more. If two hikers found themselves together inside the gentle hurricane of caramel time, maybe they could *merge*?

I studied Raina. "Are you feeling it or what?"

"Cut it out," she said. "Hikers are walking around us."

At least it was possible. If two hikers on the same trail could merge and read each other's thoughts and not know who was who, then, who knows, maybe they wouldn't feel so damn alone? I know this, launching air sculptures into the airways is pretty sick. Making your salmon nautilus hum is even more ballsy. But hiking your way into *caramel time*, the sacred dimension, is the most pissa good out there 'cause it transforms the so-so, let's-do-a-chore present into a Jimi Hendrix wah-wah pedal solo. That's when I first experienced what a mint song can do. A mint song can retrace a person's steps to caramel time.

I ran across the summit, leaping and doing 360s. I got so sweaty my eyes began to sting. I leaped off an outcrop. In the air a gust of wind pressed against my body. I spread my arms and tried to glide through the wind, but my body sank. Landing on wet lichen, I began skidding across the granite. Hitting a lip in the granite, I fell forwards.

Next thing I know, I was tumbling down the mountainside towards a huge cliff, scraping the hell out of my elbows, knees, and face.

"Kuba!" screamed Raina, running down the mountainside and jumping over a ravine. I tumbled past a boulder. Raina leaped onto the boulder, ran across the top of it, and hopped off the other side. She continued to chase me down the mountain. Twelve yards before the cliff, Raina dove towards me. In mid-air she grabbed my shirt and pulled hard, slowing my fall slightly. I tried to grab a root and missed it. I tried to cram my fingers into a crack in the granite. Instead, I scraped the skin off my fingertips. We continued tumbling towards the cliff. A few yards from the edge a root dug into my belly. I wildly reached for the root and managed to grab it. My body jerked to a stop. I heard a loud ripping sound as my shirt was torn off my back. Raina tumbled past me, clutching my shirt. She disappeared over the cliff.

An electric shock surged down my spine. I frantically looked around for what I know not. "Somebody get some help over here!" I yelled as I climbed up the steep incline towards the trail. "Injured hiker. We need help." At the foot of the trail, I grabbed my backpack and began running down the trail, blood dripping down my face and legs. After a steep descent, I swerved off the trail and ran into the woods towards the cliff. At the bottom of the cliff, my sister's body lay motionless. Her leg was bent in a horrible way. Her forehead looked so much like hamburger that vomit poured from my mouth and covered my shorts. But Raina's skin wasn't cold. It wasn't cold like Donk's skin.

Remembering my Cub Scout manual from fourth grade, I kicked over two dead spruce saplings and pulled them out of the ground. Whipping out my jackknife, I cut off the branches. Then I tied my windbreaker and shirt to the tree trunks and built a makeshift stretcher. With my belt I fastened Raina to the stretcher, lifted one side, and began dragging her down the mountain.

"Somebody get the heck over here!" my voice echoed through the forest. "Injured hiker."

The trip down blew. My legs buckled a bunch of times. Luckily, another hiker caught up with us and lifted the other end. We nearly jogged down the whole monadnock. I imagined Donk was blocking for us. My salmon nautilus hummed like mad. When it got dark I removed my coalminer's hat from my backpack. A beam of light lit the ground in front of us as we jogged down the trail.

At the trailhead the paramedics carried Raina to a waiting ambulance and sped off down I-93 South. I tailed the ambulance in my Chevelle to a hospital in Nashua. I didn't have the seeds to call Mom.

In the waiting room, Flathead's "Till It Breaks" played on the radio. It's weird, the shift that happens in my head at times like this. When a person's alive, all I can think about are the things that person did to screw me. But when she's in a hospital hooked up to plastic tubes and nine machines, all I can think about are the cool things that person did to make the world glow. As hard as I try not to, that's the way I think.

Mom and Aunt Bee hurried into the emergency ward.

"You should have called me immediately," said Mom. "It's a good thing someone at the front desk did." A half-hour later Mom transferred Raina to Children's Hospital in Boston.

With only stitches to gain, Raina rolled off a cliff for what? How dumb was I? Believing people should only hitch rides from drivers who offered a lift with a smile. Then I started thinking about snobs. Maybe there was more to snobs than I had originally thought? Maybe some snobs were stuck up 'cause they were guarding something real like the curves on a '66 Vette? Maybe that's why they kept their helmets on so long. Go figure. Because Raina rolled off a cliff for me, there were salmon alleys in my chest humming that only yesterday were rivulets of pure ice.

Track 48
The Inner-Compass

FOR SOME COOL REASON RAINA DIDN'T DIE. SHE spent the next six weeks at Children's Hospital with a level-3 concussion, bruised kidney, compressed lung, four cracked ribs, and a busted wrist.

Back at our house in Arlington a melody floated through my mind. I grabbed Donk's Telecaster, switched on his amp, and tried to play it.

I heard a knock on our front door. I switched off the amp, walked downstairs, and opened the door. Coach Brewer stood on the front step.

"Hi, Coach."

"Can I come in?"

"Sure."

Coach Brewer walked into our kitchen. "I'm pleased as hell to hear that your sister's going to be alright."

"Me too. I'm psyched."

"If you haven't heard, I'm no longer coaching Merriam Hill."

"No way."

"Moving on." Coach Brewer took a wad of papers from his brief case.

"Oh yeah, where?"

"You're looking at the new head football coach at Dartmouth College."

"Traitor. Just kidding. Have you told Pushkoff? He'll be pumped."

Coach Brewer shook his head. "Just signed the contract. Pre-season starts tomorrow. Heading up there right now." Coach walked over to the coffee maker, sniffed the pot, then poured himself a cup. "Staying in the dorms till Karen finds us a place. Not looking forward to that, I tell you," said Coach, drinking his coffee. "Thought I was going to retire here. Can you believe it? Just wanted to stop by and say goodbye."

"Thanks."

Coach shuffled through his wad of papers. "Just one problem. Last year's place-kicker flunked out and they didn't recruit a new one. Can you believe it? No kicker on a Brewer coached team. Last year alone we won four games with field goals. Where am I going to find a kicker at this late date? Haven't done a stitch of scouting." Coach Brewer stood real close.

"Too bad I wasn't accepted. Check out these quads." I flexed my quadriceps. "Been hiking a ton. I should get a permit for those guns."

"Always a commercial with you Brices." Coach Brewer glanced at my quads. "Shame you can't stand Ivy Leaguers 'cause when I went over to the Dean of Admissions and showed him the sports page from Thanksgiving, and explained how it was Brice against the whole history class in Jeopardy, and told him how we needed a place-kicker, he pulled out your application and reconsidered it."

"He did?"

"Sure he did." Coach handed me a letter.

Dear Mr. Brice:

Based upon further examination of your application and due to a higher than expected number of students who chose to attend elsewhere, the Dean of Admissions has accepted your application for admission to Dartmouth College for the upcoming Fall Semester. Please let us know by August 1st if you will be able to accept.

Sincerely,
J. K. Franson,
Assistant Dean of Admissions

I looked up at Coach Brewer.

He handed me another letter. "As you know, Dartmouth doesn't give athletic scholarships. However, courtesy of the Booster Club, you've been hired to paint the stadium for twenty-hours a week. What do you say?" Coach Brewer killed his coffee and set the mug on our counter. "To hell with you if you don't take this opportunity 'cause there's plenty who would."

I was blown away. College ball was pretty sick for a twig like me. "How big are the players up there?"

"Spare me the tap dance, Brice. I've got a three hour drive ahead of me."

Next thing I know I was shadowboxing: *Jab, jab, fake, step inside, hook.* For the first time, I had those soulstealers on the ropes. *Circle, jab, fake fake, haymaker.* For the first time, I was winning.

But what would Donk say? He'd say I was selling out. But how did he know? Did Donk ever visit Dartmouth?

"What about all the snobs up there?" I asked.

"What about them?"

"You know, they think they're better than us."

"So what if they do?"

Coach had a point. "But don't you just wanna punch 'em?" I said, thinking about Donk.

"I want to punch *you*," said Coach.

"Why?"

"Because you always have a smart aleck answer, but it never comes from here." Coach hit my sternum with his open palm, knocking the wind from me.

That's when I first felt it, something in my gut pulling me towards New Hampshire, some kind of *inner-compass*. From that day on when my brain whiffed (which it did a ton), I let my salmon flesh make decisions for me. To tell you the truth, I'm a little pissed that it took me nineteen years to find the friggin' thing. Now, for some strange reason, I could feel the needle move. It took Donk zero years. Straight from the womb, he could feel the needle move. It sorted through the bajillion choices a person faces and pointed Donk to one. It told him most rules were pure fudge, but not knowing which rules were real and which rules were made up, Donk broke them all and broke himself in the process.

"Look, am I going to see you at practice tomorrow or not?" demanded Coach Brewer. A light breeze flowed through an open window by the sink causing the white curtains to gently flutter.

All my life I've been rolling Donk's tires onto my Chevelle, but what good were Nova tires on a Chevelle? What good were the gifts Donk handed out like a Santa Claus at Macy's if they kept me from knowing who the heck I was or stopped me from climbing through my own trap door to caramel time? What good is talent when it wasn't good enough to fix Donk? The same pilgrim pigheadedness that led Donk to his finest riffs, banged into shape by his original energy, also made him deaf to cheers, and certainly any choruses of our help. What did it matter what people thought of Donk's salmon nautilus, his trance, or his Aloe Vera rivers, if they couldn't pass through Donk's own private fudge detector? In the end, all we could do was watch as Donk's life became another episode of "Six Million Dollar Man," only this time without the bionic rescue. I say, in order to compete with the Ivy League ballet boys, I needed to become one first and figure out the friggin' rules so I'd know which ones were silk pajamas and which ones were polyester socks. Then I'd have a better chance to move the medicine ball a quarter-inch. That would be a ton.

"I will be at practice tomorrow." I bear-hugged Coach Brewer (tightly so he didn't think I wanted him). "This is the third-best thing a person's ever done for me."

Coach Brewer looked around the room. "Okay, don't get carried away. I get the point."

I didn't give a crap and held on. "I'm going to be the Babe Ruth of placekickers. You'll see. From thirty, forty, even fifty yards out—automatic like the Sunday Globe. I'm not talking trash either." I pointed to my legs. "These tree trunks could run through a brick bank."

"Okay, okay, I appreciate your enthusiasm. Now get moving. You've got to pack your things and get a measles shot. They won't let you practice without one."

"Where am I going to crash?"

"We'll find you a bunk in the dorms. See you in the morning at seven—not a minute later." While walking through our den, Coach Brewer paused in front of our bookcase. He pointed to a pair of navy blue books. "Those mine?"

"Oh yeah, Donk borrowed them."

Coach B. slid his *Oxford English Dictionaries* off the shelf. "Bunch of used car bandits—all of you," he said as he walked out of our house. In our driveway, he set the navy blue books in the passenger's seat, slapped his car in reverse, and disappeared down Merriam Street.

Upstairs, I slid a suitcase out from under my bed and stuffed it with clothes. I grabbed Donk's dictionary, his Telecaster, and my amp, and loaded them into my car. In the garage I grabbed my three-ring binder of songs, my football gear, and Raina's P.A.

After leaving Doctor Van Dyne's office, I was driving up I-95 North, about to turn onto I-93 North, when I felt my inner-compass pulling me towards Boston. So I took the I-93 South exit and headed into Beantown.

At Children's Hospital the elevator opened. I stepped out and walked towards Room 410. Raina sat up in bed with a lunch tray. On the radio Crispin's voice wailed above Ferranti's bass. Swirls of trance guitar riffs blended with Janota's hi-hats, snare, and toms. I admit, it sounded pretty sick. I wanted to kick Crispin's amp over and trash Janota's kit.

"What's going on?" I asked.

"Can you believe this?" said Raina. "Restless Records re-released our CD with Crispin singing. It's selling like crazy at Strawberry's. Noy told me."

"Forget about those guys. What did Dr. Van Dyne say about your concussion?"

"They don't know yet. If the tests go okay, I could be out of here by Friday. How does my forehead look?"

I surveyed the railroad tracks of stitches and black-purple scabs. "A ton better," I lied.

A nurse with a clipboard came in and checked Raina's blood pressure, temperature, and oxygen levels.   "What

~ 382 ~

you did was really stupid. Next time, just let me fall and call for help."

Raina looked up surprised.

"That's right. What would Mom have done if both of us had died? Didn't think about that one, did you?" I tightened my lips. "You had to go and hog all the attention."

"Phhth," Raina laughed.

So did I. "Guess who just left our house? Coach B. He's the new football coach at Dartmouth, but he's got a little problem." I snagged a roll off Raina's tray and took a bite. "Their kicker flunked out and they didn't recruit a backup, so guess who's moving up to New Hampshire?"

"You're screwing with me," said Raina.

I shook my head. "Got a job painting the stadium too."

Raina's eyes got glassy. "You're going to college?"

"Yeah, and I'm taking all the music equipment—if it's okay with you."

"I don't want any of that crap. Take my P.A. too."

"I did. Aunt Bee told me Dartmouth has a sweet music program. I'm gonna study all the big boys too: Rachmaninoff, Stravinsky, Rossini, Bach, Vivaldi, Saint-Saëns, Elliott Carter, Brahms, Hayden. Then, I'm going to swipe all their stuff. Starting my own band too. Screw having to beg musicians to play my songs. Besides, I have enough songs for ten CDs."

An intense expression appeared on Raina's face.

I scoffed down the roll, then went at the fruit cup. "Only one thing missing: Dartmouth doesn't have a voice major—just a minor—so most singers go to Berkley or Hart."

"Maybe you should sing," said Raina.

"Yeah, right. How do you expect me to write decent songs if I'm singing scales all day?" I walked over to the radio and turned it off. "I was hoping maybe you'd want to come up to New Hampshire too. You could crash with me in the dorm till we found you a place. I bet they'd even let you sit in on a few classes."

Raina frowned and finished her meal. We said nothing for the longest time. It was like there weren't any words to say. No words for this *exact* moment and this exact situation. It was really freaky. For some reason Donk's dictionary popped into my head. Then it hit me: why Donk practically slept with that stupid thing. 'Cause if a person was really going to tune into her inner-compass, really going to make her salmon nautilus hum, really going to experience caramel time, really going to merge back into the Aloe Vera river, that person needed to come up with her *own* words. Words had a way of making things true. The used-up, borrowed words had to go.

"You'd do that for me?" asked Raina.

"Frigginay, I would." I leaned over and hugged Raina.

She turned her head. "Don't it hurts."

That night in my dorm I opened Donk's humongous red dictionary and almost blew chunks when I discovered that Donk—the sick unit—had been scribbling his own words in the margins for who-knows-how-long. So I began scribbling in my own words too, adding them to Donk's. I flipped through so many pages that my fingertips got chaffed and began to burn. But I kept going and didn't stop till a ray of sunlight split the darkness and the licorice night dissolved into a ginger ale dawn laced with grenadine.

Track 49
Stop-Time
(Eight months later)

On Friday, April 17th, Raina, a bassist who lived on the 3rd floor, a drummer from Ripley Hall, a violinist I met in my *American Civil War* class, and I lugged our gear down into the dorm basement. Pushkoff rolled in a keg. Students gathered around us as I tuned Donk's Telecaster. At the soundboard Noy talked with my roommate Colton. Raina passed around the song list. First on our list was a new tune called "Orpheus With A Guitar." We fired up our amps. The drummer raised his sticks. Raina walked to the microphone. The violinist brought the bow to her strings. In the silence before the first song, the unheard melodies are waiting to be born.

"One two three, one two three, one two three."

The drummer brought his sticks down: Ti ti tuh. Ti ti tuh. Ti ti tuh—whoosh koosh. Ti ti tuh. Ti ti tuh. Ti ti tuh—whoosh koosh.

The bassist's chestnut notes spilled onto the floor: Doo doo doo, dee dee dee, doo doo doo, dee dee dee.

A melody swirled from the violinist's fingers: Ah la na, la ma na, hum ma na, la na na, ah la na. Ma la na, la ma na, ma na na, la ma na, ah na na.

A step below, I strummed a counter melody: Om nom nom, shom nom nom, oo oo oo. Om nom nom, shom nom nom, sheen noo, oo noo.

Raina sang the first verse:

> *The sky is smeared with ink and gin.*
> *A barbed wire fence digs in my skin.*
> *The sun-blush berries bump the ground.*
> *A child's laugh will soon be gone.*

I stopped playing, then rejoined the violinist and drummer in the climb. A wave of sound rolled through the basement. Then, we cranked out the first chorus:

> *I've been sleeping in my car,*
> *Singing to the stars,*
> *So I travel on. I am Orpheus.*
> *I can bend the branches of an elm.*
> *I can wake the turtles on a log.*

Surprising the heck out of myself, I ended the chorus on a Dsus13. The chord floated through the basement, waiting to be resolved. I winged it, playing a Csus9, then an Em9+11. Raina made up the lyrics:

> *Firefly meadows, barefoot friends,*
> *Jam jar prisons, pajama runs.*
> *Hands and rings, our summer lanterns swing,*
> *The blades of grass they sting.*
> *Moss-filled pillows, mom's first son.*
> *I think penguins look like nuns.*

Increasing our volume, we cruised into the intro. This is when it happened. Just before the second verse, everyone stopped playing. Silence filled the basement, but in my mind the song kept going. After a few seconds, we resumed playing. It's called *stop-time*, sudden injections of silence, strategic volume shifts, dramatic reversals of complexity. It was a boast, really, that we could carve up time, act like Hercules and divert a river of air. We returned to the intro. Circular arpeggios flew from the violinist's fingers.

Raina sang the second verse:

> *Crickets rub their wings*
> *Bats in dark night drop*
> *Stolen kisses from your cheek*
> *As squirrels count their acorn clocks*

Again we stopped. This time on a Bsus13. The unresolved chord hung in the air. My mind did pirouettes to resolve it. Then it hit me. That's what a mint song needs: stop-time and unresolved chords so listeners could supply their own notes and resolve the chords in their *own* minds. Hand holding never helped. But sudden silence while riding in a musical car was a chance to lift off into untraveled space. A cluster of moments passed. We began playing the climb. Just before the chorus, we stopped, but something in my body kept hurtling into the silence. And in the silence, I could hear my salmon nautilus humming—warm, pink, and pliable as the day I was born.

In the sky above Hitchcock Hall, the unknown constellations began to shift. A space opened. The perfect length of time passed. I began jamming on a solo. First, I tapped a phrase. Then I played triads and dyads. Then I floated quarter-notes and half-notes over the audience. My mind began to spin with all the choices. I got dizzy, then nauseous. Diving into my belly, I let my inner-compass find the best possible notes, notes that fit the needs of each unique moment, each distinct feeling, each clear-cut idea. My fingers began climbing up the fret board, freeing notes that were stuck in my salmon nautilus. Now, all songs were original, every time we played them. Very slightly, my sneakers lifted off the floor. I don't think anyone noticed. With secondary and tertiary hooks—whatever was needed—I propelled the melody skywards towards the newly-opened space. My body began to rise. Did anyone see? I was nearly two inches off the floor. Super-strings of helium notes flew from my amplifier and lifted my body. My fingers raced up and down the neck. Each perfect riff rose upwards and fit into the new constellation. My body floated higher. Why wasn't anyone freaking out? I played a chordal melody. Starfish-shaped knots of sound floated through the basement. But just as quickly, my connection to my inner-compass weakened. I played a slightly-flat note. Then another. My body stopped rising. Hurriedly, I played the refrain. No luck. My body began to drop. I tried trance, but my body grew heavier and dropped faster. I broke into freeform, but the stage shot up and I fell onto the floor. The violinist stopped, then the bassist, then the drummer. Everyone was staring at me. "What the heck happened to you?" asked Raina.

"Not sure," I said as the bassist pulled me to my feet. I brushed dust off my shirt and checked Donk's Telecaster. A long crack had formed in the body. I felt the neck. At least the neck was okay. I plugged my guitar back into my amp and fiddled with the knobs. It still worked. Talk filled the basement. A girl in a plaid skirt stared. I looked away. During my sick solo, the pale orbs inside me had begun to migrate back to the hyaline river of pure awareness. The orbs were shedding mass, trying to escape time and place, then I played the wrong series of notes, the mystical swing in the song was lost, and gravity grabbed me back.

"That's friggin' Spaz for you," said Raina. "Are you ready to play another tune or what?"

I nodded and glanced at our song list.

"One, two, three, four," Raina counted.

Glowing chords leaped from my amp as I strummed the intro to "Short Supply." The drummer furiously tapped his hi-hats and snare. Bullfrog burps bulged from the bassist's amp. Six bars later, Raina opened her mouth and, I swear, finches flew out. The race was on.

The Sacrifice

Standing on the portico of Sigma Nu, I knocked on the front door. A guy in khaki pants opened the door.

"Is Scott Pushkoff there?" I asked.

"Don't know." The guy turned and hollered up a flight of stairs. "Hey, Scott, you up there? Someone's here to see you."

"I'll get him," a voice called down. "He's in the shower."

A few minutes later, Pushkoff came thumping down the stairs with a towel around his waist. He'd been lifting a ton and it showed. Pushkoff flashed his twenty-tooth grin. "Little Brice, what are doing?"

"Wanna go on a hike?" I asked.

"Take a look at these bad boys." Scott began flexing his pecs in sync with the refrain from Tchaikovsky's "Waltz of the Flowers." "Na na na, nah, na-nah, na-nah—dah da da da. Nah, na-nah, na-nah—dah da da da."

"Want a couple band aids for those mosquito bites?" I asked.

"Yeah, right. Look, I've got to hit the gym first. Why don't you come to the gym with me? Then, we'll head out after." That's what I loved about Pushkoff. He was never too busy to spend time with one of his buddies.

Inside the weight room at Alumni Gym, metal clinked against metal as students raised and lowered barbells and steel plates. Coach Brewer walked around the room with a clipboard.

At the squat machine, Pushkoff slid a 50-pound and a 20-pound plate onto each side of the bar. Then, he screwed on each nut.

"You nutcase. How much are you squatting?" I asked.

"540 pounds." After wrapping a towel around the bar, Pushkoff dipped under the bar and pressed his upper-back against the middle of the bar. Gripping the bar tightly, he took a deep breath and lifted the bar off its hooks. His feet pointing at ten o'clock and two o'clock, he squatted until his thighs were parallel with the floor. Squeezing his glutes, Pushkoff lifted his hips straight up until he was standing. He exhaled. Then, the sick unit did twelve more reps. When he was done, Pushkoff set the barbell on its hooks and walked toward the bench press. I followed. He pointed to his torso. "Can you imagine this in a Volkswagen? I can't. I won't be able to fit into a car again. Kick him out of the gym," Pushkoff hollered. "He's too huge." Adding his own lyrics to "Who Are You" by The Who, he began singing and flex-dancing around the gym.

> *Who's too huge? Who, who? Who, who?*
> *Who's too huge? Who, who? Who, who?*
> *The girls really wanna know.*
> *Who's too huge? Who, who? Who, who?*

I admit, it was pretty ballsy 'cause the gym was packed with ripped guys. Girls too.

At the bench press, Pushkoff slid 100-pound, 50-pound, and 35-pound plates onto each side of the bar. Laying down on the bench, he took a deep breath, lifted the bar off its hooks, and lowered it to his chest. He began raising the bar.

"Listen, Little Brice, you've got to know what you want in life. Then, you've got to do something every day to help you get there. I'm going to finish up here in a few years—then head to dental school. They're not easy to get into, so I've got to get good grades. That means-"

"What if you don't get in?" I asked.

"Who's gonna stop me?" said Pushkoff, finishing his reps. He stood up and flared his lats, pecs, and traps. "Take a long look at *this*."

"Save me," I said, but inside a feeling of jealousy surprised me. Pushkoff's confidence came from a place I didn't know. It wasn't because Scott went to a fancypants college or that he lived in a snob palace. It was because he had a plan and he worked on it every day. Sure, Pushkoff was ripped, but it was the fact that he was trying to get ripped that mattered. He had a purpose. The rest was just Cheese Whiz. I looked around and noticed there were a bunch of kids like Pushkoff at Dartmouth. That was the advantage. In my ribcage I felt the needle move. "Step aside," I said, brushing past Pushkoff. "Give someone else a chance."

"All right, Little Brice. I'll spot." Pushkoff slid the 100-pound plates off the bar and put them in the rack. Then he slid the 35-pound plates off the bar.

I lay down on the bench, slid my head between the mounts, and gripped the bar. Maybe if I felt strong on the outside, that feeling would flow into my inside?

"Spread out your hands so your forearms are vertical to the floor," said Pushkoff.

I spread my hands, took a deep breath, and lifted the bar off its hooks. The barbell wavered. Pushkoff steadied the bar. I began to lower the bar.

"Tuck in those elbows," said Pushkoff. "Keep a straight line from the bar to your wrist to your elbow."

Straightening my forearms, I brought the bar to my chest.

"Ok, now bring it up slowly."

I pushed up on the bar as hard as I could. It didn't move. The barbell felt like Neptune and Jupiter had been added to each side.

"Come on, Little Brice, you can do it." Pushkoff placed a finger under the bar. Slowly, the bar began to rise.

"I see he's rubbing off on you," said Coach Brewer, walking up to us.

"Trying," said Pushkoff. "Keep your back on the bench."

I lowered my back and pushed harder. My face shook violently. The barbell clinked against the hooks.

"Not bad," said Pushkoff. "Kid benched 145 first time out."

"Can't hurt to put a little muscle on you," said Coach, watching a group of offensive linemen doing dead lifts.

"Hey, Coach?" called Pushkoff. "We're hiking up Red Feather Ridge—you coming?"

Coach Brewer shook his head. "Haven't got time to go playing in the woods with you boys."

"The way I see it, you haven't got time to not come," I said a bit devilishly.

"That is, unless you can't make it to the top without an oxygen tank," added Pushkoff.

"Is that right. I'll beat both you blowhards up the ridge."

"No motorcycles allowed," said Pushkoff.

Coach Brewer gave Pushkoff a once-over. "When are you going?"

"Right after this."

Coach Brewer began walking towards the group of lineman. "Pick me up in an hour. I'll be in my office."

Scott and I looked at each other.

On I-91 south, I stepped on the gas. My Chevelle flew past a school bus. "Spread It Around" by The Bags poured from my speakers.

"Turn down that god-awful noise," said Coach Brewer.

I turned off the music.

"So, are you two keeping up with your classes?" asked Coach.

"I'm pretty much caught up," said Scott from the backseat.

"How about you, Brice?"

"It's a lot of work," I said.

"Well, don't let yourself fall behind. They won't let you play if you do."

"I won't."

"Taking any history classes?"

"One," said Pushkoff.

"All history classes," I said as pine trees flew past us in the car windows.

"Is that right."

"Yeah, I figure if I only take classes I like I won't blow out of college."

"Any seminars?"

"No," said Scott.

"Yeah, American Civil War," I said.

Coach Brewer turned to me. "Is that right. What are you doing in class?"

"Working on an essay."

"What about?"

"The reasons the Civil War ended," I said.

"What does your professor think?"

"She thinks the cotton embargo bankrupted the South."

"Ah, the idiotic cotton embargo. The British simply planted more cotton in Egypt and East India, while the Confederacy lost its largest source of revenue. What else?" Coach Brewer looked at me.

"The North's bigger population," I said.

Coach Brewer nodded. "I think so. The South had nine million, while the North had twenty-two million. When Grant halted prisoner exchanges, the Confederacy's fate was sealed. In fact-"

"What about the Union's huge industrial advantage?" Pushkoff chimed in.

"Can't argue with that," said Coach Brewer. "When war broke out, almost all of the U.S.'s firearms, pig iron, and textiles were made in the North. When the South did make something, there were few ways to transport it since most of the railroads were up north. Eventually, the South realized that victory was impossible, so they laid down their guns and the country was unified again. It's one thing to have-"

"No, I don't think that's true," I heard myself saying.

"Come again?" asked Coach Brewer.

"It was the sacrifice," I said.

"I don't follow."

"The sacrifice of 620,000 soldiers ended the Civil War."

Coach fiddled with his beard. "But what did each side gain from such a sacrifice?"

"Suffering," I said, putting my blinker on and guiding my car down the off-ramp. "The sacrifice caused suffering which broke through people's stubbornness and connected them in a chain of despair. When people looked around and saw that everyone was suffering, it soothed their anger and rekindled empathy in their bellies. This led to reflection and planted seeds that grew into a new understanding."

Coach scrunched his eyebrows. "The sacrifice didn't wake people up. It tired them out. They grew weary, so they stopped."

I shook my head. "They grew weary, but they kept going: citizens kept waving flags, politicians kept lying, generals kept playing chess, and soldiers kept fighting. Everybody refused to accept that morality had changed." After turning onto Route 12, I stepped on the gas. "The Confederacy clung to state's rights in a brazen attempt to keep slavery, whose huge profits blinded them to the human costs. The Union fought for federal rights, but it was the abolitionists gathered in their churches who provided the moral compass for the U.S. to grow. What changed?"

Coach Brewer shook his head. "The ideas perished with the soldiers."

"But those men were replaced with fresh-faced recruits," I fired back. "It was the sacrifice." A family of deer looked up from the road. I lifted my foot off the gas and pumped the breaks. "Suffering brought people face-to-face with their own limitations. It made their illusions seem trivial and caused them to seek wisdom with a new urgency," I said as my car swerved around the deer. "It was the-"

"It only brought more anger and more denial," said Coach Brewer.

Coach had a point, but to retreat—mid-sentence—is fatal, so I kept driving. "It was their chance to learn life's most elusive lessons. Suffering minimized their differences and magnified their shared human bonds, so the Civil War ended."

Coach Brewer pulled a can of chewing tobacco from his pocket and began thwapping it against his thigh. "Something sapped their will to fight."

"What kind of nutcase dwells on all the bad stuff that happens," said Pushkoff.

"Donk did," I replied. "Donk used to say, 'we're born into this world with nothing.' But I think we're born into this world with everything, only we don't know it. But just as the Red Sox always choke and Harvard barneys always win, we lose the world bit-by-bit as we get trapped in the worries of daily life, but if a person becomes master of his suffering, then he re-inherits the world, and earns the chance to become truly alive."

Coach opened the can and pinched a wad of tobacco. "Finding wisdom isn't the same thing as walking up to a butterfly and catching it with your net. *Here, I've got it.* Wisdom doesn't work that way. It's shedding the ideas you've picked up over a lifetime. It's having the guts to leap into the Atlantic in December, completely naked, without a wetsuit." Coach placed the wad of tobacco between his cheek and gum. "Every morning, a person should wake up, crawl out of bed, and go to the nearest mirror and repeat these words: I don't know, I don't know, I don't know, I don't know. There, it wasn't that hard."

"A person can also *create* wisdom," I said.

"Name one person!" demanded Coach Brewer.

I thought real hard. For some reason, I really needed to believe that *one person* could piece the whole puzzle together. "Lincoln," I finally said.

"Lincoln was turned into a god because his life was cut short," said Coach Brewer. "Had he lived, the radicals from his own party would have compromised Lincoln and turned him into just another wartime president."

Coach had me pinned and was drumming a John Bonham solo on my nuts. "But don't you get the feeling that Lincoln couldn't have lived past the Civil War? I mean, the sins of the U.S. were too great: war, slavery, what we did to the Indians, secession, woman couldn't vote—the Saint of Illinois had to go," I said.

Coach Brewer spit tobacco juice into an empty soda can. "So, you think Lincoln was sacrificed."

"Lincoln sacrificed himself," I said, tapping the steering wheel.

Coach Brewer exhaled loudly. "How so?"

We drove down a slope and into a valley. On the right, a moose stood in a pond, chewing on lily pads. My mind slowly turned like a Ferris wheel, trying to explain what I felt. The moose stood there munching on his greens. Was the joke on us? I slipped Joe Satriani's "Andalusia" into my CD player. The song opened with an acoustic guitar in 2/2 time. Helium riffs flew from his acoustic. Then, Satriani switched to electric guitar. Melodic rivers of liquid cigarettes flowed from his fingers. The Ferris wheel began to spin. Soon, I was floating in my seat. I kept my foot on the gas. "When Prometheus stole fire from the gods and secretly brought it to earth, humans ignored it and kept going with their old ways. They ate their meat raw, slept in cold caves, and sat around in the dark as fire sat there burning in its loneliness. In fact, Prometheus gave fire to humans many times, but it was only when he chained himself to the rocks and called the eagle to do its terrible business did humans notice. A kid heard Prometheus's groans, so he hiked up the mountain where fire snapped and burned and carried a glowing coal back to his cave. The kid showed his parents and was soundly beaten. But the coal landed in a leafy bed and burst into orange tongues. When his mom saw how fire

~ 398 ~

lit the walls of the cave and warmed their bodies too, she asked the boy to keep the fire lit. Soon, fire spread to every nook and cranny on earth. But did Prometheus ask to be released from his chains? Did he ask to be spared from the eagle's razor beak? No, he didn't. Prometheus kept quiet, knowing that once he undid his sacrifice that fire would be snuffed out, leaving humans huddled in darkness once again."

"Oh look," said Pushkoff, pointing to the sky.

In the distance, Red-Feather Ridge rose high from the forest. A peaceful wave washed across my body. To my right, Coach Brewer stared up at the mountain. In the backseat my best buddy scoffed down our hiking snacks. To tell you the truth, I felt lucky.

Coach Brewer spit tobacco juice into his soda can. "Are you really buying that? Humans wouldn't be so foolish as to give back fire."

"Oh no, I'm not buying," I said, stepping on the gas, my car accelerating towards Red-Feather Ridge, the highway twisting through the forest like a gray snake, its yellow lines bleeding into one stripe stretching into the horizon. "I'm selling."

Coda
In The Distant Post Offices

DO YOU KNOW WHAT IT MEANS TO LOVE MUSIC? ON Route 12 in Jaffrey, New Hampshire, my Chevelle barrels towards a granite-domed monadnock as a ten o'clock sun rises above the treetops. I am dizzy to be wise.

At the trailhead, we hike into the woods. Along the trail, fiddlehead ferns unroll their summer flags. In small streams, swirling whirligigs spin off momentary circles. Every instant a new series of notes emerges.

Fueled with oranges and spring water, we hike the black diamond trail that winds up the mountain. In the krummoltz the knee-high spruce scrape our shins. The spruce grow shorter, then are gone. With each measured step, my blood transports more oxygen through my body till my salmon nautilus hums.

We hike on. High in the alpine zone the trail disappears. We study the map lichen covering the granite. No luck. We listen for other hikers. No sounds. But in my chest an inner-compass points to a steep incline. We crawl up the incline and hike on. Soon, we are walking up the ridgeline towards a fire tower. On both sides the blue forest unrolls itself. We listen to songs that have not been written yet.

At last, we reach the summit and rest on a boulder, its edges worn smooth by time and rain. We open our canteens and drink. Tracing a path across the valley, up Red Feather Ridge, and past the granite crest, I launch myself into the summer sky. The unheard melodies are floating through the air thicker than jam.

After the sun drags its tired face across the sky, star-stitched patterns emerge in the dusk. Are they music? In distant pines, great horned owls *hoo* as campers crash in their tents. Are they music? How can I tell when every minute the true magnetic-north shifts? I know this, before I am wise, I am a pilgrim. Before I find music, beneath the ribs there is a thumping.

What is music? From tinhorn radio stations, millions of disc jockeys are spinning songs. Are they music? On makeshift stages in Unitarian Church basements, dozens of unsigned bands are improvising perfect sounds. Are they music? How can I know when every day one-hit wonders are soaring up the charts? Maybe music is the shell of a scallop or a hollow-body Gibson that holds something you didn't think could be held.

Donk disagrees. He used to say, "music cannot be passed from one person who has it to another person who does not." He can pound sand. After all, music is a sort of car, isn't it? Donk even said, "a mint song is a '63 Corvette split-window coupe that has 2,327 independent parts working all at once to achieve 360 horsepower of propulsion." That's what I say. A mint song lifts you up from one state and plunks you down into another. So let the magnets sing and lure the steel scraps from a hillside of spare parts and piece together an ageless car that whisks us off to caramel time.

Besides, these songs aren't about Donk! I guess, they're not about me either. They're about music, the many ways we try to find music, and the many ways music finds us.

They're about the messed up places music lives and all the places we never even think to look. I admit, I was hoping these songs were about me. After all, I'm the kid who witnessed that everything we love is swallowed back into the earth.

A mint song is different. Donk used to say, "after the last chorus, a mint song builds and builds and builds." It doesn't dip down like a drunk goose. It's not a deer in deep snow forging towards silence. No way. A mint song spirals upward in a colloid of perpetual rising. In its final flurries "a mint song builds and builds and builds," then it *climbs.* Then the track stops, but in the distant post offices of your salmon flesh, in the electric sea juice inside your skull, and across the sonic freeways flowing through the universe, the song never ends.

I hate Donk.

Biography

Robert Rowe grew up with seven brothers and sisters in Lexington, Massachusetts, where his Dad ran a Chevy dealership. Rowe attended high school in Rangeley, Maine, spending his free time playing guitar, hiking, reading, and ski racing. During his senior year, his high school ski team won the state championship. Rowe studied writing at the University of Maine, Farmington with Kenneth Rosen, Wesley McNair, and Bill Roorbach. Later, Rowe studied songwriting and drama at UCLA. He received an M.F.A. in Creative Writing from the University of Massachusetts, Amherst, studying with John Edgar Wideman, Noy Holland, James Tate, Mary Reufle, and Dara Wier. After college, he worked as an English teacher, car salesman, musician, and dressman. In 2017, he co-founded the Rowe School of Writing. Rowe is the editor of the New England Journal of Poetry and Fiction. His short story "The Violin Player" appeared in the *Sandy River Review*. He lives in Natick, Massachusetts with his wife and three sons.

Photo by Holly Hinman

Acknowledgements

My name is listed on the cover, but this novel has hundreds of authors and composers. Any utterance, quip, sales pitch, lyric, poem, late-night philosophical rant, riff, sing-songy phrase, putdown, novel, sermon, biography, song, magazine newspaper or website article, coach's gameday urgings, movie scene, sports commenter's phrase, bedside epiphany, business journal, and high school game of one-up-manship that I've ever read or heard influenced me as I wrote this novel. Foremost, thanks to Michael Jones at Bellhorn Press. Thanks to my peers at the University of Massachusetts Amherst MFA Program: Tom Kealey, Carry Comer, Kendra Borgmann, Ben Alsup, David Roderick, Mathew Kashorik, Robyn Heisey, Jon Haner, Nick Montramanaro, and Mathew Zapruder. Thanks to my professors: Kenneth Rosen, John Edgar Wideman, Noy Holland, James Tate, James Haug (from whose poem I got this title), Wesley McNair, Shahid Aga Ali, Dara Wier, Mary Ruefle, and Bill Roarbach. Thanks to writers: David Maraniss, Thomas McGuane, Dava Sobel, Joan Crothers, Jay Davis, Philip Levine, James Wright, Carmeron Crowe, John Irving, James Joyce, Russ Sargent, Charles Dickens, Mark Twain, and J.D. Salinger. Thanks to Gordon MacDonald, Reverend Patricia Jones, Jason Slaughter, Harry Davis, Tim Taggart, John Wardwell, Coach Ralph Brewer, Scott Douglass, Mark Douglass, John Rowe, Lois Flannigan, Joan Macbeth, George Rowe, Bill Belichek, Larry Levesque, Mike Rowe, the unknown composers and of ghost dances, the unknown author of an essay on the ghost dance, unknown translators of ghost dance lyrics, Merriam-Webster Dictionary, the OED, and the theorists of serialism. Thanks to the bands from Boston: Crispin Wood and Jim Janota of The Bags and The Upper Crust, Mark Ferranti of Bim Skala Bim, The Neigborhoods, Green Magnet School, Dinausaur Jr., The Pixies, Dispatch, The 360s, Slag, Aesthmatics, Flathead, Suzanne Vega, Shawn Colvin, and The Titanics. Thanks to Jeff Ament of Pearl Jam, Glass Tiger, Joe Satriani, Dream Academy, Bourgois Tagg, Jeff Buckley, and more.

New Voices in Fiction Series

Bellhorn Press is accepting submissions of unpublished novels, plays, and screenplays for our New Voices in Fiction Series. Submissions should contain strong elements of comedy, but may also be dramas with comedic situations, coming-of-age stories, tragicomedies, philosophical comedies, or stories with elements of irony, sarcasm, youthful indiscretions, pretensions unmasked and more. Screenplays should be movie-length or three episodes of a television series. We are looking for well-written and well-crafted manuscripts that have the potential to appeal to a broad audience of readers, viewers, and producers. For more information, contact:

Bellhorn Press

P.O. Box 812142
Wellesley, MA 02482
Website: bellhornpress.com
Phone: 781-214-0425
Email: info@bellhornpress.com

Made in the USA
Middletown, DE
19 June 2018